THE CHANNELER

THE
CHANNELER

—— BOOK I ——

THE **CONTINUUM** SERIES

JENNA RYAN

TCK PUBLISHING.COM

ISBN: 978-1-63161-066-0

Sign up for Jenna Ryan's newsletter at
www.jennaryanink.com/free

Published by TCK Publishing
www.TCKpublishing.com

Get discounts and special deals on our best selling books at
www.TCKpublishing.com/bookdeals

Check out addtional discounts for bulk orders at
www.TCKpublishing.com/bulk-book-orders

To my parents, who knew I could.

CHAPTER 1

THERE ARE THINGS ABOUT THE universe we may never understand. I've been told I'm a complex person, that I think too much. I don't disagree with that; I've been having an existential crisis every day since I left my mother's womb twenty-one years ago. My head is always busy, always wondering, always curious. I think some people, like me, just happen to be born with minds that go into overdrive.

But in their head, there's a whole world separate from the one they live in. People like us—people like me—just think differently.

I always believed something was out there, in the vast unknown. I wondered what went on beyond the borders of our planet, or our galaxy, or whatever is outside our galaxy. Was there life on other planets? Was it anything like what we see in sci-fi films, where different species fight for survival? Are their lives anything like ours? What about parallel universes, or worlds that are alternate versions of our own?

I also think about what is outside the universe. Is there an afterlife, or are we just gone once we're "gone?" Is there a God? Multiple gods? Is the whole universe some ancient, all-powerful being that runs the whole damn show?

Or is there nothing at all?

This is the profound topic I'd settled on torturing myself with while getting dressed for class one autumn morning.

"Caleb!"

I jumped, startled from my thoughts by my aunt's obnoxiously high-pitched voice. I rubbed my eyes and groaned, trying to talk myself into leaving my bedroom.

"I'll be down in a minute, Nikki!" I called out to her, reluctantly sliding a blue t-shirt over my head. I stepped out into the narrow hallway and dragged myself back into the bathroom to finish getting ready. I looked in the mirror and scowled.

Standing at six feet tall, I could only see from my mouth down in the glass, the top of my head cut off by its frame. I ducked a bit to be more level with my reflection, and an exhausted college undergrad stared back at me. I examined the terrible shadowy bags beneath my electric-blue eyes, dark bruises I bore every day of my life, a constant reminder of my insomnia. I was a light sleeper, so every bump in the night, every creaky stair and floorboard in this godforsaken house caused my eyes to snap right back open. I never really knew why I was like that. I always assumed it was because of the random drop-ins from my unearthly winged friend, Gabriel.

And he wasn't the only one of them I'd seen.

I'd never been able to figure out what they were exactly—Gabriel and the creatures like him. The first one I'd ever seen was Gabe, and he first came to me was when I was a toddler. And I remember it all vividly, because it is the first memory I have of anything.

It was late in the day, sometime in the evening. I was in my footie pajamas, the kind that have snaps down the leg, and I was standing on my tippy-toes trying to peek out the window. It was snowing hard on the front lawn, and I could just barely see the main road. My mother was making dinner for us in the kitchen. I think it was macaroni and cheese, because she'd kept reminding me not to go near the stove.

It had always just been my mother and me for as far back as I could remember. I never knew my father, but people my age being raised by a single parent was simply the social norm. My mom did her best to be happy all the time, but I had always felt my father's absence. No one ever spoke of him, and after my mother died I didn't care to ask. I always resented him for abandoning me and leaving my mother alone.

So, obviously, I was beyond confused when some random man—Gabriel—made a sudden appearance for the first time in my home that cold, winter evening.

Like a ray of sun through open blinds, I felt an intense heat on the left side of my face. It wasn't painful, but it wasn't quite pleasant, either. I turned in the direction of the warmth and saw a man, an unfamiliar stranger, towering above me.

He was by no means, however, an ordinary man. He was lean, muscular, and wore an ancient-looking set of armor that could have been fashioned only by a blacksmith sent from the gods themselves. And yet, his attire was nothing like I'd read in storybooks or seen in those cartoon gladiator movies. He had dark eyes, and I could feel the wisdom and experience they carried. But the strangest, most incredible aspect of this man in my home was the enormous pair of silver-feathered wings growing out of his shoulder blades.

An overwhelming sense of calmness filled the room. He smiled, his face chiseled and perfect, not a crevice or scar to be seen. I could sense he was as confused as I was; who was he, and how did he get into my house?

"Caleb."

The winged man's voice was so deep it vibrated in my chest as he said my name. I blinked and teetered on my feet, losing my balance briefly. The man chuckled and kneeled down to my height.

"You can see me." His statement sounded more like a question.

"Yes," I squeaked. "Hi!"

This time, he laughed heartily, his voice rattling my chest again.

"Hello. My name is Gabriel." His brow furrowed, and he tilted his brown-haired head curiously. My gaze traveled to the silver, shining wings on his back. The feathers looked light but tough, each one perfectly placed next to the other.

"Can I touch?" I reached my hand toward his wings.

He smiled and nodded, taking my tiny hand in his. He leaned close and placed my hand on a group of feathers.

They were soft on my skin, but I could tell they weren't the feathers you would find on a bird. As soon as my fingertips brushed against them, they held a type of power that surged; it was almost as if they were coated in something protective, like the wood sealer my mom used on our kitchen table she built. Smooth but unscathed. The feathers were firm and strong, and they didn't bend or break apart. My eyes widened.

"Wow!" I dropped my hand.

I peered over my shoulder, hoping wings would sprout, then looked back at Gabriel, whose face was still full of wonder and uncertainty.

"I have to go now, Caleb Swift." He rose to his feet. "I must return home."

I grimaced impulsively, staring at the floor, so the man wouldn't see the disappointment in my eyes. He was leaving already, and he had only just got here.

Gabriel placed a hand on my shoulder. "I can try to come back sometime if you would like." He smiled down at me.

My head snapped up, and I grinned widely. "Okay."

He nodded, gave a little wave goodbye, and vanished from right where he stood.

The warm feeling was gone, and goosebumps crawled up my arms. I shuffled over to the kitchen for dinner.

"Mommy." I tugged on her sweatpants.

She gazed down at me and smiled. "Dinner's almost ready, sweetie. Who were you talking to?" She bent down and lifted me into her arms.

I touched the side of her face, and she leaned into my hand.

"Gabe!" I exclaimed happily. "Gabe had wings."

She giggled and kissed the palm of my hand. "That's nice, baby." She carried me over to my booster seat and placed me inside it, ruffling my hair.

That was the first and last time we ever had a chance to speak of Gabriel before my mother died. She had been diagnosed with breast cancer just after I was born, and she passed after I turned five. I've held on to the memory all this time, not only because of the mysterious winged man who arrived at my house so unexpectedly, but because it is one of the few memories I have left of my mom.

Since that first day I met him, Gabe would come by unannounced, often when I needed him most. He showed up at the funeral when my mother died. When I was eleven, he was at the hospital when Aunt Nikki took me to get stitches in my lip after hockey practice. And there was one time in high school, when I came home after I bombed my calculus test, and he was waiting in my bedroom, asking if I wanted to talk.

But no one except me could see Gabe. I can remember asking him about that at my mom's funeral after I'd wandered away from the crowd.

"When I came to see you the first time, it was an accident," Gabriel had explained. "I didn't know I would be meeting you that day. It just happened." He gripped my shoulders firmly but gently. "Listen to me, Caleb. You are special in ways you can't even imagine. Something caused me to appear in your home that evening. Something causes you to see me, where in other instances, I purposely and knowingly reveal myself to others. Whatever this force is…it is beyond my control, and I cannot explain why."

My face wrinkled in confusion. "What do you mean?"

Gabe shook his head. "Caleb, you're the only human who has ever seen me without my intending you to." He paused. "Think of it as me being able to hide, but you can see me no matter the hiding place. It's hard to explain to you, boy. I wish I could. But I am not sure what...this is. I hope to understand it better as time passes, but for now, all I know is what I am experiencing." Gabriel looked to the side slightly then, as if someone called his name. He glanced back at me as he stood. "I have to leave now, but be assured I will try my best to come visit. I feel we were supposed to meet for a reason."

"What?" My voice cracked. "No, you can't leave me now. I'm all alone." Tears flowed from my eyes. "Everyone left me. Not you too!" I covered my face angrily.

Gabriel reached down and pried my hands off my face. He placed them on his wing, just as he had the very first time we met. I stared at the feathers and rubbed my thumbs across them.

"You are not alone, Caleb," he reasoned softly. "You will never be alone. And I will do my best to watch over you and stop by whenever possible."

I looked him square in the eye. "Promise."

He nodded and placed his hand on my head as he stood. "I promise."

Gabe kept that promise; I had seen him many times throughout my life. Sometimes he visited often, and other times, I wouldn't see him for months.

But the older I got, the more I noticed how many winged creatures—beings like Gabriel—were hidden all around me. And the more I grew, the more I realized I shouldn't really talk about Gabe to anyone, because people might think I was hallucinating. At some point, I started to wonder if he and the others were actually there at all.

Until I started having the visions.

"Cay!" Nikki called again. "I refuse to pay your tuition if you don't show up to class!"

"Gavin texted me that he's running late anyway!" I shouted back.

I leaned against the wall behind me and poked at my swollen eyes, feeling a familiar dull ache in the back of my head. I tried to ignore it and shook out my messy hair. Ignoring the pain didn't help at all; in fact, the pain only got worse, as it always did. My heart jolted, and I clutched my chest. I gasped and struggled to breathe for a moment, trying to force the feeling away.

It was happening again.

I staggered to the sink like a drunk, my head bumping against the mirror. I gripped the sides of the sink, shivering, my eyes squeezing shut. I silently prayed that this one wouldn't last long.

Different pictures filled my brain, flashing scenes of things I didn't understand, things I really couldn't explain even if I tried to. I could see some things quite clearly, such as a grassy area shaded by the trees of a forest, and a quick flicker of a girl who looked about my age. Other images were pretty ugly as well. The girl in the forest sometimes stood with her blood-spattered hands splayed out in front of her, face frozen in horror. I could see scenes of red liquid sprinkling onto the grass and other visions of an empty casket in an open grave surrounded by people crying. Unbearable things.

A deafening, high-pitched noise like a kettle whistling mixed with nails on a chalkboard filled the air, a sound so loud it caused me to let go of the sink and clutch my ears. I couldn't get away from it. I could only hope it would all just stop.

And it did.

Everything came to an abrupt halt, as if I never suffered that headache and chest pain and took a wild trip on the crazy train. I opened my eyes cautiously and observed my surroundings. I was on the white-tiled bathroom floor, on my knees, panting and shaking. I tried to regulate my pulse, breathing in and out repetitively at a slow pace. After a few of those deep breaths, I relaxed a bit.

I removed my hands from the sides of my head and cursed. They were stained red from the blood dripping out of my ringing ears. I could feel more of it moving from my nose to my lips, and I swore again, scrambling to my feet. Still shaking, I turned on the faucet and rinsed my hands and face and wiped my ears with the towel before any of it spilled onto my shirt. I looked in the mirror and tried to fix my wet, rumpled hair again. I really wanted to take another shower, but I knew I had no time. So, I let my hair lazily flop over my eyes as I wore it every day, and I brushed my teeth, trying to wipe the images in the vision from my mind.

Yes, it was true—I was clairvoyant. But I hadn't always been. The visions started the summer prior to my junior year in high school, when I was sixteen, and they only got worse as time passed. The first time I'd had one of those visions, I'd been lying in bed on a regular school night, casually tossing a tennis ball up and catching it. Then, out of nowhere, came the chest pain. I had started seeing all those deranged things, and gravity had caused my seemingly harmless tennis ball to whack me in the face. I had seen so many images, felt so many emotions, and after about ten seconds, all of the pain had ended with that same screeching sound echoing in my ears. I had snapped out of it to find blood staining my hands and my clothes, just as it had this morning. Just as it had after every bad vision between that first one and now.

Once I had that first "attack," I was terrified something was wrong with me. Sometimes, the visions would come with no warning. Not long after the first one, I started seeing other visions, little blips of things here and there, things I ignored for fear of accepting that I must be insane. If I pretended they were hallucinations, like Gabe, then I could at least try to live like a normal teenage kid.

That wishful thinking was short lived, though, because the visions started to come true.

When I finally talked to Aunt Nikki about it, she suggested maybe I should see a therapist. She thought the trauma of losing my mother so young and that I never had a father had resulted in me having some suppressed emotional issues that were arising in the form of hallucinations. She found me a therapist; someone kind who always nodded at every word that came out of my mouth. After a few sessions, nothing had changed. Nothing improved. I still wouldn't break down over my mom and dad, I still hung out with Gabriel, and I still kept seeing the future.

Once, when I was eighteen, I kept seeing numbers—the same foggy numbers behind my eyes, over and over. It was disorienting, and it got to the point where I couldn't even focus at school. So, I did what any guy my age would do with a repetitive set of numbers, and I played the lottery.

I won. One thousand dollars.

On three separate occasions.

Nikki finally believed I had a "gift" after I handed her that first winning stub, and she pulled me out of therapy.

Some visions I had over the years were positive, like that one, or insignificant and uneventful. But others were so bad, I could do nothing to prevent them. These visions were impossible to stop from happening, like the bus crash in the next town over or when Nikki's father was diagnosed with Parkinson's disease. I tried my best to ignore those kinds of premonitions and live my life as normally as possible. Aunt Nikki never forced me to talk about my ability, allowing me to continue living a regular and comfortable life. I cared about what happened to people, and I felt guilty when I knew things ahead of time that other people didn't, but just because I carried this burden didn't mean I was obligated to use it or anything.

I was just glad I wasn't losing my mind, and Gabriel was probably real. I still kept him secret from Nikki though, just in case for some reason he wasn't.

A few of the images I had seen this morning were ones I had actually seen many times before, during previous vision fits. This one had come to me more frequently lately, showing me the same forest, the same girl, and a lot of blood. Something about her and this vision didn't sit right with me.

"Caleb Michael Swift! Your ass is going to be grass if you don't get going!" Aunt Nikki shouted to me a third time. Knowing her temper, it was going to be the last time she called me before she came up and dragged me downstairs herself.

I ignored her call and went back to my room to grab my school bag and swing it onto my shoulder. I slipped on my sneakers and went down the hall to the stairs.

Nicole DeCarlo wasn't actually my blood relative, and anyone would know that just by looking at her, since she was part Jamaican and I was whiter than milk. I just called her my aunt because she had been my mother's best friend since high school, and I had grown up respecting her as a family member. My mother had picked her as my legal guardian if ever she passed away from the cancer, and Nikki had taken care of me ever since Mom died. She paid for all my schooling and doctor appointments and food and clothes, and she treated me as she would her own child. She was a hard-working registered nurse at a local clinic and currently paying for my college tuition all on her own too. I could never thank her enough for all she'd done for my mother and me.

Nikki stood at the bottom of the stairs, wiping her tiny hands with a violet-colored dish towel. She had a small frown planted on her face, and she cocked her head quizzically. "What's wrong, buddy? You don't look so good."

I trudged down the stairs and tried to brush past her. "Nothing. Just a headache." I wasn't exactly lying.

She stepped in front of me, blocking the front door, and preventing me from proceeding any farther. I turned my head away, attempting to conceal the pained expression on my face. I knew how shitty I must look.

"Caleb…" Nikki muttered, stepping closer to me. "Hon, what happened to your ears? Did you have a vision this morning?"

I didn't answer, and with all the strength a petite, five-foot-tall woman in her early forties could have, she grabbed my face with one hand, forcing me to look at her.

"Hey." She frowned with worry. "Something's not right, and you're going to tell me what it is."

I pulled away from my aunt's grip. "Nikki, it's nothing. Really. I slept crappy last night." I avoided her eyes—those large, brown eyes that pierced my soul and begged me to tell her about the visions. But, as usual, I really didn't want to talk about it with her. "Please, don't worry."

She patted my hair gently. "Is there something going on at school then? Is it drugs?"

I laughed. "Nikki, no, it's not drugs."

I smiled reassuringly and looked out the window behind her, seeing my best friend Gavin McDaniel pull into the driveway in his old, sky-blue 4x4. It was truly perfect timing.

"Gavin's here," I stated.

Aunt Nikki narrowed her eyes at me, and I swiftly kissed her cheek.

"Really," I protested, "I'm okay."

I sprinted out the door without another word.

This is what my life had been like for five years. I'd seen winged people and had visions of endless possibilities, a thousand different futures. For five years, I tried to rationalize why I wanted to be normal. I tried to convince myself I could ignore the future and just let bad things happen without feeling guilty about it. There had to be some unspoken rule about messing with the future, right? Regular people weren't psychic, and I was defying the laws of the natural world by having the ability to see ahead. If I didn't have this burden, I wouldn't have to justify it or feel this unwavering guilt.

But I *was* psychic. I *did* see different ways the future could turn out.

I tried to avoid my clairvoyance though. I wondered if being able to see the future had any purpose at all if I didn't plan to change it. I knew, deep down, there must be something I could do to reshape the images I saw. There had to be a way to help people without completely messing up the entire future of the world or breaking any "rules." I had seen this girl in my mind so often lately, more than anyone I'd ever had a vision of.

And after five years, I finally realized why.

CHAPTER 2

WHEN I REACHED THE PASSENGER side of Gavin's truck, I tore the rusty door open and scooted inside, shutting it quickly. Before my pal could greet me, I said, "Drive, Gavin. Hurry." I groaned, resting my head against the window and closing my eyes.

Gavin's tires squealed as he peeled out of the driveway, and we journeyed down the main road. He cleared his throat.

"Sorry I'm late, bro. I missed my alarm."

I sighed. "Don't worry about it. I just wanted to get the hell out of there. Nikki was on to me, and I didn't want her to come out and interrogate you."

He chuckled slightly. "When isn't she suspicious? She's your parent. She tries to protect you." He paused. "Dude…you look like hell."

Ugh. "Thank you, Gavin, I appreciate the words of encouragement."

"Really, Cay, you look like you just crawled out of the literal bowels of hell. Was it a bad one?" Concern tinged his voice.

I sat up in my seat and shrugged. "It seems like they're always bad lately."

Gavin was the only person I trusted with my life besides Nikki. He had been my best friend since kindergarten, my brother, and the only person I knew I could tell anything to. He was an ordinary, vision-less guy with messy, short-layered auburn hair and emerald-green eyes that girls frequently seemed to be attracted to. He was about my height and just as fit, considering we both were on the college ice hockey team, and his personality was golden. As much as I didn't like talking about my visions with anyone, not even Nikki, I was able to tell him all of them in detail without feeling like a freak. He also knew about Gabriel and how I could see creatures like him, and Gavin still believed me even though he'd never seen the winged beings himself. He was always a true friend. Sometimes, you just want your friend to be the one you rely on, and he had always supported and been there for me.

"How come you don't have visions about your dad and stuff?" Gavin lowered his voice slightly. "He's got to be out there somewhere, and you'd think your visions would show more people who are…relevant in your life. Right?"

I winced. Gavin knew the topic of my father was a touchy subject for me, but he could never help his curiosity.

"Most of my visions appear to revolve around events that have yet to happen, not about the past or anything like that." I tugged on a wet curl in my unkempt hair. "Unless, my future involves my past, then maybe I'd have a vision of him? I don't know." I shook my head. "And anyway, I don't even care about him. You know that. He could be dead, and I wouldn't feel a thing. He's *irrelevant* in my life."

"I know, I just wonder…" Gavin frowned and shrugged, not finishing his thought.

"I do, too, sometimes, but as far as I'm concerned, he left my mother to die alone. So, fuck him."

The rest of the ride to campus was quiet. Gavin and I were just starting out our third year of college. We attended a local university, so we constantly saw people we knew from high school. Our town was small, sat near the Appalachian Mountains in North Carolina, and went by the name of Divinity. Therefore, we had attended Divinity Elementary, Divinity High School, and now—yes, you guessed it—Divinity University.

I glanced over at Gavin, who had a dreary look on his face.

"What's wrong?" I asked him.

"I just feel useless sometimes, you know?" he muttered. "You have these crazy visions, and I can't really understand what you're going through. It's not a regular issue. Like, it's not girl trouble or ice hockey problems or some big paper. This shit is beyond all that." He suddenly stopped short as a doe and her babies sprinted across the road.

"Look," I said, once we began driving again. "I didn't ask for any of this, and I've never wanted it to affect you the way it affects me. I appreciate that I can talk to you about it, but if ever you feel like you can't handle—"

"No, man, I can handle it just fine! I only wish I could do more than just listen."

"You do plenty." I smiled hearteningly, even though I, too, wished someone could do more to help.

Once we pulled into one of the parking lots and got our stuff together, we hiked up the ridiculously mountainous hill toward University Hall to pick up some bagels. Then we headed out toward the science building for Planet Earth class, where we would sit for two hours and learn about the glorious planet we inhabited. I actually didn't mind the class, but the professor sucked and seriously made the time drag.

As we walked through the halls to our designated classroom, Gavin was complaining about the commuter parking situation, like most students did at least once a day. Out the windows, I could see threatening clouds forming in the sky, and rain started to pour on panicking students outside.

"Shit, we're lucky we missed that, right?" Gavin stared out through the dripping glass. We entered our classroom and slid behind our lab table before Professor Sampson started taking attendance. He was the only professor who even took attendance; most didn't care if we showed up or not these days.

"Nice of you to join us, boys." The husky teacher didn't turn from the whiteboard. "Glad you missed the rain."

We both laughed awkwardly and pulled our notebooks out. I began jotting down the notes from the slideshow Sampson provided via projector screen, while Gavin aimlessly doodled on the border of his notebook. He was a smart kid with incredible memory. He would highlight his books or make a mark next to what he needed to remember, and it would be filed into the contents of his mind for whenever he needed to use it. I, on the other hand, always needed to write down the facts on paper or I'd never remember them.

About a half hour into class, the door to the lab opened slowly, and a drenched, flustered girl stepped inside. She had long, curly, caramel-colored hair that was plastered to her face, and she stared at the floor as she shifted into the room. She obviously didn't feel at ease standing there with everyone staring at her.

"Hi…?" Sampson said with disregard. "Are you the new transfer student I was expecting to arrive on time?"

The girl muttered a "yes," and Sampson motioned her over to his desk.

"All right, let's see…" He put on his reading glasses and studied his attendance list. "Miss Adair, is it? Darla Adair? Gee, that's a mouthful." He rummaged through papers in search of the semester syllabus we'd all received back in September.

The girl nodded and glanced up, her piercing-blue gaze locking with mine.

It felt as though something was caught in my throat. As soon as our eyes met, I totally recognized her. Her anxious appearance gave it away.

She was the girl from my countless visions.

I was sure of it.

And I was also pretty sure I was creeping her out with my incredulous expression, so I quickly looked down at my notes.

"Perfect!" Sampson located a copy of the syllabus and handed it to her. "Take a seat by Doug over there, four tables back."

Darla proceeded to Doug's table, which would be an unfortunate partnership for her, considering he was the biggest prick and dumbest jock I knew.

Gavin elbowed me in the side, startling me slightly.

"I call dibs!" he hissed at me.

I rolled my eyes and leaned toward him. "That girl...she's the one who's always in my visions."

Gavin whipped his head around to look at me. "You've got to be kidding—"

"Enough chit-chat!" The professor clapped his hands and changed the slide to the next one without even explaining anything the new girl had missed.

Doug was already trying to flirt with the girl, his whitened teeth blaring out against his dark skin as he innocently offered his notes for her to copy down. I couldn't help but glower; it wasn't that I was into her or jealous or anything like that, but I felt a sense of protectiveness because of all the terror and agony I'd seen her go through in my visions. As far as I knew, I could be fully responsible for her safety or have to prevent the future I'd seen for her.

But this had never happened to me before, where someone I'd seen in visions and didn't know personally literally walked into my life. How would I even go about telling a complete stranger that she could be in danger? Would I just approach her and say, "Hi, I'm Caleb, I'm a psychic, and I've seen your future, so I just wanted you to be careful every day for the rest of your life?" I couldn't do that. She'd think I was nuts. But who was she, and why was she here?

Darla turned her head in my direction slightly, and for a moment, I thought she'd heard me. But that was stupid of me to even consider, since I clearly wasn't thinking out loud. She glanced my way for another second before returning her gaze to the board. I released a breath that I'd apparently been holding longer than I normally would, then continued writing down my science notes.

Class was so slow today. My hand was cramping from the note-taking, and I was getting a headache from straining my eyes to see the projector screen. Every so often, I'd peek over at Darla Adair and miss important notes Sampson would rush through as he clicked through his slideshow. At one point, Gavin ripped paper out of his notebook, scribbled something down, and then passed it over to Darla. She opened it, smiled, and slipped the note into her jeans pocket. Gavin looked at me and grinned sheepishly, and I smirked, giving him a subtle fist-bump.

Finally, at long last, Sampson released us from class. Gav and I slid out our chairs and pushed past everyone to get into the hallway. Exiting the stuffy room felt like stepping into the fresh air, even though we were still in the building.

I stretched as Gavin and I walked.

"My ass is actually sore from sitting there for so long," I groaned.

"I feel you." Gavin scanned the crowd, obviously looking for the new girl.

As if on cue, I felt a tap on my shoulder, and I turned around.

Darla was standing there, a little over five feet tall and hugging her science notebook close to her chest. She smiled at me then looked at Gavin and blushed.

"Hey." She ran a hand through her frizzy-from-rain hair. "I'm fairly new here, and I still don't know what I'm doing or where I'm going." She lifted her shoulders shyly. "Will you guys be on campus around noon still? I only had Planet Earth today, but I figured, you know, since you"—she gestured toward Gavin—"gave me your number, maybe if we got lunch or something—"

"Yeah!" Gavin blurted out, cutting her off. "Of course, we would love to help you out. We both only have one other class today before noon anyway." He was definitely pleasantly surprised by her forwardness.

Darla beamed. "I really appreciate it! It's hard meeting people, especially in college." Her smile faltered a bit, and she leaned in close to us. "And that guy I was partnered up with in class was so egocentric, a total creep. Not a good start to my first day."

"Yeah, I totally get you. Just meet us in the quad for lunch." Gavin smiled his best smile for her. "Stick with us. We promise to be un-creepy."

I nodded cheerfully in agreement, hoping this would be a good opportunity to find out more about her. I wanted to have some idea of who this person was before I saved her life.

Or ruined it.

"Great." She then pulled out a note from her back pocket and handed it to Gav. "Oh, and this is for you."

She bit her bottom lip as he grinned at her, then turned and disappeared into the wave of students.

"She wants me," Gavin said triumphantly.

"So much for not being a creep." I laughed, and he punched my arm hard. I shoved him toward the exit. "Let's just see what the future has in store for you both."

Gavin rolled his eyes heavily. "Your psychic jokes are so funny."

I chuckled in response, but part of me was completely serious.

"You know, I'm going to admit this right now," Gavin said as we sat on a table outside beneath an enormous umbrella. "I wasn't really thinking straight when I told her to meet us out here while it's raining."

I sighed. "Text her. That note had her number, right?"

He nodded. "Yeah, but I shouldn't text her right away. That would make me look too eager, you know?"

"But you are eager."

Gavin blinked. "Fine, I'll just text her." He narrowed his eyes at me, whipped out his phone, and unfolded the note Darla had given him.

As he typed away, I stared at the people walking past us, bustling this way and that to get to their classes or meet with friends. To the left, under a nearby table umbrella, sat two guys and two girls strumming on guitars, creating a harmonic tune that seemed to suit the current weather. Looking to my right, I saw a short girl who looked like a freshman light up a cigarette in the designated smoking area of the quad. She stood alone in the rain, struggling to keep her cig lit. For more reasons than one, I felt bad for her.

I couldn't help but think of how completely normal this was—people playing guitar and smoking. Nothing was special or strange about them or their actions. These people didn't see winged beings or have visions of the future. They just woke up, went to class, played guitar, and smoked.

The sky began to clear, the rain fading to a drizzle and the clouds parting, revealing tiny splotches of blue sky. Leaves blew around the quad, and people emerged from wherever they'd gone to take cover during the rain.

"Should I tell her *never mind?*" Gavin's voice cut through my thoughts. "I'm going to text her *never mind* since it's not raining anymore."

I couldn't help but laugh at him; he always worried too much. He showed confidence on the outside, but in reality, he was just as awkward as anyone else. I shook my head as I pulled out my sunglasses, continuing to observe the people around me while we waited. I liked that I could watch everything while keeping my eyes hidden.

Darla emerged from University Hall to our left, shielding her eyes from the growing sunshine. She looked around until she spotted us, and Gavin waved her over. A lump formed in my throat, possibly from nerves, mostly from anxiety. How did one go about telling a complete stranger they could see their future?

My cell buzzed in my pocket. I reached in, pulled it out, and unlocked it, revealing a message from Nikki.

Hope you're okay, kiddo. I don't have work tonight, so come home after practice. I'm making eggplant!

She must've been having a great day because eggplant was one of my favorite foods. I texted back a reply and looked up through my shades in time to see Darla take Gavin's clearly flexing arm. He was already starting Darla's campus tour as he gestured around, boasting about the lovely landscaping surrounding the quad. I got to my feet, and she glanced at me and smiled.

"Hey," she said quietly.

I muttered a hello and followed the two of them silently as Gavin gave her quite possibly the grandest tour I'd ever seen of our magnificent university.

I was beyond distracted, and it showed at hockey practice.

We were playing some four-on-four; Coach Lancer was nowhere to be found, and we didn't want to waste a day. We could at least practice for a couple hours. Hockey was usually one of my many means of escape from reality, and I enjoyed it immensely.

Unfortunately for me, Gavin had decided to invite Darla to watch us play, which made me skittish for some reason. I was one of two goalies for our team, the Divinity Falcons, but today I was sucking so badly as goalie that Coach, when he appeared, swapped me in and put me on defense. Team captain Gavin McDaniel, of course, was grinning ear to ear and performing better than usual. He was playing against me, and he frequently checked me into the rink wall in order to impress Darla. I rolled my eyes in response and flipped him the bird almost every time. In fact, I flipped him off pretty much whenever he just so happened to look in my general direction.

Once we decided to call it a day, Gavin and I went to the locker rooms to rinse off and change. We swung our duffel bags over our shoulders and headed for the bleachers, Gavin's eyes scanning them for Darla. To my surprise, she was sitting at the far end with one of my closest friends, Ava Westley.

Ava turned our way and waved playfully. The corners of my mouth turned up in a smirk, and I watched her twirl a strand of light-brown hair around her middle finger. Ava and I were friends, but on some occasions, we had been more than "just pals." We'd been close since high school, and we'd gone out together a few times. We'd *made* out more times than we'd *gone* out. But we were only friends, and we'd never been an actual couple. And that was fine, because we liked things the way they were.

Ava pinched my butt just before I plopped down next to her, and heat rose to my ears. She squinted at me and smiled mischievously, then wrapped her arms around me. I hugged her back. As usual, she smelled of liquor and sadness. At first glance, a person would see a bubbly college student with her whole future ahead of her. But there was a lot more to Ava than most people could see.

"I was just meeting your new friend!" Ava piped up as she released me. "I like this girl already."

Darla nodded and shuffled her feet. "We're going for coffee in a bit if you guys want to join."

"I would, but I have dinner waiting for me at home." I avoided eye contact with Darla. "Maybe tomor—"

Suddenly, for the second time that day, I felt that familiar pain in my chest, and my voice caught in my throat. I wheezed quietly and stood, giving Gavin a look. "I'll be back. I forgot something in the locker room."

Gavin nodded, the expression on his face filled with concern. Before anyone else could ask what was wrong, I excused myself and hustled toward the locker room.

I tasted blood in my mouth, and I ran toward the back of the locker room near the showers. Lucky for me—if lucky was the right word for it—the last few guys were packed up and heading in the opposite direction. As soon as I entered the last stall, I spit down the drain and fell to my knees, clutching my throbbing head.

I was expecting my usual visions of Darla in the woods. But the first thing I saw was the open grave and casket being lowered. I saw—through first person, as usual, with my own eyes—myself walking up to the hole in the ground. As I peered in, I saw the casket was no longer empty, and inside it was the outfit—just the clothes—my poor, deceased mother had worn as we'd put her in her grave. I was reliving a nightmare, one of the worst days I will ever remember.

The image shifted until I was standing in front of a house. It was a brief visual of a rustic, large place in the middle of the woods. I was waiting at the front door, staring at a brass knocker in the shape of lion's head. I lifted my hand, reaching for the knocker, feeling both at ease and filled to the brim with anticipation. The door opened, but before I could see who was behind it, the scene swirled in a dizzying array of color.

My body was wracked with pain, and the vision changed to a fuzzy image, a black shadow of someone with wings—Gabriel, I assumed. He was reaching out to me, flying above me, his majestic wings glistening in a blinding light behind him. He was shouting, but I couldn't hear him or see his face. My ears were ringing too loudly for me to understand what he was saying. I reached for his hand. His fingers clasped around my wrist, his touch so realistic that I was momentarily unable to distinguish between the vision and reality. Gabriel pulled me slowly up toward him, his shadowed face still unrecognizable as he shouted one single word, the only thing I was able to hear over the extreme ringing in my head.

"No!"

I came out of the vision violently. I was leaning against the shower wall, my hair plastered to my forehead. I was covered in blood that had poured from my nose, ears, and mouth. It was all over my hands, and my head spun at the sight of it. I reached up to the shower knobs and turned the water on, not bothering to strip off my clothes. I let the lukewarm spray soak my ruined hoodie, and I rubbed my face in anguish.

"Fuck this." I slapped my hands against the tile wall. I spit more to get the metallic taste out of my mouth then gargled the water. I shut the shower off and exited the stall.

Gavin was sitting on a nearby bench by some lockers, holding my duffle bag in his lap, which I'd forgotten when I'd left abruptly. He was frowning and stood when I approached him.

"Man, two nasty visions in one day?" He poked at my saturated sweatshirt. "You look like shit, worse than this morning. You're soaked. Here." He went to his duffle bag and pulled out some clothes. "You can't go home to Nikki like that."

I was grateful for the extra threads. "Sorry about that. What did you tell the girls?"

"They took off." He sat back down onto the bench while I changed. "But Darla was acting real sketchy. I probably wouldn't be saying that if we didn't know who she really was, but…"

"Sketchy, how?" I pulled on a pair of dry sweatpants that were a little too long but would suffice.

"She acted like she wanted to go after you. When you got up, I mean." He tapped his foot nervously. "Not like just to check on you. It was more…weird. As if she knew you were hiding something."

I threw my wet clothes into my bag and licked my chapped lips. "But why would she have any reason to believe I'd be hiding something from her? We've only just met."

"I don't know, man. Maybe she's got women's intuition. That's a thing, right?" He ran a hand through his hair. "I could've been reading it all wrong, but you know I get funny feelings sometimes. And girls always know when we hide shit from them."

I didn't respond. I hoped he was wrong, that she wasn't judging me based on my introversion around her. I was naturally the brooding type, as outgoing and social as I tried to be. But I'd read somewhere that it only takes a few seconds to make an impression on someone, and if she thought I was totally screwy now, there was no way she'd believe me when I told her I was psychic. If I had already made a bad impression on her, it would be extremely difficult to warn her that she was in some kind of danger. It was going to be hard enough to tell her all of it as it was, and she would probably be skeptical when I did.

My head ached, and I dragged a hand down my face. I had seen this girl countless times in my visions, but I had never thought about what would happen once I actually met her. I never rehearsed a speech or even thought about the way we'd come into contact. I just figured I would plan things out when the time came, *if* the time really came. I suppose in retrospect that may have been the dumbest conclusion I had ever come to. But now the time had come, and she'd moseyed on into my classroom today, waltzed right into my life with no idea of what I'd seen in her future.

I had bigger choices, harder decisions, more at stake here than I imagined. A person was in danger who, for once, I might have a chance to save. I had put this particular vision off for so long that I hadn't even prepared for the day it would come true. And now that day could be just around the corner. So what was I to do? Just sit her down and tell her, whether she believed me or not? Could I really just ignore this vision like I had so many others?

Not everything happened exactly as I saw it in my head. Some visions were unclear, and there were too many paths to be traveled. Once in freshman year at DU, I had multiple visions about this big fight Ava had with her dad. I saw three different ways it could go. Her father kicking her out being one, and in another they made up. The third was her running away. Out of all these paths I saw, she chose to run. It was none of my business to get involved, obviously, but I saw how the vision ran its course. Maybe this was like that, where there were several ways Darla could escape this bad path. Maybe Darla Adair wasn't in any grave danger after all.

But I couldn't know that for sure since I hadn't seen any variations of her future. I had no idea what the future actually held for her, and that was exactly why I had to at least try to warn her. If she listened to me, we could come up with a strategy or something, a way to get her on a different "path" and out of danger. I had to explain all of this to her somehow. I knew in my gut I had to tell her about what I'd seen. And soon.

Damn. This would be so much easier if clairvoyance was normal.

"Listen, Cay." Gavin rose from the bench and nudged my shoulder. "I know you've only just figured out who she is, and we both know she's here for a reason. This confirms that your visions obviously serve a purpose. You saw it coming; no pun intended."

I lifted an eyebrow at him.

"But now that she's here and we've actually met her and spoken with her, I think there's no reason to put off telling her the truth. Her life could be at risk." Gavin confirmed my concerns.

I made a face. "But maybe if I gain her trust first—"

"What if it's too late by then?" He adjusted his duffel bag awkwardly, glancing over his shoulder as if to make sure we were alone. "What if, while you spend all this time trying to get to know her and be her friend, she ends up dead? That could happen, right? Because even though you can see it all coming, she can't."

I sighed. I knew he was right. Even though he was my funny, laid-back pal, he always got me through hard decisions and moments like this. Well, nothing quite like this, exactly. This was a hell of a lot scarier than my typical visions-come-true. But regardless of the situation, Gavin was a logical thinker, a problem solver, and he hated seeing me struggle through anything.

Gav took my bag from me and swung it over his free shoulder. "Come on, let's get you home. We'll figure this all out."

I thanked the universe for blessing me with a friend, a brother, like him.

CHAPTER
3

"CALEB, YOU HAVEN'T EVEN TOUCHED your eggplant."
I stared down at one of my favorite meals, pushing it around
with my fork, leaning my cheek into the palm of my hand. I
didn't really have an appetite. Nikki was washing dishes already, watching me
with a worried frown.

I shrugged. "Sorry," I murmured.

She sighed and looked out through the glass back doors. The rain had picked
up again and lightning flashed across the night sky, illuminating the backyard.

She cringed as thunder boomed. "The rain is coming down hard today. It
got to my hair." She pulled her brown locks into a ponytail. "It got to yours too.
I see those little black spirals popping out behind your ears."

"You know what they say." I patted my jet-black hair down self-
consciously. I followed her gaze out the doors. "When it rains, it pours."

She shut the sink off snappishly. "Okay, what is with you today? You're all
doom and gloom." She put her hands on her hips and walked over to the table
where I was sitting. "When it rains, it pours? Tell me what's wrong."

I didn't even know what was wrong, really. I was clearly not new at
this psychic thing, yet it always confused and depressed me. It was all too
much to handle sometimes. Nikki thought of it as a gift, but she didn't know
enough about what I saw to understand how I felt about it. It was honestly
a curse, something that was always there, and I felt its presence every single
day. It was a burden to know things ahead of time that normal people just
shouldn't know.

Nikki pulled a chair out and sat, clasping her hands together. "You can tell me anything, you know."

I felt uneasy, even though I knew that was true. But I had other things on my mind. My thoughts buzzed with topics I wanted to discuss—specifically, one I had never really asked about before tonight. I pushed my plate of food to the side and set my chin on my palms.

"I feel like I don't know enough about myself," I stated boldly, unsure of what I even meant as the words left my mouth.

"What?" Nikki's eyebrows lowered. "What does *that* mean?"

I closed my eyes, searching my brain for answers. There were missing pieces in my life that had to be the reasons behind my ability to see the future or beings like Gabriel. "I feel like some things are just missing from my past. A story. I don't know. Stuff about my mother. Or who my father was."

"Uh…Oh." Nikki cleared her throat awkwardly. "Let's see…"

"Please, Nik, you have to know something." I put my hand on hers. "It's about time I asked, and I'm sorry I haven't done so sooner."

She stared at me for a moment, her eyes squinting with sorrow. I knew she knew something. I had always known, but I had never felt ready to ask. I should've been ready for a long time now, but the idea of talking about any of it still troubled me, even more than not knowing anything.

After a minute, she exhaled slowly and nodded. "It was a long time ago, you know. I don't remember much. I didn't know him that well either."

I didn't believe her entirely. Was she trying to protect me from what really went on between my parents? It could be that her memory actually was poor. Or, maybe she didn't want to remember. But that was neither here nor there, because I still deserved to know the truth.

"I'll take anything."

She hesitated, biting her fingernails for a minute before she finally spoke. "Caleb, I'm sure you've discovered throughout your young life that you are obviously very special and very different from others."

I fidgeted and cracked my knuckles. "Yes, I'm aware."

She swallowed hard and played with a bangle on her wrist. "I knew something was going to be different about you the day you were born. Everything leading up to your birth was…different." She looked sad again. "And when I took you in, I didn't know how I would handle all of it. Telling you about all these things that made you who you are. I didn't know where I would begin."

"So, start before I was born."

"Yes, I suppose that's a good place to start, isn't it?" She chewed her fingernails again anxiously, which was making me nervous. Finally, she went on.

"Okay. Let's see. Your mother—dear Tessa, may she rest in peace—we used to go out a lot whenever I was home from college. We would have parties on your grandparents' old farm, back when we lived in New York. She was a very carefree woman. Always adventurous, and the boys always chased her. She was such a doll. One night, we had an open-house party at the farm. We were young. We just loved to party. The more the merrier." She laughed. "You would've loved it all, Caleb. Definitely your kind of scene. Music, the outdoors, cool nights, and cozy bonfires. So, yes, one night, we had an open house, and your mother caught the eye of a stranger."

"My father, I assume," I said.

Nikki nodded. "Yes. He was friendly, very gentlemanly. Handsome. Not someone I pictured as the settling down type, though. He had a wild look in his eyes—the same blue eyes you have, honey. They're identical to his." She reached up and brushed one of my stray hairs from my face. "Anyhow, your mother and this guy hit it off pretty quickly. But we knew there was something…abnormal about him. He gave off strange vibes, and he had these big scars, one on each of his shoulder blades. Violent scars. Don't get me wrong; the feeling we got from him wasn't necessarily negative, per se. It was just weird."

"I get a 'negative' feeling from him." I grimaced, a pang of hatred in my gut. "He left my mother, and she died alone, Nicole."

"There's just more to the story, Caleb. You need to set aside your anger. This is important. It's about time we talked about it."

Aunt Nikki was being stern with me. She must be serious, so I shut my mouth.

"His name was Michael—hence your middle name. Your mother hooked up with him that night at the party. She wasn't responsible, clearly, not as responsible as I know you are, Caleb."

She narrowed her eyes at me, and I blinked awkwardly, gesturing for her to continue.

"She got pregnant. Your grandparents weren't thrilled about the situation, and they pretty much stayed out of it. Your mother was independent and old enough to do everything on her own without their help, and she sure as hell didn't need Michael's.

"But we didn't see him for a long time after that. Not until the day Tessa went into labor. Then he was right by her side, as if he'd never left. Only, he looked like he'd been beaten or was very ill. Or both. Wherever he'd been had to be hell or worse. But the strange part was that we hadn't told him your mother was in labor that night. He just showed up." Nikki scratched her head.

"As if someone had contacted him or something. He just knew. And I think he really did know somehow, because I didn't have time to get Tessa to the hospital; we had to get you out in the barn on the damn farm, and that's where Michael showed up!"

"She had to give birth on the farm?" I leaned forward. "Wow. That had to be so terrible for Mom."

"Caleb, you don't even know. It was a total nightmare. I thought she was going to die." She choked on the word *die*, and her eyes watered. She wiped them with the back of her sleeve. "Damnit, Tessa. Anyway, your mother went into labor while we were hanging out in the barn. Your father burst in not long after, battered and wearing ratty, torn clothes, and he kneeled by your mother and gripped her hand. It started to storm that day, a crazy storm, and I wasn't sure what we were going to do with only a rickety barn over our heads. Michael just kept looking at the sky and apologizing over and over. It was utter chaos. It was like the world around us was crumbling. Something unlike anything I have ever seen." She stared off, shaking her head.

"I don't understand why Michael bothered to show up that night if he wasn't planning to stick around." I never felt comfortable referring to him as *Dad* when in reality, he had just been a participant in the process that made me. "It's like he never existed. I never knew his face, or his name, or saw any photos of him."

Nikki's gaze was far away. "He wanted to be around. He just…couldn't. I don't exactly know why. He seemed like someone who was a good person, but also troubled in a way. Maybe he was bad news. We simply didn't know him well enough to say. You both were probably better off without him, and I think he knew that." She sighed. "The storm put Tessa and me in a panic, but he managed to calm us down as he helped bring you into the world. He told us to trust him and allow him to take control of the situation, and it'd all be okay. Michael was persuasive, and his need for us to believe him was enough for us to let him help. His decisions that night—and even the ones that followed—felt like they were the right choices. Like they were exactly what was best for everyone involved."

Her eyes flickered to mine. "That's why I wish I could help you forgive him. I understand why you can't. I carry a resentment toward him too. But I think part of the reason you are so special and the fact that you actually survived the way you were brought into the world…I think it was all because of him."

I rubbed my forehead in frustration. "It doesn't make sense, though. Not really. I have psychic abilities. That's not just something that happens to people."

Nikki had that sad look in her eyes again, but this time, it was combined with guilt. She waited a long time before speaking again, and when she finally did, she spoke very lowly.

"Caleb, there's something else. It's so hard to say this now after so much time has passed. Please, understand that whatever we did was for you, to protect you. There are reasons I didn't tell you things until you were old enough."

My heart fell to my stomach and began to pound. "Nicole..." My voice was barely audible. *Hold your ground, Caleb.*

"Sweetie, have you ever heard stories where, in some cases, a set of twins are born when the mother was only expecting one child?"

I nodded slowly. Where was she going with this? "Yeah, plenty. Happens all the time, apparently."

"And sometimes one or both of these babies are born with"—she paused, chewing on the inside of her cheek—"heightened senses? Maybe an otherworldly connection to each other or to things beyond what normal people can sense? They have unusual abilities sometimes."

"Sure, I've heard of that happening before...in *comic books*." I stared hard at her. "I don't understand what this has to do with me, Nikki."

Tears escaped Nikki's eyes. "Caleb, there was a twin. You were not the only baby born in the barn that day."

"W-what?" I leaned back in my seat, feeling dizzy. "He or she is dead, I'm guessing. The baby died at birth?"

Nikki looked at the ceiling. She, too, leaned back in her chair and grabbed a tissue from her pocket. "She. It was a girl. And she didn't die. She was, and may still be, very much alive."

"Oh my God," I whispered. I had a twin sister—*a twin sister*—and she was out there somewhere, alive in the world. I couldn't believe it. "Well, where is she? Does she know about me? Is that where Michael is? Why aren't we together?" I had so many questions boiling under my skin. I was getting chills. It couldn't be true. This sort of thing didn't just happen to people. But Nikki would never lie to me, at least not about something so serious.

Nikki rubbed the sides of her head. "God, Caleb, I really don't know the answers to any of those questions. I had only seen her the day of your birth. And then Michael took her and left."

I was taken aback. "What? What do you mean, he took her?"

Nikki shrugged. "Your mom was young, single, and unemployed with no help from her parents. One baby was already too much. But two?" She shook her head. "The pressure was on, and Michael was offering. He asked us to let him take one of you off Tessa's hands. Begged us, in fact. How could we deny the man one of his two children?"

"So, you just…what?" I stumbled over my words. "Flipped a coin over who parented who? Or did one of them just decide which one of us they wanted more?"

"It wasn't like that, Caleb. Don't be ridiculous." Nikki frowned at me. "It was in your mother's best interest, and also yours and your sister's. Your mother had no money, no support. She anticipated one child, planned for one child. Michael could've left her to fend for herself, but instead, he offered to take one of you and raise you. They both knew they weren't going to have a real relationship. One-night stands rarely lead to a happily ever after." She sighed, crossing her arms over her chest. "And an unhappy relationship based solely on the fact that you have children together? Think about it, Cay. After a couple of years, your parents would've separated, one of them taking one or both of you. Then you two would've been raised in a broken home, a broken family. What kind of life is that for a child?" She reached for my hand. "Your mother needed help. She needed to make an immediate decision before she became too attached to the idea of keeping both of you when she knew she couldn't. You have to understand."

I yanked my hand out from beneath hers. I didn't want to be touched or consoled. She gasped sharply, a surprised look upon her face. Tears sprang in her eyes again. She was probably hurt by my coldness, but I didn't feel bad. I couldn't feel bad.

"Caleb, please." Nikki's voice was the one she often used to coax me. "Looking back now, maybe there were better options. Maybe we could've done something else. But we were scared. Tessa was so *scared*, honey. She just wanted to be okay. She wanted her babies to be okay. We were all just trying to protect you."

"I just can't believe my own mother was okay with this. Giving up one of her own children. Taking one and not the other." I rubbed my eyes with the heels of my palms. I was getting a pounding headache, not like my vision headaches, but from stress. "Although, I guess I didn't really know her all that well, did I?"

"Caleb!" Nikki glared at me through her puffy eyes. "Show your poor mother some damn respect. She did her best!"

I stood, my chair scraping against the kitchen floor. I stared at her in disbelief.

"Respect? How…how can you even say that!" I had been wrong about myself, thinking I wanted to hear the truth. I couldn't handle this. "She gave one of us up to a complete stranger. Michael took…he took my sister away. He was a stranger who took a woman's baby and left with her without a second thought! Did my mother even ask for his contact information, did she even consider that my sister and I might want to find each other at some point in our lives?"

Heat rose to my face as I saw Nikki look down at the floor silently, confirming my suspicions that my mom didn't bother with any of that. There was no contact information. I had no way to find my sister or even Michael. My hands shook with fury.

"It was supposed to be as if she never existed, wasn't it?" I said slowly. "Mom took the easy way out of a tough situation and erased my sister's existence entirely. How could I possibly have 'respect' for that?" I paced around angrily. No matter how hard I tried, I would never be able to understand this.

Breathe, Caleb. A sense of ease from my subconscious tried to push its way in, but I couldn't listen; my rage was stronger. "I can't even believe you right now. I can't even fathom what could be so fucked up in your minds that you could give some one-night stand, a clearly dangerous stranger, my mother's child and just be totally okay with it!" I gripped my scalp. "I mean, who the hell does that? Was there even an actual legal agreement? Did my mother even miss her other child?"

"Of course, she did!" Nikki rose to her feet, blinking wildly. "But she couldn't think about it. She had you to worry about. She couldn't dwell on the past. She did what she thought was best at the time. Caleb, you have no idea. I know this is hard for you to understand—"

I gaped at her. "Understand? Understand that somewhere out in the world I have a twin sister? Understand that my mom chose to forget she was ever born? Understand that you handed her over to some lowlife like, 'oh, here you go, you want one? Sure, take the one kid, they'll never know the difference. It'll be fine?' Bullshit!"

"Caleb Michael Swift, you watch your mouth! It wasn't like that at all—"

"I can't do this. I can't be here." I backed away from the table. I was becoming unhinged in this room, and I had to leave. I needed air.

"Sweetie, please, it was all out of love. It all turned out for the best, didn't it?" She attempted to smile, but it looked more like a grimace. "Your father obviously cared enough to help Tessa and take care of one of his own. I'm sure he thought of you. You weren't there. You can't judge him when you never knew him. I don't think he was a lowlife, and your mother was such a good person—"

I put my hands out in front of me. "Just stop. I really can't do this right now. I need to go for a walk."

Nikki's face was stained with tears, and she sniffed. "It's raining. You'll catch a cold."

"I'll wear a jacket."

I stormed out of the kitchen and grabbed my coat and hiking boots from the closet. I headed back into the kitchen to the glass doors and sprinted into the rain toward the forest behind the house.

I ran so fast through the woods, everything sped past me in a distorting blur. I was practically gliding up the mountainous terrain, avoiding rocks and branches effortlessly, in such an unusual way that made me think it was just that—unusual. My feet thudded on the wet forest floor, and it was good to be far away from everything. It felt rectifying to be able to run away from a problem for once. This was a problem I actually *could* run from—at least, for now.

When I finally stopped to catch my breath, I pounded my fist into a wet tree trunk, cursing at the sky, until my knuckles were split and bloody. The rain had slowed to a drizzle, and I clutched my freshly wounded hands to my chest. As I continued to stumble up the muddy, rocky path, I began to feel the protection of the tall trees. Being in the woods always calmed me, even when I was a kid. I had the ground to explore, countless trees to climb, the fresh, earthy smells. I always felt hidden and safe there.

I finally couldn't go anymore, not because I was tired but because the mountain was becoming too steep. My knuckles were throbbing, but the pain didn't stop me from reaching for the lowest branch of a nearby tree and hoisting myself up onto it. The tree was kind of slippery, the bark soggy from the rain, and I had to clutch the branch above it to hold myself steady. My legs were tingling strangely, as if they were aching to move faster. I lifted myself onto the higher branch, then up onto the next one until I was within the tree.

Calm down, Caleb.

A chill ran from the back of my head and down my spine, like someone was with me, in my mind. The thought didn't feel like my own. It was soft and distant, and it sounded like someone else. First the visions, and now I was hearing voices? I was losing my shit. But I heeded the voice's warning, taking it as my subconscious trying to get me to settle down, and I took a deep breath before continuing my escalation. I faced a thicker branch on a tree that was a few yards away and a couple feet higher than I was, and I considered whether I could make the jump or if I'd fall to my death.

My instincts told me to jump.

My legs tingled still, an electric sensation that seemed to propel me upward and forward, almost inhumanly, similar to the swift movement of a flying squirrel. I tasted the rain, for a moment feeling one with the air, and I reached my arms up, so they'd hook onto the branch. I braced for impact, and the bark scraped my palms as I gripped it. I dangled there, surprised at how I'd actually made that jump, a feat that should have been impossible. What was going on with me?

I hoisted myself up with ease, feeling adrenalized. That's what it had to be—adrenaline. All the earth-shattering news and my extreme anger had caused me to have an adrenaline rush.

But if this was true and I was defying the laws of physics, then I wanted to get higher up this mountain. I stood on the branch, steadied myself, and then sprinted to the edge. I stared straight at the branches sticking out from the rock face of the mountain ahead of me. The world around me slowed down as I pushed off the branch I stood on, grabbing the next and sliding my feet into the crevices in the rock. I was being stupid, and I was well aware of it. But something seemed to be guiding me up the mountain, far away from all the uncertainty and fear. As if the mountain was calling me, and I was prepared for the clarity it would bring.

I continued up through the trees growing out from the mountain, climbing effortlessly. I felt as if the high was endless, and I had the ability to do anything. Being unstoppable—that was every child's dream. Though I'd had to grow up a little faster than most, I'd always dreamed of being able to fly or become invisible or something. Having superpowers and protecting the world. When I was little, I always thought that if I'd been a superhero, maybe I could've saved my mother.

But instead of having fun, heroic, unstoppable superpowers like those, I was stuck with seeing futures I may or may not be able to change. I was stuck with an ability that hurt more than it helped. I couldn't fly, and I couldn't turn invisible. I could only watch the future like it was a show on television, unable to really figure out how to use this to save others. I could only see ahead as horrible things unfolded, unsure if I could really do something about it. Or I just chose not to do anything at all.

I guess that made me more like a villain than a hero.

I went faster and faster, scrambling up the face of the mountain. The branches and rocks whizzed and whirled past me in a blur. The rain, a gentle drizzle just seconds ago, pelted away at my face, and it stung my skin from the speed. Climbing so easily, moving this fast felt so natural, so instinctive, and almost comfortable; I felt as though I could keep climbing up with my eyes closed. I wouldn't try it, since I was obviously not superhuman. I burst through a green bush and slowed to a halt when I realized only flat land lay in front of me. I'd reached a plateau near the top of the mountain.

The rain stopped abruptly. The full moon lit the grassy floor, which sparkled with dew as if there had never been a storm. This clearing was an area that had been untouched by man—any man—until I placed my dirty shoes upon it. The wind whipped around me, not harshly but warm and soothing, drying my wet clothes and skin. I cautiously leaned over the edge of the cliff, peering down at the world below.

I was so high up, I couldn't see my home or campus or even our town of Divinity for that matter. The concept astounded me; I was standing on this mountain, a piece of land that was untouched by human life, with the moon so large above me it made everything else seem so small. And it didn't feel lonely...it felt beautiful.

Being alive is such a beautiful gift, don't you think? The other voice, the foreign voice in my mind whispered so quietly the words seemed to fade with the wind.

I smiled, feeling secure inside, as if a blanket were wrapped protectively around me. A droplet of water rolled down my cheek, and I touched it, for a moment thinking of how the rain had stopped. Another rolled down my opposite cheek and over my lips, tasting salty and warm. And then another. And another.

CHAPTER

4

EYE CONTACT HAD ALWAYS BEEN something that completely fascinated me.

I never liked looking people directly in the eyes. I just felt awkward, I suppose. But awkward wasn't quite the right word to describe it. I couldn't keep my eyes from wandering when I talked to people. No one had ever pointed it out to me; I'd just noticed it one day. Of course, Nikki would call me out on it, thinking I wasn't listening since I wasn't looking directly at her while she spoke.

I had never been in love before, nor did I ever care to be. I'd never even made eye contact with Ava or other girls I had liked in the way people who like each other do. I wanted to find love someday, obviously, but I didn't make it my lifelong mission to lock eyes and feel something. Doing so just felt funny to me, and whenever I would accidentally make eye contact with someone, anyone, I felt as if they knew all my thoughts. My heart would jump and fall into my stomach, like the world had stopped. And then I'd look away really fast. Maybe it was an insecurity or something. It just amazed me what looking into someone's eyes made a person think and feel.

It was a sunny Tuesday afternoon. The fall air was a comfortable temperature—jeans and t-shirt weather. I was outside sitting in the quad on the stone wall with Gavin, talking. He was talking; I was listening. Well, half listening—I couldn't stop thinking about my conversation with Aunt Nikki the night before. She'd called me a bunch of times after I'd run off, and finally, I'd made my way down the mountain and back home, apologized to her with a quick kiss on the cheek, and retreated to my room to sleep.

I wanted to tell Gav the story at some point. But my mind was deep in thought, and I wasn't quite sure what he was even saying anymore. My gaze roamed the quad, and I observed people in the way I usually did, this time without my sunglasses.

That was when I accidentally locked eyes with someone at a nearby table. A girl with a fairly large novel open in front of her. She had long, golden, beach-wave curls framing her face and eyes bluer than the damn Caribbean Sea. I had seen her a few times around campus and town before, but I had never spoken to her. I wasn't shy around girls and didn't mind talking to them, but the thought of going up to this particular female always made my stomach turn and my face warm. So, I didn't.

I wasn't sure if she was looking at me first or if I looked at her first and she caught me. But there we were, making eye contact, and I couldn't look down. I wanted to, but her eyes made me feel like she was invading my head. Not in a bad way, I just felt very vulnerable. And part of me liked it.

I kept blinking in the hopes I would snap out of this trance. She kept blinking, too, her soft red lips parting a bit in confusion. I felt strange, almost numb to everything around me. My heart did that funny thing where it fluttered in my stomach. It almost felt as if I knew her, but I knew I didn't actually know her. A memory was trying to surface, but I couldn't pinpoint where or when or if I'd seen her before. She was beautiful, and warmth flooded to my face as always.

She tilted her head, her face full of fascination, then broke the eye contact for a moment to squint down at her book, as if we'd never had this weird but normal human interaction. She glanced up at me again, peeking through long eyelashes. I frowned, suddenly aware that I must look like an ass, gawking at her, and I finally pried my eyes away from hers. I stared down at my shoelaces, and the world sped up around me.

"And then I thought I should drop out of college and dedicate my life to trekking the Appalachian Mountains," Gavin said loudly, trying to get my attention.

I chewed my lip and looked at him sheepishly. "Sorry, dude. I stopped listening."

His eyebrows lowered. "It's okay. You seem a little bummed out today." He looked at his watch. "We've only got fifteen minutes until class. We can talk about it after or whenever you're ready."

"Hmm." I shook my head, smiling at the fact that he always, always knew when something was up. "Yeah. Just warning you now. It's a lot."

"Well, don't get me all excited now. I won't be able to wait!"

He grinned, clearly trying to cheer me up and make light of whatever I was going to tell him. Today was one of those days I greatly appreciated his lightheartedness.

"Cay, I'm so sorry. I can't even believe it." Gavin's emerald eyes were wide like saucers and his chin rested on his arms.

We were sitting at a table in the corner of the student cafeteria. I told him everything Nikki had said about my parents and how I'd felt after learning about what they did. I'd left out the part about the mountain-climbing adventure, though. I felt like that was more of a personal experience.

"I know." I took a bite of turkey wrap. "I was so pissed. I'm still pissed."

"I mean, yeah." Gav sat up and shook his head. "I would be too. I feel pissed for you. This is all so crazy, man." He looked down at his salad and picked up a spinach leaf with his fingers. "What are you going to do now?"

I bit into my food again. "About what?"

Gavin rolled his eyes. "Well, are you going to try to find your father now? Or your twin sister? What are you going to do?"

I stopped chewing for a moment, put my food down, and swallowed. "Nothing."

"What do you mean, nothing?"

"I mean, I'm going to keep living my life. I'm not going to stop everything just because my father may be out there and have some sort of explanation for what he and my mother did." I crossed my arms. "I'm not going to drop everything just because I have a sibling I know nothing about. It's not like this proves anything about my clairvoyance, either. I'm still different, with or without this news. The world will keep on turning."

I knew Gav wanted to know why I didn't plan to pursue this lead. But he knew not to press any further. He gave me an apologetic look, and I shrugged.

"I know how important this news could be in someone else's situation," I said. "But in my case, I can't let it complicate the life I already have. I'm fine with the way things are. I can live with the fact that I have some whacky past and weird psychic abilities."

Gavin tugged his shirt collar awkwardly. "Yeah," he muttered, leaning over to glance around me. His eyes lit up for a moment, and he smirked.

I turned to look behind me. Darla Adair had entered the cafeteria, bag slung over her shoulder, her body slumped in a way that conveyed pure exhaustion. I immediately empathized with her.

"She should sit with us. Get her attention," Gavin hissed at me hopefully.

I looked back at him, lifting my eyebrow, then turned to wave Darla over.

She gave a weak smile, scampered our way, and sat down, rubbing her temples. "Hey, guys."

Gavin moved his seat closer to her. "Rough day?"

She nodded. "You noticed?" She placed her hands on her lap. "I get a lot of migraines. Too many thoughts swimming in my head. College sucks." Her eyes flashed to Gavin briefly before she swung her bag onto the table and dug through it, pulling out a granola bar.

"I hear you." Gavin's voice was laced with sympathy. "How was class today?"

"I had Roman Civilization at ten a.m., and my other class is online. I like Roman Civ."

Gavin continued nodding in agreement to every single thing Darla said thereafter, and my eyes literally rolled back into my skull. After a bit of small talk, Darla then excused herself for a moment, heading out of the cafeteria.

I watched Gavin ogle her as she walked away, and I shook my head. "Could you be any more obvious?"

He turned his head to glare at me. "What if I'm trying to be obvious?"

I snorted and rolled my eyes again, but as I did, a slight pressure hit the base of my skull. "Shit, not a vision, not now." I winced and rubbed the spot.

Gav scooted closer to me. "Do you need me to do anything?"

I closed my eyes. "Maybe I can control it somehow, prevent it from happening." That was wishful thinking. The pressure started to twitch, getting more and more persistent, and I was beginning to feel a slight pain. "No, maybe not."

I rose to my feet as my chest began to constrict, and I abandoned my worried friend at the table. I started walking faster as the pain increased and my eyesight blurred, mentally trying to convince myself to keep the vision at bay until I reached the restroom.

As I rounded the corner to the hallway, I suddenly collided with Darla.

"Oh!" She jumped back in surprise. "I'm sorry, Caleb, I didn't see—"

She paused, I'm assuming because of the grievous look on my face. I couldn't even see her anymore, my sight was so fuzzy, like snow on an old television screen when the cable goes out.

"Caleb, are you all right? You don't look well."

Her voice was muffled; I could barely hear her.

"Help," I managed to say before the vision took control.

And then I hit the ground.

I stirred. The vision had ended, and all I could see was the blackness behind my eyelids. My back was leaning against a cool tile wall and I was sitting on a similar tile floor. I was in the bathroom. I opened my eyes.

Darla sat across from me on the floor in the handicap stall we were locked in, arms around her knees, hugging them to her chest.

I gasped and moved to sit up, but I felt too dizzy and held my head. "Darla…how—?"

"You fell on the floor just outside, and I dragged you in here as fast as I could." Her voice was quiet, even though it appeared no one was in the restroom with us. She was looking at the white wall behind me, her head leaning back against the stall. She was strangely calm for someone who had just witnessed…whatever she had just witnessed. "I figured you didn't want anyone seeing you. This is the ladies' restroom, by the way."

I squinted at her. I figured she'd want an explanation for what happened. Was it too late to pretend nothing was wrong? Probably. Maybe this was the time to be honest. But where would I begin, and shouldn't we leave the bathroom?

"You don't need to explain anything, Caleb."

"Okay." I blinked at her, confused. "Why…why didn't you call emergency services? Or bring me to the health center? Why bring me in here of all places?"

"You don't really want me to take you to the health center, do you?" She rose to her feet, reaching her hand down to me. I hesitated then grabbed it, shaking my head no as she pulled me up.

She kept a hand on my shoulder to steady me until the feeling returned to my legs. "We should probably talk."

A lump formed in my throat. "O-Okay." What did she mean by that?

Avoiding my eyes, she unlocked the stall, and we snuck out of the restroom.

As we headed back to the cafeteria, I wiped my nose with the back of my hand, checking for blood. Nothing, thankfully. After I checked my ears and made sure I was physically unharmed, I smoothed my wrinkled shirt awkwardly, feeling a cold sweat.

This was so weird. She had to think I was insane. I mean, I couldn't blame her; *I* still thought I might be insane.

"So, I…" I cleared my throat. "Thanks for not letting anyone see me like that. How long was I out for?"

Darla shrugged casually. "Not long. Maybe about a minute or two. At first, I thought you were…I don't know. You were so pale, I thought you might be sick." She paused. "I was about to text Gavin to see if maybe you're, like, anemic or something and needed help, but then you woke up."

We walked toward the back of the cafeteria to where Gavin was waiting. I glanced at Darla's face, which was twisted in the kind of expression I assumed I have when I get my pre-vision headaches.

"Are you okay?" I asked her.

"It's loud in here."

But it wasn't, really.

We both sat down silently, Gavin glancing between Darla and me skeptically. She returned to her granola bar, and I picked up my unfinished turkey wrap. So, were we going to talk right now? Or did she mean later? What could she possibly want to talk about with me?

Ugh. Everything was weird now.

"Uh," Gavin murmured, seemingly stunned.

I imagined he was just as uncomfortable and tense as I was at that moment. We glanced at each other, and I could tell he knew something was off.

Darla fiddled with the wrapper in her hands, the crinkling momentarily distracting Gav and me, and we both stared at her. She looked at each of us, then at the ceiling, and then at her wrapper. After she swallowed her food, she placed her hands on the table.

"Okay, it really wasn't that weird until you both were thinking it was weird." She squeezed the wrapper into a crumpled ball and tossed it onto the table.

I was baffled by her comment, and Gavin and I briefly looked at each other again.

She sighed heavily. "Please, just voice your thoughts."

"Uh," Gavin muttered stupidly again.

I placed my food down. She wanted to talk? Then I needed to lay everything out on the table, metaphorically speaking.

"Listen," I started, "what happened back there…I know we just met and all, and this might sound wild, but I get these visions—"

Darla closed her eyes. "I just want to know why I am in them."

I sat back in my chair. "Excuse me?"

She rubbed her forehead and grumbled. "It's not weird that you're psychic. It's weird that I was able to see what you saw. In my mind. And I saw me."

"Not weird?" Gavin stammered, saying my exact thoughts aloud.

I swallowed hard. "I don't know why." I shook my head, bewildered by this whole conversation. Her tone made me feel as if she was accusing me of something. Um, hello? Why was I being interrogated here? "Why were you able to see what's in my head?"

Darla pursed her lips. "I can hear people's thoughts, and I left the cafeteria because it was getting too noisy in my mind with all the people in here, and then you bumped into me in the hall and had a vision, and I was able to see it and—"

My jaw dropped slightly. "You hear thoughts? Like, you're a mind reader? So—"

"I didn't actually think you were anemic. I heard you thinking you were going to have a vision just as you dropped to the ground, and I figured you'd want to be somewhere not so public when it happened, but I didn't expect to actually see it. It was so freaky!" Darla exclaimed, putting her hands up. "Clear as day, I could see everything going on around me while I dragged you into the stall, but in my head, I could see everything you were seeing and—"

"Can we please slow down for a moment?" Gavin looked between Darla and me, his outburst startling us. "Let's all just chill out for a second. What the hell are you two talking about?"

Darla and I both got quiet. I don't think either of us knew how to answer his question at that moment.

Gavin looked flustered and he spoke again. "I think you both need to start from the beginning."

I looked at Darla and nodded once. "You first."

She rolled her eyes. "Of course." She moved her chair closer to the table and rested her arms on it. "Since I was in high school, I could hear thoughts, read minds, I guess. Whatever you want to call it. But not in a way where I just hear everything a person is thinking." She tugged on one of her curls. "Usually, the voices come and go. I tune them in and tune them out, kind of like when you channel surf on the radio. I can't always control it. There's a lot more to all of that, and I'm not going to go into the details right now, but…" She trailed off. "I know I heard Caleb's thoughts in Sampson's class my first day here. I just didn't really pay attention to them. I ignored his thoughts like I ignore all the others. They become distant hums in the back of my mind."

"So, you knew I was psychic when you came to class yesterday?" I asked cautiously.

"Not at that moment. I mean, I got a strange feeling from you that piqued my curiosity. I thought you might be different, like me. So I introduced myself after class. Regardless if you were or not, I would've anyway." She tilted her head and looked at me. "You know, initiated conversation and made friends with you. Or we would have bonded over abilities people wish they had but we are inconvenienced by. Normal college shit." She waved a hand. "But I knew there was something off about you for sure when you left so quickly at your hockey practice."

I studied her face. She seemed serious, as indescribably bizarre as this all was. She had approached us yesterday with good intentions.

"I figured we'd talk about it eventually." She continued, "I know a lot about being different, and it seemed like you thought you were the only one in the world who was. And the fact that Gavin knew about what you could do made me wonder how open you'd be to discussing it all." She looked at my astounded friend, biting her bottom lip. "I thought it would make things easier, having friends outside of my own bubble who are okay with the 'ability' thing. I've never really talked about it with anyone but my family before, so I just thought it would be good for me to try at some point.

"But then last night when I was home, I was, I don't know, zoning out, I think." She squinted, as if she were remembering. "I started daydreaming, I guess, or maybe I had fallen asleep. I had a dream where I felt like I was in your head, trying to help you be calm. I know I don't know you at all, but seeing people upset makes *me* upset. I didn't know what was wrong or why your emotions were running hot. I only tried to ease your stress because it was making me stressed. And then I saw you flying up a mountain, Caleb."

She paused, and I felt beyond embarrassed. What I thought had been a personal experience, I had actually, technically, shared with someone else. She was obviously reading my mind now, though, probably realizing that the previous night hadn't been a dream, because she didn't go into detail about it.

"You seemed really upset, so I *thought* to you to make you feel better. I tried to send you a message with my mind. The whole thing was strange. I mean, I thought it was all just in my head, but—" Her mouth snapped shut.

I flashed back to the previous night when I had heard a distant voice that didn't belong to me. Had it been her voice in my head when I was climbing the mountain? I'd thought I was losing my mind. Thinking back now, it had to have been hers. I had a tingling sensation in my spine, and a voice—her voice—had told me to calm down. And I did; she'd helped a little. And then she'd said, *Being alive is such a beautiful gift, don't you think?*

I thought the phrase to myself, all the while knowing she could hear it from across the table.

"Yeah," Darla muttered, staring hard at the granola wrapper. "Anyway, it didn't seem real. I thought nothing of it. Until just now in the hall...."

"Okay, so now what?" Gavin crossed his arms, looking cynical. "What do my man Caleb and I do with your information?"

Darla frowned and blushed furiously, and I glared at my friend.

"Gavin..." I began.

"Don't you guys think this is too unbelievable? No—too coincidental that you both have these special abilities, and you both live in the same town, attend the same college? I mean, what are the chances of that happening, really?" He shook his head at me. "This isn't normal."

His comment made me wince. I knew I wasn't "normal," and he usually worked hard to not remind me of that. He must have seen the hurt in my expression because his face softened, and his lips tightened.

"I'm sorry, Cay. And Darla."

Her face was still red, but she shrugged it off. "No biggie. And to answer your question: the chances are pretty high, considering there's a whole lot more of us out there than you both realize."

"Oh." Gav awkwardly stared down at his arms. "Well, I just hate not understanding things like this, not having control or having an answer for Caleb's...thing. I have a fear of the unknown."

"Doesn't everyone?" Darla practically whispered.

The three of us sat in silence for a while. I think we were all really overwhelmed by our revelations. I couldn't stop thinking about how I wasn't the only person who had an ability. I was more than just overwhelmed. The very idea that there was a whole world out there with people like me in it blew my mind.

This must be how Darla and I were supposed to meet, why I was having visions about her. She was different, and I was the only one who might be able to help her if she was in trouble. That should make things easier, right? My heart was racing. I was sure anyone in my situation would've been thinking, *okay, what next?* Or perhaps, *let's evaluate the situation.* Something along those lines.

But all I could think, over and over in my mind—and I knew Darla could probably hear it—was the word *why?*

Gav suddenly pushed his chair back. "Well, I could use a drink." He rose to his feet and gathered his belongings. "Care to join me?"

Darla and I looked at each other for a minute, and then she stood as well.

"Let's go. Someone's got to show me where the good bars are," she said.

My shoulders relaxed as if I had been holding my breath the entire time. Some normalcy sounded good. I murmured in agreement and followed the two of them out of the cafeteria.

We didn't talk about it at the bar. But Darla and I exchanged numbers when we parted ways so we could talk about it later. This was all so new to me, meeting someone who had a gift—or, in our opinions, a burden—similar to mine. I wasn't looking for, like, a support group or anything. But it would be good to have someone who understood what I went through when no one really understood. And it would be so much easier to protect her now that she knew I was psychic.

Gavin drove me home around dinnertime. He kept asking questions I didn't have the answers to. I didn't feel like talking, but I felt bad for him, considering all he ever wanted was to help me.

"And I'm also wondering if she heard my thoughts when she came into class that first day," he continued, running a hand through his auburn hair. "You know what I was saying about her, but you don't know what I was thinking, dude."

"I don't think I want to know." I raised my eyebrows at him. "But I have no idea if she heard or not. Whenever she calls me, though, I will be sure to ask her."

Gav's face reddened. "I would rather you didn't. I'd like to think if she did hear my thoughts, she won't talk about what she heard."

I laughed, and he pulled his truck into the driveway behind Nikki's car. As I opened the door to get out, Gavin grabbed my arm.

"Hey, I'm sorry for being short with you guys before." He let go of me and gripped the steering wheel, staring at his knuckles. "It was strange having someone in the loop, especially someone we've only just met. I got defensive."

I shook my head. "Gavin, it's fine. I know you're just trying to protect me." I felt self-conscious then. I didn't want him to feel guilty for anything, and I didn't like ending our conversations so somberly. "I know it's all because you care so much about me," I cracked like a wise-ass.

Gavin wrinkled his nose and rolled his eyes. "You wish I loved you that much, man."

I grinned and shut the door. As I walked across the lawn, he wailed on the horn before speeding away. I put the key into the door, shaking my head, which pounded for a brief second from the loud sound of his siren-like truck horn.

Upon entering the house, I smelled the tangy scent of black-bean burgers. My stomach rumbled, and I kicked off my sneakers, calling out to Nikki to let her know I was home. She yelled back something inaudible, and I threw my bag on the stairs, heading for the yellow-painted kitchen.

She was standing over the stove, flipping patties, her back facing me and hair in a messy bun. "Hon, can you set the table for me?"

The smell of food was overwhelming, and I was aching with hunger. "Of course." I took a step toward the silverware drawer and grabbed the knob.

And somehow, I was suddenly standing outside the front door again, holding the house key in the lock.

I gasped and jumped back, almost stumbling onto the walkway. I looked around me frantically, not comprehending the fact that I was standing outside the front door to my house, school bag still slung over my shoulder, sneakers still on my feet. "What?" I gasped. It felt like an awfully severe bout of déjà vu.

My heart pounded heavily. *Calm down. Take a deep breath.* I inhaled and exhaled, trying to get my thoughts together. I walked back up to the door, unlocked it, and stepped inside.

It smelled like black-bean burgers.

"Nikki?" I called out to my aunt.

She yelled back, and I couldn't hear what she said.

My stomach growled with hunger, just as it had the first time, and my eyes widened, watering in shock. *What's going on?* I didn't bother taking my bag and shoes off, and I walked to the kitchen.

Aunt Nikki was standing in the same spot as she had been when I'd first entered the kitchen—or when I'd thought I'd already entered the kitchen—over the stove, back facing me, hair in a messy bun, and a hand on her hip.

"Hon, can you set the table for me?"

Her voice made me jump slightly, and I stared at her.

"Um." I murmured, "Of c-course."

What the hell just happened?

CHAPTER 5

I SAT ON THE EDGE OF my bed. The lamp on my desk provided the only light in my room. I stared out the window at the mountains, my eyes bulging so much they burned. My hands clenched and unclenched my blue-and-black plaid comforter as I tried to make sense of the chaos in my thoughts. My head was swirling; I couldn't understand how it was possible that I'd had a vision without warning, without any indication, of something so insignificant. I had felt a slight pain prior to the moment it began, but I had assumed it was from being startled by Gavin's horn. The discomfort had been so subtle, as opposed to the horrible throbbing I often endured, and I would've never thought it was a pre-vision warning.

Now, I was second-guessing myself. What if this happened all the time and I never knew it? What if it happened again?

What if I actually couldn't tell a vision from reality?

I stood abruptly and began pacing. I prayed the visions would go away and never come back. I didn't want anything to do with them. I didn't want to be "gifted" or "different" or responsible for others' lives. I started panting and developing tunnel vision. I was panicking, and I needed to keep myself busy. I glanced down at my phone in my hand, considering calling Gavin or even Darla. But I wouldn't even know how to explain this. I didn't understand it myself.

I moaned, tossing my phone onto my bed. I moved over to my window and leaned against it, pressing my face to the cool glass. I just wanted a minute of peace.

I then felt a sudden warmth pressing on my back. I was overcome with a sense of ease, and I turned to face it, knowing all too well what—or who—was standing behind me.

"Gabe," I breathed with overwhelming relief.

He stood there, tall and immortal, glowing in a light that wasn't from the lamp on my desk. His silver wings rippled, and he rolled his shoulders, rubbing his neck. His dark eyes were confused, as they always were when he visited.

"Caleb." His deep bass of a voice sounded, vibrating my eardrums.

I leaned the back of my head against the window and closed my eyes. "Your timing could not be more perfect."

"Is that sarcasm?" I heard him shuffle over to my desk, and he sat on the chair. "You're frequently sarcastic."

I chuckled humorlessly and shook my head, moving to sit on my bed. "No, I'm being serious." I frowned. "There are strange things happening to me."

"There are many strange things happening in many places." His gaze roamed my room. "You changed some of your knick-knacks." He smiled.

I shrugged, ruffling my hair. "It's been a while since you've stopped by."

Gabriel leaned forward, resting his forearms on his legs. "The timing is always so erratic." He looked at my face, eyes displaying worry. "What happened?"

The words flooded out of me as I told him about meeting Darla and how she was most definitely the girl from my terrible visions. I circled my room while explaining how she was different, like me, and I discussed her abilities and how I learned about them. Then I explained the vision incident that had occurred before dinner.

Gabe nodded and scratched his square jaw as he listened. "The more I visit, the more I become befuddled. I understand a lot of things, Caleb." He looked me in the eyes. "But I struggle to understand you."

I looked down at my hands, as I naturally do when someone makes eye contact. He sighed and scooted the chair closer to me.

"It makes me feel youthful. As if I have yet to learn all things. And I know I have much to learn." He stared off, obviously deep in thought. "I just wish I had some answers for your sake."

I narrowed my eyes at him. "I don't really understand you all that much, either."

Gabe smirked, a dimple forming under his left eye. He leaned back in the chair, folding his arms. We sat in silence for a little while; I knew we were both trying to just figure it out. Figure each other out. I never knew what to believe or what any of this was. All I ever knew was what was right in front of me. All my life, Gabriel had literally appeared in front of me, and, as far as I was concerned, he was real.

Gabe sighed. "There are greater forces than us at work here."

I blinked twice. "Like, higher powers?"

Gabe nodded. "There are many forces out there, light and dark. A higher power, higher purpose. There is always a higher something." He paused, tapping his finger on his arm. "This is much bigger than us. And now there's this girl."

"Darla, yes."

"Yes, the telepathic. A telepathic and you, a seer. You both have the mental capacities of oracles—something your world hasn't seen in many, many centuries. But it doesn't explain…" He trailed off, shaking his head.

I could tell he was getting frustrated. I understood why, though. I'd known him my entire life, and every visit with Gabe just added more mystery on top of the mystery.

"Explain what, Gabe?" I inquired timidly.

He shook his head again. "It doesn't explain why I came to see you in the first place. And how you can see me and others like me. And why I have no real control over when I come to see you. Maybe our connection has something to do with your abilities, but your clairvoyance is not the reason behind it."

"You've visited me plenty of times without reason."

"Yes, but it is extremely difficult to do all on my own. It usually happens randomly, completely haphazard. There's this feeling I have whenever I know something is wrong, or you simply need a friend. There are times when I wish to visit you, and it happens. But more often, I am brought here by force."

I frowned heavily, feeling a slight pang of hurt in my chest. "By force."

Gabe looked at me with surprise. "I don't mean that I am forced against my will to come to you." He leaned toward me. "I mean I am brought here by some kind of force, that I just don't have a choice in the matter sometimes, that's all. It's sort of like a rope around my waist. It tugs on me hard, consistently, until I follow it to you. I'd never experienced anything like that in all my years until you came along." He rubbed his forehead. "I am fascinated by you, and there must be a reason I was brought to you originally, specifically you."

I breathed deeply. "Yeah, I know what you mean." I paused, thinking. "Do you remember back in January when I had to get my tonsils out?" I asked him. "And I was stuck home for, like, ten days?"

"Mmhmm." He nodded.

"And you came to see me almost every single day. That was the most we'd hung out."

He smiled. "If you call me attempting to learn how to play your electronic gaming machine when you had no voice to teach me with 'hanging out.'" He shrugged. "What about it?"

I plopped down onto my bed. "How did you know to come then? How were you able to stay so long?"

His nose wrinkled, and he looked down at his palms. "It wasn't easy. You know how challenging it is for me to stay in one place when I am tethered to another."

"But what is it like?" I pulled my knees to my chest. "I've always wondered what it's like for you, trying to get here from wherever you're from."

"I've figured out some things as time goes on." His gaze drifted to the wall behind me. "It's kind of like a window, you see. When you need help or just have me in mind or I just want to check in, the window opens a bit." He tried to shape the description with his hands. "Just a bit. And if I try hard enough, I can squeeze through the crack. Some days are much easier than others, like when you had your surgery. But most times, I'm not quite strong enough to get myself through." He dropped his hands. "I think it's because my kind doesn't really belong here."

"What about the times you can't get through?" I asked. "What does that look like?"

"It feels like something is blocking my way out. I can still feel your presence on this other plane, but it is weak." He sighed. "Maybe I'm not physically strong enough to travel, like some of my kind can, though I am stronger than I used to be. Or maybe there's actually something in the way. My original instinct when I first came to you when you were a child was to push until I made it through." He lifted an eyebrow. "Perhaps you open the window for me?"

"But that would mean I also keep it closed," I said quietly.

"We've gone over this many times, Caleb. You struggle with letting people into your life. As open as you are with me and your friend Gavin, you still put up walls and lock yourself inside." Gabe studied my face. "But you trust me. And I you. This is not a one-way connection, though it may seem that way, considering I suddenly appear wherever you are. But regardless of the how and why we've been connected for about two decades, it developed a good foundation for our friendship."

I nodded slowly. I looked up to him, sometimes like a father figure. I respected him, felt he was family to me. I had known him all my life, and he had always been there for me, whether I actually needed him or not. We were friends.

But despite his answer, there were others I needed. I was always curious about the world he was from and the rest of his species. He always skirted around the topic, and I tried to respect that he may not want to tell me anything. Or maybe he really didn't know enough to give me a straight answer. Either way, my curiosity always got the best of me.

"I still see others like you. From afar," I said. "We don't interact, ever. I see them, and they see me, but there is no acknowledgment."

Gabe sat up straight. "Perhaps they are afraid."

I snorted. "Afraid of me? Okay, Gabe."

He lifted a dark eyebrow. "I'm serious, kid. They certainly know of your gift, I'm sure. Even I can feel it developing in you as you age. You have a very powerful chess piece in your hands. And they must feel vulnerable to it, just as I feel vulnerable to our unanswered questions." His shoulder blades shifted, wings glistening. "It almost seems as though our worlds are intersecting differently than they have in the past."

"Like where you're from and where I'm from are connecting?" I was intrigued by the thought of something so much bigger than what I knew. "It's happened before?"

Gabriel nodded. "Yes. My kind typically isn't seen by human eyes unless we reveal ourselves willingly. So, there must be some break in the normal cycle. I really believe something like that could explain things." He held his hands up. "What else could it be? Your abilities, you and this Darla girl. Your seeing the others regularly and them seeing you. Really, what else could it be?" His wings shifted at their base through the slits in his t-shirt.

"Are you an angel, Gabe?" I blurted out then.

He smiled. "That's a funny question to ask."

"How so?" I leaned forward, awaiting an answer.

"You've never asked me specifically what I am before, that's all."

I shrugged. "Children think they know everything. Then they grow into adults who have a shit-ton of questions."

Gabe nodded, his smile broadening. "You make me feel pride."

I didn't visibly react to his statement, even though it made me feel a lot better about myself. I'd always wanted to know more about what he was. Now that I had asked him, I hoped I would finally have some idea of what lay beyond what we knew as human beings.

He scanned my face as he always did. Then he nodded. "We are divine beings. We answer to even more divine beings, who answer to something more divine, and so forth. We have many names. You might call us angels, and if that is what you wish to call me, then that is what I'll be. But your idea of what these 'angels' are may not be true to what I really am."

He moved to sit on the bed next to me. His left wing brushed against my biceps, leaving a trail of goosebumps behind. He leaned his elbows on his kneecaps and continued.

"I was an 'angel,' and I once was not. And then I was again. And then, for another time, I was not. I was never a human or an Earthling. I was never alive, and I was never deceased. I will not be forever, but I will 'be' for a long time. It is how my species exists. We come and go to different places. Sometimes, we make mistakes, and we're exiled. We have to work to get back home, work at being worthy enough to rejoin our own. That is how things run where I am from. Some of us remain perfect and never leave home, but I was not one of them." His face was distressed for a moment. He swallowed hard. "But I earned back my place and my position. I can be reckless, too... much like you." He glanced at me and smirked, a look of nostalgia on his face. "You and I are not so different."

I stared at my friend. He was answering my question, thoroughly, but at the same time, he had answered nothing. I wondered if maybe he didn't quite know the answer himself.

I returned the smile, satisfied with his response. For now.

He then rose to his feet, respectfully pushing my chair back under the desk. "I believe it is time for me to take off."

I stood, too, a sinking feeling forming in the pit of my stomach. I hated saying goodbye to Gabe.

He turned to face me, towering over me. "I'll come by again soon, and I will continue to try to find a better path to get to you. It's relatively easy for me to come to your world, but tracking you down, that's a different kind of adventure."

I looked up at him. "You definitely have to go?" I was feeling lonely again already.

He tilted his head, a sad, hesitant look on his face. "As I said before, it is never really my choice."

I reached out my hand to shake his. "Then I guess I will see you later, Gabriel."

He regarded my hand, lifting his eyebrow, and then grabbed it, pulling me into a tight hug. I was surprised by this gesture, but I shouldn't have been; just because I was older now didn't mean I couldn't use a good hug. We patted each other's backs, a typical, man-to-man embrace when friends won't be seeing each other for a very, very long time. My hand lingered on his feathered wing for a second; I didn't want to forget what it felt like in case I didn't see him for a while. Or ever again.

Gabe gripped my shoulders and gave me a slight shake. He looked me square in the eye. "Did you know that your name, Caleb, means *faithful* in some human interpretations?"

I hadn't known this. I shook my head and grinned. "Sounds pretty damn accurate."

Gabe slapped my shoulder and laughed. He gave it a squeeze. "For now, talk to Darla. Learn about her and see if there is a way you can stop that vision from coming true. Spend time with her and your friend Gavin."

I nodded. "She said she'd call, so we could talk—"

My cell on the bed behind me started to ring. I turned away from Gabe and climbed onto the mattress. The screen read *Darla*, and her number displayed below her name.

"Good timing. It's her, Gabe." I looked up to where my winged friend had been standing, and to my dismay, he had already gone.

"And sitting with that Doug guy yesterday was just torture. He was trying to flirt with me, and his thoughts were repulsive." Darla's voice rang over my phone speaker. "So that's when I told him I was a lesbian!"

I was laying on my stomach, my phone next to my laptop, and I wasn't really paying much attention to the assignment I had started working on. I grinned. "But are you a lesbian?" I asked.

She laughed. "No, no, I'm straight as an arrow, thank you. But damn, that barely got him off my back!"

This was all so not what I was used to. We had started out our conversation, talking very vaguely about our pasts first, considering we were only just starting to get to know each other, and then we jumped into everything we had been through with our otherworldly abilities. She found my clairvoyance interesting and insisted her telepathy wasn't as "cool," but I felt it was the other way around.

"It would be awesome to know what everyone was thinking," I had said. "I would just finish people's sentences all the time."

Now that we had moved past the awkward stage of the phone call, we laughed about things that shouldn't be normal but felt completely normal to talk about. And for once, I didn't feel like a freak or at least, not the only freak in town.

"I just want to know"—I paused from typing out the first paragraph on my essay—"Last night, when you were talking to me through your mind, how did you do that?"

"I don't know." Darla said, all humor gone from her voice. "It's never, ever happened to me before. Telepathy for me has always been a one-way street."

"But I heard you, without a doubt. You've never, like, sent your thoughts to someone else?"

"If I did, they definitely never heard me." She was quiet for a moment. "Maybe it's because you have a consciousness thing too. Maybe our minds are just that complex, that advanced, that they work together."

I pursed my lips. This was getting interesting. Not only were we capable of generally having our own unique abilities, but there could be a possibility of accessing them in different ways, using them to our advantage. Maybe it was somehow possible to control my visions and find out how far into the future I could really see. I'd never tried anything like that before, nor had I ever wanted to, but now that I knew I wasn't the only one like me, maybe I could start trying.

"I don't suppose you can try it again?" I asked. "Communicating to me in our minds, I mean?"

She was quiet once more then said, "I'm going to hang up the phone."

There was a beeping sound and the call ended.

At first, I thought I'd offended her somehow and I considered calling her back. But suddenly, a chill ran down my spine, and I sat up on my knees. The sensation was a continuous, tingly feeling, sort of like my back had fallen asleep. I tried to ignore it, but it came again and again in heavy waves, making me feel as if I needed to just allow it to take over my body.

The moment I relaxed, I heard her.

Calling Caleb. Hello? Do you read me?

My mouth fell open, and I shook my head spastically like I had a bug in my hair. "Oh!" I was startled by the sensation of someone else's thoughts actually being inside my head.

The tingling stopped for a moment, and I felt something in my brain. Something that reminded me of someone stepping on a hose and cutting off the water, like the connection between my mind and Darla's had been blocked.

I waited again. The tingling started up after about a minute, and my instincts told me to block it, to shake it from me. Beside me on the bed, my phone buzzed with an incoming text. I glanced down and saw a message from Darla.

Let me in, dammit.

"Let you in?" I stared at the message, still trying to ignore the strange chills, but then I realized what she meant. I relaxed and let the tingling flow through me.

Caleb, this is your conscience speaking. She spoke again inside my mind.

"Very funny," I responded, soon realizing she couldn't hear me. I rubbed the back of my head and thought the words instead.

Very funny. Can you hear me?

Oh my gosh!

I couldn't help but laugh, first, because my inner child was excited, then because of how crazy-ridiculous the situation seemed, and then I laughed out of shock.

I cannot believe this is happening right now.

Me, neither; now we can talk shit about anyone all we want.

I laughed again. I felt giddy—not only was this the coolest thing ever, but for once, I truly didn't feel like my clairvoyance was something that was wrong with me. This was all real, and we were both experiencing it.

We can totally mess around with Gavin now, too, you know, she said in a mischievous tone.

You're already enjoying this too much. I think you need therapy, I replied jokingly.

I think we both need therapy.

"I almost—oops."

I spoke out loud again accidentally, breaking my concentration, and I felt the "line" cut. I was going to have to get used to using my thoughts to respond. I took a deep breath and focused on the incoming, tingling connection.

Knowing there's someone else who is going through this…stuff…I almost feel normal.

Ironic, considering this is the weirdest it's gotten so far.

I rolled my eyes at her statement.

Did you just roll your eyes at me?

Yes.

My phone buzzed and lit up, and our connection broke. This time, I'd gotten a text from Ava. I snatched up the phone and opened the message.

Party at Sigma Delta Pi's house a week from Friday. It's their first open house of the semester! I know it's the week of Halloween, but costumes are optional. Bring your new friend!

I smiled, and the phone buzzed again as another text came through from Ava.

Gav needs to get laid.

The time on my phone read one o'clock in the morning. I closed my laptop, realizing there was no way I was going to get any work done, and put it on my side table. I rested my back against the headboard, wondering if I'd be able to make a connection to Darla myself or if she had to initiate the conversation. I closed my eyes, waiting for the tingling to start.

Nothing.

I huffed in annoyance and typed to Darla on my cell.

How do you get into my head? I want to try.

I watched with anticipation as Darla typed back a response.

I have no idea.

I made a face, but then another text popped up.

Just clear your head. I pictured you, so picture me in your mind, and a door, and then knock on the door. You know?

WTF are you talking about? I wrote back in response.

That's just how I did it! I pictured you in my head and kept pushing at you what I wanted to say. There was a mental wall, and I couldn't break through until you let me. Get it?

I thought I did. Okay, BRB.

I closed my eyes again. I pictured Darla in my mind and thought something, then repeated the phrase in my mind. My head felt funny, and I was getting that tingly sensation, but, as Darla had said, there was some kind of wall, some blockage in the way, and my phrase kept bouncing off it.

Darla? You there?

I waited a moment, feeling silly.

Finally, *Is this my conscience?*

I bolted upright. *It worked!* It seemed this telepathy did in fact work both ways for us. Though she didn't have visions, and I couldn't read minds, this was something we actually shared.

Good job, you made it into my head. Now get out; I'm tired, she joked, feigning a yawn.

Before I go, Ava wants to know if you want to party at one of the sorority houses a week from Friday.

That sounds awesome, yeah.

Cool.

I closed the link between our minds, then I responded to Ava's invite. I placed my phone in my charger and turned off the side-table lamp. Though I was nowhere near tired enough to sleep, I did feel content for the first time in years. But that didn't last long before I began thinking of how much had happened in the past two days. I mostly thought about my visions and about what was going to happen to Darla.

I spit blood into a sink for what felt like the millionth time that week.

Some scrawny freshman with round glasses and bulgy eyes was gaping at me from the urinal he was using, and I had to suppress the urge to ask him what the hell he was looking at. I was sure I looked insane with a bump on my head after having hit it on the corner of the ceramic sink and coughing up blood; no doubt the kid thought I was on some kind of drugs. I avoided his eyes and just stared at my own in the mirror.

It was funny, looking into my own eyes, considering it was something I never did—I felt as if I was looking at a stranger. I didn't know when I'd grown up, but it seemed like yesterday I was this awkward, lanky, fourteen-year-old boy with a puberty-induced, cracking voice—a kid who had a crush on every girl with a pulse. I still pictured myself as him, blue eyes round with inquisitiveness, black hair completely untamable, and not a care in the world.

But now, each time I looked into a mirror I was surprised. It seemed as if the image was different, always different. I was so much older, and not just physically—my eyes showed how much the stress of the past few years had aged me. My gaze reflected back the sheer exhaustion of someone who has seen too much, knows too much. Had it not been for the five years of visions— seeing futures near and far, good or bad—that interrupted my everyday life, maybe I'd appear less grim. Or less aged. I looked and felt as if I had lived a thousand lives.

I grunted in dissatisfaction, wiped my mouth with a paper towel, and left the gawking freshman in the restroom. Pushing through a herd of students leaving classes, I got a sense of claustrophobia, and I just wanted to get out. I'd had no classes the day before, which always threw me off, and now that it was Thursday, I was aching for the weekend. I finally reached the exit of the building and stepped out into the fresh, invigorating, fall air. Walking in the direction of the quad, I couldn't help but be grateful for the good weather. Everyone was out and about—the guitarists were on the stairs, the chain-smokers were happily lighting up.

And that pretty blonde I'd locked eyes with the other day was sitting at another table, reading the same thick book.

I swallowed hard, sliding my sunglasses down from the top of my head and over my eyes. I walked slower, so I wouldn't draw attention to myself and went to go sit on the wall where I usually met with Gavin. Her table was closer than it had been the last time, and I could see that the book she was reading was actually the complete works of the poet Edgar Allan Poe. An interesting choice—I had always been a big fan of Poe, but I never really knew anyone who read it just to read it. I watched as her ocean eyes shifted back and forth across the page, her eyebrows low while she scanned the text intently. Her chin jutted out, bottom lip pouting, and I could tell she was absorbed in whatever poem she was reading. I smiled; I found her and her Poe-reading so intriguing, and maybe even a little endearing too.

I heard the familiar voices of Gavin, Ava, and Darla as they approached, and I quickly composed myself, shifting so I was leaning back on my hands. The girls were talking about what to wear to the party at Sigma House, and Gavin was trailing behind them, glancing down at Darla's backside every so often. She had to know he was doing it, being a mind reader and all. I shook my head.

Once they reached me, Ava hopped up on the wall next to me, taking my sunglasses off and putting them on her own head.

"I heard it's going to be a huge rager." Gav tried to sound casual, but his lopsided grin only made his anticipation more obvious. "Their house is really big too. And I met this chick there last semester at one of their parties who said I was hot—"

Ava cut him off with a loud, "Ha!" And then she pulled out her pack of cigarettes and plucked one. "First of all, she was drunk, so—no offense—that girl would've thought a brick wall was hot." She placed the cig between her lips and flicked her lighter.

Gavin frowned and crossed his arms. "She was not that drunk! And she was cute."

"She was seventeen, Gav," Ava said out of the corner of her mouth, still struggling to light her cigarette.

Despite my personal dislike of cigarettes, I cupped my hands around the flame for her, and it finally lit.

"Thanks," she muttered, taking a puff and blowing it away from our circle. "She was seventeen, and she should not have even been there."

"So? Seventeen isn't that young, and I was only hitting on her," Gavin protested, ignoring Darla's snickers. "Nothing even happened anyway." Usually, he didn't argue with Ava, but he clearly didn't like being teased in front of our newest friend.

Ava lowered my sunglasses to her nose and looked at him. "You're delusional. I remember after you realized she was underage, you almost drank yourself into forgetting about the whole thing."

Darla leaned against the table across from me and smiled at Gav. "Don't worry about it. Shit happens. You know, a great poet once said in one of his pieces that foolishness and self-confidence are technically one in the same. So, just believe that what Ava saw as you acting like a fool was actually confidence you had in yourself."

I froze at the familiarity of her statement. *A great poet…?*

Darla looked straight at me, tongue pressed against her cheek as she tried not to crack up.

Did you just…are you referring to Edgar Allan Poe? I thought to her, my nostrils flaring in annoyance.

She smiled, glancing at the blonde I had checked out twice that week. *You were still subconsciously thinking about her after we walked over.*

My face grew warm, but neither Ava nor Gavin seemed to notice the interaction.

Gav raised his eyebrows. "Which poet came up with that?"

"Edgar Allan Poe." Darla and I responded simultaneously, and I glared at her.

She smiled pleasantly back at me. *Sorry.*

Gavin looked at us and disregarded the comment. "Whatever. Fool or not, I'm a different person than I was last semester."

Ava laughed and returned my sunglasses to my head, which was currently throbbing from my fall earlier.

"I'm going to head home. I'll see you bitches later." She slid off the wall and saluted us before strolling away, flicking her cigarette butt onto the ground.

Gavin came over and sat where Ava previously had. "I'm ready for the weekend, man."

Darla nodded in agreement, crossing her arms. "Would you guys want to come over to my place to hang out tonight? My godfather is taking my younger siblings to a soccer tournament, and they'll be back pretty late, so I have the whole place to myself."

I saw Gav straighten up out of the corner of my eye.

"He wouldn't care if you had two strange guys over?" he asked.

"You're not that strange." She batted her eyelashes innocently.

I smiled, and Gavin looked at me expectantly. I knew what he wanted to do, obviously. It sounded like a good idea to me, more of a chance to get to know Darla personally, and maybe I'd get a better feel for her future and what was to come. We really needed to talk about it soon, especially since I had no idea how much time we had before that vision came true.

Before I could give her a chance to hear my remorseful thinking, I responded cheerily, "Do you want us to bring anything?"

She grinned. "Maybe something to drink? I'll order pizza." She then leaned closer to me, her eyes suddenly filled with concern. "Cay, are you all right?"

I frowned. The only way she could know I wasn't okay was from reading my mind again. "Stop doing that!"

She lifted her eyebrow. "Doing what? You have a huge knob on your head."

My hand went to where I had bumped it in the bathroom during my vision. I winced when I realized how big it actually was. "Oh. Right. Sorry."

"You know," Gav said, tapping his feet against the wall, "we should really attach some pillows to you in case you have a vision, and there're a lot of sharp objects around. Maybe bubble wrap." Darla laughed before he finished speaking, and he turned to her suspiciously, his voice thin. "Also, I don't think I like this whole mind-reading thing."

Darla smirked at him impishly. "I think it's very…informative."

Gavin's face blushed beet red. "Yeah, well, stay out of my thoughts, D."

"Maybe if they weren't so loud, I would."

The two of them went at it, and I impulsively let my gaze wander back over to the Poe-reading girl. She was twirling a blonde curl aimlessly around her finger with the book closed in front of her. She was scanning the crowds of students, just watching them, and it reminded me of the way I observed people whenever I hung out in the quad. I followed her gaze to see who was capturing her interest until she glanced at me, and I quickly pulled my shades over my eyes.

CHAPTER 6

I WAS UNSURE WHY I FELT so uneasy in Gavin's truck on the ride to Darla's house that evening. Some rock music played on the radio, great classics, though the occasional static that crackled through was starting to give me a headache. I had a twelve-pack of beer sitting on my lap, which I clutched tightly. Gav was humming to the music, bopping his head to the beat of the bass drum. We were stuck in traffic near the university, since a lot of classes got out around eight o'clock. Everything was pretty ordinary. But I think my anxiety was stemming from the fact that I was very much aware of the winged being perched on top of one of the smaller buildings on campus.

It wasn't my winged friend, definitely not Gabriel. But this one was staring right at me. I had rolled the window up in the hopes of blocking his view of me, but he kept staring, squatting on the edge of the roof, hands gripping the gutter as if he was getting ready to fling himself from it. His wings were a dull gray, feathers shaking, and his gold hair was whipping in the breeze, revealing curious yet angry, dark eyes. He appeared young, but I knew he was probably much older than he looked. My heart was skipping—I didn't like the way his eyes were fixated on me. I swallowed a lump in my throat.

"What is it, Cay?"

Gavin's voice made me jump in the seat.

I pried my eyes away from the vulture-like being to stare dead-straight ahead through the windshield. "It's one of those *things*."

Gav grunted. "Like a Gabe-thing?"

"Yeah, but not really. This one doesn't look friendly."

The road congestion decreased as we passed the campus exit, and we picked up speed. I looked in the side-view mirror to see if the winged guy was still there, but he had gone.

"I figured all the angels looked friendly," Gavin said quietly.

"I wouldn't call the one I just saw an angel." I loosened my grip on the twelve-pack and sighed. "He was watching me. Besides, I'm not sure if any of them even are angels. And whatever that one was, he didn't look like Gabe at all."

"Well, I wish I was able to see the bird people," Gavin said, glancing in the rearview mirror. "I would've flipped him off for you."

I relaxed then, and the rest of the ride consisted of Gavin and me singing along to "Highway to Hell" by AC/DC. Following the directions Darla had texted Gav, we turned off a road not too far from campus that was surrounded by forest on both sides. Gavin clicked his high beams on, squinting at the darkness ahead of him.

Leaning forward, he gripped the steering wheel. "Do you think she can read my mind from here? I keep thinking she's taking us to a secluded spot to kill us both."

I felt a tug at the back of my mind, and then her voice floated its way into my thoughts.

Yes, if I try.

I laughed loudly, and Gav looked at me sideways. "Yeah, she can hear you from her house. We're close anyway."

Gav shook his head. "How do you—?"

"I forgot to tell you, she and I can communicate telepathically."

Gavin slammed on the brakes, and at first I thought it was because the news surprised him, but as it turned out, he had missed the road we had to take to get to Darla's place. He turned around in someone's driveway, and then we were back on course.

He raised his eyebrows at me. "How did you forget to tell me that?"

I held my hands up defensively. "I don't know, I just forgot."

For a moment, I thought he was mad, but the look on his face told me otherwise.

He puckered his lips, leaning back in his seat. "I'm a little jealous. Does she answer your telepathic calls faster than she answers my texts?"

I snorted, half relieved he wasn't angry and half hesitant to respond to the question since I didn't actually know the answer to it. Before I could distract him with a joke, we drove onto the correct driveway and pulled up to a fairly large house that had brown and beige accents and large windows adorning all sides. It was the size of a classy mansion but not quite as overstated and ritzy. It seemed to suit the surrounding forest, like the house had sprouted from the ground and the woods had grown around it. The driveway looped around, a second entrance/exit on the other side, and we parked there so Gav's truck wouldn't be in the way in case Darla's family returned home.

We hopped out and walked down the driveway to the massive residence. As I looked more closely at the house, I realized something peculiar about it.

This home, this place, was something I'd seen before.

I'd had a vision of this exact house when I was in the locker room after practice the other day. I knew I'd never been here before, never seen this house outside of my vision. And yet, here it was. I was standing in front of it in real life, never having done so before this moment.

Gavin walked ahead of me, and I gaped at the familiar-yet-unfamiliar house, clutching the half case of beer. I followed him wordlessly, taking in the details of the house's exterior as I recalled my vision. If I remembered correctly, the door would open before I had a chance to knock.

"Nice place," he muttered, eyes twinkling. "Should we have brought more booze?"

I blinked, trying to recover from surprise and gather my thoughts. "There's still only the three of us, dude. The house isn't drinking with us."

As we stepped up to the front door, I recognized its dark mahogany. There's a knocker, I remembered, and I noticed the brass, lion's head door-knocker sitting right beneath the peephole. I reached for it, but the door whipped open before I could even touch it.

Whoa.

"Hey." Darla stood in the doorway, smiling widely and beckoning us in. "Oh, good, you brought beer!"

Gavin and I stepped inside, and she shut the door behind us. We stood in a high-ceilinged entryway, a chandelier glittering above our heads. A wooden staircase sat to our right, curving as it ascended to a balcony leading to the second floor. I saw an illuminated hallway ahead of us, and I could smell the scent of pepperoni pizza wafting in the air. My stomach growled obnoxiously loud, and my two friends turned to me.

I grinned sheepishly. "I was saving room for pizza."

Darla guided us down the hallway to a brightly lit kitchen that had stainless-steel appliances and granite countertops, mahogany accents matching the front door, and an island in the center adorned with several pizza boxes. The walls were a pale yellow, similar to that of the kitchen in my house. Everything looked clean and new, like someone had gutted the house and redid the interior. It was homey, and I felt comfortable despite being in a new place.

"I texted Ava to see if she was around, but she said she was busy dealing with her father." Darla waved her hand nonchalantly. "Make yourselves at home."

Gav grabbed the beer from me and clanged the box onto the island, before sitting on one of the stools. "This is a very nice place, D."

She smiled. "Yeah, Leander—my godfather—makes a lot of money as a commercial real estate broker, and he gets paid to travel. I need to watch the kids when he's away, but it's no big deal. I get the space I need." She went over to a cabinet and pulled out some paper plates. "The entire attic is my bedroom, and it has a balcony, a skylight, and a full bathroom with a shower. It's like my own apartment."

She distributed the plates and some napkins. She then glanced at Gavin, and her face briefly turned red, but Gav didn't seem to notice. I could only assume she'd heard some inappropriate thoughts floating out of his thick skull.

I cleared my throat, reaching for one of the pies. "How many siblings do you have?"

"There are four of us altogether," she said as I handed her a slice. "There's me—I'm the oldest. Then there's Tucker, who's eighteen. He's kind of shy sometimes around other people, but we hang out a lot. Then there's Arlo, who is fourteen, and the youngest, Olivia. She's ten."

"Wow, full house, huh?" Gav said, his cheeks already stuffed with food.

Darla nodded, pulling a hair tie off her wrist and throwing her locks into a ponytail. "Leander really provided us kids with everything. And we all get along really well with each other. Although, Arlo seems to be going through a grunge phase right now, but I mean, we all do at some point." She bit into her slice.

I twisted the cap off a beer bottle and took a swig. I was glad Darla was open to talking about her personal life, especially since I hadn't been sure if it was something she'd want to talk about. "Is Leander your uncle?" I asked.

She hesitated and put her slice down. She grabbed a napkin, her gaze following her hand. "No. It's complicated. Well, not really." She smiled. "Leander is a distant relative, a cousin to one of my parents. They assigned him as my godfather, and then when they evidently decided they weren't fit for parenthood, they dumped me on him. He took me in willingly as his own, of course. He adopted me and the others as well. The only one who's really his kid is Olivia. Arlo and Tucker were a bit older when we welcomed them into our lives, so it was hard for them to adjust to a new family. Lea's like a father to all of us, though."

"That's amazing!" Gavin exclaimed, some crumbs spitting onto his plate as he bit into the crust. "He must be a great guy, especially to have taken in four kids. No wife?"

D shook her head. "Nah. He once had an on-again, off-again girlfriend in college for a short while when I was little. They were friends for some time I think, but I never had the chance to meet her before they went their separate ways. He dates here and there, but it's not much of a priority to him." She tossed her plate into the trash. "We move around a lot. The only reason he found Tucker and Arlo was because we moved from place to place. He's got a big heart, you know. He wants to help everyone." She smiled, admiration in her blue eyes.

"What about Olivia?" I wasn't sure if I was prying too much. No turning back now. "Where's her mother?"

Darla scowled, "Yeah, poor Ollie. I guess it's partially Leander's fault. He hooked up with one of his dates, and nine months later, she showed up with baby Olivia. She practically shoved her into Lea's arms and took off for good."

I felt full all of a sudden. Or maybe I had just lost my appetite.

It's really okay. Darla's voice rang in my head. I guess my face had displayed my obvious dislike of parents abandoning their children.

Gavin looked sympathetic, his vibrant green eyes showing genuine sadness. "That must've been really hard for Olivia."

D tilted her head to look at him, and they locked eyes. I glanced back and forth between them, feeling as if I was invading something personal. Darla's gaze shifted over to mine, and she coughed awkwardly.

"Anyway, it hasn't been that rough," she said while clearing the island. "We're all really happy together."

"You and Cay have similar stories—" Gavin started, but snapped his mouth shut after seeing my scowl. While Darla might be open to discussing her past, I surely was not.

The look of surprise on D's face told me she was interested.

"How so?" she asked.

I had to answer now. I'd make it brief. "My father knocked up my mom, left us when I was really little, then my mom got breast cancer and died. Now I live with my godmother, my mother's best friend." I popped my knuckles. "We're good together, she and I. Life is excellent. But it got hard after the visions." I decided not to discuss the daddy issues any further and chose to leave out the part about the long-lost twin. No need to make myself look pathetic, and I didn't need or want sympathy. But my shortness caused a weird silence between the three of us.

Gavin spoke first. "Sorry," he muttered to me. "I didn't mean to bum you out. You know me. I'm curious about everything. I figured since we were on the topic…"

"Don't worry about it." I interrupted.

A thought flickered in the back of my mind. I had to ask, especially now that I knew visions and mind-reading were all real things. Besides, it was time for a topic change.

I turned to Darla, crossing my arms, trying to appear blasé. "Hey, D?"

Her eyes lifted and met mine, and in response, I looked down at the thin hair on my arm.

"Yeah?" she said.

"Other than us being able to share telepathic conversations and your ability to read minds," I began, trying to be cautious with how I phrased my question, "do you ever, you know, see things? Like strange things?" I looked up at her through my eyelashes, trying to keep my mind empty, so as to not give anything away, just in case.

Darla narrowed her eyes at me. Her gaze was unwavering, and this led me to believe I might already know her answer.

"It depends what you mean by that." She spoke carefully.

I licked my lips, avoiding Gavin's uncertain look.

"Do you see things people don't usually see?" I asked.

"Yes," she answered, so softly that I wasn't sure I'd even heard her correctly.

My heart skipped a beat. *I'm not crazy. I'm definitely not crazy.* Happily, the tension in my shoulders released. I kept my face straight as I tried to think of how to open up further dialogue.

"So." Gavin ran a hand through his shiny, auburn hair impatiently. "Are you both talking about the same thing then? Can we openly say what the thing is, so this isn't weird anymore?"

A smile tugged at the corners of Darla's lips. She was amused by Gavin, as always. "I'm guessing we're talking about the same thing. I'm not sure what they are, if they're angels or aliens or—"

"Yes." I practically sighed with relief. "Yes, I'm not sure what they are, either. Mine answered the question ambiguously when I asked—"

Darla put her hand up to stop me. "Yours? What do you mean? Your what?"

I scrunched my face up with doubt. "My…being. His name is Gabriel."

Darla's lips parted in surprise, and she looked at me like I had five heads. I felt very self-conscious then.

"You…you've spoken to one?" she breathed.

I mirrored her expression. "You haven't?"

She shook her head wildly. "Never! They're always off in the distance. Doing stuff or just sitting there. Some of them are so beautiful I can't look away. But sometimes, they watch me." She shuddered. "I just got a chill thinking about it."

Gavin and I made eye contact. Maybe I was the crazier of Darla and me.

"They've never communicated with you?" I asked.

"No. Not ever. You know one? Personally?"

I nodded vigorously. "If I'm being perfectly honest here, Gabriel is my best friend next to Gavin. I've known him my entire life."

D's eyes filled with wonder. "That's incredible. What's he like?"

I proceeded to explain how I met Gabe and about all the times he'd visited after that. I even told her about his visit to my room the other night. She sat there quietly, both her and Gav resting their chins in their palms. It felt really good to talk about it all and not feel like something was wrong with me.

"That's just…wow." Darla shook her head, opening a second beer. "Really, Caleb. That's indescribable." She laughed. "I just can't…wow!"

I smiled widely. I was glad she thought it was cool.

"Does your family know about you?" Gavin asked D suddenly, smooshing his cheeks together aimlessly. "I mean, do they know what you can do?"

Darla chewed on her bottom lip, looking to the left. "Yes, actually, that's another thing."

"Is there any pizza left for me?"

A male voice from the entryway behind us caused Gavin and me to both bolt upright and turn. Peeking into the kitchen was a tall, lanky guy with dark brown hair styled in a pompadour, and soft, gray eyes. He had high cheekbones and a prominent jaw, and he looked like he might be half Japanese. He was wearing a white t-shirt and jeans, a hand casually slid into his pocket. He seemed delighted by the fact that Gav and I were so startled by his presence.

"Hey." He lifted his eyebrows and waved with his free hand. "I'm Tucker."

Darla came around the island, hands on her hips. "Tuck, what are you doing here?"

"Not a fan of soccer. You know I'm more of a boxing buff, Darla." He grinned lopsidedly and approached us.

"Well, why didn't Lea tell me you were home?"

"I'm eighteen. I'm a legal adult. He knows I don't need a babysitter anymore."

"I beg to differ."

Gavin and I each reached out to shake his hand and introduce ourselves. He responded politely, with a firm handshake and a quiet "hello," then opened one of the pizza boxes. He grabbed a slice then climbed up onto the counter by the fridge to sit.

Gav scooted his chair closer to the island, its legs squeaking against the floor. "You snuck up on us. We didn't even hear you come in."

Darla rolled her eyes heavily. "Yeah, like I was saying before—my family knows about what I can do because they can do unique things too."

"They know?" Tucker looked at her wide eyed, his cheeks already full of greasy pizza.

"Tuck here has an ability too. He's able to adapt to his surrounding environment." Darla's eyes rolled again, as if this were something a typical, eighteen-year-old could do. "You know, like camouflage. Show them, Tuck, it's fine."

She crossed her arms, and Tucker smiled mischievously from his seat on the counter.

Then he was gone.

"Shit!"

Gavin's eyes lit up when he said the word, and I was all but catching flies in my gaping mouth.

"I'm like a ghost. I'm like the wind." Tucker's sarcastic voice came from the air. "Oh, and I can turn intangible too."

He reappeared right beside Darla, whose hand flew to her chest in alarm. "Christ, Tucker," she grumbled.

"Intangible?" I asked. "Like, you can phase through solid objects?"

"His ability doesn't fuck with his mind like ours do, Cay," Darla explained.

I felt a pang of jealousy.

"He gets the fun power," she added.

"You could do a lot of damage with that kind of ability." Gavin raised his eyebrows at Tucker.

Tucker wiggled his eyebrows back at Gav. "I did take a few trips into the girls' locker room at my old high school."

Gavin smiled like the Cheshire cat and leaned over the island, lifting his hand. "Up top, my brother."

Tucker gave Gav a high-five, and Darla and I simultaneously shook our heads, silently judging.

"Unbelievable." She faced me. "That's part of how Lea found Tucker. Lea has a way of finding people who are like us or who could potentially be like us. He's different too."

I unintentionally entered her mind. *Your entire family is...?*

"Advanced, yeah." She responded aloud. "It seems our abilities develop around our late teen years. Arlo's hasn't shown yet and neither has Olivia's. We only assume hers will because she is Leander's flesh and blood."

She swatted away Tucker's hand as he reached for a beer.

"That's how Lea was able to take care of me so easily," she continued. "I am a blood relative of his, so he was prepared for me to be different."

"And he just goes around adopting anyone he feels may have abilities?" Gavin blinked, his nose wrinkling. "Sounds like he's building an army."

"He just didn't want us to end up in the wrong hands." Tuck's voice was slightly defensive. "Come on, man, you've seen the movies! Imagine if the government or people with abilities who didn't use them for good knew about us. We'd be tested on, probed, dissected, or maybe killed on the spot. Lea protected us because we needed him." He turned to Gav, leaned on the counter, and tapped his fingers on the granite. "So, why is it that you two know about us?"

"Caleb is like us, Tucker," Darla said, finally allowing him to snag a beer. "He has a special ability like you and me. He's psychic."

Tucker's face brightened. "Holy shit! That's so wild!"

I shifted, my face flushing with embarrassment. I remembered how Gavin had thought it was really awesome until he saw how much it tore me apart.

"It's...difficult to handle," I mumbled.

"I can imagine it is." Tuck's gaze wandered off. "It must be intense." He nodded at Gavin. "What about my dude over here?"

Gavin shook his head. "Sorry, your dude is one hundred percent normal."

Darla laughed obnoxiously. "He wishes."

Gavin glared in her direction. "I'm the most normal one in the room."

"I rest my case." Darla winked at him.

I chuckled, but my head spun momentarily, and before I could react, the image of Tucker knocking over a beer bottle and it shattering onto the floor shook my brain. I squeezed my eyes shut.

Gavin gripped my biceps. "Cay?" His voice was panicky.

I opened my eyes, seeing that the beer bottle was still intact and on the island.

"I just had—" I started.

Tucker's elbow knocked into the beer bottle as he moved for another slice of pizza. It tipped, falling off the edge, and I leaned over the island and snatched it before it even came close to the ground.

"A vision," I finished.

Tucker, Darla, and Gavin all stared at me with incredulous expressions. I slowly returned to my seat, placing the bottle closer to the center.

"That was outstanding." Tucker beamed. "Great catch!"

"Thanks," I muttered, scratching the back of my head.

"No bloody nose, no pain?" Gav finally let go of his hold on my arm. "A vision that doesn't cause you physical harm? What kind of wizardry is this?"

"It's happened before." I suddenly felt guilty that I hadn't told him about the other night when I hadn't known I was having a vision. "This one was obvious. I actually felt that it was a vision. But there was one time recently, when I couldn't tell the vision from real life."

"That's scary." Darla gave a slight frown. "The not knowing the difference part, I mean."

I agreed with her. It was scary, but at the same time, I wondered if I was just changing, my body adjusting to my aging, growing mind. Maybe the visions were finally becoming less violent and more natural. Maybe I would finally stop blacking out. I had hoped, after the first year of experiencing them, that my visions would become more in tune with natural intuition and that I wouldn't need to experience the pain and abruptness. But, honestly, I would never know if or when I'd learn to manage this. I was still just as confused and afraid as I was five years ago.

For the following two hours, Tucker, Darla, and I shared stories of how we discovered our powers, while Gav listened intently and asked all the typical questions; some of which included, "If I poke you when you're intangible, can you feel my touch?" or "When I have a song stuck in my head, can you hear it playing in yours?" Tucker spoke of a time when he'd had to hide from a bully who was chasing him when he was fifteen, and then suddenly, the jerk couldn't see Tuck anymore. Darla found out what everyone's Christmas presents from Leander were when she experienced her first telepathic reading at age sixteen—I imagined Leander hadn't been pleased.

As the two of them laughed over pranks and accidents, I couldn't stop myself from feeling a sense of longing for a life like they'd had. Not that Nikki hadn't been beyond perfect, but it was hard on her too. She didn't know how to handle me, ergo, I didn't know how to handle me. Darla and Tucker had Leander, who had been prepared for dealing with them and their supernatural abilities, and he knew how to make them feel normal. They had each other. No one was the odd man out because they were all odd. Maybe, if I had met them prior to my first vision, things would've been different. But as someone who had seen so many things in my head—past, present, and future—I knew all too well that this timing had been right.

I stiffened suddenly. Someone was watching us.

The hairs on the back of my neck tickled as they rose. My intuition, natural or unnatural, kicked in. No, someone wasn't watching; they were approaching. My body grew rigid, and as I looked over at Darla, I felt the urge to say something. But my vision blurred and swirled, and I then saw a man and two adolescents hopping out of a black Cadillac SUV in the driveway outside.

"I think your godfather is back early," I breathed quietly as my eyesight came back into focus, and I loosened the ridiculous hold I had on the edge of the island.

Darla blinked at me, her lips twitching as if she was trying to suppress a smile. "You're starting to freak me out."

The four of us turned at the sound of the front door clicking open and voices traveling down the hall. Gav patted me on the back, for what reason, I didn't know, but I guessed he was just making sure I was all right.

"Lea?" Tucker called, shoving his beer bottle into D's hands. "Is that you, man?"

Two figures rounded the corner and filed into the kitchen. The first was a small girl, who I deduced was Olivia. She was a tiny thing with hazel eyes and pin-straight, white-blonde hair. She bounced around the island, grinning ear to ear with the most defined dimples I had ever seen on a child, and wrapped her arms around Darla's waist.

Darla hoisted her up into her arms and pecked her on the cheek. "What are you guys doing back so early? I thought you wouldn't be home until later."

"They lost," grunted the other youth who had entered the room. He frowned heavily, arms crossed and shoulders raised. "So, we decided to dip early."

"Arlo was super annoyed the whole game." Olivia pouted and gazed up at Darla innocently. She tossed her white-blonde hair over her shoulder dramatically, then shot the disappointed teen a glare. "I think that's why they lost. He kept booing."

"Well, you kept cheering for the wrong team," Arlo growled. He glanced over at me then, his dark eyes peering through a raven-black faux-hawk, noticing Gavin and I were in the room. He appeared to be almost as tall as Tucker, making him look much older than he sounded, considering his voice was still in its cracking stage of puberty.

"I wanted everyone to have a chance to win!" Olivia stuck her tongue out at Arlo. "Maybe, if you weren't so grumpy, your team would've won. Can I have some pizza?" She squirmed in Darla's grasp so she could be placed back down.

"It's way too late for another meal, Ollie." Leander finally entered the kitchen, shrugging off a brown suede jacket.

He stood over six feet tall and had short, black-gray hair—kind of like salt-and-pepper—and a goatee to match. He wore a dark-green sweater that made his chestnut-brown eyes prominent. I had a sense of familiarity when he walked into the room, but I couldn't quite place the feeling. He smiled warmly at Gavin and me and waved as he rolled his sleeves up.

"I see we have company."

Darla gestured to us. "These are my friends from school, Lea."

Gavin and I both stood and introduced ourselves courteously. As Leander shook my hand, his lingered a second longer before he tilted his head curiously. He glanced over my shoulder at Darla, and she cleared her throat.

"They're the ones I told you about the other day," she told him.

"Ah!" His smile revealed pearly white teeth. He grabbed a bar stool and sat on it. "Which one of you is the clairvoyant?"

"That would be me, sir." I glanced down at the floor. *I'm already uncomfortable.*

Relax, he doesn't bite. Darla's voice sounded in my mind, interrupting my thoughts.

"We have so much to talk about." Leander beamed warmly.

Darla glared at him. "Go easy on him, Lea." She spoke with authority. "The abilities aren't new to him but being in our world is."

His smile wavered a bit, but it didn't fall. His eyes went from excited to apologetic, and I stared past his head at the fridge to avoid eye contact.

"You've been alone?" he asked. "You've been alone all this time?"

I shook my head, eyeing Gavin, who nodded at me encouragingly from across the island.

"No, not alone. I've had Gavin and my aunt to support me."

Lea inclined his head respectfully at Gav. "Of course. What I meant to say was, you have dealt with these changes on your own with no one to guide you through them."

I glanced down at my hands, tapping my thumbs together. "I guess you could say that. Yeah."

Leander looked at Darla then returned his gaze to me. "There's a lot you need to know about all of this. It's much more than just being someone with extraordinary abilities."

I looked up, and his expression was extremely serious.

"You are a part of something much, much bigger than yourself," he said.

No kidding. I'd figured that out when I'd had that deep conversation with Gabriel the other night about "mysterious forces" and "higher beings." But I politely listened as he continued.

"I would really like to take the time to talk with you, about you, and tell you everything I assume you've already begun to question in your life. A lot of this is about heritage and a lot of this is about different worlds. Most of it is learned through stories, which I am more than willing to tell you."

He leaned toward me, his brown eyes holding mine in place. I was feeling overwhelmed until he placed his hand on my shoulder. A calmness settled in me, just as it did whenever Gabe was around. Leander smiled then leaned back, turning his head toward Olivia, who was resting tiredly against the island.

"But it will all have to wait, as it is way past my daughter's bedtime," he said.

Olivia's head perked up, and she frowned. "I'm fine, Daddy. I'm awake."

Lea shook his head and slid off the stool. "You have ten seconds to get upstairs and…"

She then took off at the speed of light, so fast she was a blur of color, and she was gone from the room.

Lea looked after her and exhaled heavily. "She's such a ball of energy."

"She's also the fastest out of all of us." Darla had a hint of pride in her voice. "She can outrun me, beat me in any race, and I've been running so much longer than she has."

"I thought she didn't have any abilities yet." Gavin lifted an eyebrow.

"She doesn't really," Lea responded. "One of our capabilities includes being faster than most people, and for reasons unknown, this specific supernatural trait appeared in her earlier than expected."

"In other words, she was just lucky," Arlo grumbled from his position in the entryway, from where he had yet to move.

Leander crossed his arms and faced Arlo. "Don't be jealous. You'll be joining us soon enough."

Arlo scowled and turned away from the kitchen. "I'm going to bed." He disappeared around the corner.

Leander faced the rest of us. "Don't mind him. He's just being a typical teenager in need of an attitude adjustment." He patted the granite island. "So,

Caleb. Tonight is not the night to talk, but if you are around tomorrow, I'd be happy to have you over for lunch."

"Oh," I said inaudibly, partially surprised by the kind gesture, and partially panicking. "I have classes until two-fifteen, but after that, I'm free."

"Cool." Leander smiled sincerely. "Just come to the house when you get out. The door will be unlocked for you."

I bit my bottom lip. "Unfortunately, I don't have my own car, and Gavin has class until three—"

"I'll pick you up, Cay," Darla piped up. "I'm done with class by noon."

I thanked her, and Lea clasped his hands together. "I look forward to getting to know you better. Also, if you leave the beer, we can have it with lunch."

I couldn't help but grin, and Gavin laughed, rising to his feet, indicating it was time to leave.

He gestured to the beer with a slight bow. "It's all yours, sir."

Leander clapped Gavin on the back approvingly.

I'd started to feel different during those last few moments I'd spent in Darla's house. Being around people who were so used to being abnormal made me feel less like a broken-up puzzle and more like I was filling in some blanks. Rather than being an aberration, I felt as if I was just an upgraded person. Better than normal, no longer needing to be normal. Because, apparently, being different was not necessarily a bad thing. This thought made me stand a bit taller as Gavin and I left the house, and for the first time in five years, I felt prepared to accept who I was.

I also thought—as we waved goodbye to Darla, Tucker, and Leander standing in the doorway of the house—that perhaps I should be mindful of who I trusted with my secret.

CHAPTER
7

TOWARD THE END OF MY last class, I started getting jittery about talking with Leander.

I met Darla at her car—lucky her, she had a high-tech, eco-friendly sleek silver BMW i3—and I tossed my stuff into the back seat. As I climbed into the front passenger side, Darla plugged her auxiliary cord into her phone, and electronic music pounded heavily over the speakers. I bounced my head to the bass and leaned back into the seat as she peeled out of the parking lot.

"Sweet sound system," I said over the music.

"It was a gift from Leander." She grinned, reaching for the volume dial and turning it down. "I'm not one to want extravagant things or feel a need to be spoiled, but a car with good bass is a totally different ballgame."

"What do you study at Divinity?" I asked casually, trying to get my mind off my anticipated talk with Lea.

"My major is in aerospace engineering and spacecraft design," she said.

She must have seen the surprise in my expression because her grin broadened.

She ran a hand through her hair and tossed her caramel waves. "I have a double minor in philosophy and creative writing. What about you?"

Attempting to compose myself, I asked, "First—aerospace engineering? What do you want to do with that?"

She lifted her eyebrows at me. "Well, duh, I want to work on rocket ships of course."

"You must be extremely brainy. Engineering is hard."

She shrugged. "Truthfully, I'm much more street than book smart. I'm no straight-A student, that's for sure." She shrugged again. "I just really love what I study. And I've always loved space science."

"Me too." I stared out the windshield. "Anything we don't have all the answers to interests me."

Darla nodded, tapping her fingertips on the steering wheel. "And you? What's your area of expertise?"

"I major in earth and environmental studies, and I have a minor in philosophy too." I felt less than impressive next to her with her engineering major. "Planet Earth class with Sampson is a core requirement, which, unfortunately for us, is why we're stuck with him. I had two of my required philosophy courses today. How come you aren't in them?"

"I'm still working out the kinks in my schedule." D rolled her eyes. "But now that I know you have these classes, maybe I can get switched into them." She glanced at me hopefully. "What are you taking?"

"My eleven-thirty is just a critical-thinking-type class, and it's really boring, considering the old man who teaches it just stands at the board and talks the entire time. But my one o'clock is metaphysics and the theory of existentialism, and that's my favorite branch of philosophy to learn about."

Darla's head tilted slightly, her gaze darting from the road to her knuckles and back to the road again. By the look on her face, she was thinking deeply about something. She looked kind of sad. I wished I could read her thoughts in the same way she could read mine.

"Existentialism? That's my favorite too," she said quietly. "I love learning about the nature of being, of existing in the world. But sometimes, I overthink things. What got me so interested in it was the fact that my existence, and my family's existence, contradicts everything I actually know. You know what I mean?"

Of course, I did. That had been my life every day since I had my first vision. Her reason for studying philosophy was the same as mine; I often questioned why things happened—not just to me but to all people. I wondered why I was connected to Gabriel and what it meant. I speculated why I had abilities no one could explain, and I envisioned a universe so big that there had to be reasons for my existence.

Darla was in my head. I could feel her there, even though she probably didn't mean to be.

"As usual, I completely know what you mean," I responded casually.

She turned onto the road that would eventually lead to her home and loosened the grip she had on the steering wheel. We were both quiet and thinking for a moment. She ran a hand through her hair again.

"It's almost…unnerving," she started.

Before I could ask what she meant, she went on.

"When I walked into Sampson's class this past Monday, I was more than just aware of your presence. I could hear everyone's thoughts, but I had this instinct, like a mental, gravitational tugging in your direction. As if—" She sighed, seemingly struggling to explain as best she could. "Like out of the twenty-something people in that class, my entire self was aware of you, and your existence was practically calling me. Over the course of the last few days, I've come to realize I am very in-tune with your thoughts and feelings. I know this sounds totally weird, and I'm sorry—"

I started to protest, to clarify that it wasn't any crazier than anything else happening around me. But she shook her head.

"But there was no way I couldn't meet you. Maybe it's because you've had visions about me—which, by the way, I am *not* ready to ask about yet—or maybe it's some weird, connected mind-thing we share. Or maybe it's kind of like the feeling Leander gets when he senses one of us nearby."

She pulled into her driveway and drove the car up to the garage. As the doors lifted, I turned in my seat to face her.

"Darla, it's really not crazy. It makes just about as much sense as everything else in my life."

She smiled thinly, tight-lipped and anxious, and I knew my face mirrored hers.

"But I'm glad we met and became friends. Now maybe I can get some closure." As I stopped talking, I couldn't help but think closure was the last thing I would find. With the answers I'd get today, I would probably only have more questions.

Darla sighed again, her aura less tense. "Don't be nervous, Caleb. Leander is protective of us. He will protect you too."

I narrowed my eyes at her jokingly, opening the car door. "It's that obvious, huh?"

"Oh, please. Thanks to you, I lost my appetite, and my hands started sweating before you even got into the car."

Upon entering the house, I could hear something sizzling and I could smell the sweet-but-tangy scent of teriyaki sauce. Darla dropped her bag onto the floor and looked at me with gleaming eyes.

"My appetite suddenly returned." She grinned and headed toward the kitchen.

I left my bag beside hers and followed her into the room.

Leander was at the stove, sweating beer in hand, tossing vegetables like a professional chef. Darla skipped up to him and kissed his cheek, before snagging a fork off the counter and dipping it into the pan.

"I assure you it will taste as delicious as it smells," Leander said.

He looked over his shoulder at me as I took a seat at the island. He snatched the fork from Darla and shoved the piece she grabbed into his own mouth.

"In addition to your visions, Caleb," he said, "your senses are more than simply heightened. You can smell, taste, hear, and see better than any average human being."

I thought about that briefly. I couldn't tell if there was a difference between the way I sensed things and the way someone like Gavin or Aunt Nikki sensed things. If he was telling the truth—which I'm sure he was—then that was something I could get used to.

Darla went over to the fridge and opened up the double doors, reaching for the remaining beer bottles. She popped two of them open, handed me one, and sat across from me. "Chicken and vegetable teriyaki is Lea's specialty."

"I appreciate you inviting me over and taking the time to speak with me, sir," I said gratefully, taking a sip from the bottle.

"No need for formalities, kid. You can just call me Lea." He reached up to the cabinets and pulled some plates down. "I hope you aren't a vegetarian. We're a family of meat eaters."

I chuckled politely. "Nope, I'm carnivorous."

Lea made up plates for the three of us and joined Darla and me at the island. We dug in, all quietly eating. I didn't want to strike up the conversation first, considering I never talked in-depth about my visions with anyone before other than Gavin or Darla. But, eventually, Leander started asking me about school and what I liked to do on my free time. He asked about Gavin as well, more so than I expected, and Darla's cheeks were flushed the entire time.

"It's good that you have someone to trust like that," Leander said. "Gavin seems like a reliable pal."

We'd finished eating and had started washing dishes. I couldn't be a guest in someone's house without offering to help, even though he protested at first. He was drying as D brought over pans to clean.

"Darla is obviously quite fond of your friend too," Lea said to me.

"Leander!" she hissed, glaring at him with daggers in her eyes.

A smile played on his lips. "What? Caleb is intuitive. He had to have known anyway."

I laughed. "It isn't intuition as much as it's just plain obvious that they like each other."

Lea snickered. Darla narrowed her eyes at us and tossed the plates into the sink with a not-so-gentle clang. She pushed herself into my thoughts abruptly.

Well, aren't you two chummy already.

I grinned, not taking my eyes off of the plates.

Once we had finished cleaning up, Lea put his hand on my shoulder. "Why don't we go talk in my study?"

We began heading for the hallway, Darla walking behind us.

"I think just Caleb and I should talk," Lea told her.

I turned to Darla, my chest tightening.

She nodded at Leander and looked at me, displaying an expression caught between concerned and untroubled. *It's fine, don't worry.*

I know.

Lea guided me around the spiral staircase, and we passed by several mahogany doors that matched the theme of the home. We branched off toward the back of the house, where at the end of the hall stood a lone door. This door was made of a different, lighter wood and had vine-like engravings along the edges of it. Leander turned the doorknob, opening the door and allowing me to step inside first.

His study, which I had imagined would be an office, was actually more of a library, a rectangular, cozy room with a vaulted ceiling and wooden shelves along the walls filled with an array of colorfully bound books. At the head of the room on my left was a wooden desk to match and a large, dark-brown leather swivel chair. Behind it was a floor-to-ceiling window with a black wrought-iron design on the panes through which I could see the Appalachian Mountains, purple in the afternoon sun. Two office chairs sat in front of the desk, ready for anyone looking for a consultation, and beneath them was a soft, maroon rug spread across the wooden floor. Between two bookshelves on the far wall stood a fireplace made entirely of stone, but there was only ash and a fresh log within it today. In the far corner of the room on the right side was a smaller version of the huge window, trees and mountains in view, and in front of it sat a big, beige, puffy reading chair that looked as if it could swallow a person whole. A coffee table sat in front of it, upon it a brewing, Wi-Fi-activated, wireless, coffee machine. There was a matching, brown-leather loveseat beside the puffy chair as well; the perfect reading nook for a bibliophile.

"Have a seat anywhere you like," Leander said, patting my shoulder. "I see you eyeing up that reading chair in the corner. Do you like to read?" He closed the door behind us and gestured to the inviting, puffy chair.

I nodded. "I don't read as often as I'd like to. College keeps me pretty occupied."

I went over to the reading corner and plopped down into the seat. Lea headed for his desk, but rather than sitting behind it, he lifted himself right on top of it. I leaned forward, elbows resting on my knees, putting my hands together and glancing over at Leander expectantly. He swung his legs slightly, back and forth, the look on his face telling me he was pondering how to begin.

He exhaled, shaking his head. "I have had this conversation four different times, and it never ceases to make me nervous."

"What are you nervous for?" I was puzzled. I should have felt more nervous than he did. But surprisingly, I felt less anxious about this than anything, maybe because I was finally going to get some answers.

Lea chuckled, his eyes crinkling at the sides. "It's the same feeling a parent gets when giving a child the sex talk—you just don't know how they'll react."

I smiled politely, waiting patiently for him to start. He licked his lips, his swinging legs ceasing. I felt Darla pressing against the back door of my mind. As much as I wanted to let her poke her way in, I kept myself locked shut, trying to think of anything other than how anxious I was. Then, Lea began.

"I'm sure you have figured out by now that there is so much more to life than just our world, the people and places and sciences we have come to know." He crossed his arms, nodding. "You've seen things and felt and experienced things many people will never understand. I don't know everything—I'm sure Darla would like to tell you I do—and everything I have come to learn about our...kind, so to speak, is through years of traveling, researching, and meeting people.

"When I discovered my abilities, I was fourteen years old, still living in the orphanage I'd spent my entire life at in New York City. I was faster than the other kids, stronger. I could scale buildings and jump across roofs like a parkour expert. I could smell and taste things more intensely, and I could see clearly even in the darkest of nights. I remember one day just watching dust particles floating around in a beam of sunlight; they were sparkling and spinning, and it was so...enchanting. I got into a fight once with one of the bigger, meaner boys, and I took him down so fast the other kids feared me afterward. I loved it at first, but eventually, life got really lonely, and I became very aware of the fact that I wasn't normal.

"One night, I was sitting upon the roof of a building, and I happened to see a woman off in the distance. I'll cut to the chase—she saw me, I saw her, and she sprouted wings, flying off into the night like an angel. That's when I knew I had to find the answers, find out everything I could about these secrets I was discovering. I had to find out how and why I came to be, who the winged people were. It was no longer all fun and games to me; this was my life, and I needed to protect myself. So, when I reached the ripe old age of eighteen, I packed everything I had—which was not all that much—and I set off on the biggest adventure of my life.

"After a few years of traveling in the States, working in different places and making as much money as a nomad could, I discovered two very specific things. One, I had a special ability that many of our kind did not have—my skill of sensing others who are like us. It's a strong tug that pulls me in the direction of the others and brings me to places unknowingly at times. The kids and I have often traveled around for undisclosed reasons because I felt the pull in those directions. But this skill especially helped me in my quest to find answers."

I interrupted. "Is that why you came to Divinity then? Did you know there were others here?" I swallowed. "Did you know I was here?"

Leander scratched his salt-and-pepper goatee, seemingly thinking. "You know," he said with a small smile, "I guess, in some way, I did." He looked pleasantly surprised. "How about that for a twist? Would you like some coffee, by the way? Tea?"

I respectfully declined. He scratched his goatee again.

"Where was I?" he asked.

"You discovered two things."

"Oh! Yes, my second discovery." His eyes lit up. "I discovered from the stories I heard from people I met and from the research I'd gathered, that my quest would take me to Norway. This was where I learned everything I am about to tell you and everything I've come to know. Vocabulary, origins, and categories of our kind—and stories older than the dawn of time. I flew out to Oslo, the capital, and spent several years researching there, and I met people who gave me more information than I could have imagined finding. I went to Svalbard and saw the northern lights, too, which was such an incredible experience." He nodded. "It was the greatest trip of my life."

"I've always wanted to see the northern lights," I said. "I love learning anything about our planet. I love reading about how Earth runs."

Leander grinned at me then. "We can take a trip to Norway one day if you'd like. I took Darla and Tucker once when they were younger. They didn't see the lights, but it was good for them to see where the stories came from. I'd like to take Arlo and Ollie there, too, so you're welcome to join us on the next adventure."

I blinked in astonishment at his gesture, a smile creeping across my face. A trip to Norway. Wouldn't that be something? I'd never been out of the country before. "That would be too much to ask."

Leander shrugged. "You're part of the clan now, Caleb. It's not as if I'm telling you all of this, all about yourself, so you can be on your merry way and pretend your world hasn't changed. We're your support system, and I'm here to help you like I helped the kids."

I was touched by his words. Never had I ever been a part of something so immense. I couldn't imagine what my life was going to be like when I woke tomorrow, knowing everything I was about to know. "Thank you. Really, thank you. You have no idea what this means to me."

Leander's face grew serious then. "Don't thank me yet. I wish it was as simple as just giving you the answers, so you could move forward with your life. But there's a lot more than just our kind and special abilities and living in this world with them. As I said, we're your support system—this means we're here not only for you, but to protect you now as well."

I waited for him to continue, a sudden feeling of dread pooling in the pit of my stomach.

Leander slid off his desk, crossing his arms again and leaning against it. "During my stay in Norway, I learned there are names for people like us and for the winged beings. But it's not as black and white as I wish it could be, unfortunately. Just like in our everyday mortal lives, there is good and there is evil. And I'll start from the beginning, before there were people like us. Those so-called 'angels' we sometimes see go by two Norwegian terms—*helliget* and *mørkeste*, which roughly translates to *hallowed* and *darkest*. Long, long ago, these terms were given to the winged beings by the Norwegians, who thought they were angels from the heavens. Holy beings and their counterparts. Which, as far as I and the rest of the world is concerned, they very well may be. It makes about as much sense as anything else.

"Now, there was a period of time where helliget first came to Earth. Some stories say they—or, rather, the good helliget—were in search of new homes and a new world to discover. Some say the mørkeste—which are helliget that have turned on their own kind—traveled the universe in an attempt to capture and conquer planets, and they would come and go however they pleased. Others say some had fallen from grace, and Earth was their landing site, where they were bound until they could prove worthy enough to return home. All of these could be viable answers, and I believe one or all of them could be true. If there is one thing I have learned throughout my years, it's that anything is possible.

"Anyway, the helliget and mørkeste came to our planet, furling their wings so as not to bring attention to themselves, roaming around, and living among the mortals—they live much, much longer than mortals, I should add. But this is where our story begins, where helliget and mørkeste mated with humans, coexisted with mankind. They lived as humans did, where the females and males interacted with human men and women—and in some cases, pregnancy was the result. We—you, me, Darla, the kids—are their progenies, known as *velsignet.* We are part-human and part-helliget. Or part-mørkeste, which, sadly, many of us are."

"Velsignet? What does that mean?" I asked.

"It translates to *blessed.*" Leander smiled sadly. "From what I learned, the children born of the helliget and mortals were considered blessed gifts from Heaven, which, I could imagine, made sense at the time. After all, we, the velsignet, grew up with special, unique abilities and lived more advanced lives than our fellow mortals. Unfortunately, it wasn't that simple; the mørkeste often had agendas of their own. Allow me to go back a bit to explain how the mørkeste even came to be. Originally, when the helliget all first came to Earth, they were still unified as a species, a united front. There was no good versus evil with their kind.

"But upon their arrival, they split into two factions. The first group wanted to live peacefully and remain hallowed, true to their helliget nature. The other group, on the contrary, wanted to disaffiliate from their species and distinguish themselves as a whole new, vengeful type of helliget—known as the mørkeste. They made a vow to take control over this new planet. They would try to find free-roaming helliget, as well as the earthbound helliget, and corrupt them into doing their bidding or convince them to join their group. From what I hear, the two sides have been at war for centuries. The only thing us velsignet can do is attempt to live our lives without getting involved with the higher beings. And, more recently, the mørkeste have been looking to capture velsignet and perform something I believe is called forced evolution."

Leander shook his head with a disgusted look. "Being half-human is difficult. We are not strong enough to stand up to the mørkeste. It could very well be our downfall. The only advantage we have, if you want to call it that, is that we are able to somewhat hide in plain sight. We have extraordinary abilities, but these will only get us so far. It would be one thing to be just human and left out of their world entirely, or just helliget, all-powerful and able to fight back. But because we are both, and many of our kind know next to nothing about what I've just told you," he sighed, "it is collectively our greatest weakness."

"What's forced evolution?" I asked, unsure if I wanted to know the answer.

Leander grimaced. "I'm not really sure, Caleb, and I hope we never find out. I've heard different things from other velsignet. But it never ends well for our kind, and we become slaves to the mørkeste. It only makes the mørkeste stronger in numbers, and they wreak havoc wherever they go."

I wrung my shaking hands. "This life is much…denser than I thought."

Lea sighed. "I know it's a lot of information to take in. But I've seen so much, and everything I've discovered only confirms my research and the stories."

"So." I ran a hand through my hair. "I'm a velsignet. Which means one of my parents was helliget? Or mørkeste?"

Leander nodded.

"My blood has the DNA of a higher being—a creature of some sort—that isn't from Earth?"

He nodded again.

"I am the child of a human and something otherworldly?"

He nodded a third time, and I blew out a breath I hadn't known I was holding. The news was so much to take in. Too much. His story explained everything, and it explained nothing. The history of beings like Gabriel, and how people like me came to be. It was out of this world, literally. Magic or science or religion—whatever it was, it made perfect sense, and no sense at all.

"This is everything I have learned from my research and from various velsignet I've crossed paths with throughout my life," Leander said. "I still have so many more questions, but what I've told you is all I know." He closed his eyes solemnly. "I hope I've been able to provide you with useful information, things that may help you protect yourself in this cold world."

"I-I…" I tried to compose my racing thoughts, all the while blocking Darla's prying mind. "I can't believe this is all real."

Leander looked down at his hands. "Since I left the orphanage, I've spent my life searching for all the answers, which has led me to where I am today. I spent much of that time in Norway, where I obtained the most information and met velsignet nomads like myself. I was desperate, and my quest gave my life purpose. And now I have the kids." He glanced over at the wooden, vine-covered door. "I have the kids to protect. And you as well." The corner of his mouth lifted, and he winked at me, obviously trying to make light of all this heavy news.

I relaxed in the chair a bit. "I appreciate this more than you'll ever know, Leander, really." I shook my head incredulously, still bewildered at all the knowledge I'd received. "I'll repay you in any way I can."

Leander waved his hand. "Nonsense, it is my purpose in life to protect and inform our kind as best as I can, especially when it's a friend."

He came over to sit in the loveseat beside my chair, and I wondered if he'd earlier sat far from me out of the fear of my reaction. He crossed one jean-covered leg over the other. "Now that you have some pieces of the puzzle, are you comfortable with telling me of your origins? About how your life has progressed?"

Whether or not I felt comfortable talking about things didn't matter anymore; this man had shared his secret—a worldwide yet closely kept secret—and I was practically obligated to tell him about my life. I chewed my bottom lip thoughtfully while he poured himself a cup of coffee from the wireless machine on the table.

"I don't know where to begin. I don't talk about myself much." My face grew warm.

"Why don't you start with your parents?" He poured cream into his mug. "Now that you know a bit about our histories, which one do you think was helliget?"

I bit the inside of my cheek. "Well, I'm thinking it was my father, since he left when I was an infant, and my mother had passed away from cancer when I was five. You said helliget live long—"

"Oh, for God's sake, I'm sorry." Lea leaned over and put a hand on my knee apologetically. "I'm so sorry. I forgot you said you live with your godmother."

I shook my head. "It's really okay. Don't worry about it." I wanted to move past this part and not think about my mom right then.

"So, you never knew your father." Lea sat back, wrinkling his nose. "You couldn't have known if he was one of the higher beings. I would suggest he could've been velsignet, which would make you more human than helliget, but because of your particular ability, I don't think that's the case." He lifted his coffee cup off the table. "Darla tells me that you have a helliget friend. I've only spoken with a few I've happened to come across over the years, but in my past, I've run into more mørkeste than I would've liked."

I perked up at the thought of my friend. "Gabriel," I said. "He's been with me since my father left. He's really like a guardian angel to me, ironically, always looking out for me and there when I need him the most."

"You're really blessed—no pun intended." Lea grinned. "Helliget are the most wonderful beings, as far as I've been able to tell, and they very rarely interact with humans in their true form." His smile faltered then. "But mørkeste can easily be mistaken for helliget, so always be cautious. Does your godmother know of the being's presence in your life?"

"Nicole knows about the visions but not about Gabe." I felt a pang of guilt in my chest. "I just don't want her to think I'm insane. Although, she recently told me she thought there was something 'different' about my father when she met him."

Lea's head tilted curiously then, and he sipped his coffee. "Nicole, you said?"

I mirrored his head tilt. "Yes, I refer to her as my aunt most of the time, but she was my mother's dearest friend."

Leander cleared his throat, tugging the collar of his gray Aran sweater as he set his mug back down. "This 'Nicole' wouldn't happen to be a small, spunky brunette with the last name of DeCarlo, would it?"

I sat up straight. "The very one!" My gaze swept over Lea. "You know her?"

He stretched his collar again. "I did! In fact, we dated for a time."

Dated! I couldn't imagine Nik dating when she'd only been on a date maybe once in the last decade or so.

Lea continued. "I met her when I was starting grad school and she was attending the University of Nevada. We'd started seeing each other not long after Darla entered my life—maybe when she was around a year or two old." He sighed, looking dejected. "I never told Nicole about Darla, though. I didn't talk much about my personal life with others. Kept to myself mostly, never got too serious with anyone. But we were quite fond of each other."

"Wow," I stated, the surprise prominent in my voice. "Small world, huh?"

"And getting smaller," Leander concurred. "I'm not someone who fully believes in fate, but I also don't believe there's such a thing as coincidences either."

A dude after my own heart. "I'll be sure to tell Nikki I've met you."

He didn't respond, and he stared up out the window behind me. I swallowed, feeling uncomfortable.

"Or not," I mumbled.

His gaze dropped to mine. "Oh, no, I'd love to see her again. It's just… um." He paused, glancing into his coffee. "Now I'm figuring out the math, and I just can't help but think that the reason Nicole broke things off was because it was around the same time she had to take you in as her own."

"Oh."

"I had been upset at the time because she wouldn't tell me exactly why she was leaving. I was thick-headed. I ignored all her emails." He rubbed his forehead. "Now I realize the pain she must've been in, mourning her best friend. I'm such an asshole."

He placed his face in his hands and groaned, and I snorted unintentionally. He whipped his head up.

"What's so funny?" He smirked as the mood lifted.

"All of this." I chuckled and waved my hand. "It's an amusing situation. You're not an asshole." I grinned. "It's just...it's funny how not coincidental this is."

Leander grinned at me in return. "You're a really smart guy, Caleb Swift."

I bowed my head. "Thank you, sir."

Nikki and Leander. I still couldn't wrap my mind around it.

After a minute, Lea picked up his coffee again. "I'm curious to know who your father was and how Nicole knew him."

I scowled. "I don't care too much about him and his whereabouts, frankly. All Nikki told me was his name and that, apparently, he ran off with my twin sister the moment we were born."

"Interesting!" Lea's voice echoed in the mug. He tilted it down to speak again. "What was his name?" He went for another sip.

"Michael. Just Michael. I don't know his last name. I actually only recently learned about—"

Lea started choking on his coffee. I hurried to my feet and moved to pat his back, and he handed me his mug to set on the table. We stared at each other, wide-eyed and startled, as he caught his breath.

"Are you all right?" I asked him, gently shaking his shoulder a bit to make sure.

His face was pale as the cream he'd poured into his coffee, and his brown-eyed gaze bore into mine. The room was dead silent for what felt like an eternity.

"You said his name was Michael?" Lea finally said, hoarsely.

I nodded very slowly. "Yeah, did you know him too?"

"Caleb, when were you born?"

The question caught me off guard. "October eleventh. Why?"

His Adam's apple bobbed as he swallowed hard. He rose to his feet steadily, making his way over to his desk. He reached over it and pressed a button on the office phone that rested on top of a notebook. "Darla."

I could hear his voice sound from elsewhere in the house. There must've been an intercom system with speakers set up throughout their home.

"Could you come into my study, please?" he asked.

I didn't realize I was still standing until I felt my knees quiver slightly from anxiety. A short moment later, Darla, eyes bulging, cracked the door open and slipped into the room.

"I wasn't listening. I swear." She leaned her back against the door, gaze bouncing between Leander and me.

Lea pinched the bridge of his nose, his face twisted into some emotion I couldn't decipher—maybe a mix between frustration and disbelief.

"Could you both sit down for a moment?"

Darla turned to me, and our eyes locked, but neither of us moved an inch. D looked at him. "Leander, what's wrong?"

He turned and placed both his hands on his desk, allowing his head to hang down over his chest. "I'm just trying to make sense of this."

"Make sense of what?" Darla glanced at me. "What's he talking about, Cay?"

I put my hands up defensively. "I'm just as confused as you are, okay?"

Leander spun around, looking back and forth between Darla and me. "I've had a revelation, and the explanation is going to be unbelievable—"

"Just spit it out, Lea!" Darla crossed her arms. "Stop freaking us out!"

He rubbed his face in distress, pulling at his goatee. He sighed. "Caleb," he said, the forcefulness in his voice causing me to look directly at him. "Your father, Michael. He was or is, I should say, a distant cousin of mine."

"Okay," I still couldn't understand what had him so stupefied.

"A distant cousin of mine," he continued, "who, about twenty-one years ago, delivered an infant girl to my doorstep, relying on me to take her in and raise her."

I could hear his words and what he was saying very clearly, but none of it was processing right in my brain. I stepped out from behind the coffee table and scrunched my face up, trying to read his features. He stared back at me as if he'd seen a ghost.

"Lea, seriously, what are you...?" Darla shook her head.

We glanced at each other again.

That's when I knew.

I looked into the biting blue irises of her eyes, and my mind raced to understand the memories I had of seeing them. I had seen her eyes in my visions of the future for five years. For five damn years, I had seen the same blue eyes as she silently screamed, her hands and face spattered with blood. I had seen her eyes in person only a few days ago, the first day she entered my class, and I knew her as that girl. But all this time, I'd been recognizing her all wrong. In that very moment, I envisioned myself looking into a mirror, the exact same eyes staring back at me.

While I thought I was looking into the eyes of a girl whose future was untold, I was actually seeing my own eyes in hers.

"I'm sorry. I should've known," Leander's voice sounded so far away, and my ears were ringing too loudly for me to focus on his words. "I should've talked to Michael before he..."

"I should've known," I repeated his statement softly. I pressed my sweating palm to my forehead, my hair falling over my eyes. "How did I not see it?" We had the same eyes. We had the exact same eyes. Suddenly, it was like looking into my own reflection.

Darla gripped the sides of her head and squeezed her eyes shut. "Caleb, please, I can hear what you're thinking, and I don't understand it."

"Darla, sweetheart," Leander coaxed carefully, "it appears I've discovered that Caleb is your brother. Your *twin* brother. You were separated at birth. Michael brought you to me, and it seems he had left Caleb with your mother."

As he said this, it made it all the more real. My heart was pounding so hard. I couldn't comprehend the fact that Darla was not only the girl from my visions, she was not only a velsignet, like I was; she was my twin sister. Michael, our father, had taken her away from my mother and me. How had my mother lived without her? How could she have just given Darla away? How could they have split us up? How could they have done this to us? All these questions violently wracked my brain, and for a moment, I thought I might need to sit down.

How could they have done this to us?

She stared at Leander, her mouth agape. "I don't... We don't even look... How is this...?" She swallowed. "Is there, like, some kind of test we can take or something?"

Her lips were pale. I could only assume she was as shocked as I was.

Leander rubbed his shoulder. "I'm sure we could, but it's not necessary. I'm one hundred and ten percent certain of this. You were brought to me the same night of your birth—October eleventh." He ran his hand through his hair. "I've never been so certain about anything before. My relative, your father, and Caleb's father are all one and the same."

Darla nodded sluggishly, the color drained from her face. A knot had formed in my stomach, and my head spun in the way it did before I had visions. But I knew this wasn't a vision; it was real life. *My* real life.

"I need to just...not, right now." She spoke barely above a whisper and then turned to leave.

She looked at me once, scanning my face, before she opened the door. Her expression caused a lump to form in my throat, but I couldn't tell what she was thinking. She slipped out of the room and slammed the door shut behind her.

CHAPTER
8

"**S**HE'LL COME AROUND," LEA SAID.

I didn't respond. I was sitting in front of the fireplace, a maroon blanket over my shoulders, a hot cup of black coffee sloshing about in my shaking hands. Leander sat near me on one of the desk chairs, and notebooks and documents and photos scattered about the floor. As he was finishing his fifth cup of coffee that evening, he reached over to stoke the fire.

"It wasn't obvious, Caleb. It's not as if we all could've seen this coming." He flipped one of the documents over. "There were missing puzzle pieces in your life. In mine and Darla's life, things appeared cut and dried. Michael came to my apartment the night of your birth and dropped off Darla without a word about a second child. I came up with the story about her parents being unfit and thought that would be the end of it."

I didn't know whether to be pissed that Michael took Darla from our mother or feel insulted that he hadn't taken me, too, or feel bad for Leander, who'd been forced—without warning—into becoming a parent. I stared into the fire. Despite the warmth of the flames, my body couldn't stop trembling.

Lea sighed. "I know you must feel…disoriented—"

"And at a loss. And infuriated," I added to the list.

"And rattled and distraught." He finished tending the fire and sifted through some of the papers. "Your world has been turned upside down many times since you discovered your abilities, and even more so today. I can't imagine what you're going through. What you both are going through."

Us both. Her and me. We. I hadn't really thought about what she must be feeling right now. There wasn't just "me" anymore. I wasn't alone in my thoughts and emotions. There wasn't just Darla's life and Caleb's life. This was both our lives connected by one unchangeable, iron thread. We had the same parents. She was my sister, and I was her brother. We were both velsignet, trying to live in a world of humans who didn't even know that people like us existed. We had connected instantaneously when we met, even if we hadn't developed a clear or obvious bond. We shared similar abilities, including a mutual telepathy that existed between us and no one else. Just today, she had told me she felt in-tune with my thoughts and feelings, and there was no way she couldn't meet me. Originally, the straightforward answer to it all had seemed to involve my visions of her future—and those visions had brought us together. Fate or some shit like that. Not a *twin* thing. But now the truth was out, the situation seemed so crystal clear.

The only difference between us seemed to have been that I was able to have a relationship with one of our parents for a brief period of time and she hadn't ever been given that chance.

Leander picked up a folder of documents and handed it to me. I gave him a funny look, trading my empty cup for the folder. They were adoption papers—Darla's, to be exact—drawn up and signed by Leander and none other than my father himself. I touched Michael's signature, tracing the loopy letters with my finger. I sifted through some of the papers and came across a hospital bill.

"Darla Rayne Adair," I read, "treated on October twelfth, 10:45 a.m., at Valley Hospital in Roseland, Nevada?"

"We brought her in to make sure she was healthy. That's where I was living at the time. And where your aunt Nikki lived and studied to be a nurse." Leander smiled solemnly as I handed him back the certificate. "Darla Rayne… Swift. Seems to flow better than Adair, now, doesn't it?"

"Did you name her?" I inquired.

"No, Michael had already given her the name Darla when he knocked on my door that night." Lea stared into the fire, leaning his elbows on his knees. "When he showed up, it was pouring rain for the first time in months—hence why I gave her Rayne as a middle name. He was holding her in his arms, a small bundle of blankets, standing on my stoop in the downpour. I hadn't seen him since…" He paused, then shrugged. "Well, that's a story for another time. But he implored me to take her. I really had no choice in the matter; he introduced her as my goddaughter, and she was my family by blood—which, I suppose, means you and I are bonded as such as well."

"All these little pieces of our lives coming together—" I started to say but then stopped. There was no need to really explain it. "It's like I'm watching a film about someone else's life."

Leander was already nodding; he understood what I meant.

"I know. It's all so surreal. But I haven't seen Michael since then. He is helliget, so there are other places for him to venture off to, I'm sure." He rubbed his chin. "It's not like we were close, really. He is a very distant relative. You and I are descendants from a long line of helliget-humans, most of whom I had only found after looking at endless ancestry books. Our side of the family has a high percentage of helliget, so much of our line is pure helliget blood, like your father. We'd met a few times, but only a few."

"He didn't say why he was splitting us up and taking off?" It was the only question that truly bothered me.

"He never mentioned you or your mother or where he was going or why." Leander scratched his head. "He only told me that if I didn't take D in, she'd never be safe. Frankly, I didn't want to know what kind of trouble he might have been in, and I didn't want to be involved. I was young, in my early twenties, and you can imagine the pressure I felt at the time, the need for me to make an instant decision."

I exhaled. I had so many answers to the list of questions I'd always had, but now I had so many things left to uncover. And Leander, who had only been a stranger yesterday, had just become my relative. Apparently, we'd both come from a long line of pure helliget who'd mated—or procreated or whatever they called it—with humans. Leander was a brave soul who had taken in my sister as his own child when he was as about young as I was now.

I suddenly wished my coffee had been Irish.

"You're a good person, Leander," I said lamely. "You didn't have to get involved or take Darla in and raise her, but you did. You didn't have to find the other kids and protect them, but you did. You didn't have to bring me into your home and help me. But you did." I stood, taking the blanket off my shoulders and folding it over the arm of the chair, avoiding his gaze. "You could've said no. And she's so lucky to have had you as a father."

"Thank you for your kind words, Caleb." Leander stood as well. He placed a hand on my shoulder and squeezed it. "I just always try to do the right thing."

I looked down at my sneakers, taking his words to heart. Just do the right thing. I frowned and looked at Leander. "What should I tell my aunt Nikki?"

"You can tell her the whole truth and nothing but the truth," he answered, "but if you want my honest opinion, I would leave out the supernatural parts.

If I've learned one thing in all my years, it's that sometimes ignorance protects the people we love."

We turned away from the fire and he patted my back.

"If I were you, I'd tell her about your sister at some point. I'm sure she'd be happy to know you've found each other. And if Nicole is still the same person I knew years ago, she will want to meet her."

"Yeah, you're right," I agreed. I'd come up with something to tell my aunt. But before I left that evening, I wanted to talk to D.

As I moved for the door, I glanced back at Lea. "I'm going to check on Darla before I go. I want to make sure she's okay."

"I think that would be a good idea. She's stubborn, so don't back down, but give her space if necessary." Leander began shifting the chairs back to their original place by the desk. "I promise she'll be fine."

"Okay." I clenched my fist around the doorknob, hesitating. I focused my eyes on its dulling silver shine. "Thank you again. For all of this." I opened the door and slid through it before he could reply.

Having this new knowledge of our heightened senses, I guessed she could probably hear me as I walked up the two flights of stairs. I hesitated in front of the attic door. I didn't think knocking was appropriate, but I didn't know how to get her to talk to me without doing so. I made a fist and held it up in front of me to knock.

I don't want to talk right now, Caleb.

"Just open the damn door, Darla," I said sternly, despite being startled by her intrusion in my head.

I heard creaking and movement on the other side of the door, and I felt she was closer to it than where she previously was.

"Come on, now," I pleaded.

She stepped closer. The doorknob twisted, and the door opened inward slightly. I pressed my palm against the mahogany and pushed the rest of the way inside.

Darla's room was the size of a one-bedroom apartment, just as she'd described the day before—one main room with a full bathroom off to the left. A large picture window, similar to the one behind Leander's desk, was located directly ahead of me, beneath which sat a queen-sized bed sporting a midnight-blue comforter. Darla sat on the edge of her bed, arms crossed, as she allowed me to observe my surroundings.

A carpet matching the bedspread covered the majority of the hardwood floor. The ceiling slanted to reflect the shape of the roof, and it held two rectangular skylights. Dark-wood furniture lined the walls—two bookshelves, a desk, and a dresser. On the wall to my right was another big window, but this one led to a balcony. Night had taken over the sky, and a sliver of moonlight slipped through her drawn curtains. The only other light in Darla's room came from a couple of lamps and some scented candles.

"Nice digs," I said, clasping my hands behind my back. "Does Romeo hit you up so you can let down your hair?"

Darla glared at me, her eyes—the eyes we shared with our father—burning a hole in mine. "Romeo is from Shakespeare's *Romeo and Juliet*, you idiot." She dropped her arms. "You're thinking of the prince from *Rapunzel*."

I blew off her remark with a wave, walking over to sit beside her. She looked down at her hands and started chewing her bottom lip. The same way I always did whenever I was apprehensive of something. I stared down at my hands. I was sitting next to a sister I never knew I had. I guess she sort of looked like me. We both had Mom's nose. This was so crazy.

"Caleb." Darla lifted an eyebrow at me.

Oops.

I smirked sheepishly, cupping the back of my neck with one hand. "Sorry, I forget sometimes."

She looked back down at her lap, and I let out a huff.

"Look, this is all fucking insane. It's hard for me to register this too. I feel…" What did I feel, really? I had been told unexpected news, the most earth-shattering thing I'd probably ever hear. But how did I feel? "I feel like nothing has changed. I feel like we both had broken pasts, and this kind of fills in all the holes. Maybe the initial shock hasn't hit me yet. I don't know." My mouth snapped shut. I wasn't used to expressing my thoughts so openly with someone, especially when I had only just met Darla less than a week ago. I just felt like—

"A part of me that's been missing all my life has been found." Darla answered my thoughts exactly. She nodded, as if to agree with her words. "It feels like some kind of void was filled that always needed to be."

I pressed my lips into a thin line, the awkwardness settling in. "Yeah."

She let out a sound of annoyance and put her face in her hands. "I just can't stop asking all these questions in my head!"

"I know," I sympathized. "I'm asking the same ones."

"Can you tell me about your visions now?" she asked suddenly, eyes wide. "You don't have to tell me, like, all of them. Just the ones I'm in for now. Is that okay?"

I blinked twice. The question caught me off guard. "Darla, I don't know if now is—"

"I know, but now that we know we're twins, it'll make it easier to figure out what the visions mean."

"I don't think it's a good idea, D, especially with all this heavy news we just heard."

"Come on, Cay, I'm tired of secrets!" She thrust herself backward onto her bed and groaned. "Now that I know you're my brother, I want to know everything else!"

I crossed my arms. "Don't throw a tantrum. Of course, I'm going to tell you everything, but I just feel like tonight we should leave things here for now."

She bolted upright and glared at me again. "Me throwing a tantrum? That's funny, coming from the guy who literally ran away from home and up a mountain the other night when he got upset."

I jumped to my feet, my mouth open. "You can't be serious. You don't even know what I was pissed about. You weren't even supposed to be in my head!"

She, too, got to her feet. "That wasn't my fault. I couldn't control my mind from latching onto yours!" She put her hands on her hips. "And anyway, it doesn't matter what you were angry about. You still threw a hissy fit, all the same."

My ears burned with irritation, and I balled my hands into fists. That little escape to the mountains had been a way for me to catch a break, get some air, and calm down from the other crazy news I had received this week. The experience had been really personal, and she had no right to throw that in my face. The heat spread to my cheeks as I glared down at her.

"For your information," I said in a calm voice that didn't sound like my own, "that was the night I realized what a piece of shit our father was."

Her tight-lipped, smug face turned soft then, which wasn't exactly the reaction I'd hoped to get out of her. But I was too annoyed with her snarky comment to feel any remorse, so I loosened my shaking hands and headed for the door.

"Where are you going, Caleb?" she said, her tone scolding, which only fueled the flames of my anger.

I paused by the door. "I was thinking I'd head to church and sing with the gospel choir," I spat, rolling my eyes at her. "Where does it look like I'm going? I'm going home."

She raised her eyebrow again. "I drove you here."

I started out of the room. "I can walk."

"Caleb—"

I shut the door behind me before she could finish.

Cars whizzed by me once I reached the main road, and one wailed on its horn, causing me to bump my knee into the guardrail. What was everyone's problem? I scowled and dipped my hand into my school bag, snatching up my phone. One missed call from Gavin and a text. I unlocked the screen and opened up my messages.

How'd it go with Dar-licious? Did Mr. Adair tell you everything? Call me, dammit.

I smiled briefly at my phone, preparing to press Call, but then I figured I'd just call him when I got home. I tossed my phone into my bag and continued on my way.

Caleb, please come back so I can drive you home.

I gritted my teeth and rolled my shoulders, trudging along. Who did she think she was? It wasn't as if we'd been siblings forever. Well, in actuality, we had always been siblings, but we barely knew each other. She didn't know me like Nikki or Gavin knew me. The way she'd judged me had been unfair, especially since she didn't really know anything about me. I wasn't one to throw a "hissy fit," ever. At least, not without a good reason. All this fighting just because she was mad I wouldn't talk to her about my visions right when she wanted me to. She had no idea what kind of snake pit she was leaping into.

It's not safe to walk around at night. Leander is worried.

I could feel Darla's emotions through the connected link in our minds, and it wasn't helping when I was trying to be angry with her. I sighed heartily. I really didn't have time to be pissed off at my newly discovered sister, especially when we needed to talk about her impending future. I was actually wasting time trying to walk—shit, how many miles? —all the way home in the dark on a Friday night. I was being stupid. And I was being asinine, standing here on the side of the road, mentally arguing with myself.

I'm sorry for what I said, Caleb.

"Ah, fuck." I grunted, my shoulders rising to my ears. I closed my eyes. *It's okay, D. I'm sorry too. I'm heading back to your house.* I turned around and started back in the direction of their home.

My chest suddenly constricted in that way I could never get used to.

I cried out, the sharp cramp causing me to stop short and bend over. My pack slipped off my shoulder as I fell to my knees, gasping and sucking in air desperately. My mind tingled familiarly, and I dragged myself off the road and onto the grass by the guardrail, so I wouldn't get run over by the nighttime traffic. Pressing my cheek to the dewy grass, my sight dimmed as I was about to be transported out of my reality and into another. In one last desperate act, I called out to Darla to come find me, but I couldn't tell if I'd telepathized it or whimpered the plea out loud.

I saw white first, blinding white. Then blue patches splattered about the glaring canvas, and my sight swirled as my vision-self rolled onto his stomach. Grass touched my cheek. But was it the real grass or vision grass? I turned onto my back again, my gaze turning toward the blinding white, the sky overhead. Everything was blurry. What was I seeing? I wanted to rub my eyes, but I couldn't move my arms. I groaned, searching for something that wasn't white or green.

Finally, my sight cleared, and I could see trees circling around me. I saw her—I saw Darla standing there, her shirt and face spattered with blood as it always was. Her hands were stained red, held out in front of her, and her mouth was open in shock. But she wasn't looking at me; she was looking just past me, her face frozen in horror. She slowly collapsed to her knees, her hands shaking as she brought them to her red-splattered cheeks. My stomach turned at the sight of her, and I thought I might be sick. My vision-self twisted his head, turning to look in the direction Darla was gaping in, but then a bone-chilling scream lurched me from the vision.

"Caleb!"

My eyes were squeezed shut, and I refused to open them, shielding myself from the outside world even though I knew the vision was over. My chest ached, sore from the near-heart attack my visions caused. I thought I heard a car door slam. I was panting and sweating, lying on my back now, the sound of cars flying past me on the road coaxing me back into the real world.

"Hey, man, you okay?"

My eyes snapped open, and the night sky was blocked by a figure illuminated by headlights. A man was bending over me, his blond hair flopping over his eyes, hands on his knees. He was blinking fast, and I thought I could see specks of gold in his brown—almost black—irises. He looked young but old at the same time, which was hard for my tired mind to comprehend. He was also extremely close to my face, which made me slowly scooch away from him in the nicest way possible.

"You all right, buddy?" He rubbed his dimpled chin and stood up. "You drunk or something?"

"N-n-no." My voice croaked. The man's accent was different; I couldn't quite place it. It sounded kind of southern. I cautiously moved to my knees. "I'm f-fine, thanks."

"Are you sure?" The headlights revealed the tiny gold specks in his eyes again. He straightened, reaching his hand down to help me up. "I was driving and saw you just lying on the side of the road here." He smiled toothily. "You sure you haven't been drinking?"

"No, not at all." I grasped his hand.

He hoisted me up. "There ya go."

I brushed off my grass-stained jeans. I wobbled a bit but covered it up by snagging my backpack off the ground. "Thanks."

He stepped in front of me then, his hands an inch away from my chest. "Now wait a minute there." He looked me in the eye. "You have blood spilling out of your ears. Why don't you let me take you to a hospital?"

I dabbed my ears with the thick part of my palm and let out an exasperated sigh. I knew this guy was just trying to help, but I really wanted to get home. I had also noticed fewer and fewer cars were passing by, so being alone with this stranger at night was making me feel vulnerable. And truthfully, he was creeping me out.

"No, man, thanks, really, but I'm just going to head home. I live just around the corner," I lied, stepping around him, trying to smile politely.

Suddenly, my shoulder was yanked backward forcefully, and I was pulled in front of the jerk again. We were practically nose to nose, and I could swear I saw a hint of a smile play across his thin lips. A weird, strong scent came off him—an odor I couldn't pinpoint—sweet but sour at the same time. I felt threatened then, and my legs twitched, aching to run, as my instincts told me to get away as soon as I could.

"Come on, now," he said through clenched teeth, his gold flecks glittering like flint sparks. "I think it would be best if you come with me." His hold on me tightened, and he began to haul me in the direction of his car.

"Hey, man, let go of me!" I struggled to rip his fingers from my arm, tugging in the opposite direction. "Get the fuck off me!"

Tires screeched to a halt behind us. A black, Cadillac SUV parked right next to the guy's car, and the asshole loosened his grip. I backed away as two people hopped out of the SUV—one from the passenger side and one from the driver's—and they hurried toward me. I squinted into the headlights, trying to see who it was, and the shape of their silhouettes brought me relief.

And then the blond bastard spun around, his fist connecting with my face with sickening crunch.

I stumbled backward, covering my left eye, which instantly flooded with heat, my ears ringing excruciatingly loud. I heard muffled commotion and steadied myself, squinting to see the mayhem in front of me. All I could see was a blur of colors moving around as my vision tried to come back into focus. I'd never been punched before, but, thankfully, it didn't hurt as badly as I would have expected. Maybe my adrenaline had kicked in—

"Caleb!" Darla shouted.

My eyes focused on her form sprinting over to me. She violently shoved the blond guy out of the way and into Leander and threw her arms around my neck. I wrapped my own around her waist and buried my face into her shoulder, letting out a long breath and a few quiet curse words, my thoughts racing to understand what was happening. My eye throbbed against her shoulder, but I didn't care. My heart was hammering hard; I was certain she could feel my frantic pulse tapping the side of her neck. I had never felt so relieved to see anyone.

The sound of a gun cocking made my head snap up.

To my sheer disbelief, Leander stood in front of the creep, holding a silver pistol to the man's head. His mouth was twisted in a snarl, but he appeared entirely calm, and the blond guy was holding his hands up defensively. I wasn't sure whether to be reassured by this or to be terrified of Lea.

"Is there a reason you were forcing this man to get into your car?" Leander asked him steadily, glaring into the gold-flecked eyes of the stranger. "Kidnapping is a felony, you know."

"I wasn't kidnapping him. I was helping out someone in need of assistance." The jerk moved to look at me, but Lea grabbed the guy's jaw and forced him to look back at him.

"Whoa, hey, relax!" the man said.

"He doesn't need your help," Lea growled, forcing the guy to lean away from the gun. "Leave him be, and while you're at it, leave town."

"Or what?"

"Or your recruitment days are over, you disgrace of a living creature."

Recruitment days?

Darla nudged my side reassuringly. *We'd never let his kind take you.*

The blond lowered his hands and squared his shoulders. "We both know it's not that simple, youngling," he sneered.

"Go," Leander said through gritted teeth, his expression infuriated as he tapped the man's forehead with the barrel of the gun. "Don't think I won't—"

"No need to threaten violence. I'm gone." The blond sidestepped Leander and hastened to his car.

He opened the driver's side door and looked me dead in the eyes, his gold-flecked orbs sparkling out from his shadow.

"Good luck with your survival." He chortled malevolently before sliding into his car, backing onto the road.

"Damn it." Leander watched the guy drive away until we could no longer see his taillights. He switched the safety on and slid the gun into the back of his jeans, pulling his shirt down over it. He gestured to me with open arms, his eyes filled with concern. "Are you okay? Did he do anything to you?"

I tapped my left eye, flinching from a quick, sharp, bruising pain. "Other than punching my lights out, no."

Darla grabbed me by the hand and pulled me over to the car. "I'm so glad we found you in time."

She thrust open the back door for me, and I slid onto the comfort of the black leather seats.

"We'll take you home." She slammed the door shut.

Leander moved into the driver's seat, and Darla hopped in the passenger side. Lea turned to look at me, his face questioning whether I was really okay. I gave him a weak thumbs-up, and he began to drive, pulling onto the quiet, dark road.

"Was that...?" I began, knowing the answer before I asked the question. "Was that one of those...things? A mørkeste?"

Darla nodded forcefully. "He was trying to recruit you—mørkeste tug on the heartstrings of velsignet, pretending that they care, that they can help them. They feed on the weak ones, normally, try to get them to willingly join their side first." She spun around in her seat. "He must've thought you were a hitchhiker or something."

"How did you guys know where to find me?" I sat forward, grabbing hold of the seats in front of me. "Did you hear me calling you, D?"

"Actually, no." Darla cracked her knuckles, looking at her hands. "I wanted to go after you. I didn't want my first real talk with my brother to end as an argument."

My ears grew hot, flushed with awkwardness, but I shook it off. "But how did you know I was in trouble?"

She pursed her lips. "I don't know."

I narrowed my eyes. She was lying. I gave her a look, and she rolled her eyes. "I'm so used to feeling your presence in my head—since the day we met it's like you're always there." She started pushing her cuticles back, fidgeting in her seat. "I knew you were in trouble because one minute I could feel you there and the next minute you were gone."

"Gone?"

"From my head. It was empty and quiet, and it felt how it did before I met you." She paused. "Like the holes were back."

I understood what she meant. Since we'd connected telepathically earlier that week, I'd felt as though she'd become a constant presence in my mind. I no longer felt as if something was missing, never felt too alone in my head. She wasn't there—not fully there all the time—but she wasn't out of reach, either. She was just one call away.

I started smiling at the thought of it, and her mouth cracked into a tiny grin as well.

"So what happened to you then?" Lea looked at me in the rearview mirror. "Why couldn't Darla sense you?"

I sat back in my seat, grimacing. "I was actually going to walk back to your house. But then I had a vision. A really awful one. Before I blacked out, I thought I called to Darla telepathically, but I guess not."

Darla shook her head. "I didn't hear anything. You were there, and then you were gone."

"I woke up, and that guy was standing over me asking if I wanted help, insisting I go with him to the hospital." I scrunched up my face. "I knew there was something off about him. I was getting a weird vibe. And he smelled different."

"Velsignet have adapted over the centuries," Leander said. "We were a bit of a weaker species long ago, but we've adjusted so we now have a natural instinct. We're mindful of dangers, threats, and energy through our usual senses, and it helps us protect ourselves. In your case, you could smell something off about that prick." He sighed. "All mørkeste are helliget, but not all helliget are mørkeste. We've been forced to learn to find differences between the two in order to survive."

I ran my hands through my hair. "That makes sense, but then, how come there are velsignet who willingly join the mørkeste? Can't they tell they're in trouble?"

Lea and Darla glanced at each other before he continued.

"Some are weak minded. They can't tell the difference. Sometimes, it's because they have yet to even understand anything about our kind and the helliget. They're alone and have no one to guide them. But there are others who do sense the danger and, like anyone else is capable of in this world, they just choose the wrong side."

I gazed out the window at the shadowy trees rushing by. "That's disappointing."

Leander grunted. "That's life."

The rest of the ride was pretty quiet, other than me giving Lea directions to my house. We passed Divinity University, which looked eerily quiet and dark for a Friday night. Usually, the campus and town were popping from Thursday through Sunday. But tonight, the roads were mostly clear for some reason. I suppose it was a good night for a mørkeste to hunt for velsignet.

Once we pulled into the driveway, Nikki's shadow crossed the side window as she peered through the curtains. Suddenly, I was very aware of the fact I'd be walking into the house with a shiner on my eye. I leaned over and peeked in the rearview mirror. My top lid was red and swollen, and I had a tiny cut and some dried blood under my puffy bottom lid. My eye was oozing clear liquid, and I inhaled through my teeth at the sight of it.

Darla winced at my expression. "Just tell her you fell down the stairs."

I snorted. "That's believable." I turned to her. "She always knows when I'm lying."

"Well, you aren't going to tell her you were roaming the streets in the dark of night and nearly got kidnapped by some creep, are you?"

"Ugh." I sat back. "Maybe I will tell her I fell down the stairs then."

Leander murmured in agreement then looked at me in the mirror again. "But when Nicole finds out you got hurt while in *my* house, I may pay for it with my life."

"Wait." Darla put her hands up dramatically, palms facing Lea. "Nicole? As in, your old college hook-up you told me about? The one I never had a chance to meet before she dumped you? *That* Nicole?" She unbuckled and leaned over the seat to look at me. "She's your godmother?"

I gulped. "Yes."

Darla looked between Lea and me incredulously before sitting back down in her seat. "Shit just keeps getting weirder and weirder."

I opened the car door and slid out. Darla rolled her window down as I shut the door and swung my backpack onto my shoulder.

"Thanks for saving me from that freak," I said.

D grinned. "Don't thank us until after Nicole spares you."

I waved goodbye, watching them pull out of the driveway before I went into the house to face my godmother.

I slept until midday on Saturday. I was mentally and physically exhausted from the events of the day before. Nikki had also kept me up until two in the morning, checking my pupils and making sure I didn't have a concussion from my "fall" at Darla's house. I was lucky she believed me, but I wasn't comfortable keeping secrets from her.

When I rose from my slumber, I rolled over and snatched my phone off the nightstand. Opening my texts, I saw I'd sent an incoherent message to Gav at 2:30 a.m. in my deliriousness once Nik had gone off to bed.

I'm home safe, I will callmdbfeuwinwufb

WTF, he had responded. And then around nine-thirty this morning, he'd said, I think I know what you were trying to say, but just in case you forget to call, I'll be at your house at noon.

I put my phone back on the table, stretched, and went to rub my eyes, forgetting I had gotten rocked in the face. I groaned, turning onto my stomach, leaning on my eye as it throbbed in pain. I still couldn't believe everything that had happened yesterday and last night. But it was all so easy to believe when it made sense of everything that hadn't made sense throughout my entire life. I wondered how Gav would take all the news when I told him.

Soon, there was a rap at my door. It opened a crack, and Gav peeked his head inside. "Morning, sunshine! I brought you up some frozen peas."

I popped my good eye open, peering at my grinning best friend.

"Much appreciated," I mumbled.

He shut my bedroom door, grabbing my desk chair and spinning it around to face me. I sat up as he tossed me the bag of peas but not before he whistled at the sight of my black eye.

"Nik told me you fell, and she gave me the peas to ice your eye, but I didn't know how bad it really was."

"I didn't actually fall."

"I figured that." Gav waved his hand, and his eyes gave me a once-over. "Nice bedhead, by the way. So, what really happened last night?"

I rubbed the back of my hair to smooth it down. "I'm going to tell you everything from the beginning, but you have to keep up, you've got to stay with me, okay?"

Gavin's eyebrows raised, and he rubbed his palms together. "Yeah, of course. Can't say I'm not nervous now, though."

I breathed deeply and went into full detail of how Friday had progressed—from the car ride to Darla's, to lunch with Leander, to our talk in the study, and Lea's revelation about who D was to me. The entire time I talked, I kept breaking eye contact with Gav and fiddling with my fingers, being cautious of how to word things and making sure I was saying everything correctly. But none of it seemed to surprise him. Until I got to the part about Darla and me being twins. He straightened up abruptly, his mouth open in bewilderment. He started to chew on the tip of his finger, and when I finished the entire story, it was the first thing he brought up.

"You and Darla are twins?" He moved his chair closer to my bed. "As in, you're her brother and she's your sister? Darla is your sister?"

It still sounded so foreign in my head when he said it. "Yep. Separated at birth. Reunited by chance."

"And I want to date your sister." Gavin shook his head slowly. "It sounds so weird. I want to date my best friend's sister. This is like a bad soap opera."

I face-palmed. How typical that this was what he focused on. "Yeah, I guess so."

Should this be weirder now that Darla was my sister? If she was some random chick, this all would've sounded completely normal. Gavin always liked chasing after girls, and it was all fine and dandy. But now the idea of him dating my sister was floating in my head, and my already prominent sense of protectiveness over her was growing. It all seemed different now.

"Caleb has a sister," he droned on. "I want to hook up with Darla, Caleb's sister—"

"Stop that!" I snapped at him.

"Sorry, sorry!" Gav put his hands up defensively. "I just can't get past it."

I grunted and let myself fall back onto my bed. "Yeah, now you've put the thought in my mind, and if you do end up dating her, I'm going to have to pretend I don't know what you guys do behind closed doors."

Gavin laughed, reached over, and tugged my arm, so I'd sit back up. He snatched the less-frozen bag of peas and put it into my hand. "I can't believe some moron-kente—"

"Mørkeste—

"Whatever. Some asshole tried to get you into his car!" Gav lifted my hand with the peas to my eye and patted it. "Doesn't he know you're a grown-ass man who has had years of experience regarding stranger-danger awareness?"

I lifted my shoulders. "He seemed to be convinced I could be easily swayed."

"How, though? Like, what in the world made him think you'd believe him?"

"He was acting like any normal human person does, Gavin." The pea bag was only melting on my eye, so I tossed it onto my nightstand. "He pulled over when he saw someone passed out on the side of the road and offered to help. Anyone could've been fooled, especially someone who doesn't have knowledge of helliget-mørkeste beings."

Gavin crossed his arms over his chest, swallowing hard. "Do you think it's possible that—?" He paused and closed his eyes. "No, never mind."

"Say it."

"Do you think it's possible we actually run into their kind all the time? Like, on a regular basis?"

The idea hadn't crossed my mind. Anyone on the street could be one of them, I supposed. A professor, a fellow classmate, my dentist—who knew how many were out there? When we'd left Darla's Thursday night, I had told myself I needed to be careful regarding who I trusted. But that had been before I knew about unearthly beings that could fool me into thinking they were normal, mortal people.

It was a spine-chilling thought.

Another tap came at my door. Gav and I both twitched in alarm, but then it opened and revealed only my innocent, little aunt checking in.

"I'm off to work," she said, her head peeking through the door. "You boys should go outside today. It's beautiful out."

Gavin and I muttered that we would, and she leaned further into the room.

"And Gav, keep an eye on Caleb for me. He's so clumsy!"

"Oh, I know. You've got it, Nikki!"

Gavin's emerald eyes gleamed as he glanced in my direction, and I narrowed my gaze at him. Nikki blew us each kisses goodbye before shutting the door.

"Get dressed, and we can go hiking. We won't take pictures since you're ugly as sin today." Gav rose out of his seat. He tapped his chin. "I wonder what your hot sister is up to."

I grabbed my pillow from behind me and whipped it at his face.

A bead of sweat rolled over my eye. It was a comfortably cool day, the last day of the third week of October, and perfect hiking weather. We had been walking uphill for over an hour, trying to get to one of our favorite viewpoints in the mountains. My hardworking heart was pulsating distinctly in my black eye.

I was also carrying a one hundred-and-something pound little lady on my back.

Ava flicked her finished cigarette past my ear and onto the ground. "Are you getting tired already, Cay?"

I turned my head, peering at her out of the corner of my bad eye. "It's not like I'm piggybacking both you and your backpack or anything."

Darla, who'd been treading backward the whole way up thus far, slowed and skidded back down toward us. She took a swig from her water bottle. "Hey, it's not her fault she rolled her ankle four and a half seconds into the hike." She gestured for me to open my mouth, which I did with gratitude as she poured water into it.

"That's not fair!" Ava slid down off my back and tucked her mousy brown locks behind her ears. She stretched her ankle, rotating it around in circles. "I just get excited when I'm outside, okay? I'm always cooped up."

Gavin appeared beside us, a bit of sweat matting his auburn hair to his forehead. "You coop yourself up, Ava. You know you can come hang out with us whenever you want."

She made a *psh* sound. "I know that. I just get lazy. I prefer lazy days."

Lazy days, as in getting high with her dealer. I lifted my snapback hat from my head, wiped the sweat off with the back of my forearm, and placed the cap on backward before walking again.

Is that really what she means by 'lazy' days? Darla's question echoed in my mind.

Unfortunately, yeah.

Oh.

"How much longer anyway?" Ava trudged behind me. "It's becoming kind of dusky. Aren't there bears?"

"Should be another ten or fifteen minutes of walking," Gav replied. "It won't be long. Just enjoy the nice, clean air, Ava."

"I get it, I get it. I'm going to stop smoking as a New Year's resolution, by the way," she said cheerily. But she had been saying the same thing for seven years now. Being friends with Ava was always an uphill slope. No pun intended.

As the sky began to turn an orangey-pink, we came to a fork in the trail and veered left to get to the cliff Gav and I frequently hiked to. We pushed through the freshly grown brush and followed the path until we arrived at the familiar clearing. The trees faded behind us as we came out onto a wide, flat ledge that overlooked much of the east side of Divinity.

"Wow," Darla breathed, squinting out from the trees. "It's so beautiful from up here!"

Gavin stepped past me and went over to the edge. "Cay and I used to come up here a lot when we were in high school. 'Hike therapy,' we called it." He plopped down and dangled his legs over the side. I came up behind him and did the same.

"Still puts the mind at ease, doesn't it?" I inhaled and exhaled slowly, allowing the fresh, woodsy air to cleanse my lungs.

The girls came over and Darla sat between Gav and I, while Ava stood over our heads, looking out at the sunset view.

Darla looked over the ledge at the impressive fall below.

"Hmm." Darla leaned back on her palms.

What are you thinking? I asked her.

"You ever been to places like this and thought about jumping?" she said aloud. "Not for any particular reason, of course." She explained herself quickly as Gavin's head whipped in her direction. "That's not at all what I'm saying."

"What do you mean, D?" Ava sat next to me and stared skeptically past me at Darla.

"Going to a place so beautiful and high up. And wishing you could jump and survive."

Her eyes looked clear as spring water in the reflection of the sky, and I wondered if mine did too.

"Like, have you thought about jumping, not because you're trying to hurt yourself, obviously, but because you want to, I don't know, feel the rush of the wind?" Darla said. "Or that adrenaline jolt in your chest and stomach you get from the height on top of a rollercoaster?" She looked between Gav and me. "You know, to see the world from a different perspective."

I peered over the edge of the landing. I knew what she was trying to say; seeing how high up we were and seeing how far the horizon was ahead of us did give me a rush of adrenaline. I'd never thought about the jumping aspect of it, how it would feel to fly away, over the trees that had just begun to acquire their autumn colors. Of course, if I could jump and not die, I'd probably do it. Darla, having read my open thoughts, smiled at me.

"Yeah, that's an interesting thought," Gavin responded when no one else had. "I'm not going to be the first to try it, though, so if you want to test it out, by all means."

Darla nudged his shoulder, and they laughed.

My eyesight whirled a bit then, and at first, I thought my bad eye was just bothering me. But a few seconds later, I knew better and sealed my mind in time to see a foggy, dream-like image of Gavin and D. He was holding her hand, his thumb grazing over her knuckles gently, a tender gesture. The sight of them didn't freak me out in any way—it was actually kind of sweet. But as vision-Darla turned her head in my direction, I saw she was crying.

My sight swirled again, transforming into the sunset I had been watching only seconds before. I looked at Darla, who was staring off at the skyline, her body tense next to me, and I could feel her pushing against my mind, harder than usual. She had to know I was preventing her from seeing my visions, blocking her out on purpose. I opened my mind to let her speak.

I've noticed your eyes do this strange thing when you have visions.

I usually close my eyes on impulse, but these new ones come on so quickly. I shook my head a bit. *Do I look crazed?*

Nah, your pupils get super-huge though. They almost cover all the blue.

I didn't respond. I leaned back on my forearms, closing my eyes. I wanted to temporarily forget about all the insane things that'd happened this past week. Just for a moment.

A crow cawed overhead, and my eyes snapped open. The bird's black, smooth, flattened feathers stood out among the green and brown branches above us. It squawked loudly, and I quickly shut my eyes again, willing it to fly away. I always avoided looking at crows; as soon as I heard or saw one, I would look away as quickly as I could. When my mother passed away, there had been crows everywhere at the funeral. In the trees, on the ground, pecking at other graves, screeching their ugly bird calls. To me, crows represented death. I liked ravens though.

Can you tell me about her later? Darla interrupted my musing.

Who?

Our mother. Can you tell me what she was like?

I didn't open my eyes. It would truly be a difficult subject for me to talk about. But Darla had never known my mother. Our mother. I had no choice.

In a way, this had to be even harder for her.

CHAPTER 9

TIME WAS A FUNNY CONCEPT.

Minutes and hours and days passed by like nothing. Sometimes, I wondered if it was because we humans always thought about what came next or what we were doing the next day or even next year. Some people had plans, and some people looked forward to things. But time always seemed to move so quickly; one day we were babies who had no worries, and the next we were grown adults trying to find our place in the world. For whatever reason, time always seemed to choose when it wanted to slow down and speed up.

The following week was all a blur. Though the school days seemed long, Thursday came and went quicker than I could process. During my classes over the week, my visions were consistent, and I was in my head a lot—as was Darla, trying to make conversation constantly. We'd touched upon my visions of her at one point and decided the best thing we could do was remain vigilant until I could get a clearer idea of what was to come. For the time being, Gav and I hung around her every day at school, and she'd go straight home, where she would be safe with her family.

My mind often ventured away from course work and traveled into the insane world I'd awoken to, a world I now belonged to. I'd sit at the lab table in Planet Earth while Sampson droned on, and suddenly, I would be daydreaming, imagining people I knew who could actually secretly or unconsciously be velsignet. In the student cafeteria, I would look around and wonder if anyone was mørkeste or helliget. Or, sometimes, I would try to think of what "forced evolution" could possibly entail. It seemed clear-cut, but as I had learned several times in my life, not everything is what it seems.

Gavin, Darla, Ava, and I spent the afternoon in the commuter lounge in the basement of the student center—also known as the Falcon's Nest lounge— in order to catch up on homework before Friday's party. Gavin and Darla had taken over the couch; Darla was reading a novel, leaning on his arm, while Gav read his astronomy textbook, prepping for an exam. Ava was sprawled out on the floor, searching online for where to purchase an inexpensive, vintage, Volkswagen van for whatever reason.

I was sitting on the floor, my back against the arm of a corduroy lounge chair, exploring the internet for an environmental crime article for next Monday's class while also looking up Norwegian helliget history. To my disappointment, I was coming up short on helliget news, but I had an endless list of environmental crime stories to choose from. I leaned my cheek on my bent knees, scrolling over pages of nature injustice I just couldn't sit through fully reading. I allowed my laptop monitor to enter sleep mode, and my reflection was all that remained. My black eye had healed up nicely over the past few days, the bruise yellowing with a hint of blue on my cheekbone and the cut almost fading to a pale pink. In the reflection on my screen, I could also see the blonde, Poe-reading girl sitting in a lounge chair behind me in the far corner of the room.

I peered around the chair I was propped up against, trying to sneak a peek at her. If she caught me this time, I'd probably have to go apologize for being a creep, but I planned to worry about that if the moment came.

She was flopped onto the seat horizontally, her noticeably long legs bent over the chair's arm. She was wearing a white cotton sweater, dark jeans, and had an enormous textbook propped on her lap. She tapped her sneakered foot to the beat of whatever music was playing through the earbuds in her ears. Her spiral hair spilled around her shoulders, as it had every time I'd seen her, Her Caribbean eyes squinted at the pages in front of her. Every once in a while, her lips would pucker as if she was in deep concentration or the tip of her tongue would poke out of the corner of her mouth when she wrote down notes. My heart ached in a way I'd never felt before, a yearning for something I didn't recognize. Just as I attempted to decipher what I was feeling, I felt that tugging in the back of my mind I knew all too well, and I was gently pulled into a vision.

I immediately recognized the scene around me and realized this wasn't a vision of the future, but a memory from my past. I was small, young, about seven years old, holding Nikki's hand while we waited in line at a smoothie bar. We had taken a trip to Newport, Rhode Island, a place Nik would often take me during the summers of my childhood. The place had no significance to me at that age—it wouldn't until later when it became a regular vacation spot—but it meant something to Aunt Nikki, which made the trips all the more special. Seeing it briefly made me miss the way things were before I had turned sixteen and everything changed. It was an unusual feeling, reliving a memory as vivid as my typical visions.

In this memory, we were next in line, and Nikki asked me which drink we should share. A little girl and her mother were ahead of us, the girl standing on her tippy-toes to reach the mango smoothie her mother ordered. The woman pushed it into her daughter's tiny hands, and the girl flattened her feet, her golden curls bouncing. A sense of recognition hummed through my present-self, and when she turned around, I slowly realized the little girl was Poe-reading girl. She smiled at me, dimples on her baby-face cheeks, smoothie straw between her lips, and my younger, vision-self looked down at his feet shyly, something I still did to this day.

The first thought that came to my mind was that my brain was playing tricks on me, distorting my memories, trying to make sense of the weird ache in my chest whenever I looked at her for too long. But then my sight faded into a new recall, this time taking me back to a week when Nikki took me snowboarding in Girdwood, Alaska. This vacation I remembered so clearly; it was late December, and I was fourteen years old, playing in the snow in a state I had always wanted to travel to. Nikki had originally questioned my choice of vacation location, not knowing too much about The Last Frontier, but once we had arrived, she'd known it would be the best trip ever.

I was sliding down the mountain on my rented board, my knees cramping and legs a bit wobbly from hours of play. I was slowing myself near the bottom, just as someone skied into my path up ahead. I tried to skid out of the way, but I wasn't fast enough and ended up bumping into the person hard, a solid crash that left me bruised. Before the memory continued, my present-self was remembering that it was *her* again, she was the person I had crashed into. It couldn't be possible, but it was. It was possible because I totally remembered crashing into her, helping her up, and asking if she was okay before I headed to meet Nik for a big mug of steaming, freshly brewed coffee. What baffled me most now was that I had seen her in places where you typically wouldn't run into someone you know, and only now was I realizing and wondering how many other times in my life had I actually bumped into her.

Whether or not there was any such thing as fate—and lately, it seemed more likely it was real—I still didn't believe in coincidences.

I came out of this unusual vision, or flashback, or whatever it was, and found myself staring into the black, sleep-mode monitor at my own image. I glanced up at my friends, who didn't seem to have noticed my wild, trippy voyage. Ava was still on page one of her search results, and Gavin still had his eyes on his textbook. I couldn't have blacked out for more than a minute. I looked at my sister then, who was still staring at her book, but her eyes paused, and she was no longer reading it.

Her gaze flickered to me. *The Edgar Allan Poe girl? You know her?*

I shook my head ever so slightly. *Not…formally.*

D's eyes returned to her novel. *I saw all of it. I'm craving a smoothie now.*

I looked back at my monitor, trying not to smile.

Why don't you go talk to her? D wasn't letting the issue drop.

My head snapped up, and I stared at her aghast. *And say what, exactly? That I've seen her before in an assortment of exotic, faraway places?*

Maybe act like a normal college boy, and tell her she's pretty and then get her number.

I grunted, glancing at Poe-reading girl in the reflection of my laptop. Darla was right, as usual, typically making me feel like I was a nimrod, completely inept at being a normal person. Before shutting my laptop, I looked over to see that she was grinning down at her book. I rose to my feet, placed my PC on the chair, and took a deep, shaky breath. My hands started to sweat—I was getting embarrassed already, and I hadn't even met the blonde bombshell yet. I shoved my hands into the pockets of my sweatpants and headed over.

Poe-reading girl was still chilling out on the chair, scribbling in a notebook with the textbook propped open on her lap and listening to music. As I approached her, I started feeling a smidgen of confidence cooling down my body; Darla was in the back of my mind, sending me vibes of encouragement. I sat down on the coffee table across from the blonde and cleared my throat.

"Hi," I said bravely.

She glanced up at me and gave me a once-over.

"Hey there." She smiled captivatingly, popping an earbud out. Her voice was soft, smooth like velvet and sweet like honey.

I swallowed hard. "I saw you reading—" My voice caught. Oh shit, what was she reading? "Something."

Smooth.

She lifted an eyebrow and turned in her seat, revealing the cover of her textbook. It was a guide to creative writing etiquette according to Divinity University's standards. Something she wouldn't be reading for pleasure, but for homework; not exactly a good conversation starter.

"It's not usually what I'd pick to read," she responded politely. "You're used to seeing Edgar Allan Poe's book in my hands."

I almost choked on my own spit. "I-I'm not—"

She giggled and closed her textbook, along with her notebook, setting them down on the table beside me. "I've seen you in the quad before. You think I'd forget eyes like yours?" She reached out a hand. "My name is Shay. Shay Bishop."

I was sure my face was scarlet with discomfort. As I took her hand, I thanked the universe that she was being nice, despite her apparently catching me checking her out. *Play it cool, Caleb.* "I'm Caleb Swift." The blood flushed to my ears. "I'm sorry for staring. I promise I'm not weird."

Don't lie to her already, Cay, D teased me unmercifully.

Shay grinned. "It's nice to meet you, Caleb."

Her eyes met mine, but I didn't look away as I usually would. I couldn't look away. I kept feeling that pulling in my heart, and there was something about the way she said my name. It was a different kind of sensation, where the sound of it rolled off her lips differently than when others had said it. Knowing her name and her knowing mine created a real, established connection.

Maybe if I stopped overthinking everything and put an end to my idiotic gazing, I could take that connection to another level.

I cleared my throat again, removing my hand from hers. "What music were you listening to?" I was genuinely curious while trying to gain back that bit of confidence.

"Oh!" Her eyes lit up, and she untangled the unoccupied earbud. "Well, I was listening to some grungy stuff, a little alternative rock. But it shuffled, and now I'm listening to 'The Sound of Silence' remake by Disturbed." She handed me the earbud. "It's one of my favorites."

I had listened to plenty of Simon and Garfunkel before, but I'd never pictured a rock band like Disturbed making a cover of that folksy song. "Disturbed, huh?"

I popped the earbud into my ear, and she nodded.

"It's really actually very beautiful, I swear." She hit play on her phone and grabbed her notebook off the table to scribble more while I listened.

The tune of this version was much different than the one I was used to hearing. She was right; it was beautiful, but I found it kind of haunting as well. Not in a bad way, but in a way that made me feel, well, just generally feel. In this version, I visualized every lyric, every word in my mind, and I was subconsciously trying to understand its meaning. I had done this with other songs I'd heard before—I'd always been involved with music and used it when I couldn't put my own feelings into words. I loved all kinds, all genres, and I could pick up any instrument and play. I'd played guitar and piano a lot in high school, but there wasn't much time for it in college.

"I could probably figure out how to play this on guitar or something," I said quietly, allowing my mouth to run, not realizing what I even said until I heard myself say it.

Shay looked up from her notes, her eyes gleaming. "You play?"

I nodded, and her cheeks turned pink. Her gaze returned to her notebook.

"I can sing, but I was never good with instruments. If you can learn this song, I'd love to hear it."

Her face turned a darker shade of red, and I started to believe she may be just as shy as I was. This made me feel better, less nervous, my confidence returning.

The song ended, and I handed her the earbud, flashing my best smile. "Sure, when I learn it, I'll play it for you. Or maybe I can teach you how to play it yourself?" I felt as if some optimistic, assured soul had graciously chosen my body to possess and now controlled every word that came out of my mouth. I could only hope Shay would take me up on the offer.

She looked up at me through long eyelashes and smiled so charmingly, and that gentle pull on my heart increased to where it felt as though it would soon be yanked from my chest.

"Yeah," she said. "I'd like that."

"Cool." I bit my bottom lip, bouncing my leg, not knowing how to end this conversation.

The party! Darla hissed in my thoughts, and I almost sighed with relief, mentally thanking her. *Perfect.*

"So, there's this huge party tomorrow night—"

"The one at Sigma House? Are you going?" She leaned on her notebook, moving closer to me, and I thought I saw a glimmer of hopefulness in her eyes.

I couldn't help but grin goofily. "Yeah, my sister and my friends"—I jabbed a thumb over my shoulder at my posse behind me—"and I are all going. Will I be seeing you there?"

She nodded, brushing a blonde wave out of her eye. "I know some of the sisters. I'll be there. Maybe I'll see you?"

"Okay, sounds good." I rose to my feet, ready to return to my friends, satisfied with how this had gone.

Her number, Caleb! D reminded me.

I spun back around. "Your number!" I practically exclaimed.

Shit. I had been so close to keeping my cool.

But the gods must've been on my side that day because she willingly lifted her cell to me without hesitation. "Make sure you save it with your first and last name, so I know it's you."

Her face was flushed, and I attempted to conceal my pleasant surprise as I took her phone.

Still grinning, I typed in my info and handed it back to her. "See you tomorrow."

She gave me a little wave as I left, and then she returned to her original sitting position, legs hung over the arm of the chair, earbuds back in place.

I returned to my group with a bounce in my step, and all three of them were looking at me funny. I picked up my PC off the chair and plopped down onto the seat. Gavin leaned on his thighs, his astronomy book shut, and gaped at me.

"Who's the babe?" He eyed Shay, his gaze shifting from me to her and back again. "Do you have a date?"

"Yes. No. Sort of." I turned on my screen nonchalantly and returned to my article-searching. "She's going to Sigma's party tomorrow, and I said I'd see her there. No big deal." Then why was my stomach flipping at the thought of it?

Gavin slapped my knee enthusiastically, his eyes wide. "You hookin' up tomorrow night?"

Darla responded to his comment with a heavy tap to the back of his head and a glare.

I laughed. "Maybe. I don't really know her."

Ava, who was filing her nails at the moment, rolled her eyes. "You don't need to know anyone to have sex with them, Cay. I know you're kind of an old soul, but this is the twenty-first century."

My smile faltered. I knew that. But I wasn't someone who typically hooked up with girls on a regular basis. When someone was interested, they'd flirt, I'd flirt back, we'd talk or kiss or whatever, and then it'd be over. Random hook-ups weren't all that thrilling to me. Part of it was that I didn't want to be "that guy" or be an asshole, and I didn't want to be screwed over by those girls, either. Seeing Gav get rejected—or him having to reject a girl—turned me off to it too. Any time Gavin got an "I'll call you later," he ended up feeling like shit about himself afterward, and most of the girls he went for weren't even good for him anyway.

Not to mention, every time I met someone new, I felt disconnected from them. Girls would capture my attention, but nothing ever stuck—no feelings, no desire to chase after a certain one. I would always just see them, check them out, and then the next girl would walk by and catch my eye. I had sort of put this idea into my head that I'd find a girl I really wanted to be with, and that I'd know I'd want her when I saw her. It was a dumb thought—or at least, Ava told me it was when I'd talked to her about it. She said relationships never happened that way, that you couldn't "shop" for love. And I knew she was probably right. But that lack of any real connection had prevented me from taking any relationships further or pursuing girls who pursued me. I was patient, and I was okay with being alone. I didn't want to waste my time, or some poor girl's time, if I wasn't going to be fully invested. That wouldn't be fair to anyone.

I looked over at Darla. She had been listening to my thoughts—her head was tilted, her face caught between a look of scrutiny and admiration. She crossed her arms and frowned down at Ava disapprovingly.

"Maybe he just wants a relationship that actually means something," Darla said defensively.

Ava shrugged, tossing her brown hair over her shoulder, turning back to her Volkswagen van search. "I just don't see the point in waiting for something that may or may not ever happen. He should just go for it and see where it goes." She scrolled aimlessly. "And if he doesn't land a date after they hook up, at least he had a little fun in the meantime."

Gavin leaned back awkwardly, eyeballing me. "Not all of us want to nookie and move on, Ava."

"I think Caleb just has a little more respect for people than that, that's all." Darla leaned back next to Gavin and nodded in my direction. "But whatever Caleb does—whether he's hooking up tomorrow night or not—it's none of our business, and we should be judgement free."

Ava shrugged again. "I'm just saying—"

"Can we please stop talking about my sex life?" I cut in, thankful for Darla's support but very much finished with the whole conversation.

Everyone muttered in mutual agreement. Gav waited barely two seconds before he began grilling me on what I'd said to Shay, and Darla went back to reading her book.

After a while, she entered my mind. *You do realize Ava is just jealous, right?*

Of me talking to Shay?

No, no. I mean, she's not overly excited about that, obviously. She used to like you a lot. Darla chewed on the inside of her cheek while she turned the page of her book. *But she's jealous that you're able to hope for love and go with the flow and all that, while she searches fervently for it by sleeping with random guys.*

I frowned, guilt seeping into my gut, and I rubbed the back of my neck. *Were you reading her mind?*

Yeah. She turned another page. She was probably just skimming at this point. *But I don't have to be telepathic to notice what she's feeling.*

I swallowed a lump in my throat. Ava was a good friend to me, one of my best friends. But she was troubled, and nothing was ever easy for her. At one point in time, I thought I could maybe help ease some of her pain. But since then, I'd started to believe that maybe she was a lost cause and all I could really do was be there for her. She always got excited about partying—she was always the belle of the ball—so at least tomorrow night we'd all get to see her shine.

I forced myself to stop feeling remorse for others and start thinking about Shay. And I started thinking about myself for once.

Thank God it was Friday.

The four of us met up at my house that evening, planning to eat dinner and pregame before the party. Nikki had whipped up a hearty, Italian pasta meal for all of us just as Gav arrived in his beat-up truck with the girls. I was aching to talk to her about who Darla really was, but tonight just wasn't the night for it. It was time for a break; I needed to have an average, wild, college party night without worrying about family trees and supernatural shit. I'd tell Nikki soon enough.

After stuffing ourselves with carbs, we all hung out in the living room to drink while D called Tucker, bribing him into agreeing to be our designated driver for the evening. She was already tipsy, slurring into the phone that she'd wash the dishes all week, and she'd let him have the BMW for the night to do as he pleased. Lucky for us, he agreed, and by eleven he was outside the house, ready for transport. On our way to the sorority house, I sat in the front with Tucker, and the girls were giggling in the back seat with Gavin, who kept saying Darla's BMW was a "beaut." He used the word over and over until Tucker threatened to turn the car around and take us home.

By the time we got to the enormous house, people were filing inside and covering the front lawn, music pounding out of every opening of the manor. College kids were walking in the streets, swarming like ants, and Tucker had to crawl to a stop a couple blocks up from the house in order not to run over anyone. We all slinked out of the car, buzzed and ready, thanking Tucker and letting him know we'd text him when we needed to be picked up.

Darla and Ava linked arms, skipping down the sidewalk through the crowd ahead of us, laughing hysterically about something that had happened in the car—something I'd already forgotten about. Gavin watched them go, a sneaky grin plastered on his face.

"I think I'm gonna go for it with D," he muttered to me as a big dude walked impatiently between us.

"You mean you're gonna go for it with my sister." I raised my eyebrows at my pal. It still felt so weird to me now that Darla wasn't just a friend. And it was especially weird because the guy who was practically my brother was going to try to "get" with my actual sister. But the look of determination set on his face only convinced me it was a fine idea to accept.

"I'm gonna go for it with your sister." His emerald eyes widened, and he laughed nervously as the girls bounded up the steps to the house. "Do I need to be worried about you coming after me?"

I clapped him on the shoulder, and he briefly stumbled on the lawn.

"As long as you don't piss her off," I said, "you have my blessing."

I turned to sneer at him, but he had come to a stop. He was staring above my head at the roof of the house, craning his neck. His eyes were glassy, his lips parted in a look of confusion and alarm.

"You okay, Gav?" I put my hand on his shoulder and squeezed. "Do you feel sick?" Maybe he'd drank too much already.

He shook his head. "Caleb, I think I'm seeing shit."

His eyes fleetingly met mine, then he looked back toward the roof, and I followed his gaze.

Sitting atop of the highest point of the shingled roof was a winged female.

My breath hitched. It was Halloween weekend, but there was no way those wings were part of a costume. Who was she and why was she here? Was she helliget or mørkeste? Why was Gavin able to see her? Was she revealing herself to everyone or just to us? Questions whirred through my slightly drunk mind, making my head spin. She had short, pixie-styled, dark hair, and the whites of her eyes practically glowed against the night behind her. Her wings matched the sky, having a deep purple tint to them. She was staring down at us, unsmiling, and I knew she could see us watching her. Her wings began to recede behind her back and disappear then, and her eyes momentarily glittered gold. Suddenly, I felt as though I knew which side she was on.

"Caleb, did you see that?" Gavin whispered.

I barely heard him above the pounding bass and shouting people.

I stepped in front of Gav, placing both my hands on his shoulders now. "Look at me."

He kept staring upward.

"Hey—look at me, Gavin."

He tore his eyes away from the dark angel and blinked at me.

"Listen to me carefully, all right?"

He nodded.

"She's a bad one. Don't look at her. Don't acknowledge her. Hopefully, she'll just leave us alone. Okay?"

He nodded, his eyes darting everywhere but up. "Pretend she's not there. Pretend I didn't just see one of those things you always see. Got it."

"Come on." I pulled him by the arm, guiding him toward the steps. "Let's just get drunk and have fun."

I led him toward Ava and Darla, who were currently getting frisked for illegal substances by a burly fraternity dude and a small, freshman sorority member guarding the door. This was routine for Greek parties—no one came in unless they came clean and had ID.

Ava, for obvious reasons, was getting frustrated with the poor sorority girl. Ava yanked her purse away from the youth.

"I said I don't have anything, okay? Just take my damn word for it!"

She shoved past the girl into the house, who then blushed with humiliation.

"Sorry about that. She's already drunk." Darla shrugged apologetically. The now-flustered sorority member checked Darla's jeans for narcotics.

Gavin and I were checked by the big fraternity guy, and at long last, we were sucked into the party atmosphere in the colossal house.

As big as it was, the place was packed; girls danced on the dual spiral staircase, plastic cups in the air, while guys shouted and banged the walls to the beat of heavy electronica. My head naturally bobbed to the music, and the three of us were pushed further into the house, surrounded by dancing bodies. Freshman sorority girls and the occasional fraternity recruits held trays of red Jell-O shots high above their heads, and before I knew it, I had a cup in each hand. Gav and I grinned at each other, and my worries were left behind, outside that front door with the people on the lawn.

Some time passed, and I ended up in the dimly lit basement, swaying with intoxication. For the first time in a while, I was feeling pretty relaxed. I had a fairly large cup of something I couldn't even taste in one hand, and I had my other hand shoved in the pocket of my jeans. I was tapping my foot to the music, the DJ playing epic song after epic song. I leaned against the graffiti wall, watching the sea of dancing bodies, observing people like I always do, sober or drunk. Darla and Gavin were against the far wall to my right, talking very close to each other, and his arm was around her waist. It was nice to know Gavin was with someone good for once. I couldn't help but sway and smile as I scanned the smoky room.

A flash of blonde, curly hair on the opposite side of the room caught my attention. My eyes locked onto the girl, and I squinted to see if she was who I hoped she'd be. The girl turned around to speak to someone, and my stomach flipped as I confirmed that it was Shay. Through the crowd, I could see she was wearing tight black jeans and a maroon cropped top, exposing her midriff and a pierced navel that glinted in the colorful party lights. Her hair was in perfect, flowing curls, and she broke into a fit of laughter at something somebody I couldn't see and didn't care to see said. My mouth shaped into a grin, and before I knew it, I put my cup down on a chair and I was walking toward her.

People parted like the Red Sea—or at least that's what my mind convinced itself was happening. I slid through the crowd effortlessly, Shay's tinkling laughter growing closer, and I pressed through the last few people who separated me from her. Her scanning eyes spotted me just as I appeared, and she ran a hand through her golden waves, tousling them to one side and smiling shyly. She was with two girls, both of whom looked taken aback as I held out my hand to her. Shay looked at me with a surprised expression and placed her hand on mine. Whether it was the booze or something in the air, confidence surged through me, and I felt myself truly coming out of my shell for once as I pulled her away from her friends, back into the Red Sea.

The DJ cross-faded into his own remixed version of some Skrillex song. I guided Shay through the crowd toward the center, trying to avoid knocking into the sweaty, wasted partiers. The people around us were typically club dancing and grinding—or, as Gavin fondly referred to it, "sex-with-your-clothes-on" dancing. But the only way I really knew how to dance comfortably—without tripping over myself or looking stupid—was by simply just swaying side to side. I wrapped my right arm around Shay's waist, took her right hand into my left, and pulled her against me. It may have looked awkward to dance this way to dubstep music, but I didn't care because I actually had her in my arms. She was beaming up at me, the lights reflecting in her bright eyes, so I must've been doing something right.

Feeling a tad courageous, I gave her a quick little twirl around, and her eyes crinkled in delight. I grinned, bringing her back in, and I wound my arm a bit tighter around her while she laughed, her cheeks flushed with warmth. I moved my hands to Shay's hips, and she slid both her arms around my neck, her eyes avoiding mine while she looked down at my black t-shirt. Her smile was wide, and I could tell by the way her eyes kept darting to the side that she was probably more nervous than I was. Ironically, her timidity was only making me more comfortable with being so close to her.

Instinctively, I leaned my face down against hers, her hair smelling strongly of lavender and something sweet. She turned her face into my neck, and I could feel her eyelashes as she blinked against my throat.

When had I stopped being the reserved Caleb Swift I knew so well and turned into this alien, uncharacteristically bold version of myself? Where had this bravery and carefree disposition come from? I was outside my comfort zone. Despite the sweaty, drunk students and heavy bass drop—and as cliché as it sounded—I really felt as if we were the only two people there. I turned my head down to her, my lips brushing against her cheek. Her gaze was fixated on my face, and she looked up at me expectantly. My heart was clobbering against my chest. I wanted to kiss her; there was no doubt about that. But she was gazing at me, her deep-blue eyes capturing mine in a trance. I sent a silent "thank you" to the universe for this moment.

I leaned my forehead against hers, and our noses briefly grazed over each other. I could smell some kind of sweet liquor on her lips, and I slid one of my hands up her back. She inhaled softly, biting her bottom lip, those Caribbean blues watching my every move. I pulled her closer.

Caleb!

My head pulled away, and suddenly, I was jerked back to reality—out of this parted-sea dancing fantasy I was in with Shay and back into the sweltering, smoky, loud basement with hundreds of other people. I scanned the crowd, looking for the source of intrusion.

"W-what is it?" Shay stammered, blinking at me.

My attention returned to her.

"I thought I heard my sister yell my name." Suddenly, I was aware of how stupid that sounded and wondered if I'd offended her by ruining the moment.

But she was still smiling up at me sweetly, so I casually twirled her around again.

Caleb, where are you?

Darla's voice sounded panicked.

Basement, near the speakers. What's wrong?

No response. But less than a minute later, a hand gripped my forearm, and I turned to see D and Gavin squeezing between people to get to me. They had perturbed looks on their faces, and immediately, I was overcome with worry.

"Hey, guys," I shouted over the bass.

Shay gave them a small wave.

"What's—?" I started to ask.

"It's Ava," Darla said loudly, her eyes sharp and jaw set. Her expression was more serious than I'd ever seen it. "Something's wrong."

"Her dealer texted me from her phone." Gavin was ruffling his sweaty hair, his skin looking pale. "Come on, he said she's out of it, and we need to go to the third floor now." Gavin grabbed Darla by the arm and he gestured toward the stairs.

I gritted my teeth. This was so typical of Ava to do this to us. Any time we went to a party, she either drank too much or *did* too much or she would end up in some kind of trouble that would force Gav and I to come to her rescue. Knowing we had to look out for her, we never actually got to enjoy ourselves.

"Ava?" Shay asked, glancing between me and my friends. "Ava Westley?"

I tilted my head and looked at her. "You know her?"

Her brow furrowed and her face mirrored Darla's worried expression.

"Yeah, I work at the Alexis, her dad's bar. I rent out the apartment above it." Shay then motioned for Gavin to lead the way. "I'll come with you. If she's in any trouble, I can let her dad know to come get her."

"Let's go already." Gavin groaned heartily, tugging on Darla's arm.

Darla's eyes were unsettlingly distant, but she followed him through the people, Shay and I trailing behind her.

We ascended the stairs back to the main floor, and the party had become more chaotic than when we'd arrived. The music was so loud I thought I'd go deaf, and the amount of people in the building was unreal. All the lights were off other than the ones in the kitchen and the violently flashing strobe light that was causing my pulse to quicken. As we pushed and shoved our way through the crowd to the dual staircase, my chest felt like it was constricting. Not in the way it does before a vision, but in a way that told me I was getting claustrophobic. I couldn't see straight, and I became acutely aware of how drunk I actually was. I bumped into someone and lost sight of the group. Momentarily panicking, I became convinced I'd be trapped in Strobe Light Hell for all eternity.

Then Shay's hand found mine. She squeezed my fingers and pulled me through the crowd into the dimly lit main hall. We paused at the bottom of the stairs, and while I swallowed a couple gulps of air, she studied my face. I nodded to indicate I was fine, and she pulled me up the stairs to catch up with Gavin and D. We took a right turn and hurried down the wing past several bedrooms, until we got to a closed door near the end of the hall. Gavin tried the knob, but the door wouldn't budge. He then shoved his shoulder against the door, and it flung open, slamming into the wall. He and Darla squeezed through the doorway and Shay went in after them.

I knew something was very, very wrong before I even entered the room.

The first thing I saw was Ava's drug dealer, Joe, kneeling on the floor, brown hair in disarray and a phone in his hand. My gaze traveled to the floor, where an orange prescription pill bottle lay empty. But the image I was trying to ignore, to avoid seeing, was my dear friend Ava sitting slumped on the black leather couch, her eyes open and lifeless.

"She wouldn't wake up!" Joe was rocking back and forth, hugging himself, flinching away from Ava like the sight of her might blind him.

"Move it, asshole!" Darla shoved Joe backward and squatted down in the spot he'd previously occupied. She took Ava's wrist and searched for a pulse.

"I'm calling nine-one-one." Shay bent down by Darla and picked up the empty pill bottle. She whipped her phone out of her back pocket while Gavin began to drunkenly pace the room.

"What the fuck happened?" Darla hissed at Joe. She gripped Ava's wrist under her fingertips, and I silently prayed, starting to feel woozy.

"I gave her the usual bottle. I didn't think she'd take the whole lot of it in one night!" He whimpered again, cowering in the corner, his pupils filling his irises. "She just wanted to trip!" He grabbed at the sides of his head. "I can't go to jail!"

Darla turned and whacked him upside the head. "You should have thought of that before becoming a drug dealer!" She turned back to Ava, leaned toward Shay, and whispered, "There's nothing, she…has no pulse."

Shay spoke into her cell, her voice steady. "Hi, my name is Shay Bishop. I'm at a party near campus on Reagan Avenue."

No…no. I couldn't hear the rest. My blood started boiling through my veins and thudding in my ears. I couldn't even think about the fact that, this time, Ava was in trouble that she might not make it out of. I reluctantly looked over at her, her limp hand holding the pill bottle cap. I backed up against the wall behind me, and everyone's voices became muffled, inaudible background noise. Gavin was shaking his fists, yelling something at Joe I couldn't hear, and then Gav grabbed the prick by his shirt collar and thrust him against the wall. Shay jumped to her feet, handing her phone to Darla and rushing at Gav. She wrapped her hands around his arm and dragged him away from the doomed drug addict. Her muffled voice had a soothing tone to it as she attempted to calm Gavin down.

I looked over at Darla while she spoke into Shay's phone to the police. Streaks of mascara tears ran over her cheekbones. The moment we locked eyes, I knew—with every fiber of my being, I knew— that Darla could no longer hear Ava's thoughts. Darla had stopped hearing Ava's thoughts and had known something bad had happened to her friend. There was nothing in Ava's head.

Nothing.

The room suddenly spun violently, and I thought I was going to be sick. "Gavin! Grab Cay!"

Gavin caught me before I hit the floor and supported me, gently pushing me out of the room, away from the horrific sight of my lifeless friend. The hallway was tilting disturbingly, and Gav was gripping on to me with all he had as we headed for a pair of glass doors at the end of the wing. My head was hurting now—I felt as if I couldn't get control over anything—not physically, emotionally, or mentally. All I could do was sag against Gavin as he pushed the doors open, leading me onto one of the balconies and guiding me to the railing.

Gavin was mumbling to himself. "This can't be happening, she can't be gone."

Cool air whipped at my skin, and I clutched the railing, finally steadying myself. My stomach churned, and every time I closed my eyes I could see her on that couch. I covered my face with my hands, rubbing my forehead repeatedly, and my mind began to work diligently on making sense of everything.

"Ava." My voice croaked, my throat dry and body dehydrated. She couldn't be dead. She *couldn't* be dead. "I didn't even have a vision." Why hadn't I seen this coming? If I'd seen it ahead of time, I could've stopped her from doing this to herself. "If we'd just stayed with her—"

"Caleb, please, stop for a minute!" Gavin was pacing the balcony, rubbing his hands together. "We can't think about that right now."

I gripped the sides of my head and let out a frustrated cry that didn't sound like my own. I felt crazy. Why was this happening? Why Ava? It just didn't feel real; it all felt like a terrible nightmare. The gears in my head turned, and I pictured the mørkeste from earlier in the night. What if she had killed Ava? What if she had something to do with this?

"That winged woman." My voice was hoarse, and I was so thirsty. "She... what if she did this to Ava?"

Gavin eyed me incredulously. "Caleb, you need to get a grip. You're not making any sense!"

Sirens began blaring in the distance.

Gavin's eyes began to water, and he moved to the railing. "Ava did drugs. She did lots of drugs. And she killed herself."

I shook my head fiercely and tugged at my hair, my scalp burning. "It was Joe. He sold to her weekly. If he never—"

"We can't keep saying 'what if' when the answers are right in front of us!" Gavin slid over by me and grabbed my shoulder. "Ava did a lot of bad stuff, okay? We all knew she didn't have much of a will to live. Ava did this to herself, Caleb. We have no one to blame but her."

Several cop cars and an ambulance pulled onto the street, and the police and paramedics rushed out of their vehicles and into the house. College students were being ushered out, and the music had been turned off, indicating the party was over. I bent forward, hands on my knees, and closed my eyes. I couldn't even think about Ava being gone. I couldn't comprehend it, even though I knew everything Gavin said was true. But I didn't want to believe it. I couldn't come to terms with this as easily as he was. I wasn't as logical as he was in situations such as this. I wasn't a "critical thinker" when it came to horrific tragedy. And I couldn't help but begin to hate myself for not having foreseen this devastating accident.

"I don't want to believe any of this is real. No," I said quietly.

Gavin squeezed my arm, his eyes wet.

"It wasn't her fault, really. I didn't mean it like that," Gavin whispered, staring at the flashing red-and-blue lights. "But she lost herself a long time ago, Cay. We couldn't have done anything."

A hush fell over the area. The remaining crowd had become chillingly silent, unnervingly still on the lawn below us. I held my breath, my hands shaking as I clung to the railing, digging my nails into the chipping wood. Then Gav and I watched as a stretcher carrying a body bag was rolled out of the house slowly through the gap in the crowd—the parted Red Sea—to the ambulance's open back doors.

I couldn't bear it anymore. I wailed loudly and dropped to my knees, reaching through the spaces between the railing for a lost girl who had never wanted saving in the first place.

CHAPTER 10

SATURDAY EVENING.
I hadn't left my room all day other than to shower. Four times. I couldn't eat, nor did I want to; I was hungover and had no appetite. Aunt Nikki had been making phone calls throughout the day to different places—parents, the clinic, and to the local florist. I hadn't slept—Darla, Shay, Gavin, and I had been taken to the police station for questioning at four in the morning. Then Tucker had picked us up from there to take us to the emergency room at our local medical center, Saint Anthony's Hospital. Just in case Ava wasn't dead.

But she was.

I walked down the hall past Nikki's bedroom toward my room. She was mumbling quietly, but with my apparently super-human hearing I could understand everything she said.

"He's all right. The three of them were friends since grade school." She paused. "Yes, a lot of problems from what Caleb Michael told me. They're beginning to suspect it was suicide, that she intentionally overdosed."

I hurried to my room in my towel, wishing I was deaf.

After I shut the door, I rummaged through my drawers to find a pair of sweats and my favorite I Need My Space science t-shirt. I changed and glanced at my electric guitar in the corner of the room, its cherrywood covered in a layer of dust. Ava had come with me to pick that one out; she'd even helped me get the seller to lower the price. Looking at that beautiful instrument only made my stomach hurt now. I went over to my side table and clicked my phone's home button. One missed call from my grandparents in Florida; they'd probably heard the news from Nik. No text messages from anyone. I didn't feel like talking, and I was sure the others didn't, either. I buried my face in my hands.

Warmth spread throughout my back, and I turned around.

My helliget friend Gabriel stood before me, his dim illumination making his brown hair look lighter. His eyes were deep brown today, almost black. He appeared dispirited, a glum frown plastered on his face. He wasn't in any armor today, nor was he dressed casually. Instead, he wore a white cotton tunic, a pair of navy linen pants, and his brown boots. I sat on my bed and stared down at my feet.

"It hurts me to see you suffer, Caleb," he sighed.

"I lost my friend last night," I said flatly.

"I know, I felt it." Gabe came over and sat beside me. He placed one hand on my knee. "You know, I was able to get here much quicker this time."

I looked up at him but didn't respond. I couldn't feel good about anything. He sighed again and removed his hand, placing it on his own knee.

"Do you want to talk about things?"

I nodded and turned to him. "There's a lot going on."

He waited for me to continue. I began telling him everything that had happened the night before, beginning to end, mentioning the winged woman Gav and I saw before the party. I even told him about Shay Bishop and how I'd met her and how I thought I'd met her more times before. He found this interesting and very possible. Which was typical of him to say, of course, considering he believed anything was possible. Then I began Darla's story—my meeting with Leander and learning about the Norwegian origins of Gabe's species. How a mørkeste had attacked me after I'd stormed out of Darla's house. Talking distracted me momentarily from the walls closing in on me. And I'd left the biggest news for last.

By the time I was preparing how to tell him, Gabriel and I were sitting on my bed back to back. I was leaning against his spine between his shoulder blades, his wings surrounding me in a protective shield. I was petting a single silver feather, so strong and soft. I'd never studied them so closely before, and I noticed each feather was speckled with brown dots.

"This Leander fellow." Gabe's wings rustled as he spoke. "I'm impressed with how determined he was to find himself through finding out about my kind. I like this interpretation of us. I think I've heard it somewhere before. It is the most accurate depiction I have ever known."

"Lea's smart. He traveled far to learn all he could." I let the feather slip through my fingers and dropped my hand into my lap.

"He is a good soul, taking in those children as his own. Taking you under"—he paused and looked over his shoulder at me—"his wing."

I smiled briefly. "Good one." I ran my hand over my hair tiredly; it didn't feel right to smile when someone I cared about was dead.

"I am wary of something, Caleb." I heard him scratch his chin, as he usually did when he was puzzled.

"What's that?"

"Our worlds should not be connecting like this. This is not one species and another simply coexisting. I knew there were—helliget?—that are more deviant than others, but I didn't know there were any that want to harm your species in this brutal way." He sighed. "It disappoints me to have my kind, my people..." He left his statement at that.

"You were right about something." I stared at my bent knees. "We are not so different. Our kinds, I mean."

"I suppose not," Gabriel said solemnly. "I must say, it is the first I've heard of such horrors being inflicted. I used to think my people hid themselves here. At first, I was not fully aware of them making lives for themselves with humans, though I was not blind to their desire to do so. It is interesting to know someone of my species created you. But now they want something more, some type of control over this world." He turned his head to look over his shoulder at me again. "I don't know how or why. Maybe it is similar to how and why I am here with you. I may not be one of the fallen, the mørkeste, as you call them," he said, turning his head back, "but I am bound to you. So they must be bound by something too."

"Hatred." I hadn't meant to say it out loud, but it was exactly what I saw in the eyes of mørkeste. "The mørkeste I saw last night, I was convinced she was responsible for what happened to Ava." Deep down, I knew the being hadn't played a role in Ava's death. I just wanted someone to blame. "I think it's hatred. I always feel it around me when I see one of them."

"Is it their hatred or your own?"

I pursed my lips. There he went again with his cryptic questions. I changed the subject.

"There's something else I need to tell you." I looked down at my hands.

He waited for me to speak.

"I discovered that Darla is my twin sister."

I expected Gabriel to gasp or to be astounded by such a shocking revelation. But he only grunted in some type of approval.

"I had a feeling her part in your life was much more important than we understood. It goes with the rest of your story. How do you feel about this?"

I spoke without hesitation. "Whole. I feel whole for once."

Gabe's spine shivered against mine then, and his wings shifted. They slowly receded into his shoulder blades, through slits in the back of his cotton tunic, and I watched in awe as they disappeared into thin scars on his skin. I'd never seen him do that before. I never knew he *could* do that.

He rose to his feet and faced me. "I wish to accompany you to the funeral."

I blinked, stunned. "What?"

"Now that I am getting better at finding you," he smiled sadly. "I wish to be there to support you."

I got to my feet and held my hands up defensively. "No offense, Gabe, but you don't exactly blend in."

"I will blend as best as I can." His tone seemed final. "My kind have done it. Clearly, they can come to this world and go about as they please."

"Why?" My hands fell to my sides. "Why do you want to go through the trouble?"

He crossed his arms, standing straight, suddenly looking much larger than me even though he only stood maybe a few inches taller. He gave off a vibe of authority. "You are not trouble to me. There are many things I would do for you."

I shook my head. "I just mean why, though. Why me? You always come back for me. You made that promise when I was young, and I know we're friends, but…" I wasn't trying to question his care for me, but I had always wondered. I straightened up like him and swallowed my feelings. "But now that I'm grown—I'm a grown man who can be on his own—why do you stay?"

Gabriel stepped up to me, grabbed my shoulders, and for a moment, the look on his face made me think he might shake me. But then his head hung, and he exhaled slowly before looking me squarely in the eye.

"A grown man still needs someone. Anyone. Any adult, younger or older, needs to know they have someone to rely on, someone they can go to when they feel they need to run. You rely on me, and I—though you might find this hard to believe—rely on your friendship some days as well."

His eyes held mine in place, so I wasn't able to look away. "If there is anything I want to teach you in your life, it is this—love is genuine when you see all their pain, all their torment, all their suffering, and you carry it with you always."

I swallowed a hard lump that had formed in my throat. Gabriel wasn't here because he had to be. He stuck around because he truly wanted to. I nodded and broke our eye contact, looking down at my feet. Sometimes, Gabe made me feel as if I didn't need to be an adult all the time, and now he let me know that it was okay to feel that way.

He straightened up again and patted my shoulders. "When is the funeral?"

I sniffed. "Monday morning. Nikki planned the whole thing for Ava's dad today."

"She's a strong woman." He unfurled his wings, allowing them to slip out through his shirt. "What of your classes?"

"I can skip them. My professors will understand the situation."

"And have you discussed your sister and her family with Nikki?"

I shook my head shamefully. I had been far from honest with her the past couple weeks. "I'm trying to protect her from some of the truth. Leander says she doesn't need to know all of it but that I should tell her about Darla."

"I feel that would be most wise." He put his arm around my shoulders and gave a light squeeze. "I will see you Monday, bright and early."

I took his hand and gave it a firm shake. "Thank you, Gabe. Thank you."

He bowed his head, and then he was gone, leaving my hand suspended in midair, where a moment ago it was clasped in his.

The morning of Ava's funeral, I'd had two visions: the one of Darla's bloodstained face and the one about Gabriel—or some other helliget—reaching for me and shouting, "No!" I was sitting on the bathroom counter, trying to gain some kind of control over my mind. My black suit was hooked on the back of the bathroom door, waiting for me to wear it. But I knew the sooner I got dressed, the sooner I'd have to go bury my friend. Eventually, I pulled on my clothes. I looked at myself in the mirror, expecting the suit to still be the baggy outfit that never fit me, not even when I'd worn it to Gavin's mom and stepfather's wedding. But today, it fit like a glove. Or like clothes that fit me.

Nikki knocked on the door, and I glanced at my reflection.

"Come in."

She stepped into the bathroom, wearing a deep-plum-colored dress and black heels that didn't make her much taller. Her hair was in a bun, and she looked tired. She smiled and came up next to me.

"You look so handsome and grown." She moved to straighten my black tie. "I never thought you'd grow into this damn suit."

I nodded. I knew she was just avoiding asking me how I was feeling on this horrible day. I felt bad that she had to go through all of it with me and that she'd planned everything because Ava's cowardly father wouldn't.

Is it okay to come pick up you and Nikki now? Darla's voice entered my thoughts. She planned to drive with us to the funeral service because Leander would only be able to make it to the reception, since he had a conference call that morning. I sighed, responded to Darla in the affirmative, and took Nikki's hands in mine. If there was one thing I'd learned over the weekend, it was that no time could ever be wasted waiting around to be honest.

"Aunt Nikki, I need to tell you something," I began.

Her eyes grew wide and her expression turned worried.

"Anything, Caleb," she whispered, giving my hands a squeeze.

"You know my friend Darla you met Friday night?"

"The girl who's nice enough to come get us today?" She tilted her head. "Yes, what about her?"

My stomach flipped. *Here we go.* "She's not just my friend. She's actually my twin sister. The one you told me about when we discussed the day I was born."

Nikki leaned back, and her mouth opened as she shook her head. "What? How did you... She can't—!"

I dropped her hands and rubbed my face. "I know it sounds crazy, but we figured it out. There's no way she's not my sister." I turned to the sink. "I spoke with her guardian, and he confirmed it all too. There's more to it, but I don't feel like going into details right now." I looked at her still-gaping face in the mirror. "I just wanted to tell you that I found her."

Nikki put a hand to her forehead, shaking her head slowly. "I can't believe it," she whispered. "Out of the billions of people in the world, out of all the sets of twins that would be separated, you two just so happened to find each other by chance because her family picked Divinity for a home." She paused, frowning. "And it seems Michael ended up pawning her off to someone else in the end anyway. What a waste. You two could've grown up together."

I faced her and crossed my arms. "I know, I know. An interesting twist of fate, coincidence, whichever. We thought the same thing when we found out." I let out a sigh. "We're together now. That's all that matters."

Nikki smiled and placed her hands on my face. "Well, you and I both know I don't believe in coincidences." She pulled my head down to hers and kissed my forehead.

More and more, I could see why she and Leander had been a couple.

"I'm proud of you, Caleb." She released my face. "I'm always so proud of you."

I put my arms around her neck and embraced her. "Thank you."

I'm here.

"Darla should be here by now." I turned my aunt toward the bathroom door. "You ready to go?"

"It's going to be very hard not to press that girl with questions about her life." Nikki laughed nervously as we exited. "I can't wait to know her better."

"Just try to act normal." I patted her back. "We have all the time in the world to talk about it. A lot to discuss. In fact, her guardian is actually someone you used to know. But I'll let her tell you about that."

"Huh. I can't imagine who that could be." She made a face at me. "I always wondered what happened to the other baby. I wasn't sure we'd ever see her again when Michael left. Seeing as you're both adults now, I'm happy you'll be able to make up for lost time." She shrugged, taking my hand. "I only wish your mother was here to meet her formally."

I waved off her comment to avoid having another reason to be miserable today. "The past is in the past for a reason. I can only move forward from here."

Her eyes glistened. "I raised a good man."

She touched my cheek, kissed it, and we headed out to Darla's car.

The ride to the funeral home was quiet, other than Nikki making small talk with Darla, asking her about what she studied, what she liked to do during her free time. It was nice, watching them get to know each other, and Nikki was doing a great job not asking too many questions. In any case, she'd probably learn a lot more once Leander arrived. I was beyond interested to see how that whole thing would turn out. To pass the time and distract myself, I tried to imagine how Nikki would react to seeing him and I wondered when or if Gabriel would show up today.

A dark cloud covered the sky as we arrived at the service. Gloomy weather for a gloomy day. The vast graveyard was visible beyond the white-painted funeral home, rolling green hills speckled with hundreds of tombstones. A sliver of sun peeked through over one of the stones way in the distance, and the light glared off a white marble statue of a weeping angel at the entrance. I wondered where Ava's grave would be.

Nikki and Darla each took one of my arms and I escorted them into the building. More people were there than I expected. Mostly family, I assumed. Everyone was filing into the room and taking their seats. Gavin and his parents were sitting near the front, and I noticed some familiar faces from school. There was also a handful of strangers I'd probably never see again. We took our seats by Gavin's family, and the three of us each hugged him and shook his parents' hands. I glanced around, finding Shay in a forest-green dress sitting between a guy and girl who looked about our age. She spotted me, and I gave her a small wave.

Surrounded by flowers, Ava's father stood up front next to the closed casket—I was thankful it was closed because I didn't think I'd be able to handle seeing her. Mr. Westley had his arms crossed and his first finger tapping his opposite arm, almost as if he was impatient and had somewhere more important to be. A pack of cigarettes peeked out of his suit jacket pocket, and I thought maybe he'd quit smoking for Ava. But that was just wishful thinking, since he'd never really done anything for her. He hadn't even planned his daughter's funeral.

A priest went up to the podium and told everyone to take their seats. He began to speak and read passages from the Bible, but I didn't care to listen. I was somewhere else, daydreaming about anything that would take me away from being sad. I thought about the party and how much fun I'd been having before Ava's accident. I looked over at Shay and thought about how I'd almost kissed her. But then my thoughts wandered to being devastated on the balcony with Gav, and I started cursing myself for being stupid enough to think that mørkeste woman was to blame for Ava's death.

Darla grabbed my hand. *Stop doing that.*

Doing what?

Blaming yourself.

I'm not...not really.

You called yourself a lot of shitty names for almost sixty straight seconds.

I rolled my stiff neck. *Sorry, I can't help it.*

She sighed beside me. *It wasn't stupid of you to blame that mørkeste.* She held my hand tightly. *Think about it; you were searching for something otherworldly to blame for a very common, very ordinary accident that happened. It was something so terribly normal in a world you know as so far from normal.*

We looked at each other. Her eyes were red and puffy. I slipped my hand out from under hers and put my arm around her. She leaned against me, looking back at the priest who seemed to be speaking gibberish. I thought about how I was more than lucky to have her as my sister. She was a rational thinker, like Gavin, always knowing what to say to help get my mind back on track. And, so often, my mind was way off track. My relationship was different with her, though, because I'd never had anyone who really felt everything I was feeling and thinking before. Like many fated things happening in my life, it was almost as if the universe had brought her to me when I needed her the most.

Once the priest finished speaking and Mr. Westley went up to read a pre-written, inaccurate speech about Ava, we followed the casket and ushers out to the graveyard. Gavin walked beside Darla and me, taking Darla's hand, squeezing my shoulder as we went outside. The gloomy clouds had floated away while we'd been in the funeral home, and the sun was shining down on the grass. At the bottom of one of the hills, in a large gap between two big oak trees, a wreath of wildflowers rested on an easel. In front of it was a hole waiting to swallow Ava's coffin. The crowd surrounded the hole, and I hung out in the back, so I didn't have to watch.

I felt Gabriel before I saw him. I had déjà vu of my mother's funeral, that instantaneous feeling of being totally okay when I knew nothing was okay. He stood on the opposite side of me near the front of the crowd, wingless and wearing a tailored suit, his hair slicked back. I questioned where and how he'd gotten a suit. It was almost comical how well he blended in with the other mourners when I hadn't thought he would. He did the sign of the cross with the rest of the crowd out of respect. Up front, I caught Darla look over in his direction.

Is...is that Gabriel? she asked.

Yeah.

I thought I felt one of them near. Her voice sounded relieved. *He came. I'm so glad he came for you.*

Me, too.

Gabriel walked slowly and swiftly through the people and came to stand by my side. He stood tall, as always, with his hands behind his back. Even though I knew I should be miserable, I was so grateful for his warm presence and his ability to temporarily make the pain go away.

"Thank you for coming," I said quietly.

"I always keep my promises." He stared at the minister, his eyes narrowing. "Humans have very strange rituals and traditions."

I lifted my eyebrow at him. "What do you do where you're from?"

He chuckled softly. "We just...worship differently." He tilted his head, the sun glinting gold off his hair. "I've seen that your kind worships with both love and hate. They kill one another over different beliefs. We don't do that where I am from. We all follow our own views relatively peacefully." He paused, glancing at the ground. "There are those who choose to take their worship in an entirely different direction, hence why some of my kind are here on Earth, starting new lives or wrecking others. But even so, back home, we worship with love."

"That's how it should be here," I said.

"I must admit to you something of great importance," he said as he turned to me. "After I left you Saturday, I began to think of everything you told me, about your origins and your sister. And your father, Michael." He took a few silent steps away from the crowd and gestured for me to follow.

"What is it?" I leaned against one of the nearby oak trees.

Gabriel rubbed the back of his neck, looking over my head. He appeared more human than I'd ever seen him—and I'd never seen him look remotely close to human. He inhaled deeply and frowned.

"I have reason to believe," he started, "that Michael, your helliget father, was also my closest and most-respected comrade."

I pushed myself off the tree and looked at him sideways. "How do you figure? Other than the fact that my father and your friend had the same name."

"Michael has been gone from my life since about the time I first came to you." Gabriel's expression was puzzled. "And I recall, several months before I met you, he asked me to do him a favor. I agreed to this favor, not quite understanding what it meant until now." He looked over his shoulder briefly, as if to make sure no one was listening, and then leaned close to me. "He told me he was going away, and he made me promise, made me swear I would take care of something he'd be leaving behind. That I would guard it, protect it forever, whether Michael came back for it or not."

I was skeptical of this theory. "And you had no idea this 'something' was his infant son?"

Gabe scratched his chin. "He never told me what it was. He only said I would know what to do when the time came. And, until Saturday, I had honestly forgotten." He put a hand on my shoulder. "But now that I have really thought about this, it explains everything—why I was always brought to you, always felt I needed to protect you, why we connected." He smiled. "Promises where I am from are like oaths of fealty. They are very serious, very sacred, and based on loyal, true relationships between my kind. He made me promise to guard you, even though I did not know you were the one I was supposed to protect."

Like an actual guardian angel. "He made you a type of godparent, like how Nikki is to me?" I wanted to be sure. "Like how he made Leander Darla's guardian?"

"It would appear that way, yes."

I nodded. It made perfect sense. But… "Why didn't he just tell you it was me? How were you supposed to know what to protect if he didn't tell you?"

Gabe's nose wrinkled. "One of the many enthralling questions I would be delighted to ask Michael if I ever see him again. Perhaps it was to protect your identity?"

I squinted up at him. "But protect it from whom?"

A recorded, instrumental rendition of "Amazing Grace" began to play over a boom box one of the ushers had placed on a nearby chair. My breath caught in my chest. Hearing this typical, overplayed funeral song only meant that the time had come to really say goodbye to Ava. Gabe looked at the crowd as they each began to toss individual flowers onto the lowering casket, and he put his arm over my shoulder.

"Come, now." He guided me back to where I reluctantly needed to be. "I know this causes you great sadness, but it's time for you to pay your respects to your friend."

As we approached the dispersing crowd, I had the urge to turn and run far away. I was thankful for Gabe's strong hold on my shoulders because without him, I would have taken off. I didn't want to do this, say goodbye again to someone I cared for. I knew death was inevitable; it had surrounded me, had been a fate I first feared and then a fate I eventually no longer feared but accepted. I had grown and learned that wherever you went after this life—or wherever you didn't go—everything you did while you were alive impacted the way you died. If you lived how you wanted to, how you should live, if you had hope and faith or loved someone or found yourself, then others wouldn't feel so bad once you were gone. They'd miss you in their lives more than they'd be upset over the fact that you were dead. They would know, and you would know, that you had really lived before you died.

Thinking about this made me realize I was more sorrowful that Ava's life had wasted away than I was about her being gone from the world. I would miss her, so much, but I had known for a while that she was squandering her time here on Earth. She hadn't been depressed or sick, but she had never made an effort to love or embrace life. Whether she had chosen to end it herself or she'd died as a result of some freak accident, she'd barely lived at all. And that's what made me the saddest.

An usher handed Gabriel and me individual flowers to throw into the grave. He gripped my shoulder supportively. I gazed down at the shiny, cherrywood coffin—the same color as my guitar—and silently sent a prayer to anyone who would hear it. I tossed the flower onto the coffin, and Gabe did the same.

Love you, Ava, I thought to her, wherever she was. *I hope you feel alive in the next life.*

Gabe and I followed the rest of the people back to the parking lot of the funeral home, where we caught up with the massive crowd. Gavin was saying goodbye to his parents, and it appeared he had introduced Darla to them because he was still clutching her hand. Nikki waved me over, looking at Gabe quizzically. As we neared her, I tried to come up with a suitable story of who Gabe was.

But it seemed he already had something in mind.

Nikki looked between us. "Who is this, Caleb?"

Gabriel released me and offered his hand to Nikki. "Allow me to introduce myself. My name is Gabriel. I'm actually an old friend of Caleb's father."

Nikki was clearly astonished and also seemed a little agitated at the mention of my father. "Nicole DeCarlo, Caleb's godmother." She shook his hand politely and gave him a once-over. "How did you and Caleb meet?"

I opened my mouth to offer an excuse, but apparently, Gabe had his story all planned out.

"Caleb tracked me down a while back when he was interested in knowing who his father was. As it turns out, Michael had asked me to watch over him in case something happened to him or the other chosen guardian." He smiled respectfully. "I didn't want to intrude on your lives. But Caleb and I kept in contact." He gave my shoulder a squeeze. "I came to support him on this tragic day."

Nikki crossed her arms, pursing her lips. "Right." She was obviously suspicious, but what was she going to do? Her eyes were slits as she watched Gabe. "Well, Caleb has been through a lot, especially lately. The more support he has the better. We appreciate it." Her statement sounded more like a warning to Gabe than expression of actual appreciation.

Gabriel continued his pleasantries and ignored her underlying tone. "I'm only just visiting today, but Caleb knows I'm only a call away if he needs me."

Nikki shifted her narrowed eyes toward me, and I dipped my head.

"Gabe has been a good friend, Aunt Nikki."

Darla pulled away from Gavin and his parents, and she moved over to our circle. Her smile seemed forced as she glanced between Gabriel and Nik. "Is everyone ready to head back to the Alexis? Mr. Westley is getting food catered."

Nikki turned from Gabe and smiled at Darla. "Yes, let's go. Does Gavin want to ride with us?"

As they continued this banter, I let out a silent breath, mentally thanking Darla for the quick rescue. They grabbed Gavin and walked to her car, and I let them go ahead before turning to Gabe.

"Thank you again for coming," I said as we embraced.

"Of course. I'm always here for you. I'll come back soon."

"Okay."

He released me, and then crossed the parking lot, pushing through a large group of people. I watched as he disappeared into oblivion, not a soul noticing he'd gone.

Watching him go made something become very clear to me—even though the helliget could shield themselves from human eyes, people generally never noticed all that much to begin with. They lived their lives in ignorance, always closed-minded and trying to make everything perfect and keep things in order. If they stopped pretending, maybe they'd see as much as I saw in this world. Maybe they'd stop living a lie and start facing their problems and fears and regrets head-on. Maybe.

We ventured to the Alexis, and the bar was packed with people. I took note of how small the place really was. I was used to seeing all the locals and college students stuffed in here, a line out the door, and people pressed together in the dark with party lights and music blaring. But with the lights on and tables set up with catered food, I could tell there wasn't much space for an actual social gathering.

I saw Shay behind the bar, handing out some beverages and clutching a white rag in her hand. From somewhere in the room, Darla telepathized to me.

Go on, ask her on a real date.

I scanned the room for my sister, so I could glare at her and found her behind Nikki getting food.

You want me to hit on someone at Ava's funeral?

She'd want you to be happy. Her shoulders lifted up and down in a shrug even though she wasn't looking directly at me. *She even told you last week that you should just go for it and see what happens.*

I looked up at the rotating ceiling fan. *But she was referring to sex, not a date.*

Different topic, same results. Just do it.

I chewed my bottom lip and headed for the bar, loosening my black tie. It was too warm in the building. I wished the fan would spin faster. I moved a barstool out of the way, deciding not to sit but to lean against the bar in case it didn't go well and I needed to make a quick getaway. Shay was wiping down the counter and sliding in my direction. When she stopped in front of me, my heart began to clobber in that way it did whenever I saw her. I licked my lips.

"Mr. Westley isn't actually making you work this reception, is he?" I asked casually.

She looked up at me through her long eyelashes and smiled sweetly. "Nah, just helping out. How are you holding up?"

"All right, I guess." I glanced around the room. "You know, Ava would've wanted a big party. She'd say this is boring and that we need to liven it up for her last hurrah."

Shay nodded. "She'd probably ask if someone died."

We laughed lightly, but it soon faded into glum silence.

I switched topics immediately. "So, what do you do here?"

"I bartend, usually afternoons and nights." She tossed the rag onto the sink behind her and leaned on the bar. "I started with waitressing, then I was trained in bartending and I made enough so that I could rent out the apartment." She gestured down the bar at the guy and girl she'd sat with during the funeral. "They're my coworkers."

The guy looked over in time to catch Shay's gesture and started heading over to us. But by the sudden scowl on her face, that hadn't been what she'd wanted him to do. The guy had a sly look on his face that made me think he was the type of dude who always had something to say, whether or not people wanted to hear it. He looked like a total meathead, wearing a too-tight, button-up dress shirt that only made his muscles bulge. I didn't like him already.

"Shay," he said.

He stood uncomfortably close to me, and I tried to stand up straighter. He was tall, well over my height, for sure, and he seemed like someone who never had to worry about a girl telling him no.

"What are you up to on your day off this week? Should we grab a bite?" He asked as he grinned mischievously at Shay. Thankfully, she clearly saw through his fake presence.

"I'm busy, Jake." She was short with him, trying to reject him nicely, but it was obvious she'd had to do this before.

"Come on, Shay." He crossed his arms over his chest, making his pecs look as if they'd burst through the buttons on his shirt.

I gritted my teeth while he pressed on.

"I'd really love to take you out—"

"She's actually busy with me," I blurted out, completely unintentionally. *Shit. No turning back now.* I stood up straighter and looked the dude in his startled mug. "She and I have plans this week."

Jake glanced between Shay and me. "Is that so?"

He looked at Shay, whose blue eyes were wide, but if she was perplexed by my outburst, she hid it well.

"Maybe some other time then," Jake said.

I thanked the universe for the quick save as Jake walked back over to Shay's other coworker and blew out a quiet breath of relief. I leaned on the bar and hung my head, feeling a little embarrassed but also a little impressed with myself.

Darla spoke my exact thoughts. *Damn, that was pretty ballsy.*

Stop spying.

I tilted my head and looked at Shay, putting on my best smolder. "I, um, hope that was okay."

Shay pursed her lips again, but this time, in a way that looked as if she were trying to hide a smile. She bent closer to me, and I smelled her lavender aroma again mixed with that something sweet. Vanilla.

"That depends," she said saucily. "Do we actually have plans?"

My face cracked into a grin on impulse, and I couldn't keep up the act. "When's your day off?"

"I'm off on Wednesdays," she said.

Her gaze dropped to my mouth and my jaw twitched.

"I get out of class at four," she added.

"That's perfect. I don't have any classes Wednesdays." Okay, keep going. "I'll make you dinner. Do you like Italian?"

"I love Italian."

Thank God, because I really only knew how to cook pasta dishes. "I'll text you my address and give you a time to come by. Is that good?"

"Perfect." She bit her lip, her cheeks reddening.

I searched my brain for a good closing statement to this, an exit strategy. As if right on cue, Leander slipped in the side entrance of the bar.

"I have to go catch up with my sister." I pushed off the counter and smiled at Shay. "Talk to you later?"

She nodded, and I used the excuse to slip through the crowd to Gavin and Darla. I had a wide smile on my face, and I was ready for any interrogation from them that followed.

Gavin raised his eyebrows at me. "It went well, I gather?"

Darla had made up a plate of food for me, and I took it graciously. She handed me a fork and knife. "I didn't want the good stuff to go before you had a chance to eat."

I noticed that my plate held three types of pasta and only pasta. I looked at her, bemused, and she blinked innocently.

"I heard you just love Italian."

You are such a little—

"Shit!" Gavin hissed at us. "Nikki just spotted Leander."

Darla and I turned in time to see Leander wave at Nikki, whose face was so red I thought she might explode. From anger or mortification, I wasn't sure which.

"The moment of truth," Darla said.

We glanced at one another anxiously.

Nikki was so small compared to Leander, but she didn't let that make her look weak. As a matter of fact, she didn't even look shocked to see him for the first time in however many years. Her stance made it clear that she wanted to make a statement. Whatever that statement was.

Lea and Nik stood very close, not by choice since it was so crowded in there, but the more we watched them bicker—or Nikki bickering and Leander taking it—the clearer it became that maybe they'd been more serious than Lea had let on. I strained my ears, trying to tap into my heightened senses and listen to their words, but it was too loud in there for me to pick out their voices from among the rest.

"What are they thinking?" I murmured to Darla, low enough so her, Gav, and I were the only ones who could hear.

Her eyebrows raised. "He's explaining you and me. He's coming up with some story about how Michael is his older cousin and how he took me in. Nikki is understanding, but she's mad he never mentioned he had a kid. She thinks that maybe, had she known, she would've done things differently. She wishes they communicated more, and so does Lea." She paused, and her lip twitched. "Oh, crap. Leander and his big mouth."

"What?" I craned my neck to see better.

"He just told Nikki she never stuck around long enough to give their relationship a chance. Oof." Darla flinched. "She's about ready to open up the whole can of worms and talk about all their unresolved issues." She paused again, and she had a look of intense distaste. "They're both also thinking a lot of things I wish I could un-hear right now."

"Oh God, please keep that all to yourself." I groaned, rubbing the back of my head with both hands.

"No problem."

Nikki may have appeared angry with Leander, but between the way she was standing extremely close to him and the coy smile playing on Lea's lips, his hands on his hips, you could tell they had once been very much in love.

I had nightmares all night, one after the other and all of them about Ava. I kept reliving the horrid scene of her death, and now that I was sober and reliving it, it was almost worse than seeing it through drunken eyes. I could see her on that couch, her eyes open and dead, her body limp. Her lips were cracked and dry—someone who used to speak who would never speak again. What was the last thing I heard her say? Oh, yeah, she'd yelled at that freshman sorority recruit. And her eyes. The last time I looked into Ava eyes, they were lifeless. But I suppose her eyes had always been like that, even when she was still alive.

What a depressing thought.

I paced my bedroom in the dark, dragging my hands down my face. The full moon spilled in from my windows, giving my room a dull white-blue glow. I needed new curtains—my blinds had finally broken and had withered to nothing over the summer, so I'd removed them entirely and dealt with the rising sun every morning. But I didn't mind the moonlight. Obviously, I could sleep through moonlight. And on nights like this, I was thankful for that calming glow.

It was four in the morning, but I was wide awake. I felt like going outside. Part of me wanted to hike up the mountain behind my house. But I wasn't a total idiot— more bears were out lately, searching for food before hibernation. I settled for opening my bedroom windows and allowing the cold air to flow in. The sky was so damn clear; nights like this made me wish I still had a car, so I could go on a midnight drive. About a year ago, Nikki had to transfer from her position at Saint Anthony's Hospital to her current job at the smaller clinic, and although she still worked as a registered nurse, the move had resulted in a much smaller paycheck. And the coffeehouse I used to work at had closed down, so we'd been tight on money. I had to sell my car. I was more than willing, since Gavin and I were always together, and he always said he had no problem being my backup. But on a night like tonight, I missed having my own vehicle.

I leaned on my windowsill, watching the forest behind my house. It was really quiet. Not eerily quiet; there was the sound of the fresh breeze. A cricket or two chirping in the woods. Trees rustling against one another. The neighbor's dog barked once, twice, three times, then stopped.

There was something else, too. Not a sound but a feeling in the air. Something in the quiet that made my mind stir. I couldn't put my finger on what it was. It made me want to think. I'd always been a pensive person, delving deep into my thoughts. Sometimes, this overthinking and analyzing was taxing; sometimes, it was something I appreciated. I didn't mind the feeling of being in my head, though. Especially when it was beautifully quiet out. It reminded me to breathe through the pandemonium.

I glanced over at my cherrywood electric Les Paul in the corner. Pushing myself off the windowsill, I walked over to it and brushed away the dust with my fingertips. Plucking the guitar pick from underneath the strings, I lifted the instrument up by the neck and brought it over to my bed. I sat down, resting it flat in my lap, wiping away the remaining dust. I then pressed it against my body, struck a couple chords, and to my surprise, it sounded in-tune after a long break from being played.

I reached over to grab my laptop off my side table and flipped it open. Pulling up the web browser, I typed in "Sound of Silence" by Disturbed. I clicked on the video with the most views, keeping the volume low, and began to match the chords on my guitar with the song as it played. I strummed unplugged and quietly, so I could still listen to the tune and lyrics. I thought of Shay listening to the song while reading Edgar Allan Poe.

It felt good to play again.

CHAPTER
11

SITTING IN THE FALCON'S NEST, I couldn't help but think about how everything paused when someone died. And then after that person's funeral, everything just resumed, went back to the way things were before. Feeling their absence was still there, of course, always lurking. But there were moments when people forgot there was even a *before* to think about.

Before long, I convinced Darla and Gavin to go with me outside to the quad to do homework. I didn't want to be in that stuffy, commuter lounge, thinking about the last time we'd all been in there together. Ava hadn't much liked the outdoors, so that was where I wanted to be now.

I was happy to be sitting outside on the wall, despite it being colder now. I was huddled in my maroon-and-navy Divinity University hoodie, reading an environmental case about the Appalachian Mountains on my laptop. Darla was snuggled against Gav, reading her book, while he highlighted the hell out of his astronomy textbook. I kept warning him no one would buy it from him if he ruined the book, but he insisted it was the only way he could remember the information, that this was the only way he would pass.

A slight twinge tickled the back of my head, and I was transported effortlessly and painlessly into a different reality, just like I'd been the night Gav dropped me off at home, and then again at Darla's when Tucker knocked the beer off the counter.

I was getting used to little blips such as this—painless visions that told me the future in seconds rather than minutes, showing me flickers of moments just before they happened or images that would happen sometime in the near future. I'd had shorter, less detailed flashes here and there throughout my years as a clairvoyant, but since they'd been getting clearer lately, I had begun to pay more attention to what I felt prior to seeing the blips. I started to prepare myself when I'd feel that little head twitch. I needed that control; otherwise, I would go crazy trying to figure out what was real and what was only a foggy image of something coming.

Of course, this current vision wasn't difficult to distinguish from reality, considering I'd just been in the quad with my friends studying. And, considering now, in the vision, my sight was blurred, my right cheek was pressed against dewy grass, and the feeling of ice-cold metal was jammed against the side of my left temple. I could tell, with a sickening feeling, that its shape and violent touch was unmistakably—and could only be—that of a gun to my head.

I came back from my vision and glanced at the live clock on my laptop, watching the seconds tick by. I had only been out for about five seconds. The visions were getting easier to deal with, but trying to decipher them was getting much more difficult.

"Lea is taking the kids and me dirt biking in the mountains the weekend of Thanksgiving break, and he wanted to know if you guys wanted to join in."

Darla swung her legs over Gavin's, and he placed his book on her thighs, never once looking up from it.

"You up for some motocross fun?" she added.

"I wish I could." Gavin snapped the highlighter cap back onto the pen. "I have to drive my grandparents to the casinos that weekend. Grandpa's gotta win big and play that blackjack." He hung his head solemnly.

"That's cute," Darla teased, grinning lopsidedly at him.

He narrowed his eyes at her.

Darla laughed and turned to me. "How about you, Cay?"

"Yeah." I shut my laptop and smirked. "Definitely. How much is it to rent?"

"Don't worry about that." She waved her hand. "Lea has a friend who runs one of the shops, so we get our bikes free."

"You're both lucky." Gavin groaned. "I love my grandparents, but sometimes I wish they lived farther away or in Florida like yours do."

"We have grandparents?" Darla squealed, her blue eyes sparkling.

I smacked my forehead. "Oh, my God." I hadn't thought about my mother's parents also being her mother's parents. She now had more relatives than just me and Lea. "Oh, my god, yeah. I totally forgot—"

She squealed again and flung her arms around Gavin, causing him to drop the textbook onto the cobblestone.

"I have grandparents!"

"It's really not all that exciting," Gavin choked, caught in her clutch. "Old people gamble a lot."

"I don't even care. I never had grandparents before." She let him go, still beaming. "It was always just me and the kids and Lea." She tugged on a strand of caramel hair. "I love my family. But there were times when, like, I dreamed about a big family—grandparents, aunts, uncles, cousins. But even just one pair of grandparents is exciting enough for me."

"They usually come up for Christmas every other year." I rubbed my chin. "I'm not sure how they'll react to having another grandchild, but our grandpa will probably forget that he didn't have two, so it might work out in the long run."

Darla laughed and shook her head, returning to her book. I couldn't imagine my life without certain people in it—Nikki, Gabriel, Gavin. Even my grandparents, who had only warmed up to me after my mother had passed. It must've been so strange for Darla to find out she had a grandma and grandpa out there when they'd never existed in her life before. It must've been a nice, strange feeling. I smiled and tugged my hood over my head.

Intuition told me to look across the quad over at the table Shay typically sat at. She was there—it was as if I'd already known that. She looked as if she'd just sat down and opened her notebook. She was searching her purse, then she pulled out a pen, relief spreading across her face. I thought about how I would've offered her one if she hadn't had one. Anything to strike up a conversation and not be so awkward about it.

That was the one thing about talking to Shay—I was totally out of my element around her. From the second I first saw her and she saw me, I'd felt different. Good different. Exposed, almost. I could talk to girls with no problem, but when it came to her, it was as if I couldn't put on that confident, cool front I put on with other chicks. She made me awkward. But not uncomfortable. It was as if my brain knew she'd see through the act, so I needed to let my walls down and just be me. It was completely instinctual.

I liked that about her.

She looked up from her notebook, probably sensing my gaze. The tip of her nose was pink, as were her cheeks, most likely from the cold. The corners of her mouth lifted into a smile and she waved at me. I grinned stupidly and waved back.

Wednesday afternoon, I hurried home from hockey practice and shaved for the first time in days, nearly slicing off the skin on my jaw. Nikki was standing in the bathroom as I razored off my scruff, interrogating me about Shay, asking things about her I would probably only learn tonight.

"You never have girls here." She crossed her arms, lifting an eyebrow. "You usually go out."

I glanced at her and grinned. "Are you really that worried about me having a girl at the house without you here?"

Her face flushed bright red and she scowled. "No! No, you're a grown-ass man, Caleb. I just…" She paused. "Sometimes I forget you're a grown-ass man. Sometimes, I still see you as the little boy who chased the girls around the playground when I picked you up from school."

I leaned down and rinsed the rest of the shaving cream off my face, clearing out the sink. I patted my face dry with a towel, turning to her. "You know, you really should've warned their mothers about me."

She laughed and moved out of the way as I exited the bathroom.

"Maybe I should've. Maybe you would've been less of a ladies' man."

She followed me as I went into my room. I went to my drawers and shuffled around for a clean shirt.

"Come on, Nik, I wasn't that bad."

She sighed. "No, you were always a good boy."

I found a dark-blue, V-neck t-shirt and tugged it over my head. "So then, what's really the difference between me having a girl here and me taking her out?"

She clicked her tongue against her teeth. "You're cooking for her. That's not your usual play."

"My usual 'play'? What is this, a game of chess?"

She huffed. "You know what I mean! You take girls to movies, bars, maybe the ice rink. You never have them over to the house." She squinted at me, her lips pressed into a thin line. "You must really want to impress this girl."

I didn't answer her while I slowly shut my dresser drawers. I wanted Shay to like me. *Really* like me. Tonight was about making a good impression on her and giving her a real date. I wasn't going to take this girl to a bullshit movie to show her I was interested in her. That wouldn't work, not if I wanted this to actually go somewhere.

No doubt, my silence only made Nikki realize how totally right she was. She placed her hands on her hips, turning to leave.

"Anyway, it's not her being here that bothers me, hon. It's that you'll be using the stove to cook while I'm at work, unable to supervise!"

I snorted and rolled my eyes, listening to her bustle down the hall and head downstairs. I wasn't a terrible cook or anything, but there might have been one or several occasions where I'd left the stove on when she wasn't home.

I started cooking once Nikki left for her nightshift at work—pulled out ingredients for homemade vodka sauce, sliced a loaf of bread—praying silently that I wouldn't mess this up. I had texted Shay earlier to let her know to come around eight, and now that the time was here, I was getting nervous.

My phone buzzed, Darla's name appearing on the screen. I unlocked the phone to read her text.

Calm tf down.

I'm fine, Y r u texting me?

You're so nervous, you're blocking me from telling you to calm the fuck down

My B

Take a Xanax or something. You're giving me anxiety. Maybe take a GasX too.

I laughed as another message popped up right after.

Let me know how it goes!

I placed my phone down on the counter and continued following the recipe I'd pulled up on the screen. With a brief twitch in the back of my skull, an image of a black Jeep Grand Cherokee parking in my driveway flashed across my eyes, telling me Shay would be here any minute. Not a moment later, I heard her pull up to my house and turn onto the driveway. I took a deep breath and reminded myself this was just a date and I was going to be fine. Tonight was one of those nights I was happy I wasn't one hundred percent human—having visions and hearing far distances had helped me mentally prepare for her arrival.

She knocked on the front door, and I gave the kitchen a quick glance to make sure there wasn't too much of a mess. I quietly went into the entryway and then hesitated, taking another breath and straightening my posture before opening the door.

All the nervousness went away once I saw her standing there.

She had her long curls swept into a ponytail, hair pulled off her face perfectly, so I could see her eyes better. She had a black leather jacket on and wore a red, V-neck sweater that dipped not too low but low enough. She was smiling broadly, a bottle of wine in each hand, and I smiled back, stepping aside so she could come in.

"I didn't know which you preferred." She handed me one of the bottles. "So I got one of each."

"Either one works, thanks." I helped her take off her jacket and gestured to hang it up on the rack behind her.

She placed it on the hook next to my own, similar leather jacket.

"Hey." She touched the sleeve and wiggled her eyebrows. "You've got good taste."

I grinned, and she handed me the other bottle as I guided her to the kitchen. I put the bottles on the counter and offered her a seat.

"So, white or red?" I asked.

"Red, if that's okay with you. I prefer red." She smiled politely. "Do you want any help cooking?"

I opened a cabinet to find a bottle opener. "No, ma'am. Not allowed." I reached over to stir the sauce before snatching glasses from another cabinet. "You're a guest in my house." I placed the glasses on the table, one in front of her. "And the line that follows is, tell me about yourself."

She giggled sweetly, and I almost crushed the cork trying to screw the opener in.

"Let's see. I'm majoring in aerospace engineering. I have a class with your sister actually," she said.

The cork came out with a pop. "She didn't tell me that."

"She only switched in this week." Shay held the glass steady as I poured. "We're partners for the class's final project. I snatched her up quick. She really knows her stuff."

"My best friend Gavin and I are into space science and all that. Darla is too. She wants to build rocket ships." I turned back to the sauce, stirring it even though it didn't need stirring. I wanted to look busy. "Is that why you got into it? Are you a science nerd like us?"

"That's half of the reason, yeah." She laughed, swirling the wine in her glass. "My mother's a pilot, actually. Dad was in the air force. So I grew up around planes and grew up loving them."

"Where'd you grow up?" I looked over at her but avoided her eyes.

"Rhode Island, in Warwick with my parents. I have a younger sister, Mackenzie, who goes to college in Connecticut, and an older brother named Elliot who's in grad school out in Colorado. I was living in a dorm at Divinity my first two years, but resident tuition was way too high. Divinity is such a good school for engineering, and I didn't want to leave." She crossed one leg over the other. "So I started working, and eventually, Ava's dad offered me the apartment above the bar." She lifted her glass for me to clink mine against. "Cheers."

We both sipped, and then she continued.

"How are you doing, by the way? I know you and Ava were close."

I nodded. "We were friends for many years. I'm assuming after some time you knew Ava almost as well as I did, so I'm sure you knew certain things were inevitable."

"Yeah." Shay frowned unconsciously and stared into her glass. "Yeah, she used to bring guys to the bar. She'd be high as a kite most times. She was a total sweetheart, but I always had this feeling, this gut feeling that someday her partying ways would be the cause of her demise."

I sighed. "Deep down, I thought so too."

We were quiet momentarily, but I didn't want to be on this date talking about my dead friend.

"I hope you like this meal. I'm not exactly a grade-A chef," I joked, breaking the silence.

She smiled at me. "Tell me about yourself now. I know you're Darla's brother, and that you have a friend named Gavin. You apparently don't cook that often..."

I stuck my tongue out at her playfully.

"And you play guitar. What else?"

"Um." I lifted a noodle from the pot and brought it over for Shay to taste and see if it was done. She nodded to indicate it was good, and I returned to the pot, shutting the burner off.

"There's not much else. I play goalie for Divinity hockey. And Darla's actually my twin, so I suppose that's interesting."

"Firstly, I'm a big hockey fan." Shay winked at me. "Secondly, I could totally see that!" she exclaimed. "I was wondering about that because you two look so much alike. Plus, she's in the same year as we are, so I figured you had to be fraternal twins. Where is she tonight?"

Huh. I hadn't thought about what to say if Shay asked about Darla. I dumped the hot water and pasta into the strainer, carefully choosing my words. How was I going to explain why my sister and I didn't live in the same house?

"I live here with my godmother, Nikki," I began. "And D lives with her godfather, Leander. Long story short, we were separated at birth. Our father is estranged, and our mother died when we were young. Only recently did we find each other." I hoped she wouldn't ask more about how.

She inhaled sharply. "Holy hell."

I caught her staring as I poured the pasta into the sauce pot.

"Well, that's incredible. Not about your parents, obviously. I'm sorry about your family getting split like that."

147

I brushed off her apology casually. "We were raised by good people. It was probably for the best."

"But finding your sister after all that time is really amazing." She leaned her elbow on the table, resting her cheek in her hand. "Are you happy? Do you like her as your sister?"

"Yeah, without a doubt." I sipped my wine. "She's really cool. We clicked instantly." As soon as we bumped into each other, and she read my vision-filled mind.

"Wow," Shay murmured, staring at my arm mixing the pasta.

I served the food on Nikki's good plates. She'd left them out for me to use, so I wouldn't humiliate myself with our chipped-ceramic, regular dishes. I asked Shay more about her life and what her home in Warwick was like. She was really easy to talk to; she asked me about growing up with Nikki and about Gavin and our lifelong friendship. She asked me what I wanted to do with my major and who my favorite philosopher was. I thought this might be the first date I'd ever been on where the girl wanted to know all about me. I wasn't usually someone who liked to talk about myself, but she made me feel comfortable doing so.

After offering several times to help me with dishes and then insisting that she dried while I washed, Shay sat at the table as I put the pots and clean plates away. I would catch a glimpse of her every so often, and she was quiet, running her finger around the rim of the wineglass, her face deep in thought. I liked the way her bottom lip jutted out when she was relaxed.

As I put the last pot away, her voice surprised me.

"Can I ask you something, Caleb?"

I swallowed, happy I was facing the cabinet, so she wouldn't see my sudden anxiety. "Sure, what is it?"

"Why do I already know you?"

Her question baffled me. I stilled, pulling the towel off my shoulder and tossing it over the edge of the sink. I wasn't sure what she meant, but I felt I knew what she was asking. "What?"

I heard her stand up and I turned to face her. She didn't look mad or anything, but her eyes were filled with curiosity. I leaned against the counter, staring at the floor, so she wouldn't be able to see that I'd understood her question the first time she'd asked it.

She stepped up to me. "I have such a strong sense that we've met before this. Maybe not formally." She flattened the top of her hair, slicking back stray frizzes into her ponytail. "I know this sounds totally weird, but I just feel like I already know you."

I didn't answer her, which was unfortunately the wrong thing to do because when I lifted my eyes to hers, she took a step back.

"You know what I'm talking about." It wasn't a question.

"We don't actually know each other, Shay." I crossed my arms, trying to remain composed. "But I've recently remembered that we've seen each other in other places."

She bit her bottom lip and crossed her arms, mirroring me. "Refresh my memory."

"I don't know..."

She approached me again, holding my gaze with hers. "You do."

She still didn't seem angry, but the intensity in her eyes dug deep into my twisting gut.

I tried to break eye contact, but it physically hurt to do so. "I didn't want you to think I was some weirdo who—"

"No, it's fine!" Her eyebrows relaxed, and she dropped her arms to her sides. "I thought I was weird for thinking I had memories of you. I didn't want to say anything in case you didn't remember me."

I exhaled, half relieved, half intrigued. I only remembered her because I had visions of the past that had reminded me. But her memory was fresher than mine—she saw me and felt we had met before. Why hadn't I seen it the way she did?

She tilted her head and crossed her arms again. "It's fine. Just tell me. I'd really like to know how and where I've seen you before."

I breathed deeply. Her lavender scent filled my nose and went straight to my brain. "Seven years ago, I was on a trip with my aunt in Girdwood, Alaska. I was snowboarding and going too fast, and I couldn't stop before—"

"You crashed into me." Shay stared past my head, her eyes recalling the incident. "I fell hard and broke my wrist. That was you?"

I flinched, guilt washing over me. "I didn't know you broke your wrist! Or that you were injured, for that matter. I'm sorry."

"I didn't know until I got back to the lodge, and it was all purple and swollen." She laughed, turning her left wrist in her opposite hand. "I told my parents that I skied into a tree. I was embarrassed and didn't want them to know I collided with someone."

"How is that more embarrassing than crashing into a tree?" I laughed, and she rolled her eyes at me.

"I was fourteen, I wasn't a commonsensical thinker. I didn't know any better!" She smiled at me then took my hand, guiding me to the table so we could sit. "There's more, though. Other times we've met." She let go of my hand and leaned on the table.

I only knew of one other time. But I wasn't sure if she'd remember. "We were very little, seven years old maybe. A smoothie bar in Rhode Island. You were with your mom I think."

"We went to that smoothie place only twice before it closed down. Once when I was little and once when I was about ten." She closed her eyes, trying to recall. "I don't really remember... Oh!" Her eyes snapped open. "I do remember. It was the first time I went. And when I left, I kept looking at you, and I bumped into the trashcan and dropped my smoothie." She looked at me incredulously. "My mom was so mad." She laughed again. "You have such vivid memory."

"It comes and goes." I shrugged, knowing she'd be weirded out if she knew my memories had actually come to me as visions.

She pursed her lips. "What about Huntington Beach? And Lake Tahoe?"

I blinked. "Lake Tahoe?"

She nodded. "And Huntington Beach." She chewed on her bottom lip again. "Five years ago. I was surfing, and I wiped out hard. I washed off in the ocean, and as I was coming out, you were coming in."

I didn't remember this, but she wasn't lying—five years ago, Nikki took both Gavin and me to California during spring break. We started in Huntington Beach and then took a road trip to Lake Tahoe, where we rented a cabin. The water was ice cold in both places, and I remember we barely went swimming.

"I did recognize you when I got to Lake Tahoe, though," she went on. "It had only been a couple days after Huntington Beach. I walked into a soup restaurant, and you were sitting on a couch by a fire. You had a Panthers football jersey on." She looked at me squarely. "I thought you were so good looking. I don't know how I forgot about that until tonight."

I couldn't stop the flood of heat to my chest and ears. She had memories of me; it wasn't just the other way around. The heat traveled to my face, and I looked down at my hands.

"It's cool." Shay's voice caused me to look back up at her, and she went on to explain. "How back then we had no idea. And we ended up at the same college, and we just had dinner together." She smiled, and her face was growing red as well. She tried to cover it by finishing her glass of wine.

Once again, her sheepishness made me feel better about myself. I returned the smile.

I rose to my feet and reached for her. "Come with me. I want to show you something."

She placed the glass back onto the table and took my hand. "Okay."

I guided her out of the kitchen to the stairs. I liked the feeling of her hand in mine; it didn't feel awkward, and it also didn't feel new. I pulled her down to the end of the hallway into my room, turning the lights on and thanking God I had decided to clean it before she came over.

"Sit here," I said, bringing her to the edge of my bed.

She did as I said, and I felt her watching me as I went over to grab my guitar.

I pulled my desk chair out and sat down in front of her, the cherrywood acoustic in my lap. "Remember the other day when I said I'd learn that song?"

She nodded, her eyes wide and her lips twisting into a smile.

"You said you sing, right?"

"Are we starting a band now?" She grinned at me.

I grinned back at her and began strumming the first few chords. She only listened at first, her eyes following my fingers as they traveled across the strings, so I repeated the chords again.

Then she began to sing.

If there was anything in this world I would want to listen to in my time of dying, it would be her voice singing this song. I expected she would have a pretty singing voice, since her speaking voice was already appealing. But she went through each verse of the song, changing tones and hitting different notes, and it was so incredible I really had to force myself to keep playing. I studied her as she sang, and she was just smiling and swaying, watching my fingers dance on the neck of my guitar. I started to wish I had something on hand to record her with just so I could listen to her later. The combination of her voice and the sad tune of the song tugged on my heart, similar to the way I felt every time I saw her; that feeling in my chest, a pulling from the inside out. I was so blown away by her that I didn't realize I'd come to the end of the song and she'd stopped singing.

My face must've looked completely dumbfounded because I was gawking at her, and she was blushing, looking at me with her big blue eyes.

"I love music. Sometimes, I get a bit carried away."

"You're amazing." I tried to shake myself back into the real world. "Really, I'd listen to you sing all day."

She put her hands on the sides of her face, as if her palms would cool her cheeks. "Stop, you're too sweet. Is it hot in here? It must be the wine. Wine always makes me warm."

I laughed and put my guitar against my desk, moving to open one of my windows. I turned to her, and she was still red.

"Sorry, I don't mean to make you uncomfortable," I told her. "You're just... stunning." Was that the right word? Yeah. But was that okay to say to a girl?

"Thank you." She sat cross-legged on my bed, beaming widely. "When our band starts bringing in revenue, I expect to be paid per song."

I sighed and smiled. I was more than relieved that she'd cracked a joke and eased my nerves. "How much are you charging?"

For the rest of the night, we talked about all the music we liked and the concerts we'd been to, until she had me pulling out dusty CDs from my rack in the corner and putting them in my stereo. This led to us analyzing certain songs and looking up their music videos on my laptop. It was fun, and she made me laugh a lot. By the time we'd finished discussing plans to see a Three Days Grace concert, it was almost midnight.

"I'm telling you, the minute those tickets come on sale, we need to buy them." She said, navigating the band's website. She glanced at her phone, pressing the home button to light the screen, and made a face. "Ugh. It's getting late. I should really get going. I have class early tomorrow."

She pouted playfully, and it took all I had not to lean in and bite her lip.

"I have an early class too. A nine a.m." I mussed my hair aimlessly. As much as I wanted her to stay later, I had to be responsible. "I'll walk you to your car." I hopped off my bed and took her hand.

We headed out of my room and down the stairs. I grabbed her jacket and held it for her to put her arms through. The leather jacket looked bigger than I remembered. She turned to me and gave me a funny look.

"This might be yours, Caleb," she said.

We laughed as she held up sleeves that hid her hands. I traded her jacket for mine, and we headed outside.

I opened the Jeep door for her, but I pivoted her toward me with a slight tug on her hand. I wasn't going to let her go without telling her I wanted to see her again. But I wasn't going to just unimaginatively say that. She looked up at me, waiting, as I basically closed and opened my mouth to speak. I hesitated briefly before wrapping my arms around her waist, leaning her against the car. I took the next step and brushed my nose against hers.

"I hope this is okay," I said softly, not wanting to scare her off. It was the second time I'd said that to her since we'd met.

But she went the rest of the way without a word and placed her mouth on mine. I smiled against her lips, her hands sliding up my chest and pausing over my pounding heart. Her hands then went to the back of my neck, her thumbs grazing over my jaw. I squeezed her gently, regretting not kissing her earlier. This kiss was short, but by the time we broke away, I was left wanting more.

She gazed up at me through her oh-so-long eyelashes and pursed her lips as if she was trying not to smile. "Thanks for dinner and a show."

I smiled from ear to ear and helped her into the car, shutting the door. She rolled down the window, and I leaned my forearms where the window disappeared.

She swiftly kissed me on the lips again and started her car, smiling vibrantly at me. "Can I buy you coffee tomorrow morning?"

"I'd like that." I was overjoyed that this confirmed a second date.

"I'll meet you at the Starbucks on campus after my first class. How's ten-thirty sound?"

"I'll see you there." I leaned forward to kiss her a third time. "Text me when you get home safely."

Shay nodded, and I backed away from the Jeep as she reversed down my driveway. She waved goodbye, and I waited until she drove out of sight before I went inside. As soon as I shut the front door, I instantly felt my beloved twin sister shove herself against my mental walls.

I sighed. *You can't even give me a minute to reflect on my evening?*

I'm sorry, I just couldn't wait to hear about it. I like her!

You neglected to tell me you two have class together.

Well, now I can grill her about your dates when you won't spill.

You're really quite a cunning little thing.

It's my best quality.

I laughed out loud, wandering up the stairs, back to my bedroom. To any outsider looking in, they'd think I was nuts, laughing to myself.

I began to think about what would happen if things got serious with Shay. Would I be able to tell her about my clairvoyance? It was a believable thing. But the rest, how Darla and I telepathize, our velsignet backgrounds? Would Shay believe me or would she think I was completely out of my mind? And if she did believe me, would she walk away or would she stay?

You're overthinking, Darla stated. *You're always analyzing everything, thinking too far ahead.*

I shut my bedroom door and began to clean up all the CDs. *I'm psychic; I can't help but think too far ahead.*

Har-har. But seriously, try not to worry about it. You need to go with the flow.

I'm apprehensive of the unknown.

Everyone is, Caleb.

I collapsed onto my bed and buried my face in my bedspread. It was ironic that a man with a fear of the unknown had the ability to see the future, to see ahead and know the unknown.

I was beginning to think my whole life was based on irony.

CHAPTER
12

THE WEEKS THAT FOLLOWED MAY have been some of the best I could remember.

Several influences in my life led me to feel this way. Classes were getting easier since the professors didn't want to grade anything over the short, upcoming break. Plus, I was going to be on break a day early since I had no Wednesday classes. Things were going great with Shay; she and I had been on a date every Wednesday since she'd come to dinner at my place—one of which had been a double date, a hike therapy day with Gav and Darla—and we had coffee multiple mornings during the week. I loved spotting her in the quad and stealing kisses from her every chance I got. Lastly, Leander had invited Nikki and me over to his place for Thanksgiving, and Nik, to my surprise, had agreed to this arrangement.

Even though I'd had several morbid, horrific, painful visions about Darla the past couple weeks, I still hadn't seen any indication of immediate danger. I had no signs, no clues as to where or when this vision would come true. It kept me up every night, and I was worried something bad could happen at any moment. I was starting to feel useless, unable to protect D, but she would constantly remind me that, just by being aware of our surroundings and being together all the time, she already felt safer. She kept telling me to relax, that I was doing my best, and she wasn't scared. She would continuously send positive thoughts my way, and it helped prevent my fears from hindering my current cheery spirit.

Following my afternoon classes on the Tuesday before Thanksgiving break, I bought Shay a hot mint tea at the campus Starbucks since she'd been stressed over a test she'd taken at noon. She once told me coffee is for mornings and tea is for freak-outs. We were sitting in the quad at her usual table, waiting for Gavin to get Darla from class, so we could get something to eat before saying our goodbyes for the holidays.

It wasn't too cold out, but Shay had a tan, knitted hat on her blonde, beach-waved hair, and her shoulders were hunched in her leather jacket. She clutched her hot tea in both her hands as if her life depended on it. To keep her hands warm, she asked me to turn the pages of her notes for her every time she finished reading a page, looking for answers she'd forgotten on the test. She didn't curse that much, so it seemed she hadn't done too badly on it.

"See? I told you you'd be fine." I shut her notebook and tucked it away into her bag.

She pursed her lips, a faraway look in her eyes. I leaned forward and pecked her puckered, red mouth.

"Your lips are like ice, Shay."

She smiled broadly at me and moved to sit on my lap, sipping her tea. "I have really poor circulation. I love the winter so much, but I'd never really survive being in a cold place for a long time." She placed her tea on the table and wrapped her arms around my neck. "At least not without you there to warm me up."

I twirled one of her curls around my finger and lifted my face to hers again. "You'll never have to be cold while I'm around." I kissed both her cheeks before returning to her lips. "I enjoy kissing you too much to let your mouth freeze."

Her blue eyes narrowed suggestively. "That's something I can definitely live with."

"Ugh, get a room, already!"

I heard my wonderful best friend's shout echo from the complete opposite side of the quad.

I turned my head reluctantly away from Shay, looking across the grass at Gavin clutching Darla's hand and pulling her along.

"You're dating my twin sister!"

He flipped me the bird, and Shay laughed into my neck.

"You know he hates it when you say that," she said.

I rolled my eyes almost all the way into my skull. "Well, it's true."

"Yes," she said, "but you make it sound like he's dating the girl version of you."

I smirked mischievously at her. "That's the *point*. I want him to be embarrassed about *dating my twin sister!*" I shouted the last four words back across campus just in case all of DU hadn't heard me the first time.

Gav yelled some profanity my way, but I ignored him and faced the angel in my lap. "What're your definite plans for break? Are you still going to fly home to Rhode Island?"

She pulled my sweatshirt hood onto my head and snuggled against it. "Yeah, my flight is early Thanksgiving morning. Mackenzie and Elliot will be home from school too. Mom has a few holiday flights, though, so it'll just be Dad, Elliot, Mack, and me for Thanksgiving Day. Then we'll see the rest of the family and Mom over the weekend." She pulled back and looked down at me. "So, you and Darla are going to have your first Thanksgiving as siblings. That's exciting, huh?"

"Yeah." I smiled. "It's usually just Nikki and me, and sometimes my grandparents come up. It will be nice to have a big family to celebrate with. And, weather permitting, we'll be going dirt biking over the weekend."

I paused as Gavin and Darla arrived.

"Nikki and Darla's guardian Leander dated a ways back," I told Shay.

Shay raised an eyebrow. "Your holiday should be very interesting then."

Darla and Gavin occupied the empty seats at the table. Gavin was wearing the same Divinity hoodie as I was, and we sized each other up. Darla had her hands shoved into her jacket pockets and nodded at Shay's tea, indicating she wanted a sip. Shay moved to pass it to her.

"What's the plan tonight, my friends?" Darla asked as she gratefully took the tea and sipped.

"I've got work tonight. I'm closing before break," Shay grumbled, taking the tea back from Darla. "You guys want to come to the bar and keep me company?"

"Depends." Gavin rolled up his sleeves and leaned on the table. "Are the drinks on you?"

I swatted his arm, and Shay laughed.

"Beer is four bucks a pitcher tonight," she said, "since we need to bring in money before the holiday. But I will provide free shots if you come before nine."

Gav and Darla beamed at each other, apparently liking the sound of this, then both looked at me as if they needed my permission.

I raised my free hand. "Hey, I'm all for cheap drinks and a hot bartender."

Gavin gave me a high-five and held up his hand for Shay to slap as well. I was ecstatic that he and D liked her so much. I hadn't been nervous that they wouldn't—Shay was easy to be taken with—but people always want their friends to approve of someone they're seeing. I glanced up at her grinning at my friends. Things were really looking up.

My sister winked at me from across the table.

The Alexis was wild for a Tuesday.

I shouldn't have been surprised, considering everyone at school typically would go out every night the week prior to semester break. Mr. Westley had the campus's favorite DJ spinning on the tiny stage by the bar and plenty of drink deals that college kids could afford. Gavin was already drunker than Darla and I combined after only an hour, since Darla had offered to be designated driver. Shay was working the bar, handing out shots and mixed drinks to anyone who threw money her way. She looked exhausted but always smiled for me when I caught her eye.

By the time I was as drunk as Gavin had been by ten, the bar had become overcrowded and sweltering hot. I loved partying, but when it gets too hot, and too many people are around me and touching me, and it smells bad, I just feel overwhelmed. I wasn't sure what time it was or where my friends were, but I needed to get some fresh November air. I headed for one of the side doors to the parking lot, one of the bouncers stamping my hand so I could get back in. I felt the whoosh of a breeze as soon as I shoved the door open. I moved along the brick wall of the building, wondering why they didn't just leave the doors open to begin with.

I rested the back of my head against the bricks and dug the heels of my palms into my eyes. Instantly, I felt better being outside thanks to the cold air. Several people were standing around the lot, trying to get some fresh air, some inhaling cigarettes. Ironic. I rested my hands against the cool brick and watched my breath come out like wispy puffs of smoke. My eyes crossed briefly while I watched.

"Jake, back off. I need to get back inside."

I pushed myself off the wall at the sound of Shay's voice. I followed the wall around to the back of the building, allowing my fingers to glide across the brick. Rounding the corner, I saw Shay standing with her back to me and one hand on her hip. She was holding a trash bag in the other, and Jake was blocking her from putting it into the dumpster.

"Is there a problem here?" I startled both of them. My words were more slurred than I'd intended them to be. "Is he bothering you, Shay?"

"I've got this, Caleb."

Her voice was steady, but the lamp overhead reflected in her eyes, and they told me something different.

"Yeah, we've got this," Jake repeated, snatching the garbage bag from her grasp and tossing it behind him into the dumpster. "We're just talking."

He reached for her arm, and she pulled away.

"No," she growled and yanked her arm back. "You were just leaving me the hell alone."

I walked up to them, still semi-using the wall to support myself. "Listen, buddy." Stepping beside Shay, I looked up at unfortunately bigger-than-me Jake. "You're both working. This is unprofessional. Also, she obviously isn't interested."

Shay placed her hand on my chest, forcing me to take a step back. "Caleb, it's fine, I can handle—"

"She doesn't need you to kiss her ass," Jake interrupted, sauntering closer to Shay, trying to grab her arm again. "I can offer that and more, if you would just—"

Shay removed her hand from my chest and used it to slap him square across his face, the sound of it echoing loudly. His head snapped to the side from the power of her blow, an imprint immediately forming on his cheek and turning tomato red. I was impressed and moved to pull her away from him. But I wasn't fast enough, and he grabbed her by the shoulders, slamming her back against the wall violently.

I didn't exactly know what happened next.

Everything felt like a blurry dream, as if I wasn't in control of my body. Something sparked up inside me that I'd never known was possible—fury. Pure rage burst from me like dynamite exploding, something unlike anything I'd ever felt. But nothing enraged me more than seeing someone I cared about get thrown against a wall by a jackass who wouldn't take no for an answer. I punched him in the jaw, and he lunged at me, hitting me in the same eye the mørkeste had nailed me in weeks before, and he shoved me against the wall with his hands around my throat. Blood red veins appeared in the corners of my eyes, my sight growing dimmer by the second. I kneed Jake in the groin, and the fire in my gut ignited.

My drunken mind started to combine visions and real life into one then. The visions hit me like lightning, flashing in front of me before my eyes in milliseconds, lightning bolts revealing every punch that would be thrown my way. It took me a minute to realize my brain was figuring out a way to protect myself, providing me with visions of how to defend from an attack. It'd never happened before, but I had also never really been attacked like this by someone before. In my head, I saw every way I would be taken down by Jake. But in reality, I was dodging every single fist Jake threw, ducking and moving like I was on speed or something. My visions warned me each time, giving me the defense I needed to prevent further injury.

The visions, the blips and bolts of the future, continued to strike me until it felt like I was lightning. I was on Jake in a flash, and I began delivering blow after blow. I smashed my fist into his face until my knuckles were cracked and bleeding, and Shay was screaming for me to stop. The visions ceased entirely once I became familiar with fighting him off and after he hit the blacktop.

"Caleb!"

Her voice cut through my blind rage and brought me back down to Earth. I was standing over Jake, who was groaning on the ground, whimpering and scooting himself away from me. A handful of people had come to watch, and one of the bouncers—a bald, pissed-off, bulky guy—was headed my way, determination set in his face. Panting, I looked down at my bleeding hands, my eye beginning to pulse and swell. I turned to look at Shay, who was clutching my arm, the one that had been pounding Jake's face in. She looked terrified—of me, of Jake, of the situation, maybe all three. But her gaze traveled all over me, concerned and searching for something.

Jake spit blood onto the blacktop. "You son of a bitch!" The words sounded more fearful than threatening.

The bouncer stomped over and looked between Jake and me. "What the hell is this? Does someone want to explain what happened?"

"It was self-defense." Shay stepped in front of me and pointed at Jake cowering on the ground. "This asshole tried to grab me. He started it. He works for Westley."

The bald bouncer narrowed his eyes at me. "This true, son?"

I looked down at Jake, his face covered in a million different-colored bruises. My chest was still heaving from adrenaline, and I was breathing in and out through my nose loudly. I looked back at the bouncer and nodded wordlessly. He nodded in reply and turned to Jake, yanking him to his feet.

"Mr. Westley has been through enough this past month," Baldy growled at Jake.

Jake flinched, and the bouncer went on.

"He doesn't need an assault report on his hands." He shoved Jake toward the parking lot. "Go home and start looking for a new job."

Jake didn't have to be asked twice. He was already pulling out his keys and searching for his car.

Baldy approached the five or six people who had come to watch the show and crossed his arms. "No one saw anything, correct?"

The crowd dispersed with murmurs of agreement, some heading back into the bar and others lighting up, walking away. Baldy came back over to us.

"Everything else okay, Ms. Bishop?" He sized me up then raised his hand, pointing at me. "You might want to get him cleaned up and sent home. Unless he wants me to escort him out of here myself."

"That won't be necessary, Rob." Shay smiled at him and started pushing me toward the back door. "I'll take him upstairs."

"I don't want to see him still drinking here when I come back inside."

We shoved our way back into the bar, which was so crowded and loud I felt as though I'd been rocked in the head again. I became tremendously aware of my body and how much pain I was really in. Shay was behind me, guiding me through the people with her hands on my hips, toward a door with a sign that read Employees Only. I turned the door handle, and she came around, took my hand, and guided me up the stairwell. We went slowly, step by step, as I gripped the railing for support.

Once we got to the top floor and reached her apartment door, she pulled a set of keys out of her pocket and fiddled with them to get us inside. I closed the door behind me and took a quick gander at the living room I was standing in. Light-blue walls, a flat screen on one side and a fairly large, fluffy gray couch on the opposite. A few posters of video games and bands were scattered about the walls, and a dark wooden coffee table sat on the hardwood floor in the center. Off to the right was a white, recently renovated kitchen. Straight ahead was a hallway that I assumed led to a bedroom and bathroom.

She pulled me over to the couch and made me sit. I leaned my back against the cushions, sloth-like, pain vibrating in my back, which had to be from when Jake had me against the brick wall. Shay rushed to the kitchen, and I heard her scuttle around, cabinets opening, water running, her sneakers squeaking on the kitchen tile floor. I closed my eyes for a brief second, and she reappeared by my side with a water bottle, a wet cloth, and an ice pack.

She cracked the water bottle open and handed it to me. "Drink," she commanded.

I did as she said and started sipping the water. I gave the bottle back to her, and she placed it on the coffee table.

She then held up the wet cloth. "Close your eyes."

Again, I did as I was told. I felt the cool compress on my eye, and it made chills run down my spine to my legs. I clasped my hands together politely, trying not to appear as beat up and drunk as I felt. She patted my eye and wiped my forehead.

"Thank you," I mumbled, opening my eyes, shame and mortification creeping into my head. I'd never fought anyone before, not like that. I should've at least made Shay go inside before I took that guy out. But everything had happened so fast. My face burned now, and I avoided her gaze.

She sighed heavily and tossed the now bloody rag onto the coffee table. "You're a damn idiot, Caleb Swift."

She held up the ice pack and I took it from her, hot with embarrassment.

She placed her hand on my leg and patted the spot. "But you're a damn idiot who protected me in a shitty situation. I'm thankful for that."

I picked my head up from the cushion and stared at the ice pack in my hands. "Shay, I'm really sorry for making a scene. But I'm not sorry for beating up that jackass. He could've hurt you."

"Don't apologize." She lifted my chin with her finger, forcing me to look into those Caribbean blues. "It was bound to happen eventually, whether I beat him up myself or someone else did." She smirked, leaning in and pecking me on the mouth twice. "I appreciate you being there for me. You really kicked his ass."

I smiled sheepishly, raising the ice pack to my eye, but she stopped me. I blinked at her and she took the ice pack.

"It's not for your eye. It's for your neck."

"My neck?" I croaked, touching my throat with my fingertips.

She replaced my hands with the ice pack, and I gasped from the burning sensation as she held it in place.

"It's bad. Jake was choking you. Do you remember that?" Her eyes studied mine.

"Well, yeah." I breathed slow against the ice. "But I didn't think he had me for that long."

She shifted the ice pack, and I winced.

"It's not how long he held you there. He picked you up off the ground by your throat." She shuddered. "It was horrible. He's horrible."

I pulled her hands off my neck, putting the ice pack beside me on the couch and took her hands in mine. I couldn't handle the cold, but I also wanted to show her I was fine. "I'm still sorry for allowing that to happen at your place of work. You could've been fired because of me."

She shook her head. "I'd rather get fired than attacked by some douchebag. I'm lucky you were there. Beyond lucky." Her eyes went to my throat. "Shit, Cay. You're really hurt. Are you going to be all right?"

I slid my hands up her arms to her neck. "You should see the other guy." I flashed a big smile and brought her face to mine.

She laughed and rolled her eyes at me. I liked when she rolled her eyes because I knew it meant that I'd broken through some of her guardedness. I liked everything she did, really. I rubbed her face with my thumbs and kissed her. She smiled against my lips and closed her eyes.

Where are you? D's question intruded on my thoughts.

I broke away from Shay and watched her face. *Upstairs in Shay's apartment; where are you?*

Gavin fell asleep while we were making out.

I heard the annoyance in her voice and tried to hide the disgust that nearly appeared on my face.

I think it's time to go, she added.

"I should probably head out," I said regretfully, still holding Shay's face in my grasp.

She pouted, and I nipped her bottom lip.

"I know," I told her. "I'd stay longer if I could. My sister is my ride home, and Gavin is passed out downstairs and staying at my house tonight."

"I should get down there anyway and make sure my other coworkers are running things okay." She rose to her feet and pulled me to mine using both hands.

I swayed heavily, almost falling back down onto the couch, and Shay caught me. The room spun a bit, and I held my head.

"You wouldn't want me here anyway," I groaned as she put my arm over her shoulder to support me. "I'm still drunk. I'm going to feel a lot worse in the morning. No one likes me when I'm grumpy." As much as I would've loved to have stayed longer—overnight, even—I sure as hell didn't want to feel like shit while I was with her.

She walked me down the stairs carefully, and we stopped by the door. She ducked out from under my arm and slid hers around my shoulders. I wrapped my arms around her waist and kissed her again, this time longer and deeper. When we parted, she was looking down at the floor.

"What's wrong?" I asked.

She gazed up at me. She didn't speak for a minute. Then she said, "Nothing. I just…it might be the first holiday I kind of wish I was spending here. In Divinity."

I processed her words. I was still pretty wasted, but I was at least clearheaded enough to understand what she was saying. I kissed both her cheeks and smiled. "You're going to miss me?"

"I didn't say that." She rolled her eyes again.

That only made me grin wider.

She couldn't hold back her own smile. "Don't be cocky, hotshot. Just because you think you're tough now—"

"I'll miss you too, Shay." I cut her off by embracing her.

She folded into my hug, her arms around my torso. I beamed into her lavender-vanilla-scented hair. It felt good to be missed. Being missed felt different coming from someone I liked in this way, as opposed to just a friend missing me. I'd felt Shay and myself growing closer over the past month, but I didn't really know how she felt toward me. We were only dating, after all. Nothing official, nothing labelled. Not yet, at least. We were having a lot of fun together.

This must've been what Darla meant when she'd said I needed to go with the flow. I felt as if Shay and I were on a great level, becoming really close, more than just friends, and seeing where things went. I wanted it to go somewhere; that was a sure thing. Ava had been right; you can't "shop" for that special someone. But I could sure as hell wait for the right person to come along.

"I'll see you after break." I brushed a curl from her eye and kissed her forehead.

She grinned. "Sounds good." She glanced down at my neck. "Call me tomorrow and let me know how *that is*."

She cringed, and I laughed.

"Will do." I winked at her and opened the door, shoving my way into the crowd.

Using telepathy to find my sister and best friend, I met them outside the front entrance, where Darla handed off Gav to me, so she could go get the car. He was completely incoherent, muttering something about a toaster and a kid who'd beaten him up in the fifth grade. His eyes were closed, and I thought he might actually be asleep. I heaved him into the back seat of the car once Darla pulled up, and then I got into the back with him. I tried to sit him up, and he collapsed half into my lap, his head on my chest. I thought he mumbled a "thank you" to me, so I shook my head and patted his auburn hair.

I was in so much pain during the car ride home, Gavin's weight not helping. I could've easily drifted off to sleep on those leather seats, though. I was so damn tired.

As I was closing my eyes, Darla spoke.

"Caleb?"

I popped one eye open and peeked at her in the rearview mirror. "Hmm?"

"Would you mind telling me what the fuck happened to you?"

Thanksgiving Day was here. Nikki had driven us over to Leander's early in the day so she could help him cook, despite his protests to let him play host. I directed her to the house easily now that I'd been there enough, and when she saw it, she gawked and asked me if Lea was rich. I told her I didn't know. She also asked me why he'd stayed single all these years. I told her I didn't know that answer either.

Darla greeted us with big hugs at the front door. She was so excited for us to be spending our first holiday together, and frankly, I was really happy about it too. The house was warm from the oven and stove and a roaring fire in their living room. Lea instructed Nikki on what he needed her to do with all the side dishes, and she willingly got to work. Olivia was bounding around the house at a normal child's speed, I assume because Lea told her Nikki didn't know we were "different." Tucker was completely charming my aunt, totally kissing up to her for whatever reason, helping her with side dishes. I could already tell he was her favorite Adair.

Arlo helped me set the dining room table, quite bitterly, I might add. He wasn't talking, and he was trying to get things done quickly. I eyed him while he straightened out the plates and napkins and tossed his faux-hawk to one side. It was a comical sight, really, watching him huff and puff while adjusting the silverware properly. I snickered unintentionally, and his head snapped up.

"What?" His prepubescent voice cracked.

I waved it off, scratching the back of my head. I felt bad for laughing. "Do you want to go toss a football outside?"

He blinked at me, flipped his faux-hawk again. "Uh, yeah. Sure."

I motioned for him to follow me down the hall to the garage, where I grabbed a ball. Arlo then showed me the way out to the backyard, which I had only seen from their back deck before. Once we got outside, the autumn air bit at my skin, and I wished I had worn a hoodie over my denim collared shirt. Arlo didn't seem to flinch at the cold the way I did, and he was only in a black V-neck and jeans.

I headed to one side of the yard with the football and Arlo headed to the opposite.

"I haven't played in a while," I yelled across the grass to him. I threw a sloppy spiral his way.

He caught it with both hands. "Me neither."

I sucked on the inside of my cheek, waiting for him to throw the ball back to me. I was used to being shy and not having to really initiate conversations, but when the person was more introverted than I was, it made things way more uncomfortable. We tossed the ball for a few minutes in silence before I finally decided to open my mouth.

"How come you're so pissed off all the time?" I asked boldly. Better to be straight to the point. I could tell he was someone who saw right through bullshit.

He caught the ball I flung and held it, his dark eyes showing his surprise at my question. Quite possibly, no one had cared to ask him this before. "I don't know." He let the ball fly.

I caught it and rolled it around in my hands. "If you don't know why, then how come you emit so much negativity?" The pattern of tossing the ball back and forth started to feel like an allusion for our conversation. Throw.

"I'm not negative. Not really." Catch. He sighed. "It's hard being in a new school. I like Divinity and all that. But I don't like moving so much." Throw.

Catch. "You know he does it to protect you guys." I tried to sound understanding. Throw. "And travel is part of what Lea does for a living, anyway."

"I know." Catch. "It's just annoying because they all seem to fit right in wherever we go." Throw. "And I don't." Arlo combed his fingers through his hair in an attempt to fix it.

Catch. I frowned. "How do you mean?"

He lifted his palms, shaking his head. "I'm not really like them. They all seem to just fit in and belong. Ollie is really Leander's kid, so they have that real parent-kid bond. You and Darla are really his godchildren; you share blood. Tucker doesn't really give a crap about not being related by blood, and he just seems to get along fine that way." He looked toward the upper deck, almost as if making sure no one heard us talking. "I don't feel like they're not my family. I just feel kind of out of place sometimes."

I knew what it was like to feel out of place. No one left me out or told me something was wrong with me or made me feel that way on purpose. But parts of me inside felt they didn't belong. I felt like there was a piece of me that needed changing. I felt this way when I first started having my visions in high school. No one would understand what I was going through, and I couldn't talk about it. After that first year, it got better. But, until recently, when I'd learned of my lineage and of a world I'd never known existed, that empty void had stayed empty.

"I can relate to that." I nodded. "But you have to see things from another perspective. Look at it differently, you know?" I bounced the football between my hands. "You're different than other people. We are part human and part something else entirely. It's really cool. And we all have each other to fall back on."

"But my abilities aren't anything, really." Arlo paced the yard. "I'm not as fast as Ollie. Tucker can turn invisible, for God's sake." He crossed his arms. "I know not every velsignet has a special ability. And sometimes, more than one can have the same kind of special ability. But I don't have anything. I can't do *anything*."

I walked across the yard to him and touched his shoulder. He stopped pacing, his mouth set in a frown. His height always threw me off, made me forget he was only fourteen years old. I wondered if the others saw him as just a crabby teenager, instead of seeing him as a lonely kid. He reminded me a little of myself.

"I'm sure you'll get your unique ability at some point, but you don't need one to prove you're worth something. Things will look up when you realize you absolutely have a place in this world. You'll see things differently, like I do now." I squeezed his shoulder, pushing the football into his arms. "You need to stop dwelling on everything you can't do and start focusing on all the things you can do, and be the best at that."

Arlo's eyebrows lifted when he looked at me. There was a beat before he spoke. "Yeah. Yeah, okay." He inclined his head and patted my hand that was on his shoulder. "Thanks, man. You're a lot smarter than Darla."

I laughed. "Don't tell her that. But I'm sure she's just used to being like a typical older sister to you." I gestured to the stairs up to the deck, and we proceeded forward. "I'm more of an outsider, so it's easy for me to sympathize with you."

"I guess so."

We climbed the stairs and walked across the deck. I opened the sliding glass door and entered the kitchen, which smelled of endless Thanksgiving scents. My stomach growled, and I almost drooled at the sight of the apple pie Tucker was helping Nikki remove from the oven. Leander commenced carving the cooked turkey, and I helped the others set side dishes around the dining room table.

Little Olivia ran over to me and tugged on my hand. "Sit by me, Caleb!"

I grinned. I liked her forwardness. "Okay, Ollie."

Leander carried the turkey over to the table. "Everyone, sit down! I'm starving."

Once we were all seated, me between Ollie and Tucker, Lea stood at the head of the table. I wasn't sure if they prayed before dinner or anything, so I waited patiently for him to speak. He rolled up the sleeves of his ruby-red sweater and looked around at the crowded table. I glanced over at Darla, who was sitting across from me, and she smiled.

"Okay, so." Lea rubbed his hands together. "Usually, during Thanksgiving, we each go around the table and say something we are thankful for." He tapped a spoon against his beer glass. "But we have a really full house this year. I'm just going to make a toast instead. Any objections?"

"Go ahead, Lea." Tucker answered for all of us. He never once looked away from the turkey, so I assumed he was as ready as I was to dive headfirst into the food.

Leander chuckled. "All right. I want to thank you all for helping out this year. Darla and Tucker are usually my right-hand chefs, but it was wonderful having my youngest kids and our guests help put the meal together this time around." He smiled at Nikki and then at me. "I want to say every year I feel more blessed than the last to have my family. And I'm so happy to have Caleb and Nicole in our lives as well."

He lifted his beer. "So, here's to family, new friends and old." He looked over at Nikki again, a different kind of smile on his face. "And here's to another incredible holiday spent with the best family I could've asked for. Cheers!"

I lifted my own beer and clanked glasses with everyone around the table. I caught a glimpse of Nikki smiling at Lea, a look in her eyes I'd never seen before. I thought maybe that look indicated she might still have feelings for Leander. I wasn't sure how I felt about that. I looked back at Darla again, and we made eye contact. She'd tell me later what Nikki was thinking.

We all ate quietly at first, trying to get some food into our hungry bellies. Then everyone started chattering and laughing, enjoying the good food and good vibes. Even Arlo was more chipper than usual; I hoped maybe I'd gotten through to him and made him feel a little better about himself. During the whole meal, Darla and I talked back and forth telepathically. At first, it was unintentional, her reading my thoughts about certain things and then answering them with her own. Then it turned into us continuing our own private conversation. I'm sure she was used to reading and hearing and picking out thoughts among others. But this telepathy thing was becoming second nature to me. I felt like it was so natural now, and it was comforting knowing I'd never really be alone anymore.

As long as she stayed the hell out of my head while I was with Shay.

Darla chuckled quietly from across the table and shook her head at me. I raised my beer glass to her before swallowing a giant gulp.

I'm thankful I have a twin sister as insane as I am.

She grinned at me, picking up her glass of wine. *I'm thankful I have a twin brother who has a hot friend to keep me busy.*

Jesus Christ, D.

I love you, too, Cay.

CHAPTER
13

SLEEK BODY, NEW TIRES, FOUR-STROKE engine, gorgeous silver-and-black paint job. Everything I could want in a machine.

It was a beautiful Sunday morning, a great day to ride over dirt mounds in the woods. The fall air was cool but not cold, breezy but not windy. It was sunny, but the trees and forest shielded all of us from the harshest rays. I had my favorite riding jersey on and the helmet I'd rented was snug on my head, inevitable helmet hair waiting beneath its protection. I was riding somewhat behind Lea and Ollie, who had rented a quad together since she was too young to ride on her own. Darla and I had similar bikes, except her bike's paint job was electric blue and black. She rode behind me but never stopped trying to pass me up.

Tucker and Arlo were bounding over mounds ahead of us—Tucker was a talented rider, steering and making sharp turns with ease. He had clearly done this many times before. I'd like to think I was as good as he was, but I was a bit more of a cautious rider since I had flipped over my bike once when I was a teenager.

We drove around the forest for several hours, only passing one group of hikers who waved at Ollie and Lea as they swerved around them. Around lunchtime, Lea guided us all to a path well off the main trail in the middle of the woods, where we rode for a while before reaching a fairly large, grassy clearing. It was slightly inclined and as wide as a baseball field. It opened up to a cliff face that overlooked Divinity. We could see the cloudless blue sky now that we had emerged from the thick forest.

We parked our vehicles and grabbed our bag lunches out of backpacks, moving to sit in the center of the clearing. It was a peaceful spot for lunch. Olivia was running around us as we ate sandwiches, too hyped up to sit. It was interesting to watch her run because she was just a blur of colors. I kept smiling while Lea scolded her to sit down and eat. She reminded me of a hummingbird; you see them for a moment, only a moment, and then all of a sudden, they're somewhere else.

"She's only getting faster with age." Darla leaned back on her hands in the grass next to me.

I tossed my garbage into my backpack, watching Tucker chase the little hummingbird, so she'd stop to eat her sandwich.

"You sure it's not sugar or something?" I asked.

Darla let out a snort. "Ha! Maybe."

Leander was beside me, watching his daughter in awe. He laughed politely at my joke. "It is baffling how fast she is. We're all fast, as you may or may not have already noticed." He wiped his hands on his jeans. "But her speed and energy are remarkable. I always wondered if the woman who gave birth to her was helliget or perhaps a velsignet like me."

I glanced at him. "But isn't your specialty sensing our kind of people?"

Lea grimaced. "Yes, but there are times when I shut myself down and ignore the sensations. I didn't know her long enough to care." He continued watching Olivia, but this time with a little bit of sadness in his eyes. I wondered if he wished Ollie had a real mother around. You could tell just by looking at him gaze at her that she was everything to him, that all the kids were everything to him.

He tore his gaze away from his daughter and lifted an eyebrow at Darla and me. "I'd like to give you kids some words of wisdom. Have you ever heard the phrase 'no glove, no love'?"

I cringed and Darla covered her ears, shouting that he needn't say more.

After relaxing in the field for a bit, Arlo came over to me and asked me if I wanted to toss around the football he'd brought. I quickly obliged, happy he was opening up to me and also quite touched by the gesture. We threw the ball back and forth for several minutes and then started whipping it at each other in an attempt to avoid Tucker's attempt at intercepting. Arlo was frustrated at first but then found it comical when our game turned into playing keep-away with Tucker.

"Caleb." Tucker panted as he jumped to catch the ball. "How come you don't have your own car?"

I shrugged. "Can't afford one right now. Besides, I have Gavin as a more-than-willing chauffeur."

Tucker intercepted a pass from Arlo. "Did you ever have a motorcycle? You look like a motorcycle kind of dude." He swapped places with Arlo and prepared to launch the ball.

"Actually, I do have a motorcycle driver's license." I was surprised by his accurate assumption. "But only because Gavin made me get it with him." I shuffled my feet. "He thought he was going to pass the driving test after he aced the written exam. I passed but he didn't. Out of respect for him—and lack of funds—I never got a bike."

Tuck shifted the ball in his hands. "You should totally get a motorcycle. Don't you think he should, Arlo?"

Arlo nodded in agreement. "Yeah. Totally. Throw the damn ball."

A motorcycle... I imagined myself speeding around on a sleek bike. "I never really thought about it since—"

That was all I managed to get out before an arm was gripping around my throat, squeezing the life out of me.

The boys yelled my name, but I was beginning to see red, and spots clouded my vision as I clawed and scraped at my attacker's arm. He had me held tight against him in a serious chokehold and was dragging me across the grassy field, shouting something that sounded muffled to me. I twisted my body, trying to shake him away, but it was no use, and I quickly began to lose consciousness. I was close to passing out—or dying, I guess—and I stopped struggling only to hold on to my attacker's arm to support myself.

His hold loosened, but only just enough for my hearing, sight, and some oxygen to flood back into me. At first, all I saw was the blue sky, and I inhaled violently, gasping and holding on to the sight of blue as if it were breathing the life back into me. Cold metal pressed to my temple—undoubtedly a pistol. I recognized the sensation from previous visions, though this particular moment hadn't been in a single one of them. I dug my nails into my assailant's arm, more to hold myself steady than to inflict pain. Everything had happened so suddenly, I wasn't sure what would transpire next. The attacker was much bigger and stronger than I was, so it was probably best not to piss him off at the moment.

I let my gaze fall from the sky, and I saw my family surrounding me at a fair distance; not too far but not nearly close enough to fight the man. They all had their hands up defensively, and Ollie was hiding behind Arlo, clutching his shirt in fear. Leander was the closest, trying to talk down the guy. My gaze darted from him to Darla, who stared at me with that same look of fear she had the night Ava died, a look that told me she already knew something was inevitable, that she knew what was going through this guy's mind.

"There's no reason to hold this man hostage," Leander pleaded, taking a hesitant step forward. His chestnut-colored eyes were wide with both anxiety and warning. "He is ours. He will not join or go with any velsignet who supports mørkeste."

"Join?" the man asked incredulously. "I am *not* recruiting." He had a slight British accent, and his voice was hoarse, as if he'd smoked a lot of cigarettes, but he sounded younger than I imagined he looked. I turned my head slightly to peek up at the face of the velsignet—early to mid-thirties, gray eyes, messy brown hair, goatee. I filed his image into the contents of my memory in case I ever crossed paths with him again.

Leander stepped forward. "Then he definitely serves no purpose to you. Leave him with us."

The man took a big step away from the group in the direction of the woods, strangling me for a brief second again, causing me to gag. "I have to take this one, old man."

His words cut me, and I felt panic rise in my throat.

"I've been instructed to take one or both of them in order to prevent a lot of problems they'll cause us all," he said.

"No!" Darla shouted.

She came at the assailant, and in response, he jammed the gun against my head harder.

"If you come any closer, I'll fucking kill him. I swear it!"

His voice croaked with doubt, and I almost felt relieved. He wasn't going to kill me.

"You will do nothing of the sort."

Leander swiped up something from the back of his belt—a small Beretta, a semi-automatic pistol I'd had no idea he had been carrying around the entire day. I guessed he needed to be prepared for problems like this.

"Give him to us, now," Leander demanded.

The velsignet made a tiny whining sound, shifting from side to side. "I need at least one of them! Him or her!" He waved his gun at Darla. "It doesn't matter which. But you must comply. You don't know what is at stake here."

Lea pulled back the hammer of the gun. "Enlighten me."

He shifted again, nudging me in the head with the cool, metal weapon. "I don't want to do this—"

"Roran!"

A voice from the forest reverberated into the field, causing my captor, or Roran, to spin around. A dark-skinned, Italian-looking fellow stomped through the trees toward us, clutching a phone in one hand and a pistol in the other. He was beefy and strong, and the tightness in his jaw told me he was in charge of Roran. He stopped close to the edge of the woods, his knees bent in a defensive stance. His gaze darted between my family and Roran, and he bared his teeth, causing Roran to loosen his arm around my neck.

"Roran," the Italian said again, this time in a warning tone. "There's been a change of plans."

He lifted his hand and then moved in a way that looked as if he was flinging something. At the same time, I felt a sudden pressure on my torso and my body was jerked backward and away from Roran's grasp. I cried out in surprise and landed hard on my back, and Darla and Lea rushed to my side. Their arms quickly went around me, and they hoisted me to my feet.

Roran put the safety on his gun and slid it into the back pocket of his jeans. "But, Marco, he insisted that we—"

"Shut up!" The Italian, Marco, lifted his hand again and made a grabbing motion, causing Roran's body to stumble violently toward him. Marco appeared much larger than Roran and showed the authoritativeness of an alpha. "You cannot be so careless. You know things can change in a single instant."

He eyed us up, taking note that Leander still had his gun held firmly in hand.

Marco jabbed Roran in the chest with a finger. "You are lucky I found you. He has chosen a different path to take. We leave at once."

"But Marco—"

"Now!" Marco shouted then bolted at warp speed back into the woods.

Roran turned to face us one last time before the image of him faded away, from the left side of him to the right. His disappearance resembled that of a piece of paper that was lit on fire and thrown to the wind, burning away.

Leander let out a whoosh of air and spun me to face him. "You okay?"

"What the hell was that?" Tucker exclaimed.

He and the others came running over to us.

"I-I'm fine." My voice was a little crackly, the bruises on my neck from my bar fight totally irritated.

Lea let go of me and turned to Darla. "What is it they were talking about?"

Darla was gazing at the woods. Her eyes were distant, and it took her a moment to answer. "They knew how to block me out."

I shook my head, rolling my neck. "What do you mean?"

"Th-they…" She stammered, clearly perturbed. "They came with expectations. They knew how to close their minds. They knew I could read them, and they knew how to shut me out." She rubbed her temples. "This has never happened to me before. Ever."

Leander began pacing. "The younger one—Roran. He teleported behind Caleb. That's how Roran grabbed Caleb before anyone had a chance to warn him."

Leander looked to Tucker, who was now holding Ollie on his back, nodding in agreement.

"And the other, Marco, has telekinesis. He seems to be the one in charge of the other. And they both share a leader." Lea stopped outside of our circle and turned to us all. "Remember their faces, guys. If we see them again, we need to be ready. We have no idea what we're up against or why we're up against them."

"They said they weren't recruiting for a mørkeste." Darla crossed her arms. "So why did they want Caleb? Or me? And how did they find us?"

"I don't know, Darla." Lea frowned heavily. "They must have a reason to want one of two siblings. Whoever is leading them knows who you are."

I mentally shivered, trying not to allow my body to react to Lea's words. Someone was out there looking for us, and not because they wanted to make us mørkeste pets. I rubbed my throat. "What do we do now?"

"Let's all grab our things and leave." Leander gestured to our vehicles and bustled us in that direction. "I'm going to make a few calls to some of my nomad friends and ask around, see if anyone has heard anything. Maybe I will contact some of my Norwegian connections as well. We will figure it out. We just need to stay together right now." His hand was on my back, guiding me toward my bike.

"I'm sorry our fun day was ruined, son," he added.

I nodded. "I'm sorry too. This was partially my fault." I really needed to try and focus on controlling my visions, to see events like what happened today in advance. Otherwise, what good was I if I couldn't use them to protect myself and others?

Leander smiled sadly. "No, it's not your fault, Caleb. Bad things sometimes happen to good people like you, and there's nothing you can do about that."

The others all went to their own vehicles, and Lea followed me to mine. He handed me my backpack and helmet and patted the bike seat. "I promised to protect you. It is my job to do so. And I keep my word."

I swung my leg over the seat and straddled the bike, sliding the helmet onto my head. I didn't want Lea to feel guilty if anything were to happen to me, and I wanted to be able to protect myself. If those velsignet knew how to shield themselves from Darla's power, then maybe I'd be able to control my abilities and make them work to my advantage.

"I'll be ready the next time I run into someone like them." I kicked the bike on and revved the engine. "I'm not going to live my life in ignorance. And I refuse to live in fear."

Leander grinned, patting me on the back twice, shaking my shoulder. "I admire your determination, Cay."

He backed away, allowing Tucker to drive in between us and into the forest.

"We'll work this problem out. And don't underestimate your ability to kick ass," Lea added.

"I won't." I lurched the bike forward, racing into the woods after Tucker, leaving my doubt, my worry, and my fears behind in that mountain field.

Darla dropped me off at home, and I walked into an empty house. Nikki must've been working at the clinic, which was perfect because I had plans and I needed to make sure I wouldn't have any interruptions. After showering and changing into something comfortable, I locked myself in my room. I mentally called upon my guardian helliget to come assist me. Luckily, he arrived shortly after my call.

"It's getting easier and easier, my friend." Gabriel stretched his wings so they practically filled my entire room. After the stretch, he forced them to recede into his back.

"Listen, Gabe." I grabbed him a chair. "I need your help. I want to try something, and I need to make sure I don't die trying it."

Gabe's chipper mood faded, and worry lines appeared on his forehead as he sat on the chair. "*Die* trying? What are you trying to die for?"

I face-palmed and climbed onto my bed. "I'm not *trying* to die, Gabe. I just need some support."

"What is it you're doing then?"

I straightened my back. "My visions come and go as they please. They're out of control, so random, so cumbersome. I know visions warn me when I need to be warned and show me things I need to see. But what I really want to do is try to force the visions upon me."

Gabriel tilted his head. "Caleb, my boy, you cannot control that. Visions happen as the future unfolds—"

"I mean that I want to be able to use them to my advantage," I cut in. "Certain visions, important ones, they come to me when they need to. But I want to be able to access my visions in times of need. Force the near-future out of hiding."

I waited for Gabe to respond, but it was clear he didn't understand what I was trying to do here.

I let out a heavy sigh. "Last week, I got into a serious fight with someone. And at one point, my body and mind reacted to defend itself by showing me exactly how the guy would retaliate. I had instant visions displaying every possible way the jerk could hit me, club me, defeat me even. I was able to totally wreck him because I had visions of the near future."

I could see Gabe's face contorting in a way where he was about to scold me, so I got to the point. "I know I will only receive visions of vital importance as they come, as the future builds and evolves and changes. But if I can access the near future whenever I need to, I really think it would help me protect myself and the ones I love, especially in the moment."

Gabe opened his mouth to say something, but then closed it. He scratched his chin, staring at my plaid bedspread. I blinked a dozen times before he finally opened his mouth again.

"You want to access the near future," he murmured, nodding and still scratching his chin. "All right." He stood, swiveled his seat around, and straddled it, leaning his arms on the back of the chair. "It sounds logical enough. Though I'm unhappy you discovered this skill while in a brawl with someone."

He squinted at me, and I shrugged awkwardly.

"So," he said, "how do you suppose we do this?"

"It all depends on me, I guess." I pushed my hair back. "It only happened as a natural response to danger. I was somehow accessing my subconscious and tapping into my full potential in order to protect myself." I paused. "Also, I was pretty drunk. So maybe my inner thoughts were, I don't know, vulnerable at the time. My mind was susceptible to letting its guard down and releasing everything I had in me."

Gabe leaned his chin on his arms. "It sounds like you regularly cause yourself some kind of blockage, preventing you from reaching that maximum power tucked away in your subconscious." He rolled the chair closer to my bed. "I don't approve of the way you were able to access your full potential..."

He lifted an eyebrow, and my face flushed with heat. Gabe shook his head and went on.

"But if you can somehow figure out a way to clear that blockage and tap into your deepest subconscious, then you may be able to really use your psychic abilities to your advantage." He smirked. "And that could prove to be a very valuable asset throughout your entire life."

I was glad he understood what I wanted to do. "Do you think I can do it?"

"There isn't anything you can't do." Gabe cracked his knuckles. "Now, what do you need me to do?"

I positioned myself comfortably on my bed, my legs crossed and my arms resting on my thighs in a meditative-like position. "I just need you to make sure I don't kill myself trying this." I didn't like the way that sounded coming from my mouth. I knew I could handle bad visions and the pain they caused, but I was unsure of how much mental and physical torture my body could actually endure. I had never forced a vision on, so I couldn't imagine what doing that might do to me. I didn't want to think about it. "Visions cause me a great deal of pain, Gabe. It's a lot of stress on my body, and considering I have a stronger one than regular human beings, that's saying a lot."

Gabriel nodded, the worry lines appearing again. "How will I know when to help you?"

"I don't really know," I said, wishing I'd actually thought this through. "Do you know CPR?"

"Are you saying, if it comes down to it, I might need to bring you back?" Gabe swallowed hard. "I don't like the sound of this. At all." He scooted the chair closer, so it bumped against my bed. "Caleb, I do want to warn you that where I come from, it is against our moral code to toy with the life and death of other beings."

"This isn't how I die, Gabe," I said, trying to reassure myself more than him. "I've seen futures beyond this day. I've seen myself beyond this day. You won't be messing up anything by saving my life." I lifted an eyebrow. "Frankly, I'm quite insulted that my guardian, who's supposed to protect me, would even consider not resuscitating me."

He rolled his eyes. "Of course, you know I will be ready and I will be here for you. I know you were born to do great things and you will live long to do great things." He tapped his foot nervously. "I just want to let you know ahead of time that my job, my obligation to your father, is to protect only you. And anyone else other than you and your sister is, well, practically irrelevant. I cannot help you if someone you care about or any complete stranger was hurt or in danger. That is not my place to get involved." He looked me in the eyes in a parental way. "I just want to tell you this, since the topic came up."

I nodded slowly. What he said disturbed me a little, that he would not be able to get involved in any lives other than mine. If someone else I cared about died, he wouldn't be able to help. I didn't want to worry about that, though. If he were an angel, and he was *my* guardian angel, I'm sure the same rule would apply. Nothing was changing now that he said it. But it still bothered me for that brief moment.

"Okay, I'm ready to do this." I moved on from the depressing topic of life and death.

Gabe smiled reassuringly, but his expression held obvious dread. "And I'm prepared to save you if you can't."

"Thanks," I muttered. I took a deep breath and closed my eyes. "I really don't know how to even attempt this."

"You thought the same thing when trying to telepathize with your sister," Gabe said. "If you could access that kind of control over your mind, then you can do this. This power is your own, it is yours alone."

My power. Mine alone. Gabe always knew what to say to make me feel invincible. I was invincible if I wanted to be. I just needed to remind myself how badly I wanted this control over my visions.

At first, I meditated on how important it was that I learn to have control. I thought about how much it would help me and other people if I knew how to control the near future. I thought about how many situations in life I could save myself from—such as that time I was attacked by the mørkeste on the side of the highway. Or when the velsignet nearly strangled me to death today. I thought about how I really kicked Jake's ass because of the visions and how I'd almost lost control of them and myself. If Shay hadn't stopped me—

"This isn't working." I groaned, covering my face with my hands. "My thoughts are straying too far from the task at hand."

"Be patient," Gabe said confidently. "Control comes with patience. It takes time to learn new things. You'll get it."

I uncovered my face and positioned myself again, keeping my eyes squeezed shut. "Darla tells me I always overthink everything."

"She's not wrong, you know."

"Hmph." I shook my head, trying to clear my mind again and focus. Instead of shooting for how important this was, I started imagining my mind as an empty box. Vacant and willing to have all kinds of knowledge filling it. I wanted control, so I put control inside the box. I wanted so badly to prove to myself that I could do this, that the power really was mine.

No one else could do what I do. No one else could see what I see. I repeated this mantra and meditated to the point where I thought maybe I'd fallen asleep and started dreaming about my big box. I noticed that it needed more than just control kept within its confines.

Control was something everyone in the world seemed to want. No one really had control over anything, though. We choose the path we take in life every time we make a choice, but we can't control what will happen in the future. Control was a lonely concept, and I needed to add more of what I wanted to my box. No one else could do what I do. I stuffed that repetitive thought in. I could protect myself and the people I care about. Tucked that one away too. I wanted this.

The box wasn't so empty, and all its contents revolved around that one goal I wanted to achieve, serving one single purpose. As the thoughts circled around my mind, I realized I was outside the box. It was closed, everything I wanted trapped within it. I needed to open those mental doors and let everything rush out, like in the story of Pandora's box, which released evil into the world.

No one else could see what I see.

Open your eyes. My own voice commanded in my head.

I did.

And I thought I'd died and gone straight to hell.

A hallucinatory vortex of swirling colors and voices and sounds and people filled my head, overtaking any other thoughts or feelings I had before. I had a splitting headache, and I could hear myself screaming, but I couldn't feel my mouth. I was existing outside my body and outside my bedroom and outside of this planet. It was too much of everything all at once, the faces of strangers, memories from my past, people I knew and didn't know, the future—so many possible and impossible futures—flying around me, trying so hard to be steady, but my subconscious wouldn't allow it.

I saw flashes of memories I recognized, and I saw images of futures that were to come. So many random, inconsistent visions, my mind violently spun with them. A car turned over on its side. An older Gavin, embracing an older Darla happily. A dog dragging a dead squirrel over to its owner. Ollie is laughing at something that is not funny, not one bit. Darla's face and hands covered in blood, so much blood, all this red. A man with dark hair and blue eyes, but they are dead, the deadest eyes mine have ever seen. Shay is with me in my bedroom, and she is kissing me. I can't catch my breath because she's kissing me like she needs me. Wings, the most indescribable, extraordinarily beautiful wings I have ever seen.

And then all I saw was snow and mountains, so much snow I was drowning in it, the white consuming every part of my soul. I thought I had seen so many visions, every one of them, and this was all that was left. Just this white limbo. That screeching sound in my ears from my usual visions sounded, convincing me I no longer existed, nothing existed anymore. My head was filled with crisp, clear white and the earsplitting, high-pitched sound. I didn't know where I was or who I was or what was real or what real was, and I thought it would never end.

Until it did. It finally ended.

I swallowed a huge, brutal gasp of air, and I clutched my head tightly as the bright white blocking my sight burned away, retreating into the corners of my eyes. I blinked ever so slowly, allowing the fuzzy image of my room to come into view. My ears were ringing, trying to adjust to the bass voice that was easing me out of oblivion. Gabriel was in front of me sitting on my bed, prying my bloodstained hands off the sides of my head and saying muted words, his eyes wide and questioning. His wings were out and draped around us protectively. The ringing in my ears eventually faded away, and I could hear his calming tone as he talked me back to reality. The endless images I had seen began to disappear from memory as I returned.

"Holy hell," I croaked. I swallowed what little spit my dry mouth produced. My lips were chapped, and I licked them.

"Caleb, one minute you were fine, and the next…" Gabriel shook his head, clutching my shoulders in his hands, his gaze darting all over my face. He moved to snatch the towel I'd used after my shower earlier off the floor and started wiping my hands. "There now."

He rubbed the blood away, leaving my palms tinted a faint red. He then started gently wiping the sides of my head, and I swayed off balance a bit.

He stopped and reached for my face. He tugged on my bottom eyelids, checking them out. "Dear almighty—" He released my face and looked at my palms. "I've never seen such torment in a being before. All in the span of maybe a minute. So much of one thing in a single minute." He grabbed my chin in his hands, and my eyelids drooped at the sudden movement. "My boy, what on earth did you see?"

I licked my split lips again. "Everything, Gabe," I whispered weakly. "I saw *everything*."

CHAPTER
14

GABRIEL HELPED ME DOWN THE hall to the bathroom. Well, more like dragged me there.

"Come on now, Caleb." He heaved me onto the floor as gently as possible, propping me up against the bathtub.

My eyes felt so heavy, my body tensing against the porcelain. I was so tired, little blips of the visions passing behind my eyelids. I didn't want to see any more of them; nothing made sense.

I heard running water and popped an eye open. Gabriel's wings were sliding into the back of his shirt as he bent over the bathroom sink, soaking a dark-colored cloth. I moved to sit up, but I felt like I was weighed down by a bag of sand.

"Don't move, Caleb." Gabriel wrung out the cloth. "Just try to relax."

"Okay." My voice was raspy, as if I'd been at a rock concert, cheering and singing for hours.

Gabriel got down on his knees beside me and started patting my face. The washcloth was warm but refreshing, slowly waking me from sluggishness.

"What happened to you?" Gabe took my chin and tilted my face up so he could wipe. "What do you mean you saw 'everything'?"

"I…I went too far, I think," I whispered, closing my eyes as the cloth went over them. "I saw the whole future. All of it at one time. I saw everything there was to see."

"Do you remember any of it?"

"No. I couldn't if I tried. I only remember colors and sounds."

I winced as he removed the comfort of the cloth from my face. He got up, ran the tap again, and this time, returned to the floor with a small paper cup of water.

"You're dehydrated. Take this," he said.

I took the cup gratefully and drank. I swallowed the entire cupful and tossed it into the trash, leaning my head against the tub, squeezing my eyes shut. "There are so many paths to so many futures, Gabriel." My words were mumbled. I felt as if I was half awake, half asleep. "So many choices to make to get there. So many ways to make it all happen."

"I can only imagine." Gabriel pushed my hair off my face. Calmness coursed out from his fingertips and into my head. "What an enormous weight to carry with you."

I looked up at him, his hand heavy on my head. There it was—the constant argument of my visions being both a gift and a curse. I barely mentally and emotionally survived each one.

And yet... *I'm still here*, I realized.

Every velsignet had a gift that separated them from the human race. Not all people had the mindset to deal with something like this. Everyone was capable of losing their minds, going crazy, turning to evil for support, human or not. But I was learning that there wasn't a separation between my visions and me. It wasn't me versus my clairvoyance. My psychic abilities never controlled me. They were all a part of me. Just like any other part of me, they made me who I was. If I could accept that, then maybe I'd be able to manage it all better.

I sat up. "I can try again—"

"No!"

Gabriel's voice startled me back to the floor. I stared at him in surprise, and he rubbed his forehead.

"I just mean, not right now, Caleb. Not tonight. You really caused yourself some physical harm. Give yourself a break."

As much as I wanted to get to work on this, he was right, and I respected his opinion.

Suddenly, the sound of a car coming down the street and pulling into my driveway hummed against my eardrums. In a moment of panic, I thought Nikki was home early, and I tried to think up some kind of explanation as to why I was half-dead on the bathroom floor. Gabriel and I looked at each other in alarm, but as the car door slammed, I heard her voice appear in my head.

Open up, bro.

I practically groaned in relief and motioned for Gabe to help me to my feet. "My sister," I breathed.

"I will go let her in." He pulled me up and waited for me to steady myself before moving out of the bathroom.

I leaned on the sink, gripping the sides of it, trying to get the vertigo I was having to stop. I stared at the silver water spout, focusing on it, so the world around me would cease its spinning. Once it did, I looked up at the mirror.

A demon stared back at me.

"Jesus Christ!" I exclaimed, stumbling back against the wall, the towel rack hitting my spine. Staring at the reflection, I let my gaze adjust to the image that was not a demon at all. Just a severely damaged reflection of me. Not bruised, not cut up, but damaged beyond anything else. I approached the mirror cautiously, as if I didn't want to scare myself off.

My eyes were bloodshot to hell, all the vessels popped and bloody, covering the whites of my eyes and surrounding my blue irises. Those godforsaken, prominent, dark circles that had always made my face appear more sunken in, looking like they were swallowing my skin—my skin, which was paler than I'd ever seen it. My lips were cracked, blood drying at the splits. But worst of all were the veins, all the blue, pulsating veins covering my face and pounding out from underneath my eyes. They made me look like a statue that was cracking apart from the inside out.

My hands went to my cheeks. I wasn't sure if it were really me in the mirror, but touching my own face confirmed it. I did this to myself.

"It's so nice to be formally meeting you for the first time, Gabe."

Darla's voice carried from down the hall, and I bent down to the sink, turning the water on and splashing my face. I was trying to wash the demon away before she came in because I knew when she saw me, she'd—

"Caleb Swift!"

"Oh, shit." I moaned into my soaked hands. I glanced up at the mirror. Color had returned to my face, and the blood was off my lips, but I still looked possessed by the devil. I reluctantly shut the water off and turned to face the wrath of my sister.

To my surprise, she was covering her mouth and her other hand was over her chest. The pain in her eyes took away from the astonishment in her voice when she came to the doorway. She had her arms flung around my neck in two strides.

"You're all right." Darla exhaled. "I felt you were in pain."

I relaxed my tense stance into her embrace, dropping my cheek to the top of her head. "I thought you came to call me a dumbass."

"She should have." Gabe stood in the doorway, arms crossed. But he had a tiny smile.

"I should've." She pulled back to look at me with my identical eyes. "But I was more concerned. Especially when I didn't feel connected to you anymore."

"What do you mean?" I asked.

I put my hand on her back, guided her out of the bathroom, and we followed Gabe back to my room.

"The connection we always feel now," she said.

I grabbed my swivel chair, which was turned on its side, possibly from Gabriel, and righted it for her. She plopped down onto it.

"I'm so aware of it. All the time. So when I felt the line cut, I thought maybe you…" She trailed off.

I climbed onto my bed and laid my head against the pillows. "Honestly, at one point, I thought maybe I did too."

"You didn't, though." Gabriel leaned on the doorframe. "It was only a moment of whatever it was you saw, and then you came out of it."

"Like any other vision." I tried to reassure Darla.

She narrowed her eyes. "Except it *wasn't* like any other vision. I can hear your thoughts on what you are trying to do."

I opened my mouth to explain, but she put her hand up.

"And it's not a bad idea. In fact, I'm impressed with your intentness," she finished.

I turned onto my side and glared at her. "I appreciate your concern, but I don't need your approval. I value your opinion, but I would've done it regardless of what you thought."

"I know that, asshat," she snapped and crossed her legs. "I just want you to know, I think it's a good idea. Smart, even. But if you ever make me think you're dead again, I'll kill you myself."

Gabe chuckled, and we both shot daggers his way.

He put his hands up defensively. "I apologize for laughing. You two argue so naturally. As if you grew up together. It is nice to see you like this."

I shook my head and smushed my face against my pillow. "She would've killed me by now if we had grown up together."

"You bet your ass I would have," Darla mumbled.

But I could hear the humor in her voice, and it made me grin into my pillowcase.

I must've fallen asleep, because my phone alarm woke me up for class.

I rolled onto my back, feeling around my side table for my blaring phone. I smacked it a few times to silence it, then picked it up, squinting at the bright screen. A few missed texts—one from Gav, one from Nikki, and one from Darla. I glanced around my room. No sign of her or Gabriel. They had probably left once I passed out.

I unlocked my phone and scrolled through the texts. I read Gavin's first.

Sampson's lard-ass cancelled class. I'm picking up Darla for lunch later. Want to grab Bishop and meet up?

Nikki's message read: Came back late from work last night and left super early this morning. Ugh. There's a new box of cereal in the cupboard for you. Hope you have a better day than me. XOXO

Darla had texted early that morning. You passed out on us last night, so we tucked you in and talked shit about you. Lol. JK. Sampson cancelled class, BTW. Going out with Gav later. Get some rest.

I dropped my phone onto my face and cursed. Rest was exactly what I needed. But first, I called Shay and asked her to lunch.

As the following week passed, I felt more confident that I'd be able to manage visions of the near future. I hadn't attempted it since the previous Sunday, but I was having natural, random-but-controlled, future and near-future visions more often. Tolerable headaches and less bleeding out of my ears. It was definitely possible to have painless visions, but forcing them on had been an excruciating experience I didn't want to suffer through again. I wanted my head clear for the next time I attempted it, and I wanted to have the proper mindset before diving headfirst into it.

Unfortunately, it was difficult to keep a clear head when I was getting slammed with classwork.

I tried meditation halfway through the week since that was the kind of state I gravitated toward the first time I attempted to see the near future. Deep breathing, repeating mantras related to my clairvoyance. I figured it would help relieve the stress of school, and I wanted to exceed my own expectations. I couldn't stop thinking—about class, graduating on time, girls, my secret origins, my new family, my aunt. I needed to breathe. It helped relieve some weight off my shoulders, but the anxiety of everything always lurked in the back of my mind, like a black, thick cloud waiting to attack.

It was Friday, and Nikki had invited Darla and Leander over for dinner. Leander said he had to leave for a short business trip that night, but he had something for me he wanted to drop off before he headed out. As I helped Nikki cut vegetables for our super-healthy veggie panini dinner, she told me to call Gavin and invite him over. And then she proceeded to ask me if I wanted to invite Shay.

So much for relieving stress.

I texted her and invited her over, but my stomach was turning with nerves. Never had I ever brought a girl home to meet Nikki. Not for any reason in particular; I'd just never dated a girl long enough to have Nikki want to meet her. I'd never dated a girl long enough to care to invite her over for dinner. I knew their place in my life would be short lived, so I'd never even considered it. Nikki must've known Shay was special, that I was acting differently about this girl. Nikki knew I liked Shay, a lot, but I didn't think my aunt knew just how much. Here Nik was, inviting Shay over for dinner. At my house. Where Nikki was. Nikki, my aunt, would be talking to Shay. Over dinner.

Gavin had picked up Shay from her apartment after her shift. I had a brief vision of them arriving at the house, and when they did, I could hear the two of them standing outside the front door giggling about something as I bounded down the stairs to open it. They stopped laughing immediately when I swung the door open, and they tried to hide smiles while I looked back and forth between them skeptically.

"What's so funny?" I asked.

"My man!" Gavin brushed past me, ignoring my question, pounding his hand on my back as a greeting. He pulled his hoodie off and hooked it on the wall. "Nikki, I'm home!" he called, heading for the kitchen.

I pulled Shay by the hand and tugged her inside. Holding her by the opening of her jacket, I leaned close to her face. "Are you going to tell me what was so funny?"

She beamed and kissed me swiftly. "Nope."

I growled a low rumble, and she squealed, leaning away.

I pulled off her jacket for her and put it away. "I just want to warn you now, Nikki is going to ask you a million questions about yourself."

"I'm prepared."

She tossed her golden curls, and I took her hand.

"I hope she plans to talk more about you than me, though," Shay said. "I'd like to hear some childhood stories."

I guided her to the kitchen, my heart racing excitedly. "That's what I'm afraid of."

Shay immediately introduced herself to my aunt when we walked in and addressed her politely. "It's nice to finally meet you, Ms. DeCarlo. Thank you for having me over."

I already knew Nik would love that. But I was surprised when she responded with, "Please, just call me Nikki!"

"Can I help you with dinner?" Shay asked, and my aunt graciously gave her the task of helping put the sandwiches together.

As the two of them began working, Nikki looked at me with a wide smile. I could tell she and Shay were going to get along great.

Which meant I was totally in trouble.

Not long after they started cooking, I heard something strange. The rumble of a motorcycle outside bounced off the insides of my ears, but instead of passing, it only got louder and stayed consistent outside the house. I heard a car pull in behind it and felt my sister's presence not long afterward. The sound of both vehicles could be heard by the rest of the household by then, and Nikki turned to look at me quizzically.

"Is that Darla?" she asked.

I shrugged. The four of us headed to the front door and stepped outside in time to see Darla hop out of Lea's SUV, and Leander swing himself off of one of the finest sports bikes I'd seen.

It was very street, painted all black with rims to match the paint job. Lime-green accents thinly highlighted the sleek edges of the bike and outlined the outer tire rims. It was a Kawasaki Ninja 300, sporty and totally built for speed. Anyone who rode that hot piece was the luckiest person alive.

Lea—that luckiest person alive—tugged the helmet off his head and rubbed his gray hair. "What do you think?"

"Sweet ride, Mr. A!" Gavin headed down the walkway over to the bike. "I didn't know you rode!"

"I didn't, either," Nikki muttered to herself.

She wasn't a fan of anything adrenaline inducing or risky; she had always been a cautious, stable influence in my life. Her arms were crossed, and Shay and I followed her over to Leander.

"I've been riding my whole life." Leander fist-bumped Gavin. His eyes grazed over me. "It's not *my* ride, though."

I stopped in my tracks. I glanced between him and the bike. I then looked at Darla, who was bouncing up and down, unable to contain her excitement. I looked back at Leander, and he busted out laughing.

"Do you like it?" He held out the helmet that matched his bike. *My* bike.

"This is"—I shook my head, practically drooling over the motorcycle—"way too much, Lea. Too much."

"Nonsense. When it comes to family, nothing is too much." He shoved the helmet into my hands. "Think of it as an early Christmas present."

"I literally couldn't wait until he gave it to you!" Darla exclaimed.

"This is for Caleb?" Nikki asked incredulously, glaring at Leander. "I'm not so sure that's a good idea—"

"We can talk about it over dinner next week." Leander sauntered over to her.

She began to protest, but her mouth broke into a tiny smile as he put his arm around her.

"But I got my license to ride a while ago. It's probably expired by now." It wasn't expired. But I wasn't going to accept a gift like this if I hadn't earned it or didn't deserve it in some way. It really was too much.

"You'll just have to get it renewed then, won't you?" Leander winked at me. "But—"

"Sorry, Caleb, there's no returns or exchanges. You get what you get, kid." He dusted his gloved hands, his eyes gleaming. "Whether you ride it or not, you're stuck with it."

I looked at the bike again. It was shining, practically begging for me to hop on it now. I clutched the helmet to my chest, completely moved by this beyond-generous present from him. He'd always made me feel a part of the family, even before he knew for sure we were actually related.

"I don't know what to say. Thank you so much," I said lamely. "I wish there was something I could—"

"Just make sure Gavin gets Darla home safely tonight and we'll call it even." He removed his arm from my aunt and reached for the SUV keys from Darla. He looked at Gav. "You think you can handle that?"

Gavin grinned and saluted. "If it means I don't have to drive Cay around anymore, then sir, yes, sir!"

Leander nodded and turned to me. "Don't let Nicole stop you from riding that bike."

"Sir, yes, sir." I grinned widely.

He gave me a salute before heading to the SUV.

Gavin and Shay walked over to the bike, and Shay ran her finger across the seat. "I can't believe he just bought you a motorcycle!"

As Lea drove off, Nikki went to examine the bike as well, arms still crossed. "It was more than generous of him."

Darla hopped up next to me. "Leander just wanted to show Caleb how much he means to him and the kids." She lifted her shoulder. "I told him just to write a nice card, but he wouldn't listen."

I stared at my reflection in the brand-new helmet. My brand-new helmet for my brand-new motorcycle. "I don't deserve this."

Darla put her hand on the helmet and looked up at me. "Of course, you do. And Leander wanted to give you something you needed. He thought a car might be overkill."

I lifted the helmet. "And a motorcycle isn't?"

She waved her hand nonchalantly. "Tucker may have had a tiny part in deciding what to get you."

I laughed. "Remind me to thank him too."

Darla smiled. "Leander wishes that we'd been able to grow up together, have the same kind of lives and all that. He feels bad. I think this is his way of trying to make sure you know you're his family and that he's fond of you."

"I'm starved." Gavin held his stomach and took Nikki's arm. "All this talk about motorcycles made me hungry."

"Let's get you all inside." Nikki was still staring at the bike. "Darla, refresh my memory. What does Leander do for a living exactly?"

Darla hugged her coat around her as we followed Nikki and Gavin inside. "He's a commercial real estate broker. He advises companies on how to raise money using their real estate as security."

"I see." Nikki turned to look at me. "He's done well for himself over the years, hasn't he?" The way she said it, it was more of a conclusion than a question.

I was still clutching the helmet as we all entered the house, Nikki asking Darla more questions about Lea's life. As they headed in, I hung back by the door and snuck a quick, final peek at the bike.

When the others were out of earshot, Shay walked up beside me, peering outside with me. "You wanna give me a ride tonight?"

Her velvet voice sent chills down my back, and my ears burned with red heat.

She laughed and squeezed my hand, pulling me back toward the kitchen as I nudged the door shut. I knew exactly what she meant, but it was the way she'd said it that had gotten me completely flustered. She was clearly flirting, and I didn't know which route to take. Usually, I was good at this game, but I hadn't expected her to say *that*.

Remember how to breathe. I raised my eyebrows at her and smirked, pulling her close to me and back into the hallway. I placed my mouth near her ear. "I promise to keep you safe if you promise to hold on tight."

I pecked her on the cheek like a perfect gentleman and put the bike helmet on the stairs before dragging her giggling self into the kitchen for dinner.

After we ate, Gavin and Darla left, and I began vigorously searching for my unused license. I found it after I completely tore my room apart, and then I went downstairs to grab Shay, so I could drive her home. I walked in on her drying dishes that Nikki was washing, chattering away about school and hobbies and whatever else Nikki asked her about. I leaned against the doorframe, watching their interaction until my name was brought up.

"Okay, ready to go?" I said loudly, making the two women jump.

Shay placed the rest of the dishes on the drying rack and turned to Nikki. "It was so nice meeting you, ma'am."

Nikki pulled Shay into a hug, which looked absurd, considering my aunt was a head shorter than Shay.

"Hopefully I'll see you soon, sweetheart." Nikki pulled away and looked at me with both eyebrows raised. "You'd better have a helmet for this girl in addition to the one Leander gave to you."

"There should be one in the garage from dirt biking." I thumbed the front door. "We'll grab it on the way out."

Nik nodded with slight approval. "Be safe. When you come back, we'll discuss some motorcycle precautions I want to establish."

"Can't wait!"

I grabbed Shay's hand and pulled her along while she waved goodbye to Nikki.

Right where I thought it'd be, I found a clean helmet in the garage and brought it over to Shay. She was straddling the bike when I came out, admiring its physique with her hands on the grips. In her leather jacket, and with an impossibly contagious smile playing across her lips, she looked the part. She was totally into this, and I loved it.

She looked up at me as I walked over to her.

"What?" she asked coyly.

I handed her the helmet, then wrapped my arms around her waist and slid her to the back of the bike. "You're in my seat, darlin'," I said smoothly in a fake Southern accent, placing the helmet on my head.

She laughed and slid her helmet on as I swung my leg over the bike. I turned the key in the ignition, watching the speedometer light up and move from side to side. I turned the headlights on and hit the start button. I let the engine warm up, revving it, all the while getting a little antsy. I was ready to ride, but I'd never ridden with a passenger before. I didn't want Shay to think I was nervous; I'd promised to keep her safe. I moved the kickstand with my heel and reached back for Shay's arms.

"You ready?" I shouted over the purring, magnificent engine.

Her arms wound around my waist, and she gave a quick squeeze. A wordless affirmation.

I squeezed the clutch, shifted the gear from neutral to first, slowly released the clutch, and twisted the throttle to give it a little gas. We moved forward a bit, and I repeated the process to get used to the feeling of riding again. I rolled us to the edge of the driveway, and we were off.

Cruising down the suburban street in the crisp night with a gorgeous girl's arms around me, I couldn't think of a better evening. It felt so natural to be riding again, and this bike was perfect for someone who hadn't ridden in a while. Once we hit the main road, I reminded Shay she should lean with the bike when we went around curves so that we wouldn't crash. I then picked up speed, shifting the necessary gears, the wind making the hairs on my arms rise.

Though my helmet covered most of my face, I could practically smell the air and taste how clean and raw it was. Growing up in Divinity couldn't have been more perfect—surrounded by nature and mountains, away from the cities and away from the outside world. It was a busy town but not overly crowded, making living here enjoyable.

I swerved into the passing lane. I could hear Shay's muffled squeals behind me, and I kept laughing. I whizzed past cars, weaving between them and switching lanes, loving every second of this, and I realized I'd never been so happy in a single moment.

Living so close to the Alexis had its benefits, but tonight it was just a drawback since I was only going there to drop off Shay. The bar was alive and loud as usual when I drove around back to park. I pulled the keys out of the ignition after settling into a spot, slid off the bike, and helped Shay dismount. We removed our helmets, and I pocketed the key.

"Thanks!" Shay grinned and held my helmet out to me.

I smiled and raised my hand. "Keep it for next time. At least until I get you a new one."

Her eyes widened briefly in surprise, which in turn surprised me. Maybe she didn't actually know how I really felt about her.

"Thanks," she said again, her face pink.

I placed my helmet onto the bike seat and put my arm around her shoulders. "Come on, I'll walk you up."

We pushed through the mass of people toward the door for the stairs. Despite the chilly air, the bar was incredibly stuffy, and I was happy not to be out drinking this evening. I guided Shay into the stairwell, and we ascended, the sounds muffled by the closing door.

"It's crazy tonight," Shay murmured, pulling me up the stairs. "Glad I'm not behind the bar."

"I'm glad you had off, too, but mostly because we got to have dinner together," I said.

We reached the second floor, and she laughed and kissed me on the cheek swiftly, before rummaging in her pockets for her key.

I felt a palpitation in my chest, and my hand flew to it instinctively. A sudden wave of dread overcame me. *No. Oh, God, no, not here.* I had been so lucky, so unfathomably lucky I hadn't had one of my violent visions in front of Shay. I'd known it was inevitable, that the visions came when there was something I needed to see. But I thought if I could hold off for a while, and if Shay and I were on a level where we could open up to each other more, that maybe I could tell her about my visions when I wanted to. It was wishful thinking, and, since the day I'd met her, I had been just plain lucky that I hadn't yet changed into a total freak in front of this girl.

Until today, that was.

She cracked the front door open, and that sound initiated the vision. The world before me fell away, and black and gray matter swirled in front of my eyes. As I was transported to another life, I prayed Shay wouldn't be scared and call an ambulance or something. She had a good heart, and she cared about me, but ending up in a hospital with the explanation of "I'm psychic" would just land me in the mental ward. Not to mention the serious impact being labelled as mentally insane would have on the lady factor.

Black lines formed, crossing over one another in a pattern on the gray, swirly background. As the vision cleared into view, I realized I was looking at a window. A large window with wrought iron lining the pane in an intricate pattern. I stood before it, the sense of familiarity tingling in my fingertips as I watched the rain outside slide down the glass. Then pure sadness erupted inside me, utter despair and sheer hopelessness, and I wanted to claw out of my own skin just to escape it.

The vision ended as soon as it began. I was looking at the floor, but fortunately not lying on it, holding my head and swaying. Shay was clutching my elbow and steadying me, searching my eyes, questioning what happened with her own.

"Are you all right?" She touched my cheek, house key still in hand.

I subtly and slowly touched my ear to see if there was blood—nothing. I couldn't taste the metallic flavor in my mouth, either. I rubbed my forehead and looked at Shay. "I'm sorry, I'm fine. I had a really bad headache all of a sudden, that's all."

Her shoulders relaxed, and she smiled as she placed her keys and bike helmet on the table behind her front door. "You had me nervous for a second. I thought you might pass out, and I'd have to haul your unconscious ass into my apartment."

So the vision had only been a second. I'd lucked out again. I was so relieved. I just didn't feel ready to tell her about that part of my life yet. It was a lot for someone to handle; I'd seen how much it had affected Gavin over the years. I wanted to tell her when I felt it was right for me and when I felt she'd be able to understand it.

She was gazing shyly up at me as I thought about this, and I couldn't help but think that—eventually—I would definitely be able to tell her and feel comfortable about it. She'd already brought a part of me out of its shell and showed me she was into this as much as I was. I could be myself around her.

I slid my hands up her neck and brought her face to mine. She smiled irresistibly against my mouth, and, as usual, it only made me want more of her. I twisted my fingers around her wavy hair, and she gripped the lining of my jacket, pulling me closer to her, her hands sliding underneath the leather. Anywhere her hands went whenever we kissed, my skin sent shivers through my body, and I'd feel like my head was surrounded by a pocket of hot air. My body had never reacted that way when I'd been with other girls. I didn't even know I could feel like that before. I couldn't get enough of her.

My phone buzzed in the pocket of my jeans, vibrating against both our thighs. I groaned and pulled my lips away from hers, but not before biting her bottom one. She gazed up at me through long eyelashes, and her eyes kept me there, preventing me from even attempting to reach for my phone. I mindlessly allowed my thumbs to graze over her cheeks, her skin making my fingertips go numb.

She glanced to the side. "I don't suppose you can stay for a while," she breathed. "I know Nikki is expecting you."

I sighed and kissed her forehead. "Raincheck?" I asked hopefully.

She rose to her tippy-toes and pecked me on the lips, once, twice, seven times. "We still grabbing coffee before class Monday, as always?"

"My favorite way to start the week." I grinned, very aware of how much heat my face was emitting.

We said our goodbyes, and I headed out of the bar, hands shoved into my pockets.

I started to question everything. I'd just had an intense vision in front of Shay, and I didn't hit the floor, but what if I had? I reached my bike and scooped up my helmet, sliding it onto my head. It was hot inside the protective gear, and my anxiety kicked in. What if I had blacked out while I'd been driving her home? No, I couldn't think that way. I needed to remember how it was back when I still had a car and I would pull over to the side of the road the instant I felt any sign of a vision. I had to remind myself that, over the years, I had learned I had enough time to get to safety before a vision hit. Crashing wasn't really the issue; it was that I would've had to explain to Shay why I was pulling over. I would've had to tell her everything I was—everything I am—under really unfortunate circumstances.

I took a deep breath and started the bike. I knew it was only a matter of time before I had to tell Shay the truth. How much of the truth was up to me, but if I really wanted a relationship with her, it might have to be the whole truth and nothing but. Was I ready to make that kind of proclamation, open myself up to someone in that way? It had been so easy to open up to Darla and her family, but she was different, like me. They were all different. It had been easy because they already knew everything before I did. It had been easy because Darla was my twin sister.

But Shay was something else entirely.

I peeled out of the parking lot and onto the road, welcoming the cool air blowing past me as I zoomed away. My head actually started hurting from thinking so much. Shay was a human being with a normal life, with normal, not-special abilities. She could run at normal speeds. She could jump to normal heights. She had a normal mom who was pilot, a dad who worked for the military, two normal siblings. She had a normal job and went to a normal college in a normal, simple town. Shay Bishop was exceptionally incredible to me, but to the world she was just another person living her life on Earth.

Now that I had entered her life, I started to wonder what kind of shock all this knowledge of otherworldly phenomena would bring to someone who hadn't known any of it existed. To uncover secrets of the world and reveal them to someone who lived a life that was so normal, so human, could be catastrophic. What did someone do when they discovered these things? I still had a lot to learn from Leander, who also still had so much to learn about the helliget and mørkeste and whatever else was out there. Shay was open minded; I knew that for a fact. I had gained trust in her and she in me, and I could see her accepting me for who I truly was.

But even so, what kind of world would I really be bringing her into?

CHAPTER
15

"COME ON, KID, YOU HAVE to give yourself a break."
Leander handed me a beer, even though I thought I should have water. I was sitting in the puffy reading chair in his study, massaging my temples, the veins in my head pulsating in sync with my heart.

"It's getting much easier, Lea." I took a swig from the bottle. "Let me keep trying."

All weekend and during the week after school, I had gone over to Darla's house to practice seeing the near future. Leander was more than happy to help but a little skeptical of how I could access my subconscious without killing myself. He had me eat a hearty meal every time I came over, so I had enough energy to withstand so much use of my brain at one time, and he kept me hydrated at all times. I had to piss every five seconds, but it was worth not ending up the way I had during my first attempt. Over the past couple of days, I had begun to pick out little moments in time that were part of the near future from among the crazy, erratic visions that surrounded them and tried to push their way to the front. I was getting better at it now that I'd tried it so many times.

"I just don't want you to wear yourself out."

Lea sat on the leather lounge seat beside me as I placed my beer on the coffee table.

"If you feel yourself getting close, then by all means, try again," he added. "But don't force yourself to see things just because you want to. That's how you'll get hurt."

"Just one more go," I said, convincing the both of us.

Leander scratched his goatee then nodded, leaning his elbows on his knees.

I closed my eyes. Almost immediately, the visions spilled from my subconscious like a glass pouring water, a steady stream of images surfacing in my brain. Originally, the scenes would come at me as if someone had tossed a bucket of water, splashing behind my eyes all at once. But I had learned how to ease everything out, slow down the process, and get familiar with the sensation of seeing all things.

Gradually, the visions came to me. An image of myself coming out of this meditative state, pissed off that I was unable to access the near future, and another of me coming out of it successful with a high-five between Lea and me. A vision of Leander getting up and pacing his study, telling me to practice when I went home tonight. Another where he asks me when Nikki gets out of work that afternoon, since she was coming to his place for a date. Me asking if he still loves her and what his intentions are with my aunt.

The scene changed to me sitting in class, receiving an A on my final paper—the future but not too far ahead. I was losing that little bit of control and needed to focus. *Easy, Caleb, take it easy.* The first few images had unfolded in front of me as if they were happening in real, present-day life, much like the one I'd had that night when I'd come home and I hadn't realized I was even having one. My mind back then had been trying to access the near future without me actually realizing it, and since it was possible, I knew I'd master this soon.

My sight morphed away from the near future and spiraled out of control, visions of the world unfolding before my eyes. And then I saw snow, the blinding white snow, as always. But this time, the snow became speckled with color, like a canvas being used for splatter-painting. Reds and oranges and greens molded together, blocking out the white until it shifted into the one vision that constantly haunted my dreams—the forest and Darla's face twisted in silent horror, her hands out and shaking, blood dripping over her cheeks like tears.

I heard the usual earsplitting ringing before I unpleasantly came out of it all in the reading chair.

"Dammit!" I growled, licking my dry, cracked lips. I still hadn't mastered the art of saving my body from the physical harm caused by my clairvoyance.

Lea wrinkled his face in distaste and handed me the beer. "I take it this attempt didn't go well."

"I just went too far, that's all." I sat up straight and stretched my shoulders. "I lost control. It was closer that time. I saw a couple different near futures."

Lea nodded and got to his feet. He began pacing around the room. "The more I think on it, the more I realize that your violent visions are typically far-future. You only recently began to see near-future events, and those visions cause you much less harm." He paused in front of one of the bookshelves, staring at the array of bindings. "I have a theory. It appears as though the farther you see, the more pain is inflicted on you. The shorter the distance, the easier it comes. Now you are accessing a whole new area of your mind and your power, and you sometimes lose control and go too far, as you say. And that's when it hurts you. Your brain isn't used to so much."

"That's an interesting thought. It makes sense that stretching my mind too far would hurt, while keeping within a smaller time frame is more manageable."

He tore his eyes away from the books and looked at me with a confident expression. "When you go home tonight, just practice a bit. I'm not worried about you losing complete control anymore, since that very first run was so quaky."

"You have a date with Nikki tonight, and I get to sleep in on Wednesdays, so it's a good night to practice. I won't have to worry about her barging in while I'm mid vision." I got to my feet and brushed off my sweatpants casually, trying not to indicate I'd already seen this moment.

But Leander knew me better than that. He raised his eyebrows and stopped pacing, smiling my way. "Of course, you already knew I'd say that."

I ran my hands through my hair, the longer pieces falling into my eyes. Did I want to know what his intentions with Nikki were? I did in my visions. But part of me felt like it was really none of my business. I wanted to protect Nikki. But I trusted Leander to do the same.

So I just smiled politely and clapped my hands. "It's getting late, so I'll just go home and rest up and practice later." I picked up the unfinished beer and gulped the rest before tossing it into the trash can on the other side of the table. "Can I trust you'll bring my aunt back at a reasonable hour?"

Leander tilted his head. "If I kept her out past curfew, would you object?"

I shrugged. "I do enjoy having the house to myself."

"I'll take that as you granting me permission." He winked and motioned to the door. "I'll walk you out."

As we exited the study and walked down the hall, I heard Darla enter the house. We rounded the corner, and she was taking off her shoes and jacket, and when she saw me, she snatched my coat off the coat rack.

How did it go? she asked.

I'm still alive, aren't I?

She rolled her eyes and whipped my coat at me. We locked gazes, and her amused face turned slightly dejected. There was no stopping her from seeing her own future in the corners of my mind. I wished so badly that I could get more details from that vision; it had come to me since the beginning, it was my most repetitive one, the vision that brought my attention to her in the first place. I wanted to protect my sister, and I always carried this unnerving sense of guilt because I couldn't even protect her from seeing it unfold in my thoughts. We didn't talk about it as much as we should, but we didn't really need to. There wasn't enough warning in it for us to interpret what it all meant. As much as she wanted to ignore it, and as much as I wanted to stop it from coming, we couldn't avoid its predestined existence. She knew it, and I knew it. But at the end of the day, all we could do was wait and figure it out when the time came.

She stared at me another second before she recovered her lost smile.

Leander glanced between us. "Sometimes, it's weird being in the same room as you two."

He reached for the door, and Darla gave me a quick kiss goodbye on the cheek before Lea escorted me out.

I stepped onto the circle driveway and walked up to my bike, which was parked like it owned that part of the road. I smiled almost every time I saw it. "She's still here," I said humorously.

Leander patted my back. "I'm glad you like it, Caleb." He crossed his arms and nodded at the bike. "You be good to her and she'll stay faithful."

I snatched my helmet off the seat. "Same goes for Nikki." I eyed up Leander, sounding aloof but partially, a tiny, little bit serious.

Leander nodded admirably and shook my hand firmly. "I respect your protectiveness over her. You're a gallant man. She raised you well."

No one had ever said that to me before. Or to Nikki. She had raised me better than anyone I could've imagined, besides my own mother. If anyone hurt her, they hurt me too. Nikki was the best, and I could tell Leander knew that. Whatever had happened between them in the past remained in the past. They were moving on from what once was. Focusing on the present and future all at the same time.

Funny, how I was trying to do the same.

I was multitasking, something I wasn't very good at. Ironic, considering it was a skill that could be gained by being psychic and knowing things ahead of schedule. I would've thought I'd develop phenomenal time-management skills with all the visions and sneak peeks into the future, exceed the academic expectations of my professors, and surpass my peers in my classes.

But it wasn't like that at all. The only thing my visions ever gave me was a splitting headache and a bloody nose. Until recently, but even so.

It was the second week of December, and I was on my bed, bouncing between studying for finals and hurrying through last-minute assignments that would be due between this week and next week. Most of it was online work, and if I got it all finished, I'd be done with the semester entirely. Darla and Shay were already finishing out their semester this week, and Gavin and I were coming up from the rear. I should've been less stressed out, considering no matter how I did in my classes, the first half of junior year was over. But I was typically an anxious person, so there was no escaping the pressure I felt.

Nikki knocked on my bedroom door, even though I had left it open. I grunted and looked up, my mouth dropping open when I saw my little aunt standing in the doorway. She was all dolled up like she was heading out to a club, her brown hair straight and down and make-up done like I'd never seen it before. She wore a flattering, red silk dress, bright against her tan complexion and heels that gave her a little extra height.

"How do I look?" She gave a little twirl, which made her appear twenty years younger than she actually was.

I grinned at her. "You're a total knock-out, Nik. Where's he taking you?"

"I have no idea," she said excitedly. "He only told me to get dressed up."

I nodded and looked back at my notes on my laptop as she came into my room. After a moment of quiet, she leaned forward and kissed me on the head.

"I know this all must be strange to you." She petted my hair. "Since you didn't know Leander before and we already had all this history—"

"It's not weird, Nik, I promise." I put my hands up. "I have nothing against you guys dating, and as long as he makes you happy, then I'm happy."

"I know." She petted my hair again and smiled. "I just want to make sure you feel comfortable with it. I will tell you more about my past with him someday. I just want you to be okay. Considering your relationship with him and how coincidentally he and I were romantically involved years ago."

"No such thing as coincidences." I winked at her.

She shook her head and walked toward my bedroom door. "Now I know where you get that from." She waggled her fingers in a wave. "Don't wait up! If all goes well, I might not come home."

I made a face. "TMI, Nikki. Just be careful, and don't do anything I wouldn't do."

She laughed and twirled back down the hall.

Once she left, I returned to my laptop. Over the next couple hours, I grew increasingly frustrated with my lack of focus, and I began to get writer's block when I attempted to finish my paper. Little flickers of near-future kept interrupting my work, telling me that my subconscious was focused on other things. It became more and more intrusive as the time passed, so I finally decided to close my laptop and have another go at seeing the near future.

It came quickly this time, once I welcomed the idea. Before, I'd been blocking it out, so I could study and do homework, but now that I didn't have any distractions, the visions flooded my head like a dam breaking. I saw myself playing guitar, making myself a snack, then returning to homework. I saw myself calling Shay. I saw myself asking Gavin if he wanted to go grab a drink.

Too soon, a million futures began to drown my busy brain, and I was ripped out of the alternate reality and tossed back into my room. I growled in annoyance and tried again. Similar images. Then I was snapped back. I could feel an ache forming in the back of my head, but I had to press on. If I didn't keep trying, I'd never get it right. I tried a third time, which lasted a bit longer, but once again, I was brought back to the present.

I flung myself back onto my pillow, feeling a tantrum coming on stronger than the headache. "What the hell is it going to take to get this right?" My heart was thudding hard from anticipation, and I was breathing heavily in response to how pissed I was with getting the same results over and over and over again.

Finally, I reached over and swiped my phone off the side table. Scrolling through my recent contacts, I hit Shay's name and held the phone to my ear. She picked up after four rings, and I already started relaxing at the sound of her voice.

"Come over when you get out of work." I spoke more urgently than I'd intended to. "Please," I added to take away some of the tension.

She agreed, and we hung up.

To pass the time, I tried to see the near future again and again. I set a timer on my phone to see how much information I could get from a vision in seconds, just to test out how quickly I could see near-future events before they happened. At one point, the near future came so naturally, so fluidly, I thought I'd finally gotten it. I let the images unveil before my eyes. It was the process of me hearing Shay's Jeep pull up to my house, then heading down the stairs to get her. I opened the door...

And I spun out of control and snapped back yet again.

I yelled into my pillow. I'd been so close that time, the minutes of a moment minimizing to two seconds and playing out in front of me with such ease. It was progress, but to make progress one needed patience, and patience was something I totally struggled with. I heard Shay's Jeep pull into the driveway, and I trudged down the stairs to let her in. I flung the door open before she could even knock.

She was still in work clothes, a black t-shirt and black jeans, her hair in messy curls. She stood in the doorway with her hand still poised and ready to knock on the door. "Caleb, are you okay?"

I didn't give her a chance to ask that unanswerable question before grabbing her wrist and pulling her into the house. Instantly, I extinguished her words with my mouth and kicked the door shut. I took her by the hands and pulled her to the stairs, and she threw her arms around my neck, respectfully not questioning my sudden need to detach myself from the world. We stumbled recklessly up the stairs, and when we reached the top, I wrapped my arms around her legs and hoisted her up, placing them around my waist. I carried her down the hall, prying my mouth off Shay's just to kiss her neck.

She tangled her hands in my hair, panting as if she was trying to catch her breath. "You sounded upset on the phone." She sighed. "But clearly that isn't the case."

I inhaled her lavender-vanilla-scented hair and carried her into my room. "I missed you."

I bumped the bedroom door shut with my butt as she lifted my face up to hers. She kissed me fervently, tugging at my hair, and I took her to my bed. I collapsed onto it with her, never releasing her lips, while simultaneously feeling around my comforter for the remote to my stereo. I couldn't remember what CD I last listened to and prayed it wasn't anything tasteless. Some alternative rock cover of "What's Up" by 4 Non Blondes came blaring through my speakers, the snare drums and symbols thrumming with the pounding of my heart. Not exactly my first choice for mood music, but it would have to do.

I felt a smile dancing across her lips, resulting in my own doing the same as I reached over blindly and turned out my side table light.

CHAPTER
16

SHAY SPENT THE NIGHT.

I slept wonderfully, of course, and I even had good dreams for once. I dreamed about her—about the way her skin felt, about her scent, and about the way she laughed and whispered and breathed. It was nice to feel all these things, especially when I'd never felt them before with anyone. The more I spent time with her, the more I saw how impossibly beautiful she was, inside and out.

I also discovered that I really liked to cuddle, so that was a whole new experience for me as well.

I woke up the next morning to the sound of a phone buzzing loudly, the shift of Shay beside me, and the cold air I felt when she rolled away and got up.

I turned onto my stomach and groaned. "What time is it?"

"Seven. My alarm is going off," she whispered.

Through foggy eyes I saw her rummaging through clothes on the floor, searching for her phone.

I moved to the edge of the bed and touched her leg. "You have class." I remembered with pure disappointment.

She bent down and kissed my cheek. "I know. I didn't expect to spend the night last night." She kissed me again. "But I'm so glad I did."

I jutted my bottom lip out. "Skip class and stay in bed with me."

She laughed and nipped my lip. "Darla and I have our final project presentation today. I *cannot* miss that. I'd fail." She pursed her lips. "Plus, your sister would have my head if she knew I'd skipped class just to sleep in with you."

Little did Shay know, Darla would find out either way by reading her mind. I dreaded the moment when my twin sister would scold me for wanting Shay to abandon her. And when she'd know I'd slept with her new BFF.

She wouldn't win that argument, though. I had Shay first.

"All right, I'll let you go." I sat up and wrapped my hand around the back of her neck. I kissed her swiftly. "Only if you wear my clothes to class."

She released my mouth with a *pop*. "Like, actually wear your clothes? As an outfit?"

I bit my bottom lip in suspense. "You don't want to present in your work clothes from last night, with that smell of beer and bar food. And besides, I'll need them back, and that gives you a reason to invite me over later."

"*You* are the reason I'd invite you over later, hotshot." She grinned that heartbreakingly beautiful smile. "But I'll do as you ask."

I beamed as she tugged on my gray sweatpants from yesterday and my navy Divinity Falcon's t-shirt. She came back over to me, and I wrapped my arm around her neck, brought her down to the bed, pecking her all over her face. She giggled and glanced down at the fierce falcon on my shirt.

"Don't you have a game tonight?"

I laid my head back onto the pillow, groaning. "That's right. I can't come over later. Gav and I have our last game of the semester."

"I know. D and I already talked the other day about going to watch you boys." She kissed my nose. "I just forgot it was this week."

"You'll be there?" She'd only been able to make it to one hockey game before, since her work schedule and my hockey schedule never synced up.

"I plan on it." She rolled off me and stood up. "If you have trouble finding me in the bleachers, I'll be the one in your t-shirt."

"Awesome." I smiled broadly, excited that my girl would be able to see me in my element. I leaned over the side of the bed, swiped my school bag off the floor, and gave it to her to carry her stuff in. She gathered up her things and shoved them inside as I moved to get up.

"I'll walk you to your car." I eyed my drawer. "Do you mind grabbing me a pair of—?"

"I'm on it." Shay walked over to my drawer and opened the top one, pulling out a plaid pair of pajama pants and tossing them my way.

I got out of bed, tugged them on, and went over to her, wrapping my arms around her waist. Her hands were like ice on my bare chest, and I pulled one of them off and kissed it. I pulled her close to me, and she shivered.

"You wouldn't be cold if you stayed," I muttered into her hair, one last attempt at convincing her.

She rolled her eyes at me—she had to know by now that I loved when she did that—and kissed me hard.

I had always wanted to be normal. I had always wanted to just live an ordinary, quiet, visionless life. But she made me feel extraordinary on an entirely different level.

Gavin and I met for lunch at our favorite sandwich shop, Déjeuner, around two in the afternoon. I would've responded earlier to the one hundred missed calls from him, but after Shay left, I'd crawled back into bed and blissfully passed out for a few more hours. When I finally called him back, he told me to meet him at the sandwich shop as soon as I "had my shit together."

I pulled up to Déjeuner on my bike and parked it right beside Gav's truck. As much as I loved my motorcycle, I missed our car rides together. Between finals week and hanging out with our girls, I was glad to be getting some one-on-one time with my best friend.

He was already ordering when I came inside. He was tugging a strand of his auburn hair, tapping his chin, trying to decide what sandwich he wanted as if his choice was a matter of life or death. I already knew what I wanted and came up behind him, cutting in front.

"I'll have the caprese sandwich, hold the chicken," I said.

Gavin kneed me in the ass and huffed, "I was just going to order!" He narrowed his green eyes at me. He looked at the confused counter clerk and muttered, "I'll have the exact same."

We each paid for our sandwiches and sat in a booth in the furthest corner of the restaurant. It wasn't busy, and the few people who were there were working on laptops or reading giant textbooks—clearly Divinity students, diligently studying for finals.

"I'm glad I never really study," Gavin said as the waitress brought over our food. "I highlight words and boom. Instant notes filed into my brain." He tapped his temple.

"Lucky you have those natural wits about you," I said sarcastically, digging in.

He raised his eyebrows at me and smiled lopsidedly. "You're an asshole. Why weren't you answering your phone this morning?"

"I'm sorry, wife, I didn't know I had to answer to your every call." My mouth was full and crumbs dribbled everywhere as I spoke. "I slept in."

Gav rolled his eyes and started eating. "You don't like to sleep late unless you were up late."

I shrugged and kept pounding my food. Unfortunately, I realized—too late—that I made the awful mistake of not responding to him. He stopped chewing and lifted an eyebrow.   .

"You can't tell me you were up that late studying," he said suspiciously. "What were you doing? Did you go to the Alexis?"

I placed my sandwich down onto the plate and snatched up a napkin. "It's none of your business what I was doing last night," I said quietly behind the linen.

Gav's eyes widened, marble and round, and he gaped at me. "Or *who* you were doing last night." Realization crossed his face. "Did Shay come over?"

I dropped the napkin and tried to avoid his eyes.

"She did! She did, you can't lie to me. Your face is turning the same color as the tomato on your damn sandwich, Caleb."

"Because you're practically screaming," I snarled at him, throwing a chip at his face, hitting him in the nose.

He picked the chip off the table and popped it into his mouth. "I knew you two would hook up soon. I've gotta say, it's about time."

"It's not like that!" I frowned at him. "We're dating. We're always together. She's not some random chick I picked up at the Alexis or whatever. You know me better than that."

He frowned in turn. "Come on, man, I'm only teasing you." His face grew earnest. "I'm sorry. I didn't know how serious you guys actually were."

"About as serious as you and Darla at this point, I'd say."

Gavin's eyes widened. "Wait. Are you…are you in love with her?"

My stomach flipped. I hadn't even thought about whether all these feelings I had for Shay were love. I had never, ever been in love before, not once in my entire life. When the topic of just hooking up had come up that day we were all in the Falcon's Nest, I had thought about how I felt that disconnection from the girls I'd met. I guessed I had a less obnoxious version of a "wandering eye"—I'd see a girl, think she was cute, and then move on to the next. I had, deep down, been waiting for someone to come along, someone who I'd be entirely invested in. I didn't want to waste my time with anyone I didn't have feelings for. I had felt back then that my heart belonged to someone who didn't exist yet.

But she did exist. Not just recently but in minuscule moments throughout my life. Little hints of a future, where we'd meet and be together. Like at the smoothie place in Rhode Island when we were kids. And in Alaska, where we'd bumped into each other, and California, where she remembered seeing me at the beach, and in Lake Tahoe, when I'd been wearing my Panthers jersey. She had always been out there, existing, while I was here in Divinity, waiting around for someone like her. I had met a million girls and never felt the way I did when I was with Shay. Maybe the reason I had so much trouble connecting wasn't because I was "shopping" for love, as Ava had put it.

Maybe—all this time—I'd been specifically searching for her.

"Oh my god, you are!" Gavin reached across the table and slapped my shoulder, bringing me back down to planet Earth. "You're in love with Bishop!"

That tug in my chest returned, the one that felt like something was pulling my heart out by a rope. I always felt it around her, even back when all we did was lock eyes across the quad. All these tiny, subtle things happened around me, all the time, and all the while I had been irredeemably falling for her. The gears in my head started turning, questioning everything I'd ever done or said around her, asking whether or not she would feel the same, what I'd do if she didn't, and wondering how to tell her what I felt and—

"Wait." My gears fumbled over one another as I came to another conclusion.

Gav lifted an eyebrow at me.

"Wait, wait, wait," I said.

I had skipped over the fact that when I had said I was as serious about Shay as he was about Darla, his response had been to ask if I was in *love* with her.

"My sister?" I asked incredulously. "You—Gavin Arthur McDaniel—feel love for my sister?"

He looked at me funny. "Well, yeah." He raised his hands, palms up, like I was the idiot for not knowing this already. "I mean, I called dibs day one, remember?"

I mimicked his posture. "You weren't in love with her before you actually knew her!"

"Same difference. She knows how I feel." Gav proceeded to eat his sandwich while I lost my appetite from the rush of emotions. "I tell her I love her, like, twenty-four hours a day, seven days a week."

The way he spoke, it was as if this was just a totally normal thing with him.

"Does she love you back?" I asked.

He shrugged, finishing the food on his plate. "She hasn't told me yet. She will, though."

"How do you know for sure?"

Gav leaned back in his seat and placed his hands on the table, as if he was about to give me a speech.

"Caleb, the way I see it, you have two choices—you can waste your life away, wondering what the hell someone else feels for you, or you can grab life by the balls and take all of the chances you want to take." He tapped his fingers and looked at me sideways. "Sure, it might not always work out in your favor, but how will you know if you don't try?"

"So, in your case, you'll just keep telling D you love her until she either says it back or ends up dissing you?" I rubbed the back of my head.

"Exactly." He nodded. "Because once I make the choice, once I take that chance, it's all in the universe's hands. I've played all my cards."

"Gavin, this is possibly the best advice you've ever given me." I was pleased that my best friend told me what I both wanted and needed to hear.

He shrugged, the corner of his mouth lifting in a goofy smirk. "Sometimes, these things just come to me."

My appetite returned, and I moved to finish my lunch. "You always know just what to say."

"When are you going to tell her? And what will you tell her first? That you love her or that you're psychic? Or are you going to do it at the same time? Are you going to tell her everything?"

There went my appetite again. "I have no idea, Gav. I just figured out less than two minutes ago that I'm in love with her."

"It's a lot to think about. If it were me, I'd just bang it all out in one go. Everything. The angel-aliens, the superpowers, Darla's family, Gabriel, and throw 'I love you, Shay' somewhere in the middle."

"It won't be easy." I swallowed my last bit of food. "I'm nervous."

"Like I said, you've got to just take that chance." He leaned on his forearms and clasped his hands together. "Because if she ends up running away screaming—from whatever you share with her—then you wouldn't want to be with her in the long run anyway."

"Yeah, you're right." As always, I was overthinking everything when really, there wasn't anything to think about at all.

Gavin grinned, lifting his water bottle up as if to toast me. "Balls to the wall?"

I grinned back at him and bumped my own bottle against his. "Balls to the wall."

Whatever the plan, whenever the time, I'd tell Shay the truth. Everything about the visions, the helliget and mørkeste and velsignet, what life was like before Darla and after. I had planned to do this all at some point anyway. Now, I had even more of a reason to, considering I had to add telling her I was in love with her to that lengthy list. It was really no big deal, despite my aching chest and flipping stomach and sweating hands over the idea of it all.

Gavin slapped the table boisterously. "All right, enough talk about balls. I want to hear about last night!"

"Actually, I think I'd rather just stay on the topic of balls, thanks."

CHAPTER
17

THE WEEK HAD COME AND gone, like all the rest since the semester had begun. And with that, I was halfway through my junior year.

To celebrate, Gavin, the girls, and I decided to go out to eat and take a hike in the gorgeous, fall-scattered, Appalachian Mountains. December had been so kind to us this year, granting us sunshiny days and chilly but bearable breezes, the leaves still hanging on in a rainbow display of autumn color. It was as if the trees were soaking up the beautiful earth as much as we were, holding onto that last breath of fall season, despite the winter already arriving.

We trekked through the incredible peaks with more ease than earlier that semester, since we'd hiked so often now. Tucker had asked to join us on our hike that afternoon, and we were happy to let him tag along. Darla telepathically voiced her reasoning—*Who else will take cute couples pictures of the four of us?*—which had me laughing harder than it should have. I really got along great with Tucker, so I wanted him to hang out with us as much as Darla wanted to use him as a photographer. He didn't care; he just wanted to be outside, celebrating the good weather and good vibes.

Shay held my hand the whole hike, pulling me along excitedly as we followed the others, tugging me up the steeper parts, eager to get to our destination. I loved how adventurous she was, taking each step with more enthusiasm than the last. The more I watched her positive attitude about life and the world around her, the more I realized how much admiration I really felt. Shay had replaced all the voices in my head that made me afraid and all the uncertainty I had with her presence, silencing all that chaos in my mind. With her, I felt free, for possibly the first time in my entire life. And as she led me on this hike, I could practically see her free spirit—it shone as bright as the sun during the day and as dazzling as the full moon at night.

She caught my incessant staring and came to a halt, squeezing my hand and pulling me back. She pursed her lips and tried not to smile.

"What?" she asked.

I turned to her, grabbed her by the hips, and pulled her to me. Her cheeks turned pink as they always did when she got all sheepish. I laughed and moved my hands up to her beautiful face.

I studied her eyes, allowing my thumbs to shape her cheeks. "You're dazzling."

"I'm *dazzling?*"

"Yeah. I can't look at you without wanting to kiss you."

She slid her palms up my arms and placed them over my hands. "That might be the sweetest—and corniest—thing I've ever heard."

I laughed again and brought her lips to mine, running my nose over hers. Like me, she was shy when it came to this kind of stuff—being "mushy" and all that. But I felt confident and comfortable every time I said these things, especially because every time I did, the look in her eyes told me they surprised her and made her feel good. Now, as I looked in her eyes and she held my hands to her face, I thought maybe—just maybe—they might hold some love for me in them.

The moment ended when I heard the sound of a camera clicking in the forest. Shay and I looked to the side and saw Tucker with his phone raised, lifting his eyebrows.

"What?" He feigned innocence. "Candid photos are the best photos."

I glanced at Shay, who was blushing, then back at Tucker. "Well, then, Tuck, you might want to capture this."

I wrapped my arms around Shay, and in one swift motion, I dipped her over my arm, and she squealed the whole time. Tucker snapped away, and I kissed Shay's neck before swooping her back up.

She flung her arms around my neck. "It's always an adventure with you, isn't it, Caleb Swift?"

We continued on our journey, catching up with Gavin and Darla, who were arguing about what movie we should all go see later. They weren't actually fighting, of course, but it was funny to watch when I knew Gavin loved her. Tucker snapped pictures of them—candid photos were the best photos, as he said—and we followed them up to a clearing at the top of our climb. The sky was so blue when the trees opened up, and a few puffy clouds spread around the blue canvas. The clearing was a beautiful spot, overlooking Divinity, much like the cliffside Gav and Ava and I had sometimes hiked to.

There was something about this place. The beauty it held gave me a sense of wonder that felt familiar. There was something about the yellow leaves on the surrounding trees, the way the forest smelled so fresh and alive. The crisp air and how crystal clear everything in front of me was. Yet a fuzzy memory of it floated around in my head, like I was standing in a dream.

Darla and Shay were running around each other while Gavin and Tucker talked on the side about how our hockey team had done this season so far, and I stood at the entrance of the clearing, trying to make sense of this déjà vu. A poking feeling in the back of my brain warned me of an incoming vision. I willingly allowed my mind to succumb to it, feeling that it would provide me an answer and hoping it wouldn't be obvious or noticeable that I had mentally tapped out.

I was aware the vision began, but I was overcome with disorientation, because I was standing in exactly the same place in the same field, with the same yellow-leaved trees and fresh-smelling forest.

And then it all came crashing down at once, like a physical blow to the chest.

It was a funny thing, how my visions came and went, and the only things I focused on and remembered were what was in front of me. It was stupid, really, that I never paid attention to details or particular aspects of what was in the backgrounds of them. I would have thought that I would have known better than to ignore all the subtle hints my visions provide. I would have thought I'd realize these details would help me figure it all out in the long run. I would have thought I'd know by then how important those types of details were.

The forest and the colors.

The way everything smelled.

The person I'd been trying to protect before I even knew her, standing in the same exact location.

The single moment I had feared the most for five years.

My vision-self turned slightly and saw Darla on her knees covered in blood.

The earsplitting screech was blasting my eardrums, and I snapped back, holding the sides of my head. This vision had been unlike itself, and before I could even process what this all meant, I knew I had accessed the near future.

This couldn't be happening. Not now. Not today.

I was panic-stricken, my heart thudding in my ears, and it totally showed. Darla and Shay had already run over, seeing there was clearly something wrong with me. Darla, especially, because I knew by the look of dread on her face, she'd seen everything I had in that short span of seconds.

"Caleb, are you all right?" Shay asked me. "What's wrong?"

As I straightened up, I opened my mouth to try to explain, but all I could release was a puff of air. I looked to Darla for help, and as we made eye contact, something happened.

Something in the air changed. That fresh, forest scent had been replaced with an overwhelming, sweet but sour smell that blew into my nostrils like a warning, my instincts causing the hair on the back of my neck to rise. Darla's eyes widened.

The sound of something tearing in half erupted in the clearing, and several individuals—two of whom looked familiar—appeared out of nowhere behind the girls. They were the velsignet from the day we went dirt biking with Leander and the kids—Marco and Roran. They strode toward us with a look of determination, Roran's gray eyes looking directly into mine. Shay and Darla turned around to face them. Darla's thoughts reached out to me, and I knew they had come back for us. This time, they'd brought reinforcements.

Out of the corner of my eye, I saw Tucker grab Gavin, and they turned invisible before the intruders noticed. Shay looked around frantically, whispering to us, asking who those men were, why they were here, how they appeared—all while Darla pushed her behind us to protect her. Shay and Gavin had no way to defend themselves in this situation, and we needed to keep them safe first.

I quickly counted how many people had come in addition to Marco and Roran. There appeared to be six; four extra men, and two young women who had chains around their ankles and wrists. I saw something in both of the women, my anxiety growing, and I knew the smell was coming off of them. They had to be mørkeste. Two mørkeste and six velsignet. The mørkeste seemed to be the prisoners in this scenario though, not the velsignet, and I took note of what we were up against. But I knew in my gut this wasn't a fight we'd stand a chance of winning.

We weren't ready for something like this—whatever this was—and this time, we didn't have Leander to save us.

I stepped in front of my sister and my girlfriend. "What do you want?"

They wasted no time before doing what they had come to do. Marco waved his hand effortlessly, and I was flung off to the side, landing hard on the grass.

"Keep him down," Marco said. "Grab the other two."

Three other velsignet grabbed the girls, one for Darla and two for Shay, and Shay screamed my name. I scrambled to get up, but I was immediately kicked in the ribs and knocked back down. A velsignet whacked me in the face with his fist, and I saw stars. His heavy boot nailed me again, so I was face down in the grass, and then he pressed down onto my spine perfectly, so if I even attempted to get up again, he would paralyze me. The velsignet bent down and punched me in the face again, at least five times more, and I was drooling on the ground, squinting through puffy eyes at my greatest fear unfolding.

I reached out my hand to the girls, who were being dragged away from me. Darla's hand freed for a brief moment, her fingers brushing against mine before one of the velsignet slapped her violently.

"Stop!" I croaked.

The moment the word left my lips, the sensation of ice-cold metal was jammed to my temple, forcing my head to the ground. My cheek smashed against the dewy grass, just like in another vision that had warned me about this day, and the velsignet leaned down to me.

"Speak another word, and we kill them now," he growled.

I closed my mouth, my face pressed in a puddle of my own drool and blood, my hands gripping the grass like my life—or the girls' lives—depended on it. My gaze traveled over to the mørkeste women, whose speckled-with-gold irises watched everything emotionlessly.

Darla pulled against the hold of her captor while the two who held Shay struggled to pry them apart.

"Why are you doing this to us? Let her go!" Darla freed one arm again and swung out to Shay.

The velsignet snatched it back again and hissed something in her ear.

"But she's innocent. She's only human!" D responded to whatever the man had said.

Roran appeared beside me, his eyes filled with that same regret I'd seen the first day. He leaned down for a moment and whispered quietly to me.

"I'm sorry in advance."

"Things will only be worse for you if you fight." Marco approached the girls, his hands behind his back as he watched Shay squirming against the two velsignet.

"Human? Are these people not human?" Shay yelled, eyes wide, looking from Darla's face to mine. "I don't understand what's happening!" She pulled against the men. "Let us go!"

Marco rolled up his sleeves. "We don't have time for this. We have to get going," he muttered to his cohorts who were holding my girl.

Darla snarled and spat curses at them while he walked around behind the two velsignet and Shay. She broke away for a brief second, reaching for Darla, but they snagged her again.

And that's when Marco produced a pistol.

"No…no!" I cried out.

The boot on my back put more pressure, causing me to gasp for air.

Marco rolled his eyes. "If you'd stop struggling, I wouldn't have to use excessive force." The gun glinted in the sunlight.

The next few seconds happened so quickly, but at the same time, so excruciatingly slowly, as if the world was in slow-motion.

Darla kicked back, causing the velsignet to stumble away and lose his hold on her. She charged at the other velsignet, Marco, and Shay. The anger and hatred in Darla's eyes practically lit the forest on fire. Then, as her hand reached out for Shay, Marco pressed the barrel against Shay's back and fired a single round into her, the bullet blasting through her front and whizzing just over Darla's shoulder. Blood splattered all over my sister, freezing her in place, her face flinching from the sudden spray.

Shay's lips parted, and dark-red ooze dribbled out.

Time sped up again.

My mind processed what had just happened.

Darla had never been the one who was in trouble.

Darla had never been covered in her own blood.

It was Shay's.

It had been Shay's blood the whole time. Shay had been the one in danger all along.

Darla's hands were out in front of her, shaking violently, and she released a blood-curdling scream that echoed in the silence of the woods. She fell to her knees before Shay, her hands going to her cheeks, touching the blood that had stained it. Shay collapsed into the arms of her captors, her eyes growing distant, the brightness of her blues turning gray. They locked on mine for one split second.

Shay. My Poe-reading girl.

As Marco slid his gun back into its holster, part of my soul left my body. I felt no pain, only numbness. Utter shock and disbelief that any of this was real.

"No…" I groaned, and the boot on my back eased up, the pistol disappearing from my temple. I struggled to lift my head. "No…no, no, no, no, no!"

I reached pathetically toward Shay, who lay bleeding and fading away as if she'd never existed in the first place.

Marco wiped his hands on his shirt, traces of blood speckled on the fabric. He looked at Shay's face sadly. "Come on now, sweetheart, it's time to go." He nodded toward the chained mørkeste women, and a velsignet threw Shay over his shoulder like a ragdoll, following Marco. Darla was on her knees, whimpering, and Roran and the velsignet who had held us both trailed the others.

"No! No!" I screamed, attempting to crawl.

Tunnel vision filled my eyes, and I watched as the group huddled together.

"No!" I screamed one last time, a helpless attempt at stopping them.

Then, Roran teleported them out of the field, the image of them burning away into the air.

"Oh, God!" I clawed at the grass, "No! Please, please, no!" I let my head fall back to the ground. "Why?"

My body quivered in pain, and my throat burned from the force of screaming. I heard the thud of feet coming toward us and saw Tucker running to Darla, then Gavin getting down on one knee beside me. Darla's whimpers ceased abruptly, and suddenly, she collapsed into Tucker's arms, her eyes rolling into the back of her head.

"Oh my god, oh my god, oh my god." Gavin was murmuring next to me, holding his hands up as if he couldn't figure out what to do with me. As if he was afraid to touch me.

I didn't want him to touch me. I moaned and gripped the forest floor, feeling dirt gather under my fingernails. The world was spinning around; all I could hear was Darla's scream in my mind. All I could see was Shay's face frozen in silent horror.

"Gav, help me with her!" I heard Tucker yell.

"But, Cay—"

"Gavin, help me!"

He left my side, and I let my eyes roll to the sky. I kept moaning, as if it were the only thing that could save me from the worst torment I'd ever felt, physically, mentally, emotionally. Every part of me ached and hummed with terrible, violent pain.

Shay.

I wanted to die. My soul was suffering. I wanted someone to end it all now, end me, so I wouldn't have to feel this anymore. *Kill me, please, kill me, take me instead,* I begged. But what I was really asking was for someone to save me from this horrid nightmare, this disaster I was trapped in. My nightmare was real, and it was way, way worse than I could have ever imagined.

It was all my fault.

Whether it was the shock of it all, the pure exhaustion, or the physical abuse I had endured, my body relaxed as I began to pass out. Before my eyes closed, I saw the shadow of someone coming down from the previously blue sky that was now covered in clouds.

He yelled, "No!" as he descended, and his blurry form sharpened into the shadow of a man with wings.

The blinding sky glinted off his feathers, causing my eyes to slowly close.

All I could think was how much I loved Shay. I hadn't even gotten to tell her before she'd been taken from me. I didn't get to tell her how I felt or even the truth about all of this. I hadn't even been able to protect her; I'd lain there on the ground, a helpless disgrace. I just never thought I'd have to worry about something like this happening, not to her. Watching her disappear with those velsignet and mørkeste had completely obliterated me, destroyed me more than anything had in my entire life. I couldn't imagine anything more awful ever happening. I'd felt her confusion and shock and fear inside me as I'd watched them hold her hostage. I'd felt a bullet in my back as I watched one blow through hers.

A part of me disappeared with her.

And it was all my fault.

Before I surrendered to sleep, I reflected on what Gabe had once said to me. *Love is genuine when you see all their pain, all their torment, all their suffering, and you carry it with you always.*

The world around me quieted, and I faded away, welcoming the sound of silence.

EPILOGUE
Darla

ICOULD FEEL ALL OF IT.

Everything he was feeling. From an outside perspective, he just looked like someone in mourning. But I knew him. I had begun to know him better than he knew himself. I knew his mind was tortured by what happened. I knew what it did to him. He was changed because of it, no longer the outgoing, elated man he'd started to become. His mind had never really been calm to begin with, but I could feel in my heart that he was deeply troubled.

I felt like my brother was dying.

After I had gone into shock and fainted in the woods, Tucker had called Leander to come get us. Leander arrived with Arlo soon after I woke up, and I had managed to gather enough strength to help them carry my unconscious brother to the car. He was beaten pretty badly, and we brought him to the hospital, the story being that he fell off the cliff onto a conveniently accessible part of the mountain. Gavin and I had run to the bathroom to wash the blood off me, and I had let my walls down completely while I was locked in that tiny room with him. I sobbed in his arms while he silently cleaned me off. I appreciated his silence though; he knew I wasn't much for expressing my feelings, especially in this way. I was usually a bit more guarded than that.

Caleb was out cold for hours, but after he was checked, he came out of it only bruised, not broken, with a minor concussion. He wouldn't speak to the doctors or to anyone, but that helped make the story more viable when

Leander told it. We got to take him home healthy with a prescription to rest for the next few days.

But I knew he was broken in places the doctors wouldn't be able to see.

Leander gave the cliff story to Nikki as well, who panicked, naturally, because she wouldn't be able to watch Caleb while he slept and work nights at the same time. But when Lea suggested Caleb stay with us while he recovered, she gratefully accepted the offer. I could hear how guilty her thoughts were, but we knew she needed our help. She trusted Leander with Caleb, and she was falling back in love with Lea, which made things easier for everyone. I didn't tell Leander that, but I'm sure he knew deep down, since he kept thinking he loved her too. Anyway, this was all in Caleb's best interest, considering the situation, and I was relieved when Nikki agreed to let him stay with us.

Some time had passed since Shay had been taken from us. It might've been a few days, maybe a week, I wasn't sure. It didn't really matter. I had lost track of time. I was sitting at the island in our kitchen, holding a cup of hot tea, as always since the incident. I wasn't eating or sleeping, mostly because I could still feel my best friend's blood on my face and see the look in her eyes when she realized she'd been shot. I relived it every waking moment. I became a fixture in that seat by the island, only ever moving to check on Caleb, who had chosen Leander's study to inhabit. He only ever left it to use the bathroom. He no longer had a reason to do anything else.

Currently, Leander, Gavin, Tucker, Arlo, Olivia, and even Gabriel were in the kitchen with me—the whole crew. We were gathered around, discussing everything that had happened. This was the first time Gabriel had been able to stop by since the incident, but Caleb refused to speak with anyone, which was understandable. Everything reminded him of Shay and what happened to her. His mind relived it even more than I did, which in turn would cause me to relive it again. I couldn't blame him for detaching himself from the rest of the world. Being a velsignet and knowing Gabriel and our origin and history... It had all led to her being gone from his world. So, what better way to be at peace than to block it all out?

I left him alone as well, because if it were me, I'd feel exactly the same. Maybe it was because he was my brother, and we were similar in many ways. But mostly, I felt as if talking about it all would make things way worse. I already felt beyond guilty that those monsters had figured out a way to block out my telepathy. It infuriated me that they were a storm that had arrived with plans I couldn't hear and protect us from. I had been able to hear only Tucker and Gavin hiding within Tucker's invisibility, Caleb's wild thoughts, and Shay's disoriented ones as she'd disappeared with the velsignet.

That was another thing. Before those bastards left with her, one of them had let the barrier in their mind fall away for one single second. Or I might've managed to break through his wall, I wasn't sure which. But whatever their plans were, Shay was not supposed to end up dead, and they weren't going to allow that to happen. That gave me a tiny bit of hope—for what, exactly, I really don't know. Maybe hope that she was still alive? That single thought in the velsignet's head gave me a sliver of faith that she might be out there, somewhere, still holding on.

I wouldn't tell the others, though. I couldn't just assume the velsignet meant anything by it. I didn't want anyone to get their hopes up, especially not Cay. We couldn't do anything with unreliable information. If we learned something new, then I'd speak up. But for now, I jotted the memory down in my mental notebook and filed it away.

Olivia didn't really understand any of it, but she politely sat with Arlo while the rest of us were talking. I had tuned out for most of the conversation; I was so tired of trying to analyze it all. Leander was trying to figure out why the attack happened, why us, why Shay, why, why, why. It was all really just irritating me now since we hadn't gotten anywhere with this. Leander had been calling nomads and old friends every day, and they would call him with whatever useless information they had. It was all just pitiful. And painful. And pointless.

"The mørkeste were chained up, though, not the velsignet," Tucker explained as I tuned back in. "I think these velsignet had them as captives or something."

Leander grimaced. "Whoever their leader is, he obviously isn't a mørkeste. I just don't understand who they serve or what their purpose is."

Tucker shrugged, and there was a moment of quiet, everyone deep in thought. I stared into my mug of tea, trying to block out all their loud theories and questions coming from their minds. My head was starting to hurt.

"What of the girl's parents?" Gabriel asked Leander. "Have you contacted them?"

"And told them what? That their daughter got shot and kidnapped?" Tucker crossed his arms.

I finally spoke up. "She was supposed to be staying here during winter break, working and making money for next semester. She wasn't going to go home at all, except for Christmas." I sipped my tea. "Her parents work often, so her absence will go unnoticed for a little while—hopefully, until we can think of a plan. It gives us some time."

"We need to find her." Gavin pounded his fist in annoyance on the island. "Whether she's alive or not. I'd rather give her parents something than nothing at all."

"That's morbid," Tucker muttered.

"Everyone, breathe." Leander glanced at Ollie anxiously. He didn't like talking about such gruesome things in front of her. "Our first priority is indeed to find her. But the only way we can even start to look for her is by figuring out what the hell happened back there."

The room was quiet again.

Then Tucker chimed in. "I grabbed Gavin because he was the closest, and I wanted to protect him. Should I have gone for Shay?"

I placed my mug on the counter and shook my head. "We can't question what you didn't do. We're lucky you were able to protect him. You thought and acted quickly. There wouldn't have been time for you to run over and get Shay under your veil."

"I appreciate you hiding me, man." Gavin clapped him on the back. "I only wish there was more I could've done."

Tucker shrugged and nodded. "I wish I could've used that crazy sword Gabe carried when he arrived. I would've stabbed all those velsignet."

Leander wrinkled his face. "What?"

Gabriel leaned forward. "What are you talking about? What is this sword you speak of?"

Leander and Gabe glanced at me, and I held my hands up. I had no idea what he was talking about.

"Yeah, that's right." Gavin pointed at Gabe. "You flew down from the sky—arriving way too late, by the way—and you had a massive sword. Some sweet armor too. You made sure Cay and D were both alive, and then you left when Lea got there." He lifted his eyebrow. "Don't you remember?"

Gabriel's dark eyes were puzzled as he shook his head. "You must be mistaken. I could see the fight ensuing, but my connection to Caleb was severed by his distraught emotions, and I was unable to locate you or come to your aid." He scratched his head. "In fact, today is the first time I've been able to come here at all."

Leander's lips parted in confusion. "I don't understand—you weren't there that day?"

Gabriel frowned. "Whoever that helliget was, it was not me."

My heart began to thud heavily, unable to comprehend what any of this meant. Of course, Gav and Tucker wouldn't have known the helliget wasn't Gabe; they'd never officially met him before today. They probably hadn't realized the two weren't one in the same. But it didn't make any sense for any helliget other than Gabriel to want to help us.

"If it wasn't you who came to us," I said quietly, "then who did?"

After everyone left that evening, I retreated to my room on the top floor. I heaved a sigh, shuffling over to my bed in my fuzzy red slippers Leander got me for my birthday this year. I sat on my bed, reaching out to Caleb through the link in our minds. As usual, he'd put up a wall blocking me from getting into his head. He hadn't let me in since that day in the woods, and he'd managed to figure out how to perfectly shield his thoughts from me. One of the ways he did this was by singing songs in his head, getting them stuck so that they were the only thing I heard in my own when I tried to link with him.

I fell back on my mattress, draping my arm over my face. Caleb's song choice of tonight was "Far From Home" by Five Finger Death Punch. I tapped my heels on the floor to the beat, humming along to it because there was nothing else I could do. He wasn't going to let me in, and I couldn't keep trying to force him to open up.

There was a light knock on my door, and I could hear Leander's thoughts buzzing about as he waited outside my room. He was frantically trying to figure out how to make me feel better by using encouraging, motivational statements. He was trying too hard to organize a speech that would cause me to smile but wouldn't make me feel any better.

I couldn't make him wait out there and overthink any longer. I sat upright. "Come in."

The door opened a smidge and Leander's head slowly peeped through the crack. He smiled softly at me before he entered, closing the door behind him.

"Hey, kid." Lea folded his arms over his chest as he crossed the floor. He cleared his throat and sat on the bed beside me. "How are you holding up?"

"Okay, I guess." I shrugged, tugging on a strand of hair that had fallen over my eye. "I'm worried about Caleb."

"He's going to make it through this. He's tough as nails, just like you are." Lea put his hand on my knee. "You know how proud I am of you, right?"

I rolled my eyes and laughed humorlessly. He was always proud of me, no matter what I did or didn't do. I loved that about him, but nothing I'd done lately was worth taking pride in. He was only trying to make me feel better.

He turned to me, pulling one leg up on the bed. "I know Caleb has shut himself away, but I can see that you are having an equally hard time dealing with this. You lost your friend, sweetheart." He tucked the loose piece of hair behind my ear. "And you need to focus on yourself before you can try and help your brother."

I nodded, then gazed down at my hands. I popped each knuckle one by one, squirming anxiously. Lea always reminded us kids to help ourselves before helping others. But Caleb's pain was my pain, so I was taking on the emotions of two minds, not just my own. I couldn't prevent that from happening.

"Do you think—" I swallowed hard. "Do you think Caleb wishes it had been me instead of her?"

Leander shook his head, smiling. "Of course he doesn't. Besides, you're the one who can read minds. You already knew that answer, didn't you?"

My shoulders slumped, and I popped my knuckles again, starting with my thumbs. "Actually, I didn't. He's been shutting me out. He keeps getting songs stuck in his head so he's alone not only physically but mentally as well. He's completely isolating himself in that damn room."

Lea's reassuring smile fell. "Ah. I see."

I gazed out the large window above my bed, trying to blink away my tears. "Yeah."

"Hey." Lea pried my hands apart, ceasing my fidgeting fingers and drawing my attention back to him. "Why would you ever think Caleb would want you to take Shay's place? You're his sister, one of his best friends. He spent years of his life worrying about you before he knew who you even were. He spent the last few months getting to know and befriend you, all the while panicking over his visions of you. He's spent all this time trying to protect you. And he succeeded in doing just that."

"But I wasn't even the one who needed saving." My chin quivered, and I shook my head slowly. "I don't know. He was so focused on me that he didn't even think he had to worry about anyone else. I blame me for that, so why wouldn't he blame me?"

"He didn't see anyone else other than you in that vision. Neither of you could've known." Leander squeezed my hands. "It's normal to blame yourself, but it's clear this is not your fault."

"It doesn't matter anyway." I pulled away from him. "He loves Shay. Like, he's *in love* with her. You have no idea the pain he was in, the anguish in his brain. It was bleeding pain, Lea." My voice cracked, and hot tears poured over my cheeks. "I would take her place in a heartbeat, you know." I looked down at my hands again. "If it had been me, I could've at least defended myself for a bit before—"

"Stop." Lea lifted my chin with his knuckles. "Things happened the way Caleb's visions played out in his head. He saw only what needed to be seen. He just interpreted them wrong, which led to the unexpected events that occurred." He exhaled shakily. "He would've been just as devastated had you been the one killed. It sucks, but everything happened the way it was supposed to."

I dragged my hands down my face then. Everyone thought Shay was dead except me. I didn't just believe she was alive out there. I knew she was. At least, when they'd taken her, she'd still been alive. I had this feeling in my stomach and my chest that told me she was out there, still living and breathing. I felt it in my gut, a sense stronger than an instinct.

Could I keep pretending she was dead? Could I keep acting as though she really had been killed, when I knew those velsignet had other plans? Could I keep lying to everyone until I had some kind of clue, some type of lead to where she was taken? A lead I may never find, because I had kept this secret to myself? I knew the truth about Shay's disappearance. No one except me had any idea she might still be alive. No one else had this kind of hope, because I was the one who had a way to see into the mind of someone who had bits of the truth floating about their brain.

Could I really take my ability for granted like that?

I scooted closer to Leander, leaning in close to him in order to whisper as quietly as I could. I had to tell him before I could tell anyone else. He was the only one in this family with a clear head who would be able to help.

"I need to tell you something." I practically mouthed so only he could hear me. I couldn't risk anyone in the household hearing what I was about to say. "You have to keep it between us. I don't want anyone getting their hopes up in case of...anything."

His eyebrows lowered, and he nodded.

"I'm pretty sure Shay's still alive," I whispered. "I managed to hear the thoughts of one of those velsignet. She's not supposed to die. They intended to take her alive."

Lea glanced at me out of the corners of his chestnut eyes. He swallowed. "Are you sure that's what you heard?" His voice was almost inaudible. "Are you absolutely sure?"

I nodded. "I don't know what's happened to her since that day. But I'm entirely sure of what I heard."

Lea sat up straight, rubbing his forehead. He stared at me hard, and I could hear his thoughts racing, bouncing off the inner walls of his skull. Every single one of them was so hopeful, so positive, that I began to feel a weight lift off my entire body.

Lea held my shoulders firmly, looking me square in the eyes. He breathed in deep, chest rising as he whispered the one thing I was praying he'd say.

"We will find her, then." He rose to his feet, patting my shoulders. A ghost of a smile crossed his face. "I'll start working on this straight away. I'll make some calls, we'll formulate a plan and start looking. I won't say anything to the others until we have more information, but we're going to find Shay." He leaned down to kiss my head. "And it'll all be because of you, Darla."

Lea quickly went to leave, his mind spinning with the friends he needed to contact, phone numbers and email addresses filling his head. He thought of the known places mørkeste liked to gather with their velsignet followers. He paused at my door then, his fingertips hovering over the knob.

"You're right to want this kept a secret for now. We can't tell Caleb anything about this until we've strategized how to go about finding your friend," he whispered, glancing over his shoulder at me as he leaned on the doorframe. "We can't have him trying to look for Shay on his own or forcing visions on and hurting himself in the process. He needs to have a level head before he finds out anything, and he needs to work with us to find her. I don't want him doing something irrational or stupid. We need to be thorough and organized. Plan first, truth later."

"Agreed." I nodded. I already felt guilty keeping something so important from my brother, but I really had no choice. If I told him now, he would jump into trying to find Shay with nothing to go on, no idea where to start. He would act first before asking questions. He'd obsess, and he wouldn't rest until he found her, because nothing else would matter.

Lea smiled at me, standing a bit straighter than earlier. "You're so strong. I really am proud of you, Darla."

He closed my door behind him and headed downstairs. I still heard his thoughts, busy with ideas and ways to buy us time so that Shay's parents wouldn't report her missing before we'd had a chance to find her. He thought about all the possibilities of where my friend could've been taken and how we would locate her. He thought about how afraid Shay must be, wherever she was.

I eventually lowered the frequency of Lea's thoughts so that they faded out of range, and my mind was quiet. I laid back on my bed again, staring up at the vaulted attic ceiling. I exhaled quietly, feeling extreme relief wash over me. It felt good to finally tell someone what I'd been holding onto since that day, to let go of what I'd heard in the velsignet's mind. I could trust Leander to keep what I told him to himself, and he'd take the right course of action when the time came. No matter what happened next, I knew I had done the right thing by telling him the truth.

Caleb always talked about the different paths he could see, that no future was so set in stone that it couldn't be changed. We hadn't been able to prevent his visions of me from coming true, but I knew now that we'd find a way to work with this path we'd been given. He and I could handle anything life threw at us, that was certain. We'd survived the world thus far, and like anyone else on this planet, a lifetime of challenges awaited us. We had to keep going forward because, even though we couldn't change what happened that day in the woods, we could still learn from the past to make the future better.

And if the path we were on seemed like it was going in the wrong direction, well, we'd just have to figure out a new one.

I closed my eyes, wiping the spots where my tears were drying. I was truly confident we were going to find her. I could feel it in my heart.

We're going to find you, Shay.

ACKNOWLEDGMENTS

First and foremost (and obviously), I want to thank my huge, loving family for being with me on this adventure thus far.

Mom—you are the person I idolize, and I would be lucky to even be a quarter as incredible as you. We both know I have a dangerous and pricey addiction to reading, but you still support me even if it (and writing) consumes my every waking moment. You drilled into my head that I could do anything if I just took that first step. You encouraged me to take what I wanted to do—what I was *meant* to do—and put it in the stars, send it out to the universe. You were adamant about telling me to live the life I've always dreamed of. And, because of you, that is exactly what I am doing.

Dad—if it weren't for you always reading "just one more chapter" to me before bed growing up, I would never have dreamed up the worlds I would create in the future, and I would've never had the passion I do for writing. With your guidance, support and all your help throughout my life—especially through this whole writing/publishing process—I feel as though I can do anything I set my mind to. Thank you endlessly for being my partner in crime, support system and my best friend.

I also want to thank my stepmother, Kerry, for having faith in me, and for all those years of sitting through my endless rambles about the stories I wanted (and plan) to write. My little sister, Megan, for always being so proud of me, even when it comes to the little things.

My friends—if only I could name you all. But the ones that have been with me from the start, showing so much excitement and support when it came to making my dreams a reality are my best friends, my best girls: Sarah, Asha, Fallon, Hayley, Katie and my "Book Babes" Lexi and Nicole.

I also want to give a shout-out to my sorority as a whole—thanks for showing me how to grab life by the you-know-whats and take on any challenge that comes my way.

My buds, Joey and Jake—I'm sorry I had to use your names for jerk characters, but the first names that came to mind just so happened to belong to two of my favorite people.

Thank you to my publisher, TCK, for saying "yes" and giving me the opportunity to share my stories with the world. My editor, Jill Noble-Shearer, my project manager Sarah Dyck, and the entire TCK team—you helped turn my book from something I wanted to throw across the room into something I am extremely proud of, and I couldn't have done it without you. Thank you for all your hard work.

Lastly, I want to thank Caleb Swift. I created you when I was the ripe age of thirteen, and ten years later, you have an entire world built around who you were in my head. To my readers: Caleb's story is your own as much as it is his. I think we all have a little bit of Caleb in us, where we feel the tug of the universe and wonder what is really out there. I think Caleb opens that door to you, and I hope after reading his story, you open your mind to the idea that anything and everything is possible.

Because, had I not believed anything and *everything* were possible, Caleb's story would not be in your hands at this very moment.

ABOUT THE AUTHOR

Jenna Ryan has been reading and writing since as far back as she can remember. *Continuum, Book I: The Channeler* is her debut novel, and she is a passionate storyteller who has a thousand worlds in her head just waiting to come alive. Jenna currently works as a paralegal and lives in a small New Jersey town. Her favorite hobbies include traveling, hiking, music, and being a total space nerd. Jenna is also planning on traveling to Mars; she is just waiting to be invited.

For more information about upcoming releases, follow Jenna on Twitter and Instagram, and like her Facebook page.

CONNECT WITH JENNA RYAN

Sign up for Jenna's newsletter at
www.jennaryanink.com/free

To find out more information visit her website:
www.jennaryanink.com

Facebook Page:
www.facebook.com/jennaryanink

Twitter:
@jennaryanink

Instagram:
jennaryanink

GET BOOK DISCOUNTS & DEALS

Get discounts and special deals on our bestselling books at
www.TCKpublishing.com/bookdeals

ONE LAST THING...

Thank you for reading! If you enjoyed this book, I'd be very grateful if you'd post a short review on Amazon. I read every comment personally and am always learning how to make this book even better. Your support really does make a difference.

Search for *The Channeler* by Jenna Ryan to leave your review.

Thanks again for your support!

CPSIA information can be obtained
at www.ICGtesting.com
Printed in the USA
FSHW011733080920
73623FS